K

THE CC   Y

Robert Ryan

Cover Design by www.damonza.com

ISBN-13 978-0-9942054-6-9
(print edition)

Trotting Fox Press

Contents

RAGING SWORDS

BOOK ONE OF THE DURLINDRATH TRILOGY

Robert Ryan

1. Death or Infamy

Brand woke. His heart thrashed in his chest. His stomach churned, and the blood in his veins ran chill. But he spared no thought for any of those things.

He lay still, wrapped in his bedclothes, while his eyes strained to see and his ears to detect whatever had roused him from forgotten dreams.

It felt cold. It was dark also, being in that last stretch of night when the hours were long and the dawn, though near, was not yet come. It was that period when the human spirit ebbed lowest, where wills were weakest and shadows pooled the most deeply.

He saw nothing out of place. He heard no noise that should not have been. Yet his heart raced ever faster, and sweat, cold and clammy, trailed down his face and onto his throat like the lingering fingers of ghosts.

All through the city a questing breeze touched and pulled and tweaked at anything loose. A weather vane creaked as it turned on some high roof. A stable door banged unheeded, and in the palace where Brand lay shivering white curtains danced palely in the open windows.

He concentrated on the breeze. He did not like it. The open window near his bed looked over the city, but he saw nothing amiss far below. Yet the air was unnaturally cold on his face. Even as the thought came to him its fluttering movement stilled. The curtains ceased their billowing, and the cobbled streets below grew quiet once more.

He let out a long breath and relaxed. All he heard now was a whisper of air down the corridor outside his room and the faint creak of doors.

The warmth under the blankets began to soothe him back to sleep. The day was not yet begun. There was no need to stir. He could rest a little while longer and gather his strength for the toils yet to come.

Nor was he even wanted here, not among this foreign people. They did not like him. They did not respect him. They thought him far too young for his high position. Yet he had spilled his blood in deadly battles to serve them, defied death for their benefit, but most would still like to see his back, to see him walk off into the wild lands from whence he came.

And that was his desire – he ached to return to his homeland – to walk the paths that once he knew and to reclaim the life that had been stolen from him. Yet ties of loyalty held him, and he would not break them. The king of Cardoroth was a great man. To him he owed much, and he would serve and help in any way that he could.

Brand stirred, restless once more. Almost he had been lulled, but he knew sorcery when he felt it. Through a fog that dimmed his thoughts he forced himself to sit up in bed. His head suddenly cleared. Many in the city might wish him gone, but not the king. Gilhain trusted him. He had given him opportunity when others had not, and respect when others offered only disdain.

Gilhain! The last dregs of confusion scattered. Sorcery was afoot and the king would be its target. Brand leapt out of bed. No time he had to don chain mail or helm or the white surcoat of his station. He pulled on trousers and boots, drew the sword of his forefathers from its ancient sheath, and ran bare chested to the door.

He put his hand to the metal knob. The cold he felt there shocked him like a blow. He flung it open anyway and let go swiftly. Immediately a blast of frigid air assailed him, and as he ran the length of the corridor he saw frost on the marble floor and the iciness of it bit his unshod feet.

"Durlin!" he called loudly, summoning the king's bodyguards who slept in rooms along the passageway.

He sprinted ahead, but he saw nobody and heard no reply.

"Durlin!" he yelled again. "To the king!"

The door to Gilhain's chamber was now before him. The two Durlin stationed there lay slumped on the ground. A quick glance told him that they were dead, though no blood marked their white surcoats.

Beneath the door strange lights flickered, and he heard the first call of any person beside himself.

"Guards!" It was the queen. Fear gripped her voice and made it shrill.

A moment he hesitated, knowing that on the other side sorcery and mayhem filled the room and that he would likely die if he entered. But he was the Durlindrath, leader of the bodyguards, and when he swore his oath to protect the king he had done so from the heart.

He kicked with all his might. The door, built of sturdy oak slabs to protect against assault, did not budge. But the metal of the bolt that held it in place shattered within its icy casing. Shards from the ruined doorjamb flew into the air, and the door careened inward on its great hinges.

Brand sprang into the king's chamber. The rapid breath from his heaving chest turned to mist before him.

Yet more vapor, like a roiling fog, swirled within the room. There was no frost here, for the floor was laid with deep carpet, but ice hung in ribbons from the windows and sheeted the marble walls.

Gilhain and the queen were held at bay against the far wall. The king grasped a mighty sword in his two hands while she raised high a long knife. Six figures pressed toward them. They were wraithlike, gray and vaporous as the fog that eddied in the room. They glided on tall legs and their long arms reached forward like creeping fingers of mist toward the king's throat. The wraiths had faces: gaunt, cold-eyed and cruel. A pale light lit their hollow cheeks and glimmered silver-white in their trailing hair.

Brand had seen enough. He leaped toward them and yelled the battle cry of the Durlin: *Death or infamy!*

He attacked. His sword sliced and cut and stabbed. The wraiths were more solid than they looked, and he drew from them shuddering screams, yet their cries came as though from a great distance, and the creatures did not die. Instead of falling, three of the six turned upon him.

They reached for his throat, and one found a grip there. He felt the cold touch of death. But his sword was a Halathrin blade, forged by immortals, and though what would have been death-strokes to a man had not yet killed the wraiths, it certainly caused harm. He drove the blade forward into the closest figure until it staggered back, and then he jumped free from more reaching arms.

The creatures pressed their attack against him. And they barred the way to the king that he had sworn to protect. But they ignored the queen. And that was an error, for she fought with animal fury, and one of her deep thrusts slew a wraith whose misty form dispersed into the air with a shriek. The king, meanwhile, held the others off with deft strokes. But time was running out.

Brand swung and stabbed, holding the enemy off but not defeating them. Yet this much he had achieved: the

9

enemy must now divide their attack that otherwise, concentrated on Gilhain alone, would by now have killed him.

He danced to the left and hewed at the outstretched arm of a foe. The blade did not sever it, but the follow up stroke drove deep into vaporish innards and Brand pushed the blade up and through to its hilt.

There was no heart to pierce, for these things drew no breath, and no blood surged through their bodies to enliven their limbs. Yet still, whatever sorcery gave them substance to kill by hand must needs also give them a physical form that might be damaged.

A moment the wraith was close to him. If it were a man they would have stood eye to eye. But in that haggard face he saw no gaze that mirrored his own. Instead, he perceived the flicker of lights and shadow coming to him as though through a fog, and he caught a sudden glimpse of a room, dark and shadow-laden, and he heard the dim sound of faraway chanting.

Before he understood whatever it was that he had heard and seen the wraith reeled back from him, but then, even as it began to sweep forward again in renewed attack, the sorcery that held it together faltered. It hissed and faded into formless vapor.

At last he heard running feet in the corridor. Light flashed from the doorway, dazzling bright. The gutted candles flared with leaping flame. The dark hearth burst with a fury of sparks and shimmering embers. Crackling flame roared to life.

Aranloth had come. He held his staff before him, and the diadem on his brow gleamed in the flaring light. The king's wizard now contended with the sorcery, and the room became furnace-hot. The sheeted ice dripped from the walls. The wraiths screeched and writhed, trying to evade the blades that now cut them with ease. Swift they died, or else sharp steel sent them back to the pit dark sorcery had conjured them from.

In the sudden silence Brand heard from afar the enemy that had laid siege to Cardoroth. From beyond the city wall the chanting of an army rose to a crescendo, but then trailed off into a din of confusion and discord. Their war drums continued to beat, holding order longer, but soon even their thrumming voices stilled.

Brand heaved for breath. Was any place now safe for the king? A host of mankind's ancient enemies gathered without, trying to break in and destroy. Yet now sorcery had slipped even inside the palace. Nowhere seemed beyond the reach of the enemy who sought Gilhain's death. And well they might, for only his brilliance and tactics had forestalled them. Without him, Cardoroth would long since have fallen, and they knew it and hated him.

Brand looked at Gilhain. It was his job, his sworn oath, to keep the man safe. And neither blade nor shaft nor poison – neither a thousand foes nor a lone assassin, not even sorcery in the night would avail against him, so long as he drew breath.

But the dead guards in the corridor reminded him that a man, no matter the strength of his will, regardless of his love and loyalty, might still be outmatched.

It was nearly so tonight. The reach of the enemy was somehow longer than it had been, and the hope of the city dwindled further. For the enemy *did* outmatch them.

The elug host was vast. The siege of Cardoroth could not be broken, and the enemy would likely prevail. If not tonight, then in a month, or six months. All the swifter if the king died, and that the enemy knew and strove to achieve – any way it could.

Brand sensed that the doom of Cardoroth was coming. By what means the enemy grew stronger rather than weaker, he could not guess. Sorcery had never yet struck so deep into the city. Always Aranloth and his like prevented it. Yet not tonight. Perhaps never again.

He saw the same understanding when he looked into Gilhain's eyes. But there was determination there also, an unflinching will, and Brand admired it.

The king might die, but if so, he would not be alone at the end.

2. Too Many Enemies

Brand had many questions for Aranloth, but his first task was the king's welfare. And the queen's, for to her he also owed much.

He strode toward the bed where they now sat together, and the sight of them holding hands and shivering from the effect of cold, or shock, having just survived a sorcerous attempt on their lives wrenched his heart. They deserved better than this. Yet assassination attempts were not uncommon. This was not the first, nor would it be the last. That the previous Durlindrath, and every Durlin who served him, was dead offered proof enough of that.

Brand pulled up a heavy blanket and draped it over them.

"Thank you," Gilhain said. The man still gripped his sword so tightly in one hand that his knuckles were white.

The queen did not speak. But she looked at him. It was a gaze that said much, for he was close to her counsels and understood better than most the mixed pride, love and fear that underpinned her marriage to the king. Her look told him that this was perhaps the closest attempt yet on the life of the man that she loved.

Brand knew that she was made of steel, a fit partner for a great king, but he knew also that even steel could break, and he saw the shattering recognition in her eyes that this could not go on. Sooner or later an attempt would succeed. But he knew also, both from past conversations and the glint in her eye now, that she would never give in to despair. She had her husband's back, and Brand wished there was a girl like that in his own life.

At that moment soldiers and servants bustled into the room. It grew suddenly loud, and Brand walked away to leave them to their ministrations. He wanted a chance to think.

He moved to the hearth. The naked blade in his hand now felt out of place, but he did not put it down. He stood close to the fire and felt the first touches of warmth return to his skin. He fed more wood to the flames, enjoying both the heat and the smell of smoke. It brought back memories of childhood campfires in a land far from here.

Aranloth joined him. The old man leaned on his staff. He seemed ordinary again, shrunken back to humanity, but it was only a veil for the power that he possessed. For he was as strong and swift as any young warrior, though old as the hills and possessed of lore and magic that could not be gathered save over the span of many lifetimes.

"That marks the third attempt this month," the old man said.

Brand stared into the leaping flames. "Yet the first of sorcery."

"Yes, and that makes me wonder. The enemy does not possess the strength to break through the wards that I and my kind use to protect the city. The walls and gate are always at risk, for we cannot be everywhere, and they are the focus of the attack. But here, in the heart of Cardoroth, we deemed it safe."

Brand looked at him for the first time. "Perhaps other sorcerers have joined the army?"

"I don't think so. There are thirteen, which is a number they favor, and I do not believe they have added to it."

"Then how have they broken through?" Brand immediately regretted that his words sounded like an accusation.

"I wish I knew. It's your part to protect against blade, arrow and poison. Mine against sorcery. Neither of us have failed – until tonight. I don't know how they got passed me, but I'll discover it, one way or another."

"I didn't mean to suggest that it was your fault. You've done more than anybody to keep the king alive."

"But it wasn't enough tonight. If not for you, then I would have been too late."

Brand ran a hand through his hair. "How did they do it? What *were* those wraiths?"

"They were drùghoth; sendings your people would call them. Something has changed. The sorcerers don't have the strength for that. Not these ones anyway, and not over that distance. It's several miles between where they lay siege to the wall and where we stand here."

Brand let out a sigh. "As you say, something has changed. But if there aren't more sorcerers, then what can it be?"

Aranloth stared bleakly into the fire. "I don't know. But if I don't discover the reason for their increased strength..." he paused, "or the artifact that they're now using, then I cannot prevent further attacks. They'll certainly try again. They nearly succeeded this time."

Brand turned, for the king had left the servants to tend his wife. He no longer looked like a man who had just faced death. There was nothing to be read in his eyes; they held the same sharp intelligence, the same wolfish stare as always. Perhaps he was used to it by now.

15

"Once more you've saved me," he said to Brand. "And my wife this time as well. What reward can I give you?"

Brand shrugged. "To serve is reward enough, My King. To defy your enemy, who is also the enemy of my people, is … satisfying also."

"Come! There must be something?" Gilhain pressed.

Brand shook his head. "The one thing that I wish above all else, my family and my rightful place among my own people, is something beyond even the power of a king of Cardoroth."

The king looked at him sadly. The wolfish gaze turned to pity.

"Those things I would give, and gladly, if I could, though it meant that Cardoroth lost its bravest man, and I a friend. But if I cannot give you that, then take at least my thanks, and those of the queen. They're heartfelt."

Brand bowed. They were high compliments, and he found no words in answer.

Gilhain turned to Aranloth. "Come, old friend. We must speak. This latest turn bodes ill for the realm, and we have much to discuss."

Brand left them to it. He had other duties now. He walked to the doorway where the bodies of the two Durlin lay.

The others of his order had gathered there. Their faces were grim, and they did not speak. Of the thirty, the *new* thirty that he had himself handpicked since the previous Durlindrath and his men were killed, there were now only twenty-eight. He did not doubt that soon there would be less. And it was hard to find good men these days. Guarding the king was a job that few were suited to, and fewer still were willing to suffer its risks.

He looked down at the dead men, and the creed of the Durlin ran through his thoughts:

Tum del conar – El dar tum!
Death or infamy – I choose death!

These men had been given no choice. They were slain by sorcery in the night. Yet they had still chosen to serve the king, to protect and guard him, to swear their oaths of loyalty. In their way, they *did* choose death, for they knew when they joined the Durlin that Gilhain would be attacked, if not how.

Brand gazed at them somberly. How long before someone looked down at his own dead body the same way, tallying up the long record of those who had died before him?

There were too many enemies, both outside of Cardoroth and inside. For there were traitors within the walls also. Less powerful than the sorcerers, but cunning, determined and cloaked in secrecy. Yet there was honor to set against it. The Durlin were legendary, and often the mere sight of their white surcoats in the city streets brought cheers from the crowd.

Soldiers arrived with stretchers, and Brand made a sign for his men to take them. They gently moved the bodies across. Brand lifted up the end of one by its wooden handles, bearing the weight of a dead man that he felt responsible for.

He made a signal to four of the Durlin. "Stay here," he said. "Keep a close eye on things, for there are now many coming to see the king, and that could be taken as an opportunity. Let no one in who does not need to be here."

"Yes, Durlindrath," they answered.

Slowly the stretcher-bearers moved down the corridor, and the remaining Durlin followed. One led them, holding a single candle in his hand, and as they

17

went the men chanted softly the words that had come down through the long years for such a procession. It was grim, but sonorous in their deep voices, and it held a certain grace.

Wherever they met palace staff in the corridors the men and women stood still and bowed their heads in respect. Some cried quietly, perhaps those new to the palace who had not seen this as often as others who had served longer.

Down they went until at length they reached the chapterhouse of the Durlin on the ground floor. They walked through the great doorway, crafted of carved oak posts and into the ancient rooms set aside for their use since the building of the palace some eight hundred years ago.

The walls were paneled with oak, broken by massive arched doorways that led to an outer courtyard. But many old hangings decorated the walls, woven in their threads the story of the Durlin since their founding and the many brave deeds that they had done.

The vaulted roof was high above, and the chanting of the men grew deeper while the ceiling threw down their voices again in matching echoes of mourning.

Brand felt the weight of the dead man that he carried. Somewhere his story would be added to one of the newer hangings.

His footsteps slowed as they came to a central dais. Here the men would be laid in state until their funeral. Carefully, they moved the bodies across onto the cold stone, the same red granite from which much of the city was built, only this was polished and carved with symbols.

The chanting of the men ceased. They stood now in a circle around the dais, joining hand to hand and standing with bowed heads. It was now silent.

Brand closed his eyes. A minute they would stand like this, showing their respect, and then their duties would call again to serve the king.

He could not help but wonder that it was a small amount of time; but not hours nor weeks would bring them back. There was no weeping as there would have been in his homeland. The people of Cardoroth were stern and proud, though death touched them just as deeply. And if they stood now in a grand building, instead of in a thatched hut; if they were silent instead of weeping, it did not change anything. There was love and respect in the room, and that was all that mattered. And that was the same whether here or at home.

But thinking of home drew memories to his mind. He wanted to walk there again, beneath its trees and sun, to once more climb its green hills and look out over its wide lands, to cross its rivers and hear the sound of the cattle lowing on the wind. But he could not. His loyalty belonged to the king. Now more than ever.

The silence was over, and the group became restless.

"Durlin," he said. "These two men have paid a high price. They gave freely of what they had so little – time. For there is always much that we dream of, and in the end much that is left undone before age, sickness or death robs us of our abilities."

The men looked at him. Their expressions showed little, but they heard his words and understood them. He was one of them, and there were certain truths that they all knew, even if they rarely spoke them. And they knew what he would say next, because they had heard him say it before.

"Yet these men chose freely, as do we all, to guard the king. But it is not so much the king that they died to protect, but the ideal of what is good in the world. Today, they served justice. Today, they struck a blow for

19

the people against the forces of chaos. Today, alone and in the dark, they gave of their lives so that there may yet be other days where truth and justice and honor and goodwill shine in the world." He paused, looking at the dead men. "We will not forget them."

The men gave the ritual reply: "Long will we remember them."

At his sign two Durlin retrieved a flag from a redwood cabinet nearby and draped it over the bodies. It was made of the same thick cloth as their surcoats, gleaming and shining, but whereas they wore no sign or emblem on their clothes the flag was woven with their insignia: seven red stars that represented the seven sons of the first king of Cardoroth, all of whom formed his guard. Three had died to protect him, and these were woven on the top. Beneath them were the other four. Separating them was the Durlin creed, uttered by the first son to die while he defended his father from attack:

Tum del conar – El dar tum!
Death or infamy – I choose death!

Brand took a last look. There was nothing else he could do for these men. Now, he must turn his thoughts to the king and how best to protect him from attack. He could not rely on Aranloth to stymy the sorcery. The enemy had somehow gained an advantage, and courage might now be asked to achieve what wizardry could not.

His second and third in command understood what he was thinking and approached. They knew him well, from even before his time as Durlindrath, and they guessed he would have instructions.

He nodded to them. "Lornach. Taingern – let's go to the courtyard. I'll feel better if I can breathe some fresh air, away from death and sorcery."

20

They followed him through one of the great arches and into the gray half-light just before dawn. The courtyard was paved with smooth flagstones, though at its further end it was grassed.

This was where the Durlin trained. A mass of weapons and armor hung from every wall. These were the tools of their trade, and Brand knew them better than most men living – else he would be dead. But he would rather hold a horse's reins than a halberd's handle. He preferred the tilling of the earth and the sweet smell of newly opened ground where things would grow instead of the hacking and cutting and bludgeoning that brought death. But few men chose their destiny. It chose them.

"What now?" Lornach asked.

Brand turned to one of his few friends in the city, and one of his oldest. He knew him better as Shorty, but that was unbecoming for the high station of a Durlin.

"The king should not be alive," he said. The two men looked at him strangely, and he gave them a faint smile. "What I mean is that our chances of keeping him alive have always been slim. And that has been the case for a long time. We fight a losing battle, one we should have lost long ago, and from now on it will only get worse."

"You paint a picture of little hope," Taingern said.

"There is no hope," he replied. "We three know it. And so do the rest of the Durlin. But they do not have our experience. They do not know that fate favors the bold-hearted, as we have learned ourselves. For we also, just as the king, should be dead."

"That may be so," Lornach said. "But how does it help them?"

"We survived our past perils, and there were certainly enough of them, by believing in ourselves. We did not despair. And a way of survival opened up. Of course, we

21

were lucky too, but a person makes their own luck. So this much we must do for them. We know they are prepared to die to try to save the king. And likely all of us will, but we cannot allow them to resign themselves to that fate, or it will come all the swifter. We must remind them at every opportunity that there is hope, even if it cannot be seen, and to fight to the last, with not only courage but also cunning. That way at least some of them may survive."

The three men looked at each other grimly. Their task was not now only to keep the king alive, but the Durlin also. It would be the hardest job of their lives, and they knew it.

They walked back inside. The Durlin had returned to their duties. The room was empty except for the two corpses. Soon men would come to prepare them for their long rest. There would be a funeral, full of pomp and ceremony. They would be praised with great praise. But nothing would bring them back. Not the gray-eyed Gernlik who could never keep his white surcoat clean, nor the red-haired Carangar, always quiet and somber, but merry as a country maid when he drank too much.

The three men went their separate ways. Taingern was in charge until mid-morning, and for a little while Brand had a chance to get some rest.

He returned to his chamber and slipped back under the covers, but he did not put aside his sword. He feared to do so, for he did not know when, or in what manner, the next attack would come. He gripped the hilt even in his sleep, and through a fog of slumber and half-waking he heard the war drums of the enemy begin to beat, the enemy that had haunted other cities, other realms and other times before this. The enemy that had harried mankind for long ages of the land of Alithoras: elugs.

The beating drums rose to a faster pace, and then the chanting of the enemy soldiers began. It too had been heard outside the walls of many besieged cities before this. Some still stood. Many did not. Brand tossed and turned as the fell words floated through the heavy air:

Ashrak ghùl skar! Skee ghùl ashrak!
Skee ghùl ashrak! Ashrak ghùl skar!

The chant flowed without beginning or end. The drums hastened. Stamping boots thundered, and dread wove itself through the shadow-world of Brand's half sleep. He heard the hateful words, and understood them:

Death and destruction! Blood and death!
Blood and death! Death and destruction!

The dark words ran through the streets and drowned out birdsong and the crowing of roosters as the dawn shone golden on the high domes and lofty roofs of the city.

In his sleep Brand heard knocking at his door. Or was it elug war drums in the palace? He leapt out of bed, sword in hand, his chest heaving for air.

But it was no attack. Aranloth stood in the doorway, the white robes of his office lit by morning sun shining through the window and the oaken staff in his hand gleaming gold. If he was alarmed by the sword levelled at him or the sudden reaction, he gave no sign of it.

"Come with me," he said. "I have an errand on the city walls, and I would like you to be there with me."

Brand picked up his scabbard from a nearby table and sheathed his blade.

"I dare not leave the palace. The king is in too much danger."

Aranloth leaned on the staff. "So he is. He's always in danger. But he'll survive an hour or two without you. I need you now more than he does, and Gilhain has given his leave. He knows whence I go and what I seek."

Brand let out a long breath and some of his tension went with it. He was still wearing his trousers and boots, so all he needed to do was put on a shirt and his white surcoat, and then belt on his sword.

When he was ready they went to the palace stables and retrieved their mounts. Brand rode his black stallion, a massive horse, but one that still mustered great speed at need and that could endure long hours of toil at a slower pace. Aranloth rode a young roan gelding.

They trotted down the streets, and the people looked at them as they went. Both were well known, and their clothes showed who they were well before their faces came into view.

Aranloth took the road to Arach Neben, the West Gate. It was chiefly there that the enemy had established its camp. They did not surround the whole city. Rather, they concentrated their force on one length of wall.

It was a long ride. Aranloth did not speak much during it, for he was deep in thought, and Brand did not disturb him. What he pondered was obviously troubling, and Brand was not eager to learn it, though he guessed that he would, whether he wanted to or not, when they reached their destination.

They stabled their mounts at the bottom of one of the guard towers that flanked the gate. Then, ascending many stairs, they came at length to the top of the tower.

Brand knew it well. In this very place he had served for some time, and the view of the walls to either side and the open lands stretching out to the west he knew well. But it all looked different now.

Below was the enemy camp. It spread out, sprawling and vast. It threw out wings to encircle the city, but these were no more than picket lines to prevent Cardoroth's scouts from entering or leaving.

The main host remained on the west side and concentrated their attack on that wall. For a month they had done so, but the city had food and water to last for years. It was a stalemate, as all sieges were, and yet by force of numbers and a persistence of effort over a long time the enemy might break through. The constant battle against fear, and the sorcerous chanting of the enemy during the night where their power was exerted to weaken the morale of the defenders, took a slow but inevitable toll.

Brand and Aranloth looked at the enemy camp. The sorcerers were in a tent in the midst of the host. They were surrounded by rank after rank of elugs, fell creatures with gray-green tinged skin, malicious eyes and harsh voices. They were a cruel people, apt subjects of the sorcerers, and they fought with an ancient enmity for mankind, born out of a time of legend, for battles had been fought with them since before the Camar races of men came east and founded realms along the coastal lands of Alithoras. And the Duthenor, Brand's own people, fought with them in ancient times also, although his ancestors migrated eastward much later and in fewer numbers than the great waves of Camar tribes.

All along the battlement wall, which the people often called the Cardurleth, the king's soldiers held their stations. They relaxed while they could for no assault was being made at present. But men skilled with blade and shaft were not the only ones who defended the wall. Spread thinly among them were white-robed and staff-carrying wizards.

Aranloth spoke briefly with the captain of the tower and he led his men away, filing down the stairs to leave the two of them alone.

"What if the enemy attacks?" Brand asked.

"The men won't be far away. They have only gone down one level and can return swiftly. But the enemy is not going to attack for a while."

Brand was alone with the wizard, and he sensed that something would soon happen, something of importance.

"So, what's our purpose here?" he asked.

Aranloth looked at him grimly. His face was unreadable, as it usually was, but there was a look to his eyes that spoke of some emotion beneath the surface, though what it was Brand could not tell.

"I'm going to attempt something ..." he said.

Brand studied him more closely. He saw no fear, but there was worry, and that concerned him. For whatever Aranloth was going to do, it must be dangerous, perhaps exceedingly so, and the wizard did not take such risks without great need.

3. Use the Sword!

Aranloth looked over the battlement at the enemy.

"Out there is the host, and it's monstrous in size and temperament, but its head is the small group of sorcerers – elùgroths to give them their proper name. They are the beating heart of the enemy, and its mind also. Not only that, they are the source of the drùghoth, the sendings that last night nearly killed the king. If I would learn whence came the power to achieve that, if I would learn more of the elùgroths' intentions, then I must seek that knowledge from them."

"And how will you do that?"

"By the only means that I can. I'm a lòhren, the oldest of the wizards, and there are skills that we lòhren have, even if we use them but rarely. One I will employ now."

Brand thought about that. "It seems obvious that the skill of which you speak is only used rarely for a reason. I assume it's dangerous?"

"Yes. It's dangerous. Lethal if done incorrectly, and even then there are perils that..." he paused, considering his words. "Let's just say that it's dangerous. But it's also necessary, and I'll risk it. For that purpose I have brought you along."

"How can I help? I'm willing to do anything you ask, but I haven't got any affinity for magic."

Aranloth gave an unexpectedly broad grin. "You're quick to agree to help given that you don't know what I'll do. That's dangerous with a lòhren, but in this case you need not fear. Only I'll be at risk."

"What exactly will you do?"

"I'll free my spirit from the shackles of the flesh and enter the otherworld, the world that hangs between life and death. There, with spirit eyes I'll enter the camp, enter the very tent of the elùgroths and discern what it is they do. And how."

Brand raised an eyebrow. "No wonder it's dangerous."

"It is what it is," Aranloth said. "But with your aid I can lessen the danger. The chief risk is that I won't be able to return to my body. If that happens, I'll wither and die. That will be your task – to call me back should I fail to do so on my own."

"And how will I know that you're in such straights?"

"I'll talk to you as I go and tell you what's happening. You'll know what I know, and should I fail to speak for any length of time you must wake me straight away. Use your sword and prick my flesh, even to the point of drawing blood. That strengthens the tie between spirit and body, and should pull me back."

Brand noticed that Aranloth said *should* rather than *will*, but he let it go. Now was not the time to show any doubt.

"I'll get you back, so long as you don't hold it against me that I strike you with a sword. The blade of my forefathers is sharp, and I'm unused to being gentle with it."

"Don't worry. You won't hurt me badly. But just remember, I'm not an elug. You need do no more than draw blood. If that doesn't work, nothing will."

"Let's get started then," Brand said. "The sooner this is over the better I'll like it. Magic always makes me uneasy."

"That's as it should be," Aranloth said. "It's what separates lòhrens from elùgroths. My kind use power sparingly, for its use is two-sided; the power affects us as much as we it. Too much is dangerous, yet the elùgroths don't forgo it, and especially they force their wills on others to try to dominate them, and the sorcery changes them according to how they use it. But enough! I'm talking now merely to put this off. We'll begin at once."

Aranloth sat down cross-legged on the stone. He let his staff rest in his lap, and he held it with his left hand while his right sought Brand's and took it in the warrior's grip, wrist to wrist.

"Do not let go," he said. "This helps me anchor into the world of the living."

Brand gripped his hand firmly. He would not let go. But he held his Halathrin blade in his right, drawn free from the sheath and ready to use if the lòhren needed recalling.

For long moments nothing happened. Aranloth's breathing was deep and long, but it grew ever slower, and he used his belly rather than his chest. His eyes were closed, the lids barely fluttering, and the clear skin on his face remained rosy with health. He showed no real signs of his age. But the grip of his hand lessened a little in intensity, and his head began to lean ever so slightly to one side.

Brand was startled when Aranloth sighed. It was like the last breath of a dying man, but the lòhren spoke to him a moment later.

"I am free," he said. "Here it is dark, but I still see the camp before us. I float down to the enemy as a leaf on the airs, though no leaf is this light. All about are shadows, and the elugs flit through them, groping forms of malice, but afar, in their midst, is a deeper shadow that not even my spirit eyes can pierce."

Brand felt his heart race and slowed his breathing to calm down. The lòhren's hand was now cold to touch, and as the words came to him of the camp and the shadows they formed a vivid picture in his mind as though they were part of a waking dream. Aranloth had not warned of that, and he was troubled, for it seemed to him that this was not quite what the lòhren expected.

"I slip among them," Aranloth continued. "The elugs do not see me, but I feel their hate, and their fear, and most of all I sense their uncertainty. That is why they do not attack this morning. They are leaderless for the moment. The elùgroths give no commands, and it seems that they were hurt last night when the Drùghoth were dispatched. They recover from their efforts."

There was a pause. Aranloth did not speak, yet Brand had the impression of sweeping movement and dark shapes lurching beneath him like a stream of water where fish swam but all that was glimpsed was the flash of tails, fins and the momentary turn and glide of bodies.

"I come now to the tent," Aranloth said.

Brand saw it. Vague – a thing of shadows deeper than all other shadows. It was guarded by power, warded with sorcery that he did not understand but still sensed.

"There is sorcery here," Aranloth said. It was needless, for Brand already knew it. That made him all the more uneasy.

The feeling of flight ceased. The tent was before them. A great construction of canvas, held in place by ropes and ties and wooden stakes.

It grew cold. The sun was so dim that it was but a shadowy patch in the sky less gray than elsewhere. Of the grass, there was no sign of green. Nor could Brand feel air on his face. But he felt the cold, both in Aranloth's handgrip and here near the elùgroths' tent.

"I go slowly now," Aranloth said.

The canvas came close. And then Brand was in it. He saw nothing for a moment but then once more on the other side dim images came to him.

There was but one room in the tent. It was bare of furniture and adornments. The ceiling was lost in shadows above. Yet at its center were deeper shadows, though he could distinguish nothing.

"They are here," Aranloth said, and his thought was a drift of nothingness on a silent breeze. "I must be careful or they'll sense me. Their wards are weak and ill crafted. My passing through did not give alarm, yet the closer I go the greater will be the risk."

The darkness seemed to gather and rush closer for a moment, and then it eased. The shadows were deep, but there was some little light from iron incense holders that smoldered a sullen red. A strange scent was in the air, sharp and repugnant. And it was clouded still further by drifting smoke from the slow burning of whatever bark-like material was in the holders.

Yet Brand could still see. Cushions and rugs covered the floor, and in a circle were the thirteen elùgroths. Most reclined as though resting. Some sat cross-legged as did Aranloth back at the top of the tower. A few muttered dully in some language beyond Brand's experience.

As though from a great distance Aranloth's voice drifted to him.

"They rest," he said. "And well they might, for the power they expended last night was great, and the destruction of the Drùghoth will have hurt them, for he who makes a thing must suffer some measure of harm when it is injured."

Brand remembered the hisses of pain from last night, and he smiled grimly. It gave him satisfaction that these sorcerers did not escape the assassination attempt unscathed.

"It's well for us that they're weary," Aranloth continued, "else they might more easily discover me."

They drifted a little closer, and Brand saw the enemy close up. They were black cloaked and hooded. Their dark wych-wood staffs rested in, or near, their pallid hands. Their skin, where he could see it, was white and blue-veined, as of a man who never saw the light of day. Of their faces, he could not see anything.

One there was who sat still and unmoving. He muttered the loudest, and at him Aranloth fixed his attention.

"Khamdar," he said. "A powerful elùgroth. Even for them he is a dark one. No evil is beyond him. Death and destruction trail in his wake, for he seeks admittance into the highest rank of their order. There is blood on his hands that all the oceans in the world would not wash away."

Aranloth paused, perhaps lost in memories of battles and destruction from other times and places. So Brand guessed. But he knew this: the lòhren's unease increased before he spoke again.

"Here we come to it at last. There is an object before them."

Brand looked closely. He could see nothing at first, but then they eased a little closer. Before them all, but most closely to Khamdar, he saw something.

It was long and dark. It rested on a thick black cloth, as though it was an object of reverence. There were marks on it, strange signs that either glowed and pulsed with a faint light of their own or else reflected dimly the smoldering embers in the incense holders.

"I am closer now," Aranloth said. "It is precious to them. It rests on velvet and is woven with marks of sorcery. It is … it is a wych-wood staff such as elùgroths use. Flexible as a whip, yet still strong enough to contain and conduct great power."

There was a longer pause, and Brand felt tension sing in the air as Aranloth's gaze swept over the elùgroths.

"Yet the thirteen each keep their staffs beside them."

There was another pause, and Aranloth drew closer still to the staff that lay on the black cloth.

"The staff is not whole. I see splinters and a shattered end. It is broken near the middle. The splinters are dagger-like and malice drips from them, cruel and potent, like venom from a poisoned blade."

The room seemed to grow colder. Or else a breeze touched their bodies far away atop the tower. Brand could not tell.

"I must get closer," Aranloth said. "This is a thing of power, and it fills me with dread. Arcane forces roil within it, trapped for many long years. They are become one with the wood, perhaps were infused into it for a purpose, designed to be one with it. It is far more than a staff ... it is a repository of elùgai, the sorcery of an elùgroth. It fills it even as a carafe is filled with red wine. It is strange sorcery ... one that perhaps I have felt before. I hope that is not so ... but I must touch it to be sure."

In the shadows Brand saw Aranloth's hand glimmer palely. It reached out, wavering and silvery, barely there and yet visible to him.

The hand stretched forth, and then paused a moment before it finally rested against the dark wood.

Aranloth cried out in sudden pain. He tried to withdraw, but his hand seemed stuck. Some power within the staff gripped him.

The elùgroths stirred. Some that were lying came to their feet. Khamdar remained seated, but his eyes flicked open, dark slits of evil. His muttering grew suddenly clear in a chant of great force.

33

"The sword!" yelled Aranloth. "The sword! I'm trapped and cannot return!"

Brand felt the hilt of the blade in his hand. He grew suddenly dizzy, swaying between two places at once, for the scene in the dark tent was before his eyes, but so also was the bright light at the top of the tower and the seated lòhren.

He fumbled, bringing his sword to bear, and he ran the edge hard along Aranloth's arm where he took his own in the warrior's grip.

The Halathrin-forged steel drew blood. It ran, bright red, dripping onto the stone floor. Or was it the dark cloth beneath the broken staff? Brand could not be sure.

Aranloth groaned. His hand gripped tightly. His strength was much more than that of any old man, and Brand felt pain in his arm. But the lòhren did not return to his body, and the grip of his hand lessened. Nor did he speak again.

Brand concentrated on the dark scene in the tent once more, and the light of the sun vanished. Khamdar's chanting was grown shrill, as though he fought some battle against another power. More elùgroths joined him, assuming their positions in the circle, hands on their staffs.

"Aranloth!" Brand yelled. But there was no answer. He sensed the lòhren's presence, but he was caught amid some struggle for life and death, and Brand knew he was losing. The elùgroths held his spirit in the tent by the power they possessed and by the force of the broken staff. He would die here unless something happened.

Brand looked around. The dark tent swam. The chill in the air grew, and frost formed on the stems of the metal incense holders. He felt sorcery, strong and dark, sure of purpose and growing. Suddenly, Brand saw the woven threads of it through the room, like a spider's

34

web, drawing tighter, growing thicker, and he knew that if he did not do something soon then not only would Aranloth be caught in this trap, but he himself would also be held by it, and they would both die.

4. The Long Hidden

Brand hesitated.

He should return to his body while he still could. But it was not in his nature to leave Aranloth behind, and he knew if he did that he would regret it. And things would go ill for the city and the king, as if they had not done so enough.

He gripped hard the hilt of his Halathrin blade and made his choice: *fate favored the bold-hearted!* With a wild yell and a mighty swing he brought the sword crashing against Khamdar's head.

The elùgroth recoiled, sprawling away, and then he rose towering to his feet, the tallest man Brand had ever seen. His head swung from side to side, his smoldering eyes, lit red like the embers in the incense holders, roved the tent seeking his assailant. On his head there was no wound, yet pain showed on his face. And surprise.

Brand had not expected to hurt him, had not even been sure that the elùgroth would feel anything, and yet he had achieved his aim. Khamdar ceased to chant. The others seemed confused by his strange movements, and their own voices faltered.

It was the chance that Aranloth needed, for a moment it was the staff alone that held him, and with a surge of effort he broke free of its power. There was a rush of air and light. And then, as if from a great distance, the voice of Khamdar followed. *You are dead, Aranloth. The city will fall about you and whoever it is that just helped you. I will know them if we meet. He shall not escape me either!*

36

Light flashed around Brand and dazzled his eyes, bringing tears to them. Yet he could see, and he knew he was on the top of the tower again. The morning was about them, and the enemy left behind below.

He turned his gaze to Aranloth. The lòhren struggled to his feet, using his staff to help him, and Brand rose also.

They looked at each other, and the lòhren shook his head as if to clear it.

"That was close," he said. "Closer and more risky than I guessed. They knew I might try such a thing, and that did not worry me, but I was not prepared for the staff. It is a thing of greater power than I expected, and that misjudgment nearly undid me."

Brand used an old cloth to wipe the drops of Aranloth's blood from his blade and then sheathed the sword.

"All is well as ends well," he said. "At least it's so in this case. We came back, and you must have learned what you needed to know about their new powers. It seemed to me that you recognized the staff."

Aranloth raised an eyebrow. "We'll get to that in a moment. Don't you know what happened in there?"

"It was all a bit vague," Brand answered with a frown. "But you were caught, both by the staff and the elùgroths working some sorcery."

"And then?"

"And then I struck Khamdar with my sword. It didn't seem to hurt him much, but it surprised him and gave you a chance to escape when his concentration faltered."

Aranloth stared at him. "And nothing about that struck you as strange?"

"I'm not sure what you mean. It was *all* strange."

Aranloth let out a long sigh. "I said when we began that I would describe things to you. But there was no need for that, was there? You were with me, as you should not have been. For someone who mistrusts magic you have a strange affinity for it."

Brand shrugged. "I *do* mistrust magic, and I want nothing to do with it. But I was there with you, and I saw what needed to be done, and I did it. Is there really anything strange about that?"

Aranloth looked like he would argue, but all he said was "Perhaps not." Then he leaned on his staff and looked out over the battlement.

"So," Brand said. "Tell me more of the staff. Where's it from, and what can you do about the power they take from it?"

The lòhren's gaze did not stray from the field below, but his eyes seemed to look back in time rather than at the enemy camp.

"It's a thing of power, that much you already know. But it has a history – one that is dark, both by the deeds done and by the long years that have piled uncounted since that time. The land of Alithoras has seen kingdoms rise from nothing and fall back into oblivion since last I saw it, and he that wielded it."

The lòhren paused and turned his keen-eyed glance upon Brand. There was anger in his eyes, but it was only the most obvious of the many emotions that swirled there, visible now as they rarely were, for the lòhren was mostly impassive. Something must have disturbed him greatly.

"The staff," he continued, "belonged to Shurilgar the Sorcerer. Shurilgar the Betrayer of Nations. Shurilgar, that once was a lòhren. It is a name not unknown to you, nor to any who dwell in Alithoras, though he lived in a past so long ago that most else is forgotten about it."

Brand knew the name. He knew it well, better than many. Shurilgar was one of the great ones, mighty among lòhrens ... and among elùgroths. He knew him, and he feared him, though the sorcerer was dead.

The legends said that he was slain by Aranloth in a great battle. The lòhren did not talk of such things. If it was true, Brand did not know. It was hard to believe that the man who stood before him now, talking and breathing, was the same legendary Aranloth from those far distant times. And yet that was what was thought in Cardoroth, though some claimed the name of Aranloth was used by generations of lòhrens as a kind of hereditary title. Brand was not inclined to believe them. But none of this, intriguing as it was, helped solve Cardoroth's present problems.

"If they have this thing of power, why haven't they used it before?"

"They did not have it before. Of that we can be certain. If they had, they would have used it. Elùgroths are always quick to exploit such things, eager to unleash sorcery, quick to dismiss the consequences, and slow to exercise caution. But every consequence is one day discerned, every secret one day discovered. In this case, the long hidden is found again. The long sought for is now in their possession. And they *have* sought this thing, since before Cardoroth was founded. Before the Camar tribes came east and founded their realms, some of which still stand."

The lòhren turned to him once more. As always, he veiled the power that was in him, but Brand sensed it near the surface now, like the sun covered by the last trailing edges of a cloud, ready to blaze.

"It was I that defeated Shurilgar, as you have guessed. It was I that broke his power and slew him, though he was as a brother to me in a time more distant than that deed now is to you. And in doing so, I broke his staff. One half the immortal Halathrin took to their realm, for they were with me and suffered more than most from his betrayal and malice. There long ages they held it secure. The other half I kept myself."

"Why wasn't it destroyed?" Brand asked.

"Alas! I wish that it was. Such was my counsel, but it went unheeded, though you will see why. For the wood came from a sacred grove of elms in the forest realm of the Halathrin. Not only that, it grew on a mound, the burial place of their great king who led them hither to Alithoras on their exodus. It was from that place that Shurilgar stole the timber for his staff. For the Halathrin do not entomb their dead in stone, even their great ones. Yet this much they knew of their own lore, and needed not my telling: the staff was possessed of an evil power, yet they deemed that its power must lie dormant without an elùgroth to wield it. There, in their forest realm, they kept their half, and they kept it in token of the living tree and the rest of the grove that Shurilgar had razed by fire and sorcery. They would not destroy the staff, for it was all that was left of something sacred to them, even though it was now tainted. I did not agree with them then, still less do I do so now, and yet I understand why they took that path."

Aranloth had grown sad in the telling of this tale. Brand guessed that he understood better than most why people clung to the last remnant of something, or someone, that was loved after they were gone. In his long life he must have suffered many such losses.

The lòhren seemed to stiffen now with some resolve or new thought.

"But some dreadful deeds must have been done to retrieve it," he said, "and I fear for the Halathrin. Not lightly did they undertake to preserve and guard this thing, for they knew it would be sought by elùgroths. And to enter the Halathrin realm by force or stealth is unheard of. They have powers of their own, not that of lòhrens and elùgroths, but a unique and peculiar magic. And when that fails they have many bright blades and great courage. Alas, all of these things must have been tested and found wanting. They will feel shame that evil has been loosed on the land, and they will feel grief that all that is left of their sacred trust is stolen again."

Brand did not really grasp half of this story. But loss he understood. And evil. It was before him now anytime he chose to look over the battlement and watch the seething mass of the dark army spread below. But something else troubled him.

"What of the staff's second half? Was it destroyed? If not, how can you know which half the elùgroths found?"

Aranloth shook his head. "The second half was not destroyed. The two halves are joined by sorcery. To destroy one is to destroy the other, for they are linked by the forces that infuse them. And I had not the heart do that to the Halathrin."

"Then where is it?"

Aranloth looked at him bleakly. "It's in the one place in Alithoras that none can go save me. There only did I trust to its safekeeping, the only secure place for such a thing. So it has proved, for few places are harder to reach than the realm of the Halathrin, yet still from there the other half was taken."

"Can we reach and destroy the half you have hidden?"

"We must!" Aranloth said with sudden fierceness. "Or else Cardoroth will fall to sorcery. I, and the other lòhrens, cannot hold the elùgroths off forever. But the reaching of it is the problem."

"Why?"

41

Aranloth turned away. "Let me think. But first, before I decide anything, the king must learn of this. And in the choices that follow he also will have a hand."

Aranloth recalled the soldiers, and they filed up once more on the battlements, oblivious to what had transpired there. Had they known, they would have shown greater fear. But Brand knew; indeed he knew better than most just how powerful Shurilgar was and that, though the lòhren had expected to discover some artefact that enhanced the elùgroths power, this was a thing greater and darker than he had dreamed.

They made their way back to the palace with little speech. The lòhren remained deep in thought, and Brand studied the city as he rode. He looked at it now in a different light, for it was always that way when something was at risk.

The people showed little worry at the siege. They had endured such trials before and they trusted the high wall, and the skill of Gilhain, to save them. Brand was not so sure. The enemy was vast. They were led by foes determined to bring the city down, and treachery bred in Cardoroth like shadows in a dark forest. It was everywhere, else there would be less need for the Durlin. And on top of it all there was the sorcery to consider. No, there was good reason for fear, but not despair. While Gilhain drew breath, the city might survive, and there were others to help him.

The hooves of their horses clattered in the palace yard and they gave their horses to the stable boys to brush down and care for.

Aranloth hastened, striding up stairs and along corridors until at length they came to the king's chamber. The Durlin guards were not there, but a maid was just then coming out of the room.

"Is the king inside?" Aranloth asked.

42

She curtsied. "No, My Lord. The king left some while ago."

"Where is he then?"

"In council with the army commanders. At least so I heard the queen say to someone else."

Aranloth strode away. He turned as he went, speaking over his shoulder, "Thank you," he said.

The maid smiled and gave another curtsy.

Brand followed swiftly. There was not far to go, however. Aranloth guessed rightly which meeting chamber was being used and in moments he stood before the great doors. They were closed, and outside waited six Durlin, two more than usual.

They gave Brand the Durlin salute, a clenched fist over their hearts. He returned it, wondering if even six guards was enough, yet the men must take turns and rest. No one could stay alert all the time. Without rest they were useless, and the palace was the safest, though not *safe*, place in the city.

"Open the door," Brand commanded.

Two of the men obeyed. One gave a knock to the timber, using a brass weight that was set in the middle of the door so that those inside knew when an interruption was coming and not to utter any secrets until it was established who was entering.

Then both men swung the door open. It was a heavy contraption of oak, carved, decorated and paneled with gold. They entered, Brand allowing the lòhren to go first, for he was of higher standing in the city.

The lòhren stood in the doorway, and his face was grim. The captains looked at him. Lornach who sat next to the king, ready to protect him and summon the Durlin if trouble started inside the chamber, studied him also. And the king scrutinized them both, his eyes curious, knowing whence they had come from and what had been his task.

"I would speak with the king," Aranloth said.

Gilhain nodded, and his gaze shifted for a moment to the captains.

"Alone," Aranloth said. "Except for Brand."

Brand had not expected to be included in the discussion. He was not a counselor to the king, but his guard, and it seemed that the captains thought it strange also. But they did not like his ascension to the position of Durlindrath. They did not like *him*, because he was a foreigner, no matter that he had proved himself more than they had. But the king knew, and that was all that counted.

The soldiers filed out, annoyed to be dismissed, more annoyed that Brand was going in. They did not look at him or greet him as they passed.

Lornach was the last to go. He rolled his eyes as he neared, and Brand repressed a smile.

"Come in and take a seat. Tell me what you discovered," the king said to them.

They sat, but it was the king who spoke first.

"So, is it good news or bad?"

Aranloth leaned his staff against the edge of the table, but he did not let it go.

"The worst," the lòhren said.

Gilhain gave no reaction. If anything, the wolfish intelligence on his face showed just that little bit more determination.

"Tell me all," he said.

It did not take long. The king was familiar with Shurilgar; it would be hard to find someone who was not. The breaking of the staff and the hiding of the two pieces were all that was really new to him.

44

"And you're sure that it was the Halathrin piece that has somehow been found and taken?"

"I'm sure."

"The Halathrin will have guarded this thing well, no doubt. And its loss will devastate them. But so too will the fact that through them a great evil has been unleashed upon Alithoras. I wonder," Gilhain said, "if they would try to retrieve the thing. I cannot help but feel that they will. Perhaps they'll even send an army. That may be the chance that we're looking for, the one turn of events that could save us."

Aranloth sighed and let go of his staff. "O king," he said. "I wish that it would be so, but it will not. The Halathrin no longer venture into the lands beyond their forest realm. They suffered greatly, as you know, in the Elù-haraken, the Shadowed Wars. The immortals died like wheat before the scythe, though in numbers far less than men. Since those times they have become reclusive. There will be no army, but *perhaps* they will send a small group of their best to try to retrieve the staff. If so, when they discover that it is held in the midst of an army, they will give up. There will be no help from them, for they will bide their time and hope to retrieve it one day in the future when the guard is not so great. They are, after all, immortal. They have great patience to wait for such things."

"Then there's little hope for us. The elug army is patient too, and it will wear us down even if it takes another year. And no aid will come from anywhere else in Alithoras. Other cities are far away, and they stand in peril of invasion also. We must prepare ourselves for the long defeat. We knew it would come one day."

Aranloth held up his hand. "O king. You spoke of a last chance for Cardoroth. It will not be the Halathrin as you hoped. Yet there *is* a chance, faint and slim. The last chance, and yet the best."

Gilhain looked at him. The wolfish intelligence of his eyes flashed.

"What chance is this? It's something new, and something to do with magic or sorcery rather than soldiers and swords, else we would have discussed it before now."

"So it is," Aranloth said. "For in every power there is a weakness. In every loss an opportunity. It is so with Shurilgar's staff. I said that the enemy has the one half. The other is not in their possession. But both are linked by the power that Shurilgar put into them. Should the second half be found, should it be destroyed, then the first will lose its potency. The power will drain from it. Perhaps even the timber itself will crumble to dust. I hope not for the latter, for I would return it to the Halathrin, yet I fear that such will be the case."

Gilhain looked at him shrewdly. "You say *if* it is found. Yet I guess that you already know where it is. Is that not so."

"That is so. Finding it will not be a problem. Retrieving it from the place in which it is hidden is where the difficulty lies. For if the Halathrin realm is well guarded, then the place where the second half is kept is warded by protections greater than all other places in Alithoras. The hope of success is so slight as to be barely there."

"And yet," said the king with his usual quick shrewdness, "if it was placed there for safekeeping, then it is possible to enter there again."

Aranloth nodded, but his face was grim, and his eyes held doubt.

Brand leaned forward. "It's time to reveal this hiding place of the second fragment. It cannot be *that* bad."

"It is worse. Worse than you could know. For it is hidden in the tombs of the Letharn."

Brand had not heard the name before. It meant nothing to him, but Gilhain sat back in his chair, a thoughtful expression on his face.

"There is a rumor, he said, "come down out of the ancient past about a people called the Letharn. Once they were mighty, the whisper says, yet their empire fell and now nothing remains of them. Are the tombs something to do with them?"

"Yes," Aranloth said. "It's to do with them, but saying they were mighty is like calling a massive old oak tree a splinter. Once, in an age so long ago that nothing is remembered save the tattered edges of legend, their empire stretched from the mountains of Auren Dennath in the north to the mountains of the Graèglin Dennath in the south. That is over three hundred leagues, and it reached inland in some places much further. But their empire fell before even the exodus of the Halathrin into these lands, and even the immortals found little more than traces of what once was great. And yet, some works of the Letharn remain, for not all that they achieved is lost."

The lòhren ceased talking, and his expression was pensive. But soon he put aside whatever he was thinking of and addressed them again.

"The tombs of the Letharn," he said, "are ancient. They began when their empire did, and the empire endured long before it fell. And in the noontide of their long rule the tombs were expanded, for ever they tunneled deeper into the hard rock of the earth where no light shines and few things live. And ever they needed more room. The wealth of nations was buried with their multitudinous dead, treasures that the cities of the Camar that came after could not match. If all that those cities

47

owned for the last thousand years were piled into a hill, still it would seem as an ant mound to the mountains of wealth the Letharn gathered. But hold, O king, I see you look at me in amazement, and I see the light of desire in your eyes, for what person, be he king or no, would not want some share of that?"

The king shrugged. "The thought crossed my mind, but wealth is no good to Cardoroth if the city falls to the enemy. That is my only concern."

"And so it must stay," Aranloth said, "for the Letharn were a mighty people, and they were jealous of their wealth, and it does not lie unguarded…"

He turned now to Brand.

"Poison covers all the treasure from the least trinket to the most sacred of their heirlooms. It rests near those who once counted it, or wore in on finger, neck or head. Even in death they would keep it that way. Poison that you cannot see or smell covers all. That poison is so deadly, even after all this time, that whomsoever touches it dies a most dreadful death. And that is but the least protection. For in their noontide, the Letharn were a terrible people. Might they possessed of uncounted arms and never-defeated armies. Yet also among them were those who delved deep into lore that few understand. Other powers they had, greater than legions of soldiers. And they invoked them to guard the tombs."

Aranloth fell silent. Brand barely dared to ask, but he wanted to know something.

"What did the Letharn do?" he asked. "What powers did they raise to protect the tombs?"

"Something terrible," the lòhren answered. "A great feat of power, for they made three creatures, or rather they drew them forth from the very powers that form and substance the earth. And those creatures they set as guardians. They roam the tombs. Bound to them, they

48

cannot leave, and yet within them they are mighty. No lòhren, no elùgroth, not a hundred combined could stand against them."

The king looked at him intently. "Yet you must have ventured into those tombs, or else you could not have hidden the staff there."

Aranloth returned his gaze. "Yes, there is a way. The ancients created an enchantment, surpassing strong, yet they also created a way to circumvent it. The powers they called forth are called the harakgar. They are bound to the tombs, but they are not bound to any particular shape or form. There are three of them, and they always appear together in whatever guise they choose. And they do choose it, for they have intelligence as well as power. They cannot be slain – they can only be held off. There are words of power that lull them, but they only work to allow entry or exit from the tombs. Otherwise, the dead and their treasures could not have been laid to rest. Yet the words lose much of their strength should someone try to take a thing, howsoever small, away from the tombs. That, the harakgar do not tolerate, words no."

Brand ran his fingers through his hair. Sorcery and wizardry were all alike to him: he mistrusted anything that he could not hold and feel in his hand.

"Has *anything* ever been removed successfully from the tombs?"

"Yes," the lòhren said. He looked down at his staff as though remembering another time. "It was done with great cost, and luck, and I had others with me to help. Things could have easily gone awry."

"Then that gives me hope," Gilhain said. "If you have done it once, if you are willing to try again, then you might well succeed."

Aranloth laughed, but it was as though at a grim jest rather than with humor.

"There's only one problem with that," he said. "I cannot leave the city. Between me and the other lòhrens, we are just enough to hold the elùgroths at bay. Should one of us leave, you would be dead within the week. Should *I* leave, you would be dead within the day. No, O king, I wish to, but cannot undertake this quest."

Gilhain did not answer for a moment. There was silence while these words sunk in. At length, he glanced at the lòhren again.

"If neither you, nor another lòhren can go, then perhaps some other brave soul might attempt the deed?"

"That may be," Aranloth said. "Yet it would be a brave soul indeed, for while the words of power may be learned, as even any lòhren on the wall would need to be taught them, even one of them would likely die. It takes more than magic to survive in that place. To ask such a thing of a person without a lòhren's training, without their power, is to ask them to risk their lives for less than the slimmest chance of success. I say this to you truly, not even an army would suffice to fulfil this task, even if you could spare the men. The many can die just as easily as the few, and the way in the tombs is long and dark. It takes a certain kind of courage that few possess, perhaps only one in an army of ten thousand men, and then luck besides. Make no mistake. Words or no, the harakgar do not permit anything to leave the tombs: not a diamond as big as your fist nor a fragment of broken pottery. The words alone will not be enough."

Gilhain shook his head. "Then we're caught in a dilemma without hope."

Aranloth let out a long sigh. "In a dark place yes, but not totally void of hope. There might yet be a way, but if it is attempted, it will likely mean death to the person who goes, and certainly it will leave me with reduced power just when I need it most."

50

"What is this way then?" Gilhain asked. "For it's death to carry on as we are. We all know that."

5. The Fate of the Kingdom

Aranloth did not answer straightaway. It seemed as though he still debated something within his own mind, and this troubled Brand more than anything, for the lòhren was usually swift to assess a situation and to make a decision.

"If I cannot go, but someone *must* go, then we have to choose a person to go in my stead – if we can find anyone willing. As I said, in such a quest one person might avail as well as an army, for it's not by mere numbers or swords or courage, but rather by strength of will that the harakgar can be survived, and the quest be accomplished, if it can be accomplished at all." He leaned back in his chair, sifting through lore in his mind that Brand guessed few, if any, in Alithoras possessed.

"And the harakgar are not the only danger," he continued. "The enemy beyond our walls is cunning. Those who command know that I have learned of the staff. They will guess my next move – to seek to break the second half in order to reduce their power, and they will be watching. The breaking of the staff is their greatest fear, not only because it will undermine their power here, but because they hope one day to recover it. If both halves are drawn together again their power would be increased. And the elùgroths' hope is my fear."

He seemed as though he would say more of that, of the intentions of the enemy, but instead he carried on with things directly at hand. It did not matter, for Brand knew as well as everybody what the elùgroths and the armies that they commanded sought: the total domination of all of Alithoras.

"One alone, or a very small group," Aranloth continued, "might slip away from the siege and avoid the watchfulness of the enemy. Even so, it would take much luck, and there will be need of magic ere the end to face the harakgar if the person gets that far."

Gilhain sat back and crossed his arms. "But you said yourself that you cannot go, and neither can any of the lòhrens. So, there is no one with the skills that you require."

Aranloth pursed his lips. "There is no one with the skills. And yet even an unskilled person can wield a lòhren's staff as a weapon. To be sure, they could only summon a fragment of the power that a lòhren might, for most of a lòhren's power comes ultimately from inside themselves and not the staff. But when a staff is used the magic takes hold of it, becomes infused into the wood, and has a life of its own. That residual power is only a small help, but on such small chances, and what a person makes of them, often rests life and death, success and failure."

The king was thoughtful. "Such a person would have to be special. Their courage, wit and luck must be unmatched."

"So it must be," Aranloth said, exchanging a veiled glance with Gilhain, "for the fate of the kingdom would be balanced on their life and every choice they made. It is a great burden, and I would trust few, if any, to bear it."

"I also," Gilhain said. "Yet there is one in my realm who has proven their resourcefulness. One who has shown loyalty beyond question. And one that luck favors. So far, anyway."

"Who?" Brand asked. There were several he could think of that might match that description. Lornach seemed the most likely. But he did not wish to see his friend go on such a dangerous quest, nor did he wish to lose one of his best Durlin at a time when they were needed most.

There was a long silence. Aranloth looked at him with his typical gaze: eyes that had seen a thousand tragedies. The king looked at him with his usual wolfish keenness. For a while Brand did not understand, and then he realized that they were talking about him.

"You can't be serious," he said in a low voice.

"We're deadly serious," Gilhain said.

"But I have no powers against sorcery, and no affinity for magic. Aranloth's staff would be nothing more than an ordinary weapon in my hands."

"I will teach you the words needed to subdue the harakgar," Aranloth said. "And the staff will respond to your touch. It will give something of its powers, though how much and in what form I cannot say."

"You said yourself that those powers would not be enough. You said that even a lòhren might not have the strength to escape the creatures in the tombs."

"I said that other virtues are needed also. Virtues that anyone could have, though few do, whether they're lòhrens or not. You have those qualities," he paused, his expression thoughtful, "and maybe you will surprise yourself if you use the staff in need. It will be more than a prop for tired legs. You will be able to tap into something that few others could, and in truth, if I cannot go, only you would I trust in my stead. I will give my staff to no other. Nor would I trust such a quest to anybody else."

Brand hesitantly reached out, looking at the same time into Aranloth's eyes for permission, and took the staff in his hand. It felt comfortable and balanced in his grip. He put it down again.

"It feels good in my hand, but as a weapon of timber and nothing else. I don't lightly say no to you, Aranloth. You've helped me so much. Your counsels are always dark, but profitable. But I *must* say no. As you trust no one else for this quest, neither do I trust anyone else to guard the king. Not as I do. I cannot go."

Gilhain stirred. "And if I, as your king, command you, will you not then go?"

"No," Brand said without hesitation. "My place is by your side."

The king gave his wolfish grin. It was not the reaction Brand expected.

"Well, I will not command you," he said. "Even kings do not lightly order those who serve them to face likely death. And yet I say this to you. Well have you guarded me. But time is running out. Not even you can protect me forever. If the staff isn't destroyed, Cardoroth will surely fall. It may well fall anyway, but the outcome is then less certain. These are facts. If you would protect me, you *must* take up this quest, but you should go of your own free will, though with my blessing. If not, then you shall stay, and we will die and fight the great dark together when it comes for us. What do you say?"

Brand did not answer. He knew it was death to stay, death if the power of the elùgroths was not broken. But this strange quest, to a place that he did not know, there to pit himself against powers beyond him, that was death too.

In the silence that now held the room he heard from afar the sound of battle renewed at the walls. It was a dim echo of screams and clashes of arms, of hurtled missiles against the walls. In his mind he imagined the rush of the enemy, the swift flight of hissing arrows, the throwing up of ladders and knotted climbing ropes, and the death that followed. He had seen battle. He was expert at it, in all the ways to protect himself and kill an enemy. He had seen battle, and he did not like it. If nothing was done, he would see it one day in the streets, and then the palace, and then finally, if he was still alive, at bay somewhere with the king. He saw that in his mind also, and he did not like it either.

Brand bowed his head. Neither the king nor Aranloth spoke. At length, he sighed and looked at them again.

"I'll go," he said. "Though I see little hope in it, yet it is better than the certainty of defeat."

Gilhain straightened. A strange look came over him. It was one of hope renewed.

"Against the raging swords of the enemy who would bring darkness," the king said, "you shall be a sword of light! You are the one hope that we set against many despairs. You are become Cardoroth's champion in her darkest hour."

Brand slowly shook his head. "But I wasn't even born here. Many in the city would be happy to see me leave and never return. It may be Cardoroth's darkest hour, but I'm not her champion. The men on the walls who defend us each day, they are each and every one of them Cardoroth's champions."

The king rested a hand on his shoulder. "Many begrudge your rise in my service. You're a foreigner, and they do not like that. You are young, and they do not like that either, but I read the people of the city better than you do. This is truly our hour of deepest peril, and as king and guardian of each and every life in this realm, I choose *you* for our hope. And should you return to this city, should it still stand, you will see that there is more love for you here than you think."

Brand was not so sure about that. He knew that the people he dealt with on a daily basis, the lords of the realm and the commanders of the army, had little love for him. They begrudged the respect the king showed him, and they would prefer that one of their own received it instead of what they considered a wild man from the tribes of the Duthenor. And yet the ordinary people seemed to like him. For the king, and for them, he would do his best to live up to Gilhain's hopes.

"Let's assume I can retrieve this broken staff," he said, turning to Aranloth. "It's a thing of power. I have seen the one half, and it's filled with sorcery. How can such a powerful artifact be destroyed?

6. A Chance at Life

Aranloth shrugged. "Sometimes you over think things. The staff is made of timber – it'll burn."

The lòhren looked at Brand with sudden intensity after his casual words. "But you must remember this at all cost. Do *not* destroy the staff within the tombs. It will enrage the harakgar beyond any hope of escape. Their sole purpose, their very reason for existence, is to protect all that is laid to rest there. If you reach the outside again, that is the place to start a fire. The harakgar are bound to the tombs. They cannot take one step beyond them, and nor should you until the staff is destroyed, for the elùgroths must *not* have a chance to reclaim it."

"None of this is going to be easy, I suppose," Brand said.

"Not much in life ever is," Aranloth replied. "Listen though!" he said. "I will teach you the words that might make it possible. Without them you will die. With them, you might lull the harakgar's powers just enough for your other talents to make the difference between life and death."

The lòhren leaned in close and whispered. He said words in a foreign tongue, harsh and strange. Brand guessed it was the very language of the Letharn themselves, a tongue now dead, unspoken by all except Aranloth and those like him. Though it would not surprise Brand if Aranloth, alone in all the many lands of Alithoras, knew this lore.

When he was done the lòhren leaned back and stared into his eyes.

"Burn those words into your mind. Forget them and you are a dead man."

Brand nodded. Having learned them, he would not forget. There were only two now who knew them, for so well kept was their secret that Aranloth had even whispered them in the presence of a king. But if Gilhain was offended, he did not show it.

Aranloth leaned in close again. "Whisper them back," he said.

Brand did so. He repeated them several times until the lòhren appeared satisfied.

"Do not forget!" he commanded. "Recite them when you wake. Recite them when you prepare for sleep. Make them flow through your mind like the blood that surges through your veins, or when you stand in the tombs you will be utterly defenseless against the harakgar, and sword and staff and even luck will avail you nothing. Do not forget!"

Brand had no intention of doing so, but he was surer of his sword as a weapon than any words. Yet he was not stupid, and the manner of the lòhren convinced him of their need.

"How shall I find my way to the staff?" he asked. "The tombs are vast, you say. It would be best to take the swiftest route."

Aranloth took up a quill left from the king's meeting with the army commanders.

"I'll draw you a map and teach you the way. It may be that necessity will drive you to venture a different path, either on the way in or out, so I'll include several. There are many however – the ways of the tombs are myriad. And it's a dark place, full of fear and nameless things. Don't stray from my paths, or else you'll wander in there, alone in the dark, until you lay yourself down to die among the already dead."

Brand watched as the lòhren drew the map and offered instructions and descriptions of the various things he would see. He memorized this also, for he trusted better to his memory of the lòhren's words than to a map. He noticed as well that he drew this in front of the king, and that Gilhain listened with interest. Brand supposed the map was useless without the words to lull the harakgar, and that reaffirmed for him their importance. Still, even the sendings of the elùgroths had proved vulnerable to a blade, and he guessed that the harakgar would be put to the same test. In steel he trusted rather than magic, and it had never let him down yet.

"So much for the tombs," Aranloth said. "But you must get there first for any of this to matter. Before you came to Cardoroth you wandered in the wild lands. But you never went far to the south?"

"No. I crossed the Careth Nien, the Great River, far to its north when it was ice-bound. I wandered in the shadow of the mountains to the north, for something there lured me, but the winter bit cold, and I was pursued at the time, so I headed south to warmer climes and Cardoroth, rumor of which has reached even the Duthenor."

"Well, from here," the lòhren said, "you must journey due south. It's some fifty leagues or more to another river, this time the Carist Nien. When you reach its banks turn east and follow it to the land of the Angle that I described. That is the place where the river splits in two. You'll not miss it. The waterfall there, and other things, are remarkable. That is a journey nearly as far as the first leg. In all it's some three hundred miles. A long way to travel on foot, but there's no way to take a horse out of the city. If you would shorten the journey, you must find a mount on the way, if you can. But the lands all about are controlled by the enemy, though no doubt most are with this army that besieges us. You'll not find help along the way, but I can't rule it out altogether, for there are other strongholds that resist the enemy. But they are along the coast – too far east for you to go. Still, the lands are wild and much may happen between here and the Angle."

"Clearly there's a way to escape this siege, albeit without a horse," Brand said. "Where is it?"

"We'll meet at dusk at the West Gate. From there, we'll show you the way."

"But the enemy is most heavily concentrated on our western wall, and the Angle is to the south."

"That may be," the king said. "But the only way out lies westward."

Brand did not like it. Westward lay the shadow-haunted pine forests around Lake Alithorin. He had been inside them, more than once, and he was not keen to go back. Every time he went there he came near to death.

"For now," the king continued, "we have said all that can be said and made what decisions that could be made. It's best for you to rest. Prepare what equipment and food you would take, though it cannot be much while traveling on foot, and then rest while you can until dusk. It'll be a long night, and you'll be glad of some sleep now when the time for escape comes later.

Brand stood up. The king shook his hand.

"This is no easy task we have set you," Gilhain said, "but do not think that either I or Aranloth would send you if we did not trust in the fact that you might achieve it. And if the worst happens, for either of us, then know this. From the wild lands you came to us, young, brash, confident – and a complete stranger. You leave now as Cardoroth's champion, and the friend of the king. Fare well, and if we do not meet again, know that nothing lasts forever. So my people often say, but we say also this: the sun is warm when it shines, and memories endure a lifetime."

Brand did not answer. But he gripped the king's arm in the warrior's handshake, and then turned and left. But from the doorway he spoke again.

"We'll meet again, Gilhain," he said quietly. "I swore an oath to protect you, and I fulfil it now in a strange way. So are the turns of fortune. But I think I'll return to this city, and to you, my king. When I do, we shall share our stories, for I think we'll both have much to tell."

Gilhain turned to the lòhren when Brand had gone.

"What fortune swept him into my realm?" he asked.

"I don't know, yet good fortune it was," Aranloth answered.

"Are all the Duthenor as he? If so, they will one day conquer the world."

Aranloth tilted his head at those last words as if in thought.

"Perhaps they could. But they are a fragmentary people at the moment. Once, one of Brand's ancestors united them. Someone could do so again, but they are not all like Brand. He is … one of a kind. Cardoroth will not see his like again."

Gilhain let out a long breath. "I hope he returns. I don't doubt that we made the right choice, for in him is our hope, and there is no other. I would bet on him. In fact, I *have* bet on him, and the stake is all our lives."

"He is our one hope," Aranloth agreed. "But he does not yet fully understand the peril of the task that we have set him. Yet if he did, he would still attempt it. Once he has made up his mind his determination builds. Normal people suffer setbacks, and he will be sure to endure many, but with them it weakens resolve. In his case, ill fortune strengthens his will instead."

"That's true," the king said. "Yet do you wonder if the task we set him is beyond accomplishment? Truly, what do you think his chances are? You know much of these tombs, while he and I know nothing."

Aranloth drummed the fingers of one hand along his staff.

"I would not send him if I did not think it could be done. Much will depend on the workings of his mind, for it is to that, and that alone, that the power in my staff will respond." The lòhren paused, as if trying to find the right words. "Magic is not made from nothing. It's a transformation of all the forces around us, a transformation inspired by the mind of a person. No magic is ever quite the same as another, for no minds are ever truly alike. What he will get from the staff, and what the staff will get from him, I cannot guess. But for all his words that he mistrusts magic, he has a greater connection to it than he knows. At least I think so, and for that we must hope, or he will not return."

"So," Gilhain said. "Even as I bet our lives on his courage, you have bet our lives that he will be able to use the magic of your staff. But you did not really answer my question. What do you think his chances are?"

"They're not good," Aranloth said. "We all know that. If I had to put a number on it, I would say perhaps one chance in a hundred, but it's the only chance we have. He'll also need luck. But he's a lucky man."

"In my experience," Gilhain said, "a man makes his own luck."

"That's true. It's a truth better realized by the old than the young, for life is also like magic. It's not made from nothing, but is a transformation of all the forces around us. But the mind has the greatest influence. Even so, there are other powers in this world besides courage and magic and determination. Men like Brand attract them, and their fates are woven through with the inexplicable. Call it fate if you will, or fortune, or luck. But whatever name you put to it, it gathers round him. That much I knew from the first time we met."

"Ah," Gilhain said. "It seems long ago now, for much has happened since then. But he is still young. *Too* young many of my advisors say. But they don't understand. In him I trust. He's never let me down, and I in turn will never let *him* down. He has become as dear to me as the son that I lost."

Aranloth sighed. "You love him, as I have also learned to do."

"Yes, and though it seems that I sent him now into great peril, it may be that he has the most chance to live, for he will escape the city. He might survive what comes after, for though it will not have occurred to him just yet, he will realize sooner or later that if the harakgar press him too hard he might live by dropping Shurilgar's staff and leaving it in the tombs."

"That is so," Aranloth said.

"It might be better that way. For I would be glad if he lived. And he would be glad to return to the lands of the Duthenor. He only stays here to help me. Otherwise he would have gone back before now. That is where his destiny is, if there is such a thing, and there he would be spared from Cardoroth's fall, as we will not. I would have it so."

"Perhaps," Aranloth said. "But his destiny with the Duthenor is linked to his destiny in Cardoroth. He's not quite ready yet for what will follow if he returns to his home. There is more for him to learn before he can face those problems – and his enemies."

Gilhain gave a wan smile. "What man is ever ready for such things?"

Aranloth acknowledged his words with a solemn inclination of his head. For a long while after, they sat in silence.

7. A Token of Trust

Night crept through the streets of Cardoroth. It came slowly, spreading shadows before it that filled the narrow alleys first.

The last rays of the sun gleamed off golden domes and then shot up into the sky to spark the first shimmering of stars. Then the darkness came. Swift it fell, as though a lamp were snuffed out, and the air stilled, and an eerie silence grew. This was no rowdy city; not tonight. It was a city under siege, and word of the dark sorcery of the previous night ran from district to district, house to house, person to person. Fear ruled the shadows tonight. The house doors were shut. The inns were empty. All the city's windows were barred.

Brand rode slowly through the streets. He enjoyed the quiet. It gave him a chance to think and to prepare himself for what was coming. He was not nervous, not yet. That would come later. But he had experienced nerves before. He acknowledged them, as always, for a man void of nerves was a man oblivious to danger, and that was a danger in itself. So, when the nerves did come, and they would, he knew how to deal with them. What froze others set his true spirit free, for was he not a wild man of the Duthenor after all? And these city folk, guarded by walls, the strategies of a great king, soldiers and laws, they did not understand that in life-and-death struggles all their wealth and privileges and culture counted for nothing. There was only strength of will.

He had put away the white surcoat of the Durlin. But the chain mail the king had given him, light yet strong,

66

whispered reassuringly to him beneath the drab tunic he now wore.

He arrived at the West Gate and found the king already there. Aranloth was with him, and also Taingern and Lornach and every surviving member of the Durlin.

He had not expected that. Rather, he had intended to slip away unseen and unknown, for farewells were hard, and he had said more than he wished to in his short life. Nor was there any need to give his two lieutenants any instructions. Both of them knew their task.

There were few others about. Only those who needed to be abroad had ventured the streets this night. For the most part they were soldiers, and though they must guess that something was happening, they did not know what.

Finding a hitching rail, he tied his horse. The black stallion was his favorite, and he wished he could ride him on this quest. He would have been more than company on a lonely road; his was a bold heart that showed no fear, and it gave of its strength without stint. The horse could run all day and still finish with a burst of speed.

He ran his hands along its flanks and over its head. "I'll be back," he said, "And when the enemy is gone, I'll take you for a long ride where the grass is green and the water cool and fresh."

The horse tossed its head and neighed. Brand gave it a last pat and turned to face the others.

Lornach and Taingern had approached. If ever there were two people the complete opposite of each other it was these. One was tall and courteous as a king of old; one was short and irreverent. Yet they both had this in common: they were his friends.

Taingern shook his hand in the warrior's grip. "Take care," he said with quiet intensity.

Lornach took his hand in the same fierce grip. "We don't know exactly what your quest is," he said, "But we know this much. You're going to light a bonfire under the pimply backsides of those pasty-faced sorcerers. So, best of luck! We all want to see that."

Brand flashed them both a grin. "I'd like to see it too. The fire part anyway."

They said no farewells, and neither did he. They pretended he would return, and he went along with that. But they all knew this was likely their last meeting, and the hard held warrior's grip said more than their words.

The gathered Durlin saluted him as he walked past, fists to heart, and then their swords leapt from their sheaths and flashed high above their heads catching the gleam of flickering torches near the gate.

Brand drew his own blade, the sword of his forefathers that had passed down from chieftain to chieftain of the Duthenor through years uncounted. Slowly, he kissed the metal, and then softly but clearly he voiced the Durlin creed:

Tum del conar – El dar tum!
Death or infamy – I choose death!

The Durlin gave a cheer, and then sheathed their blades. The city was quiet again, and Brand moved through the ranks of his men until he came to the king and the lòhren standing within the light of the gate torches.

"The time is nearly upon us," Gilhain said. "The evening grows dark, and the enemy is settling down for another night. But before you go, we have some gifts for you. May they help you on the road."

Aranloth stepped forward. He held the lòhren staff in his hand. "This I give to you until we meet again. You will find it useful at need. Trust in it, as I trust in you, and you will draw more from it than you guess."

Brand took it. He had never heard tell of a lòhren parting with their staff, but what Aranloth did next surprised him more.

With steady hands the old man reached up and carefully took the diadem from his head. It was a delicate thing of silver, plain and yet beautiful. Most of the time Brand never even saw it, but he knew that sometimes it flickered with its own light when the lòhren put forth his power.

Brand was not sure what to do. He did not want anything to do with magic. The staff and the diadem would be useless to him, and yet the lòhren kept no trinkets and would offer nothing without purpose. So, Brand removed his helm, the horned helm of the Duthenor that their enemies had learned to hate, and allowed the lòhren to place the diadem on his head. The silver centerpiece came to rest on his forehead. It was so light, and fitted so well, that he barely felt it there, but it was cool against his skin and there was something about it that seemed calming.

He put the helm back on, covering it. "Two gifts," he said to the lòhren, "and I know they are not lightly given. I will care for them as best as fate and chance allow, and return them if I may."

Aranloth gave a bow. "You will need them – more than you think. Remember most of all the harakgar charm that I taught you, and between the three things you might yet return. If it helps, I think you will."

Brand glanced at him sharply.

"Nay," the lòhren said. "I have not had a vision, and I offer no foretelling. Call it wishful thinking if you will. Or call it trust. But the words are no more lightly given than the gifts."

"Thank you, Aranloth," Brand said. "I fear that my skill lies in blades and the art of war, and that the virtues of staff and diadem will prove beyond my reach. I have no desire for magic and mistrust it, but time shall tell its own tale."

Aranloth gazed at him intently. "I would give you neither gifts if they would not turn to some benefit in your possession. And you mistrust magic, you say? Then you are already wiser in its ways than many who possess it and use it daily. But as you say, time shall tell its own tale."

The lòhren stepped back a little, and Gilhain came closer. He drew from the pocket of his robe a sheathed knife.

"This," the king stated, "is said to have come down through my line from the days of old, even from Carnhaina, that great queen of my people. It has no special value, or none that I know of save for its great antiquity and that her hands once held the hilt, but it's believed that it brings luck to all of our line. So it has proved for me since first my father gave it to me. May it prove so for you, and yours. If nothing else, it will be a sharp knife in the wild."

Brand bowed low. He looked carefully at the hilt and the sheath. It was Halathrin made, of that he was certain, though he had never seen their workmanship except for his own sword and the helm he wore.

The hilt was decorated with a strange design. Two small gems gleamed in the dim light, the sign of the Lost Huntress, the constellation of Halathgar. It was the same design as on the ring he wore on his finger, a gift itself after saving the great queen's tomb from ransacking. Well did he believe that once she had owned this thing.

He took the knife, drew it, and held it before him. He liked it. It felt good in his hand. But the king's words reminded him that he was not married nor likely to continue his own line.

"No," he said. "I cannot accept this. It's too kingly a gift, and a thing of your own family. Most especially, it brings you luck, which surely you need more than me. You'll be hard pressed while I'm gone, each and every day without stint."

He tried to hand it back, but Gilhain would not take it.

"We both need it," the king said. "But only one can have it. Accept it from me as a token of my trust in you. You cannot gainsay a gift of your king. It's mine to give, and I give it to you."

Brand could not refuse. It was a great gift, and one of more than knife alone. It would be churlish not to accept. He bowed again, deeply, but found no words to say. He was humbled.

Next, the king drew forth a great diamond, large as a child's fist, from his robes. It glittered in the torchlight, catching the dancing flames on its many surfaces and throwing the light back with a shimmer.

"This is no ancient thing," Gilhain said, "Nor is it an heirloom of my house. But it is of value, and you will find it so wherever you travel among Camar or Duthenor or further lands still that kings of the east know not, but perhaps the wandering feet of a bold man might tread. I give it to you, for you may survive, even if Cardoroth falls, and then I would ensure you had money to support yourself and to further your aims among the Duthenor when the time is right for your return to them."

Brand grinned at him. "Another kingly gift! But if I come not back here, then I am dead."

"That may be," Gilhain answered. "But not even a king knows what road he will walk until his feet are upon it. Take it on the chance that you survive and Cardoroth does not. For despite all our efforts, so it might come to

71

pass, and I would not have one that earned such great reward leave my service without a token of recompense."

Brand took the diamond. It was no token. He suspected it was worth a king's ransom, yet the knife was still the greater gift.

Aranloth led them through a side door into the base of the tower. It was dark inside, the torches meant to burn in here were extinguished.

They went down a flight of stairs, near stumbling in the dark, but halfway down beyond sight of the entry a soft light sprang from the tip of Aranloth's staff.

The Durlin did not follow them. They were alone, and the noise of the city, such as it was, was dimmed to a far distant mutter.

There was nothing in the basement of the tower save an old rug and a table and chairs. All was covered in dust, but the furniture had recently been moved and the rug exposed.

Aranloth bent and pulled it aside. The stone floor was revealed, and set within it was a small wooden trapdoor. This was the secret exit from the city.

The king himself took hold of the brass ring in the timber and opened it, exposing a rickety ladder that descended into the dark.

"I thought I knew this tower," Brand said. "But this was under my nose for quite a while, and I never knew it."

"Cardoroth is an old city," the king answered. "It has many secrets, and even I don't know them all. But don't be dismayed that you worked here for a while and didn't know. Few do. It's well hidden and better guarded."

They walked along a narrow passage. It was a confined place, hung with webs, covered in dust, and it showed no sign that anybody had ventured here in hundreds of years. Ahead, the tunnel came to an abrupt end.

Brand looked around. The stone was bare of ornament or sign. There was no opening, at least none that he could see, but the king pushed at a certain place on the far wall, and the stone turned at his touch like a door. And so it was, for at once he saw hinges recessed with skill and precision, and that what he had taken to be stone was in fact heavy timber painted by some art to look like the other walls in the tunnel.

They moved through the door. On the other side were two guards. They did not speak, evidently having been prepared for tonight's unusual events at some earlier time.

Before the guards was a strong metal gate, a replica of the grand gate above, though much smaller. Yet it was strong, and obviously whoever had had this built did not rely on secrecy alone to protect the city from any chance that the enemy should discover this route and attempt to use it.

Gilhain produced an ornate key. With a click and a rattle he opened the gate and they walked through. The way was now a little wider, but the guards did not follow them.

There were six more gates. Each guarded, though now by lone soldiers. A bell was at each station to provide advance warning should some enemy try to break through.

Brand wondered why the tunnel was wider than at its beginning. It did not really make any sense, but then he noticed the pillars that studded each side. A long chain was attached to each and ran the length of the tunnel. He guessed this was another defense. At need the tunnel could be collapsed, thus preventing entry into the city but also killing, in mass, whoever was attempting to force their way inside.

They came to the last gate after what seemed nearly an hour of travel, though it was hard to tell in their strange surrounds. At a sign from the king the guard there withdrew.

"This is it," Gilhain said. "The last gate. From here your quest begins."

"And your danger," added Aranloth.

"The one goes with the other," Brand said. "But we all knew that from the beginning." He paused, and then took the king's hand in the warrior's grip, even as he had done with the Durlin.

"Stay safe until I come back," he said.

"And you also," Gilhain answered. "We'll await your return, for if you're successful it'll tip the advantage back to us. I don't think Cardoroth will remain besieged if the enemy suffers such a defeat. But if you're not successful, there are other choices than death, whatever the Durlin creed says. A man can only do so much. Fate shoulders the rest. If you can, live well off the diamond, and, maybe, you can reclaim your rightful place among the Duthenor."

"It's better," Brand said, "to serve a great king than to lead a small people. I'll return."

Aranloth shook his hand. "Don't forget that a small people can become a great one. But fate will be what it will be," he said. "Good luck, and may the sun ever rise on your face and set at your back."

They spoke no more. Brand moved down the shadowed passage, leaving behind two that he loved and a city that had become home.

The passageway swiftly narrowed. It became dark, wet and dirty. At times he had to crawl, worming his way forward, but at length he felt the whisper of fresher air and the sounds of nightlife. The rough floor now turned at an upward slope, and he climbed slowly; not because of the rough passageway, but because he did not know with certainty what lay at the end of the path. And that was near.

Crawling on his belly he neared the exit. It was only a crack in the rock; whether natural, or man-made and given the appearance of something natural, he could not tell.

He listened and looked from within the last foot of the tunnel, but it was too dark to see much, and he could not hear anything out of place. He crept further forward, and his head now stuck out. He could see a little better and discovered that he was somewhere amid piled and tumbled rocks on what seemed to be a steep hill.

With drawn sword he climbed out, but there seemed no cause for alarm. Yet his life among the Duthenor, where he had been hunted for many years by his enemies, and his trials in Cardoroth, had taught him caution.

He saw ahead of him that the slope rose to cliffs, but there was a path, barely perceptible, that led up to the top of the hill by a less steep route. This he took, and then looked out on the night-darkened lands below.

Cardoroth was there, the great city itself alight with a glow from tens of thousands of windows. It was still, but before it was great movement. On the flat lands near the west wall he saw the shadowy mass of the enemy, lit by their cooking fires, seething and roiling with movement for the evening meal was being taken after the long fighting of the day.

But even for this time of day there seemed too much movement, as though they were in disarray or some strange event had occurred in their camp. This was confirmed when he heard the wild blast of a horn. It was no call to end hostilities for the day or to signal the movement of troops to sentry positions: it was an alarm. But for what?

It was a question that disturbed him, and he did not like the feel of things. Something was wrong.

But what? He studied the activity below as best as the darkness allowed. There was certainly a movement of troops, though it appeared disorderly. It was possible the enemy was sending out some sort of patrol. If so, it was a large one, and it was coming in his direction.

Could they possibly know that he was here? He could see no way that they would, although Aranloth had said they would anticipate the move. Yet they could not know in what direction the attempt to escape the city would be made. Coincidence, or knowledgeable action? He could not decide, but the possibility that they knew of his movements could not be ruled out. There were traitors in the city, and they may well have a means of communicating with the enemy. He could have been seen. Guesses might have been made.

None of it mattered. Brand decided not to wait to find out what was going on. He had not liked the thought of the westward exit earlier, but now it pleased him, for the hill was in range of the pinewoods that surrounded Lake Alithorin. He knew those dreary woods, and though he did not like them they offered a great place to find concealment or lose any pursuit, so long as those who followed were not too numerous.

He moved back down the slope and toward the tree line. It was no accident that the exit was here. It was placed for the very purposes that he had used it for: to spy on the enemy and then to disappear. And yet he could not travel fast for he had no horse and his pack was laden with food.

The ground levelled. Rocks gave way to grassy earth, but the trees thickened around him swiftly, and soon he was lost in another world. The pine forest surrounding Lake Alithorin had a sinister reputation, and he knew better than most why. He paused as he entered its deep shadows, but from behind him the horn sounded again and he had no choice. He stepped forward, but he did so quietly and with his eyes wide open.

8. The Enemy is Everywhere

Brand looked up through the deepening tree canopy. He could no longer see the sky, and it was very dark. So dark that his pace was become slow, and that worried him. But should there be any kind of pursuit, the same problems that he was having would also hinder those who followed.

He moved ahead. The forest was quiet. The gray trunks of the pines rose like silent statues all about him. The fallen needles were soft beneath his boots, but there were many broken and rotting branches that he had to be careful of, and outthrust roots that turned and twisted in the dark as though to trip him. He ducked beneath a long trailer of moss that hung like a beard from a massive branch, and there he paused in mid-stride.

A sound drifted to him. Perhaps from close by, perhaps from far away; it was hard to tell amid all the trees. But wherever it came from, it was a wolf's howl, long and torturous, and it prickled the hair on the back of his neck.

When the long howl ceased the forest was left deadly quiet. He heard nothing save for his own breathing and the gentle trudge of his boots along the dim trail, if trail it even was. He could not see properly, yet he knew that he was headed deeper into the forest. Not a place that he wished to go, and yet if he persisted and passed through the timber the path would eventually lead to Lake Alithorin.

If the forest was an uncanny place, steeped in ancient tales and drenched with brooding menace, then the lake was its opposite. It was a place of beauty. Its pale shores were soft and sandy, surrounding a great basin of silver water alive with flashing fish, gently lapping waves and a sense of peace at odds with the dark forest around it. That was where he was headed, for it was safer there and he could turn south on its verge and follow it for many miles on the beginning of his quest.

But the forest was where he was at the moment, and he kept his mind on it instead of wandering too far ahead. There were noises now. The wolf was silent, but many small animals scurried in the deep shadows and near-noiseless wings beat over his head, passing shadows in the deeper shadows of the night.

And then he heard a different type of noise. It came from a distance, and it was not some small animal. It was the crashing through the woods of a great number of things, and he guessed what they were: elugs. He had little doubt of it, but then the horn sounded again, closer this time, and what uncertainty there was died even as its last urgent echoes were swallowed by the dark forest.

There was nothing to do but keep going, and this he did, but he moved at a swifter pace. Yet it was dangerous to move too fast in the dark and without due caution for what lay ahead. *Fire and blood!* This was not turning out as he expected. Or at least it was falling apart more quickly than he guessed.

Aranloth had warned him the enemy would be watching for such a move as he now made. But how could they possibly react so quickly? The more he thought of it the surer he was that some traitor had stumbled onto their plan, or at least a part of it, and the elùgroths did the rest.

It was beyond him how a person could betray their own city, and all the people in it. Yet where there was

79

temptation of wealth, or power, or inducement by fear, all things were possible.

He decided to stop thinking about it. His best chance to get through the next few hours was to forget about everything behind him and move forward with a clear mind.

He was not skilled at tracking, or the hiding of his own trail. He was not skilled at hiding and finding concealment. He knew only what any hunter knew, or any herdsman of cattle and sheep, about trails, cover and hiding scent. But that knowledge would hardly serve against a host of enemies. What he did have in his favor were long legs and a willingness to endure the physical hardship of a desperate march. With luck, and the wild ways of the wood to help him, it might be enough.

It grew even darker, but there was no fog yet, and that was what he most hoped for. But fogs generally only rose from Lake Alithorin in the late hours of the night, and there were many miles he yet had to tread before he would benefit from that.

For many reasons his best course of action would be to head, as directly as the twisting trails through the trees allowed, to the shore of the lake. The closer he got, the thicker the fog would be, when, and if, it came. If necessary, shallow water would hide both scent and trail.

As a last resort he could also swim, something that he doubted the elugs could do with any proficiency, if at all. They came from desert lands, or at least the arid south of Alithoras. But that was truly a last resort, for the lake was massive, and strong as he was he would not endure long wearing mail and helm, nor survive any great length of time in its cold waters.

The night lengthened. The hours passed in sweat and toil and the taking of several false trails. Yet if he, who knew these woods was having difficulty, it would be worse for the elugs. Yet the noise of pursuit in the distance did not abate, though it drew no closer. But that noise was probably coming from the greater mass of those who followed. Ahead of the main group would be the fleeter footed, the stronger and the more eager for blood. It was a disturbing thought.

It was impossible to tell amid the trees and dark how close he was to the shore, but he knew now that he must be getting near. The ground often sloped a little downward, the trees grew thicker, the earth seemed lighter under foot as though there was sand in it. But there was no fog, nor yet even the first signs of one.

Suddenly, he burst through into the open. A white strand shimmered beneath the starlight of an open sky. Beyond the bright shore lay Lake Alithorin. It was, as ever, magnificent. But its beauty was not what attracted him now. He wanted water, for though he had a waterbag in his pack he had not yet drunk. That must last him through times when water was harder to find.

He moved to the shore carefully. There was no sign of anything about, but he was in the open now and it unsettled him. But nothing moved while he went forward, and reaching the water he knelt down and scooped up a double handful to drink. He studied his surrounds after a sip with the intensity of a shy deer, but everything seemed normal and he drank again.

He had nearly had his fill when he heard the elug horn blow again. It was closer this time, and then other horns answered it. They too were just as close, and they were not far from each other. The elugs did not seem to be throwing out a wide line and scouring the forest for him; rather they were on his direct trail, yet he had heard no dogs barking. How else could they track him other than by scent? Unless ... unless by sorcery.

81

The thought sent a chill through his body. But again, having come to the realization that such a thing was a possibility, he must not worry about it. Worry, anger and fear were his enemies as much as the elugs. He must concentrate only on himself and his next move.

It was time to turn south. If he stayed on the shore he could move much faster. There was more light, and there were no obstacles to swift walking or even running. Yet he would leave a trail that even a blind man could follow. Alternatively, he could ease back into the verge of trees and travel parallel to the lake. What was more important? Speed or concealment?

He chose speed. It seemed to him that it was useless to hide his trail. The enemy was already following him. His best chance now lay in outpacing them. He set off at a jog along the shore.

The sand was moist and firm beneath his boots. He moved at a good speed, and yet one that he could maintain for hours. He was less used to running than he once was, but the duties of Durlindrath kept him strong and fit.

Each day he trained with some of his men. They fought hand to hand, or used knives or spears or halberds. They fought with long swords and short, with staffs and daggers, with two-handed swords and one handed. Sometimes they trained with two swords, sometimes a sword and shield. They practiced archery, and they practiced defending against attack by arrow, spear or hurled dagger. They practiced everything.

None of this was new to him. He learned such things in his homeland. He had needed to, for he was hunted there by his enemies just as the king was a target now. But if he ever returned to the Duthenor, things would be different. He was older, more experienced. He was ready to claim back the life that was stolen from him.

The thought spurred him to jog a little faster. But at that moment he heard more noise in the forest. It was close, very close, and he stopped thinking about ever returning to his homeland and wondered instead if he would ever see another sunrise.

There was a greater clamor, and a sudden shout, but whether he had been seen or not he did not know. There seemed only one thing left to do: he must enter the water. He was a good swimmer, and that did not frighten him in itself, but he could not discard his sword or his chain mail. He would be weighed down and unable to swim, yet that did not mean that he could not find concealment somewhere in the shallows. Perhaps the search would sweep him by. If so, it would have to do so swiftly, for the water was fed by mountains and it was cold. Maybe dangerously cold for more than an hour.

He prepared to go in. His feet turned in that direction, but he had only taken a few strides when three elugs broke from the tree line ahead of him. They had bows, though no arrows were fitted to the strings. For a moment they did not see him, and then one gave a shout and the others looked. Their faces broke into hideous grins and they cried out in some harsh tongue. Answers came from all around and then there were horns. They blew and wailed and brayed, filling the forest with a ferocious din. The enemy was all around him.

A moment he hesitated. But the water was no longer an option. The three elugs were already drawing arrows from their quivers. He could not hide in the water, and being visible he would be easy prey for arrow shot. He must head back into the trees where their bows were useless and they had to fight him sword to sword. That, he might survive, if there were not too many of them.

He darted to the left and into the dark shadows of the trees. As he did so he heard more horns. These were so close that the sound of them hurt his ears and there was a great crashing in the timber nearby.

The enemy was everywhere. He drew his sword. The thought struck him that this would be the end. He had failed the king. He had failed Cardoroth. Not that there had ever been much chance that this quest would succeed. They had all known that. But no one, least of all him, had expected it to fail so soon.

He slowed and took some deep breaths. All about him needles rustled, branches moved and the sound of tramping boots filled the shadows. He would be found at any moment, yet whoever did so would regret it. He would take them with him into the great dark. But he knew in his heart that even if he cut a swathe through the enemy, leaving a hill of elug corpses, still more would come. The forest seemed alive with them, and that spelled his death, whether sooner or later.

9. Dust on the Wind

Gilhain surveyed the night.

His view from the tower, looking westward toward Lake Alithorin, was clear. Yet his eyes, though they gazed in that direction and saw whatever could be discerned amid the darkness and shadow, were not really seeing what they looked upon. Or rather, his mind was elsewhere.

In his youth, the land was fair and free. Now, it was surrounded by war. Everything he did, every thought he had, every choice he made was touched by that reality. And he did not like it. No matter that men said he was good at it. No matter that they called him a great strategist and that he preserved the city from destruction. No matter that these things might even be true. He still did not like it.

He would rather the lordships of old where his forefathers had ruled in peace, and their skills were used to improve trade between lands, broker alliances and build the wealth of the nation. And Cardoroth *was* wealthy.

His forefathers had been masters of their skills, each and every bit as much as he was a master of war. But without their actions, he would have no money to provide the soldiers with the best training available. He could not pay them, nor supply them with excellent weapons and armor. Without financial prosperity, his ancestors could not have raised the Cardurleth that protected the city now.

Wealth was the foundation of the city, the basis of the happiness of the people. They did not starve in winter. Their fairs and tournaments were resplendent, their clothes and food and entertainment among the best that he had seen in Alithoras. And he had travelled to many realms in his youth before responsibility weighed him down. He knew it was not so in some cities. He knew that Cardoroth was lucky, though that luck was built on good management. Yet the people, living sheltered lives, did not fully realize how close they were to total destruction. If the enemy prevailed, little would remain of them, or the things they loved.

The name of Cardoroth would endure in memory. The language of the people would still be spoken. Cardoroth, in some way, would survive in the wild lands among far-flung homesteaders and hunters. But those who were not killed in the city would still be cut off from civilization, would soon live a desperate life. They would starve in droughts. Cold would wither the young and frail with sickness and death. Banditry would rise. Knowledge would dwindle, and those folk would regress into the scattered tribes they had once been before the Camar came east, before they learned from the immortal Halathrin. Their past would be black and burned. Their future dim. For they would be hunted too. The enemy would not stop at razing Cardoroth. Its armies would turn to other cities, and would not cease warfare until all Alithoras fell before them. And scattered bands of marauders would linger in each land they conquered and destroyed. The enemy would not leave them to grow again.

There were enemies everywhere, also. Not just outside among elugs and elùgroths. But also inside the city. Lust, greed, abuse of power and the forces of chaos were growing. He had seen the first signs in his youth, and his father had spoken of it often. He did what he could to combat it. But it was a part of humanity and would never be overthrown. As the threat from outside forces grew, so too did it. For some people sought to survive what they thought of as the inevitable fall of the city. It was cursed, the legends said. They called it Red Cardoroth, believing a prophecy that spoke of its utter destruction. And the sorcerers who had been defeated long ago in Queen Carnhaina's time fed it. Their spies and agitators were always at work. And promises of wealth and power came swiftly to their glib tongues.

And if Cardoroth fell, then what next? Faladir? Camarelon? The Free Cities furthest southward that had longest resisted the enemy? The lòhren keep, where the lore and wisdom of Alithoras was preserved, and where lòhrens were trained and then sent out all across the lands as counselors, advisors, healers and resistors of sorcery in order to protect the innocent?

No. None of that could be allowed to come to pass. Cardoroth must survive. It must rebuff the enemy, show that they were not invincible, and help foster resistance among the free peoples of Alithoras. It was his job to ensure that happened, but he needed Brand in order to succeed. He had placed great responsibility on him, but Brand knew all these things as well as he did.

Brand's mind was as sharp as any sword, and his heart was big. He knew how important it all was, and regardless of the fact that most of the nobles of the city called him a wild Duthenor tribesman, he was smarter than they were, more courageous, and had a deeper sense of loyalty. And if the nobles did not like him, Gilhain knew that the general population did. They saw in him an ideal of their own courageous past, for though they dwelled now in prosperity, before their ancestors had founded this realm they had lived a hard life, and the traits to survive that life were important. They were important then, and they were important now, and all the more valued because they were rarer.

But Brand knew little of that. He dealt mostly with the nobility, and they did not hide their attitude. Of the city people he saw little, but Gilhain heard word from trusted servants and gatherers of information what the great majority thought. And they loved him. Gilhain sighed. So did he.

There was movement in the army below, and it recalled Gilhain to his more immediate concerns. What would the enemy do next?

He considered them carefully. They were not just elugs. There were men among their ranks also. The Azan were fierce warriors, and they often marched with elugs. They lived in the same lands far to the south. Usually their elders commanded elug armies, but not this time. This time, the enemy was led by sorcerers; a sign of how committed they were to Cardoroth's destruction.

But elugs, Azan and sorcerers were not the only enemy. There were other dark creatures as well, chief among them the Lethrin.

They were few in number, perhaps only several hundred, but their danger lay in their abilities rather than their numbers.

The Lethrin stood over seven feet, and though Gilhain had never seen them before, rumor carried their tale. They were immensely strong and filled with an implacable hatred of their enemies. Legends said that they were born from the stone of the Graèglin Dennath mountains in the south. Maybe that was so, maybe it was not. But he had seen their skin from a distance during some days when they came to observe battles at the wall, and even from afar he could see that it was tough like hardened leather and would resist the hack and cut of blades. They were miners that hewed tunnels in the rock beneath their mountain homes with massive picks and unwearied arms. Because of their ferocity and overwhelming strength, they usually formed the vanguard of an army, though in this case they were still held in reserve. Over black tunics trimmed with precious stones, they wore silvered chain mail vests that left their arms free. Their mighty hands gripped massive iron maces.

Such were the enemies arrayed against Cardoroth, nor yet had the sorcerers thrown all at them. But that would come. They were slow, but they were relentless. Hatred drove them. And the richness of the north lured them. And there was a shadow behind it all. That much was becoming increasingly clear, Aranloth had warned him. A malevolence controlled things: growing, waxing, nurturing its strength, testing the courage and resilience of the north.

So it had been once before. Ancient enmity lay between north and south, stemming from the time of the exodus when the Halathrin came into Alithoras. They sought to redress a great evil, to defeat it, and so they did, though all of Alithoras was drawn into the Eluharaken, the Shadowed Wars, of that time. Perhaps that evil was defeated but not destroyed. At least Aranloth hinted that it was so.

Yet even all those were not the only enemies he must counter. His half-brother was somewhere outside Cardoroth, hiding after treachery. He wanted the throne; he had always wanted the throne. He would do anything to get it, and had proven so not that long ago.

Maybe it was not so any longer. The line of the kings had come to an end. A fallen realm needed no king – his brother knew that as well as any.

Gilhain gritted his teeth. His own son had been killed in battle two years ago. When Gilhain died himself, he wanted the crown to pass, assuming the kingdom survived, to his granddaughter. But that was against Cardoroth's traditions. Should he try to force the issue by decree before his death, it might lead to civil war. There would be factions for one side and factions for the other, and his half-brother, much younger, would take advantage of that and assert his claim. But many would never accept him for his past acts of treachery, and his willingness to deal with the enemy.

Gilhain closed his eyes and sighed. The future was bleak, even if the city survived. Unless ... unless whoever came after him as king was someone strong, both in a military sense and in the political sense of bringing the people together. His son might have done that, but ill fate had taken him away. There was steel in his granddaughter, but the people of Cardoroth would not be ruled by a woman. Carnhaina was the only ruling queen in their history, yet she was special in many ways, not least of all in having command of a terrible magic.

But his great grandson was a possibility. He was too young of course. He would need a regent, and Gilhain did not trust any save Aranloth or Brand for that job. Any of the nobles would end up assuming the crown in their own name. Yet Aranloth would not be tied down to one place in Alithoras for that long. He would be needed elsewhere. That left Brand, and it was an intriguing thought. He could rule for a time as king, and no other would be better suited, and he trusted him in the end to pass the authority on to his great grandson. Yes, there was an idea there, and though the military commanders would fight it, the ordinary soldiers would all be behind Brand. He had fought with them, spilled blood beside them. Yes, they would be on his side. And that would be enough, assuming Brand was prepared to do it. He had his own problems to solve in his own lands. But ahh! Such thoughts were dust on the wind. It would never happen.

Gilhain started as he saw further movement in the enemy camp. And then the horns began to blow.

Aranloth, standing nearby and looking out, lost in his own thoughts, stood erect. His hands were on the battlements, and they gripped hard until they went white.

"This bodes ill," Gilhain said softly. "There is no attack – not against us. I think they have seen Brand."

Aranloth did not relinquish his fierce grip on the stonework.

"If so, it was not by the vision of mortal eyes, but by sorcery. They guessed our plan, as I thought they would, yet too swiftly. They spend their energy on sorcery now. I can feel it throbbing darkly through the earth and reverberating even in the foundations of the tower on which we stand, but it is not directed at us." He hesitated, thinking with a frown on his face. "The staff gives them powers I do not guess at." He paused again, and he cast down his gaze. "I should not have sent Brand. The powers raised against him, one man alone, are too great. And they will only get worse if he reaches the tombs. I have sent him to his death."

Aranloth bowed his head. The strength left his fingers, and for once he looked what he was: an ancient man who had lived so long that misery, evil, despair and sorrow littered his past, and he could not escape from it.

Gilhain drew a deep breath and steadied his voice against the emotions welling up inside him.

"If he dies," he said, "then we also are dead, and the city and all it protects. And the north is more vulnerable. You're right. It's too much responsibility for one man to bear – too great a trial, and yet, and yet, not for nothing

91

did I make Brand a captain in the army. Not for nothing did I appoint him Durlindrath. He earned those positions by blood and daring when he first came to Cardoroth. I'll not give up until I see a token of his death. If they capture or kill him, the enemy will prove it to us in order to subvert our morale. When they bring forth his corpse, only then will I believe that he is dead."

Aranloth slowly shook his head. "I have seen much death in my long life," he said. "But seldom have I so erred. I should not have sent him, and his blood is on my hands."

"Alas!" Gilhain said. "His death would now be like the death of my son, for so have I come to think of him. But courage, Aranloth! We are two world-weary old men. Brand is young. He is strong. He has luck and courage that I have seldom seen. Let's not second-guess our choices in a moment of doubt. Instead, let's trust our instincts, as he trusts his. A bright day may yet come after the long night."

Aranloth stirred. "May we live to see it."

They spoke no more for some time, lost in their own thoughts once more. But ever their eyes watched the movements of the enemy below. Time passed. Troops moved off into the dark and disappeared from their straining sight. A dim rumor came to them of noise in the distance. Eventually it concentrated, grew louder and clearer, and revealed itself as the rising chant of elùgroths. The sound swelled, and not only were there elùgroths but the fell voices of elugs also.

Aranloth lifted up his head, tilting it as if listening with great care.

Gilhain felt his heart pound. "What new deviltry is this?" he asked. "Will they now attack the wall with sorcery?"

"Nay," Aranloth answered. "This is sorcery, but not what you think. The elùgroths work some new spell. Some summoning, I think. And they augment their power with others. The elugs possess no sorcery, yet the elùgroths are using them in some manner that I have not seen before. But it is not directed at us."

"If it's not directed at us, then—"

"It is for Brand. And may fate grant him mercy."

10. Speak True or Die

Brand took a firm grip on the hilt of his sword.

The enemy was everywhere, and there were perhaps only moments before he was seen. There was no hiding from so many. Nor could he fight them all, though the sword felt light in his hand and his heart raced with anticipation. He would wreak such destruction upon them that they would rue finding him – though they outnumbered him a hundred to one.

Some dark form, tall and lithe, moved from within the concealing shadows of a nearby tree. He prepared to leap and attack, but the soft voice that came out of the dark stilled his feet.

"Come with me – if you want to live."

Brand stood motionless. A dark figure loomed out of the shadows. He saw, revealed now in the dim light, the last thing that he expected. It was a girl, and she was tall and striking. She was clothed in the white robes of a lòhren, yet he saw no staff, but a sword hung at her side.

He hesitated. But the noise of the searchers was loud all around him, and she was no elug. She was as far from that as could be possible. And yet he knew nothing of her, and a mistake now, of any kind, meant death.

He caught the glint of her eyes: anxious, impatient with him and fierce with intelligence. He made up his mind and stepped toward her.

She waited no longer but ducked down beneath a branch and skirted the tree next to her. He followed and found himself racing behind her lithe form along some animal trail that he had not noticed before.

They had gone no further than a few hurried paces when two elugs burst unexpectedly onto the trail from the left. Brand slashed, cutting deep across the throat of the first. It reeled away, but the second shouldered into him, sending him sprawling to the ground and knocking the sword from his hand.

The elug drew its own blade and moved toward him, but Brand whipped out the knife the king had given him and flung it with great force. The gems that formed the sign of bright Halathgar flashed as it flew. It was not a throwing knife, yet it still struck point first, lodging deep in the elug's leather jerkin and sending the creature reeling away. It was not a deathblow, but a bad wound nonetheless.

Brand gathered his sword and stood. The elug staggered away into the dark, the knife still sticking into its body, and Brand made to follow.

The girl had turned and she reached back, grabbing him by the shoulder and pulling him forward.

"We have only seconds!" she whispered. "Let's go!"

Brand knew that she was right, but he felt the loss of the knife as a wrench. It was such a precious gift – gone so soon. Luck and fate were against him this night.

He sheathed his sword and they ran ahead. The trees were dense, and the trail wound through them finding some secret path that no more elugs stumbled onto.

The girl crouched and paused a moment for some reason that he could not tell. Then she stood, tall and still, but seemingly ready to move at the slightest reason. Magic dripped from her fingers as flaming drops, and then she raised both hands and sent flame blasting into a thick stand of bracken.

He could see no reason for her actions, but he had thrown in his lot with hers and must trust to his initial choice.

The foliage was dry, and it erupted in bright fire for several moments, and then thick plumes of smoke billowed from it.

She took his hand and led him into a narrow gully. It was overgrown with more bracken and also many tall ferns. Noise from elugs was all about them. So too was the crackle of flame, but it covered whatever noise they made, and the roiling smoke, spinning, turning and filling the shadowy forest, but especially flowing along the gully, obscured them from view.

They ran ahead for a minute, but then she stopped abruptly again and crouched down. Some way ahead of them a string of elugs crossed the gully, scimitars sweeping through the brush and clearing a way. They pressed on, disappearing into the smoke and shadows, and the girl led Brand forward once more.

They moved faster, for the smoke grew thin and the gully widened. The noise of the elugs was mostly behind them now, somewhere near where the fire had been started.

They moved ahead some more, and then cautiously she led them out of the gully, clambering over some rough ground and then she circled about, heading back to the north and away from the direction Brand wanted to travel, and yet also toward the shore of the lake.

Within several minutes they came to the beach again. She paused there, looking around. She seemed satisfied that the elugs still searched the area of the fire, though it was now fading. Much noise came from there, and it was not that far away, yet there seemed no sign of the enemy just where they were now. Yet still it seemed to him that all she had done was trap them between the water and the forest.

"What now?" he whispered.

She looked at him, and her expression changed. Her hands trembled at her sides, and once more fire dripped from her fingertips.

"Now, you speak the truth or die. You carry Aranloth's staff, and you wear his diadem. Is he dead? Did you have something to do with it? Speak! Or I will blast you to ashes where you stand."

Brand was taken aback by her sudden ferocity, but he held his ground and spoke calmly. This was no time for misunderstandings.

"He gave them to me."

She shook her head and stared at him, if it were possible, even harder.

"That's a lie. You're no lòhren – that much is plain. He would not give you these things. They are precious beyond your understanding."

Brand felt anger surge within him, and his hand found the hilt of his sword.

"Kill me, or try to, if you must. But don't call me a liar."

She considered him. "Kill you I may well yet do. And if I choose so, you will surely perish even as the sun must rise tomorrow. Understand that, and tell me all."

Brand thought hard, and all the while his hand squeezed tightly around his sword hilt. He could not trust anyone with the truth of his quest, least of all a stranger that he had just met. And yet he sensed that her words were not idle. If he tried to deceive her, or tell her less than the truth, one of them would die.

Could he prevail against her? Perhaps. She was confident of her abilities, but she had never met him before and knew nothing of him. He was not easy to kill, magic or no. Yet if she did kill him, and well she might, then Gilhain and Cardoroth were lost.

97

He looked into her eyes. He read many things there. She was young, but her gaze was that of someone much older. She was a person of great passion, someone who always believed she was right even when she was not. But he also saw concern there. Not for herself; she believed she could kill him easily, but rather for Aranloth. And that was what decided him.

"I told you the truth. Aranloth lent them to me. Why? You had better ask him if you ever get the chance. I don't think they'll do me much good. But he gave them to me for a purpose. That, I will tell you, though once I do, you are at risk of death by not only elugs … but others also, including sorcerers. Think carefully before you insist."

She looked at him sternly. No flicker of doubt crossed her face. All he saw was disbelief – either at all or part of what he said.

"I insist. And don't think that your veiled threat carries any weight. I have little fear of elugs or sorcerers. And less fear of you. Speak!"

Brand told her what he must. He spoke swiftly of the siege of Cardoroth, of an artifact that the elùgroths used to enhance their power. He explained that Aranloth must stay there, with the other lòhrens to hold the enemy off. She seemed doubtful at all this, not convinced that Aranloth would do such a thing, but she did not interrupt.

He told her all that he could, even saying that he must retrieve the second half of Shurilgar's staff, but he did not tell her where he must seek for it.

She listened, but did not lower her hands. "That isn't everything. Tell me all, and then I will decide your fate."

Brand hesitated. Here was a dilemma that none in the city foresaw, not even Aranloth. Yet it was for him to decide now what must be done, and the lòhren and the king could not help. But if he misspoke, then secrets long held could be revealed to the wrong people. Yet there was little in any of it that the enemy did not already guess.

"The second half of the staff has long been hidden in the tombs of the Letharn," he revealed.

At that name a hiss escaped her lips. She stared at him, doubt showing on her face for the first time.

She shook her head. "What could Aranloth possibly be thinking? I don't understand any of this," she said slowly. "You have certainly not revealed all, but you have said enough, at least for the moment. Few know the name that you have just uttered. If nothing else is true, then at least I believe that he told you that. But the staff and the diadem…"

As she spoke she lowered her hands. The fire at her fingertips snuffed out and she straightened.

"Well," she said. "It seems that I must save you after all. But you'll not survive the tombs. That place is dangerous beyond your reckoning, no matter how much Aranloth warned you. The quest will not succeed. You should turn aside from it now, while you still can."

Brand let go of the hilt of his sword, but he did not take his gaze from her.

"I'll not turn aside," he said, suddenly riled. He glared at her for a moment before adding, "And I *will* succeed."

She looked back at him squarely. "So sure?"

"I must be sure," he answered. "Too much depends on it for me to fail, and I will not. Now, what of you? You have magic at your command—"

"Lòhrengai," she interrupted. "The power of lòhrens. Magic is a term which the uneducated use."

Brand gritted his teeth. He had heard the word before, but even Aranloth seemed content for people to say magic.

He shrugged. "Call it what you will. Yet you name yourself a lòhren, and seem keen to prove the point, but where is your own staff? Are you *really* a lòhren? The better now that I see you, and the longer that I talk to you, the more I begin to doubt it."

She looked at him contemptuously. "Maybe I carry no staff just at the moment, but I am, and always will be, a lòhren. Then she added, "My staff was broken."

Brand might be a wild man of the Duthenor, as some in Cardoroth called him, but he knew a lie when he heard it, else he would have died long before he ever came to the city. And that had been a lie. Whether she possessed a staff or not, and whatever might have happened to it he could not know for sure, but he sensed this much at least: it was not broken.

But she need not know that he discerned that. "I must go," he said. "It might still be possible to evade the elugs. You've given me a greater chance at that, so thank you."

He started to move away, truly thankful for what she had done but not wishing to continue their involvement. His instinct was to trust her, but everything she said led him away from that.

"Wait," she said, holding up her palm. "I'll take you away – you won't escape without me. And I'm heading toward the Angle myself, so we may as well journey together, at least part of the way."

Brand looked back at her and showed nothing of what he thought. Yet those words were her second lie. She had not intended until just now to go anywhere near the Angle. And while lòhrens might withhold information, they did not lie.

She might be less than a lòhren, or perhaps in some ways more. But one thing he knew for certain was that she was not what she made herself out to be.

100

But the question was, what was he going to do about it? He needed help, but dare he trust her?

11. The Gleam of Eyes

Brand had little time to think.

The smoke had dissipated, and the elugs now moved on with their search. He sensed also that there were more of them now. The ones that he had seen so far were just the leaders of the pack – the elùgroths were not taking any chances on his escape.

Before he could do anything there was noise from close by. The two of them hunkered down and remained still. A few moments later several elugs crept through the trees near them, scimitars drawn, but they moved on without pause and soon disappeared into the gloom once more.

Brand waited until he had heard no sound from the group for several minutes before he stood.

The moment of choice was on him, and there would be little time before the next group of elugs came their way. The noise of many nearby told him so.

He gave her a quick nod, signifying that he was willing to join forces, at least for the moment. He would have spoken, but she understood his agreement and lifted a finger to her lips.

She looked around, perhaps using senses other than sight to locate the elugs, and then she leaned in close and whispered softly in his ear.

"They are all around us," she said. "They fill the forest, but they cannot search the lake. Stay silent. Watch. And learn."

She stepped back from him, leaning against a tree trunk and almost disappearing even from his own view.

And though he could barely see her, he could hear her. She muttered under her breath. He could not catch the words, nor even the language, for her voice was so soft as to seem little more than the faint rustle of leaves or the slow creak of branch and root in the forest.

She was not speaking to him. Rather, she softly chanted into the night, for though he understood nothing of what she said, he heard the rhythmic rise and fall of her voice. What she was doing he did not know, except that it was some kind of magic – or lòhrengai as she would have him call it.

He looked about him in the dark. He saw nothing happening, but then again he did not know what to look for. Whatever else she was, she had power at her command, and she was invoking it now for a purpose. He must watch and wait to see what it was.

Harsh voices drifted through the forest. The elugs called to one another. Perhaps they had seen some mark or track of those they pursued. The night grew darker. Everything seemed breathless, and the pinewoods brooded in shadowy stillness.

He looked away from the forest and out over the beach, and then to the lake. The first tendrils of fog were rising from it. He nearly looked away again, but then he realized something was wrong.

The silvery tendrils moved ahead and rose up onto the beach with purpose, probing their way toward the tree line. He had seen fog like that before, and recently. It reminded him of the sorcerous attack on the king.

Even as he watched the fog gathered speed. It grew thicker too, rising now in clouds above the lake like steam from boiling water.

Long vaporish arms reached out, stretched into the trees and caused things to become even darker. It sailed

103

above their heads, blotting out the starlight. Soon it was so thick that very little could be seen at all.

It was cold and clammy. But then he felt her hand, surprisingly warm against his own, and she led him away from their hiding spot and down through the thick fog onto the beach. No one could see them now, but the water would be dangerously cold and he saw no real hope of escaping that way.

She led him over the rough sand. They were nothing more than two fleeting half-shadows in a world of mist, and for the first time in a while he felt safe. Yet with that thought came the realization that fog or not, there were very many eyes that sought him. Safety was scarcer at the moment than light itself.

The rough sand gave way to a muddy surface. The actual water's edge was still a little way off, but guiding him firmly with her hand the girl did not lead him to it but parallel with it. That puzzled him.

Reeds grew about them. They rustled as the two of them entered, and the noise grew louder but it could not be helped. The reeds swiftly grew tall and thick, but go as slow as she might yet still every movement sent a shiver up their stalks and shook down cold drops of water.

He knew it would be hard to spot in the murk, but they had left a trail over the sand and into the reeds. It would not be hard to follow once seen, and he did not like it. Still less did he like not knowing what her plan was. Yet she had one, of that he was certain.

She paused, becoming suddenly still. He stood behind her, barely daring to breathe, but he heard nothing. Nor could he see anything, for the reeds and fog obscured all. There was only her firm handgrip: warm, strong, confident.

He realized that it was not just quiet. It was *too* quiet. There was no sound among the trees of searching elugs, either close at hand or far away. There was no noise of shouts and harsh voices. There was nothing save the whisper of wet reeds close by and a brooding menace from the dark of the trees further away, which he could not see but still felt.

"There's something wrong," she whispered. "The enemy is close, for all their silence, but it's as if they're waiting. For what, I cannot guess."

Brand knew she was right, and he had no desire to *try* to guess. Whatever reason they had, it was unlikely to mean anything good.

She sensed his mood and began to move again, drawing him forward more swiftly now, almost careless of noise.

The reeds gave way at length, and they stood in a kind of clearing. Wet sand and gravel churned beneath their feet, but the reeds were still all around. It was like a little glade in the forest. But the reeds now seemed ominous rather than their friend. While they were in them, they offered cover. In the open, surrounded by them, they were a place where their enemies could hide – could be hiding even now, peering through stems and fog to study their prey.

She moved to the left. The shore was there, the silvery water of the lake still and placid. She stepped into the water.

Brand wondered if he should discard his chain mail. He was loath to do so, for it might yet save his life, but it might also kill him in the water.

But she did not lead him in any deeper than a foot or so. She moved back into the reeds, though he saw these were now of a different kind: taller, thinner, more grass-like.

Within moments she found what she sought, and he better understood her plan.

105

"I didn't know you had a boat," he whispered.

"It's a shuffa," she corrected. "At least, that's what my people used to call them."

She took hold of the craft and deftly undid the rope that held it to the base of some bunched reeds. The vessel was strange to Brand's eyes, nearly round, and made of some light timber over which was stretched hide. It hardly looked like it would serve as a boat, but he did not question her. That, he guessed, would prove fruitless.

"Are you any good with boats?" she asked.

Brand shook his head. His people were farmers rather than fishermen. He'd had little experience of such things, and as usual, she had a knack for pinpointing his weaknesses.

"Never mind," she answered shortly. "I'll take us out into the water. Step carefully, and don't turn us over as you move around."

She took the only oar in the shuffa and steadied herself with it while she stepped in and gracefully sat down.

Brand gritted his teeth and followed suit. He moved carefully, yet still the boat wobbled dangerously in the water.

The girl stared at him, but held her tongue until he was seated.

"Ready?" she asked.

But then she began to row without waiting for his response. With slow but powerful strokes she got them underway. She took great care to paddle smoothly so that there was barely any noise and no splashing of water.

The shuffa moved into deeper water. It floated very well, surprisingly well to Brand considering it was little more than a near round shell, but it was hard to steer. At

106

times she rowed with her back to the shore, at others the craft spun around in the water and she rowed facing it. Yet slowly and surely they drew away from the bank.

The land was now a vague line. The beach stood out, a pale strip in the fog, and the forest beyond was nothing more than a dark smudge. But from that smudge elugs suddenly emerged. They paused, saw their prey, and then drew their bows to shoot. It was some distance, yet not so far that arrows could not kill, though the accurate aiming of them would be harder.

Brand hunkered down, lifting up Aranloth's staff and lowering his head so that his helm would better protect him.

The girl paddled faster now, careless of the noise. Secrecy and quiet no longer served.

Arrows whistled past in the dark. Some struck the water nearby. Some flew wild into the fog. One would have struck him as the boat tilted sideways but with a deft movement and surprising reflexes the girl flicked the oar and deflected it.

After that, the arrows began to fall short or go wide. They were now very nearly out of sight, and deep within the fog that still rose from the cold waters of the lake.

The elugs stopped shooting. Not only that, their dim forms seemed to part: some moving left and others right. Brand thought it strange, for they might yet have continued to shoot a few moments longer.

The girl slowed her rowing a little. "Once again I've saved your life. Am I going to have to baby you all the way to the Angle?"

Brand felt his patience slip. Yet what she said was true. She *had* saved his life several times tonight. He owed her, and he did not take such debts lightly. Yet it was irksome, for it meant that she held power over him. Despite her manner, there was something about her that attracted him also: she was dangerous, strong willed, beautiful and mysterious. He wanted to see her in the light of day, and that line of thought upset him. It was another way that she might hold power over him, and he did not like that. He did not like it at all

He looked back at the barely visible shore, and thought that they were free. But it was not so. Through the parted ranks of the elugs he saw a shadow. Swift it came onward, and the elugs recoiled further away from it. And then he realized that it was not one shadow, but three.

Whatever they were, they leapt out from the shore as one, and though they made no sound of themselves, their huge bodies crashed into the water with a great splash. Foamy water frothed all around them and great waves spread out.

The girl rowed faster. Brand studied the creatures, but he could not tell what they were, except that they were not elugs. They were something else entirely.

As he watched they continued to swim, pressing closer. He saw that they were four legged, for they had the form of massive hounds, yet they held their heads high up out of the water, and there was a look to them that was not as of a hound, but rather of an elug – or a man.

A chill ran up Brand's spine. Foul sorcery! For whatever these creatures were, they did not swim or tread the earth of their own volition. They were made, called forth as were the drùghoth, and he sensed in the growing gleam of their approaching eyes a desperate madness.

The foul beasts drew closer. The elugs, closing ranks again, began to hoot and shout.

They faded from view, but the beasts came on faster than the girl could row. Or else they still ran, their great paws reaching down to the lake bottom, for he saw that they were massive, much larger than any wolf or hound that he had ever seen.

He cast about desperately for something to do to help the girl, but he had no bow, and there was only one paddle, and she was more skilled with it than he.

The shuffa came to deeper water. The fog thickened, but the beasts were closer, and he saw malevolence in their blood-shot eyes. And he felt the ill will of the sorcerers who had created them, looking out and staring at him hungrily.

12. We Do Not Yield!

Gilhain was surrounded by the Durlin. He trusted them. They called him by name, and he knew as much, or perhaps more, of their everyday lives as their friends did. Yet without Brand among them, at one moment solemn and deadly serious, at another laughing and carefree, but ever-watchful, he felt suddenly vulnerable.

The Durlin had courage, but when necessity demanded, pure ice ran through Brand's veins. He knew fear, as any wise man did, but it never stopped him. Where other men hesitated, he acted. Where other men were cowed by terror, he stood tall. Where other men broke, he found strength within himself to endure. He had proven all these things, or Gilhain would not have made him Durlindrath.

Without his constant shadow, ever-present but always in the background, Gilhain realized how easy it would be for an assassin to kill him. The Durlin were good, the best bodyguards in all of Alithoras, but without Brand to lead them they were lessened. For it was not skill that made the difference, nor friendship, but a deep and abiding affection more like that between father and son.

Gilhain shrugged his worries aside. He could not function if he dwelled on the risk to himself, and Cardoroth *needed* him to function. The attacks of the enemy had stepped up. It was the next day after Brand had left, and something had stiffened the enemy's resolve. All night their sorcerous chanting rolled and echoed through the city. At dawn, the attacks began. Wave after wave of maddened elugs sought to take the walls. Aranloth claimed the elùgroths used sorcery to work them into a frenzy, and Gilhain believed it.

Another attack was forming now. The war drums beat louder than ever. The elug chant, not sorcerous as was that of the elùgroths, yet still a powerful sap to morale, rose and beat at the Cardurleth like a physical assault:

Ashrak ghùl skar! Skee ghùl ashrak!
Skee ghùl ashrak! Ashrak ghùl skar!

The chant ran without beginning or end. The drums became one with it, or it one with the drums. The elugs stamped their iron-shod boots. Terror rose like a dust cloud, choking the air and making it hard to breathe. All along the walls men stood still, heads down, ashen-faced and scared. That chant had signaled the fall of many cities before now, and they wondered if it was their turn. Everyone knew what the words meant:

Death and destruction! Blood and death!
Blood and death! Death and destruction!

But Gilhain was no longer prepared to let the chant go unchallenged. If the will of the defenders was sapped before the fighting began, the wall might well fall. And the attack that was building was a great one. He felt that in his bones. People called him a strategist. That might be so, but most of his strategy was simple. Attack when he had an advantage. Defend when he was disadvantaged. And never allow the enemy to have everything their own way.

He stepped forward and gestured to his standard-bearer. The man lifted up high the flag that all the kings of Cardoroth had used: a sable background threaded with a gold eagle, one taloned claw lifted and raking at an invisible enemy, the wings half stretched out.

At the same moment a blast from one of the great Carnyx horns, a relic of the ancient Camar past, sounded. It was a challenge in itself to the enemy chant. But Gilhain added to it when its long notes finally died away. His deep voice rolled far along the walls, carrying to many of his men and also the front ranks of the enemy:

Death and destruction. Blood and death.
Red shall elugs bleed! Swift shall elugs die!

His men lifted their heads. Some laughed. Some gripped their swords tightly and raised their heads to stare angrily at the enemy. Some repeated the cry until it was taken up by many and rolled from the walls to smash against the chant of the elugs like two great waves crashing against each other.

The elugs stamped their boots faster. A horn sounded from somewhere amid their host and the front ranks of the enemy broke away from the vast mass behind it. The charge toward the wall had begun.

The men on the wall were ready for it. Gilhain watched from the west tower. Aranloth stood beside him.

"That was well done," the lòhren said.

Gilhain shrugged. "A small thing, but effective."

"A small thing, you say. But useless if done at the wrong moment. You didn't invent your twist on the chant just then. It's been on your mind for days, perhaps even weeks. You waited until now to use it, on the day when the enemy bends their will most strongly upon our destruction."

Gilhain shrugged again, but this time a smile flickered across his face before he answered.

"But the real point is this – why do they bend their will on our destruction? I mean, why today more than any other?"

The lòhren cast his gaze out over the wall at the charging enemy. "I don't know, but it's so. That much we can both feel."

There was no more time for talk. The great mass of the enemy drew near the Cardurleth. The sound of so many tramping boots, of wild yells and the incessant pounding of drums from within the main host rose in a menacing din that seemed to shake the very stone of the wall. But those who held it did not flinch.

The men hefted spears, drew bows and grasped rocks. The arrows sped forth first, swift-flighted darts that hissed through the air and struck death from afar. The elugs wore armor, though many only had leather jerkins. The great bows of Cardoroth were strong, and hardened leather offered little protection even from a distance. Many fell, tripping and hindering their fellows. But the mad rush continued and none slowed, for to slow was to become a target for the bowmen.

On the dark ranks raced. Arrows sang among them, but now also the spears were hurled. They were heavy, and sharp tipped, and they rained a deadly hail upon the enemy. Yet still the elugs came, trampling over their dead or wounded, screaming in rage or fear and especially for the sheer madness that the elùgroths had instilled in them during the night by sorcerous chanting.

The rocks came next. Some were thrown like balls. Others, so large that two men had to heave them, dropped over the wall. Just as the elugs reached the Cardurleth this latest defense assaulted them, but they had reached some measure of safety now, being so close to the wall where arrows and spears were of less use.

113

The elugs threw up the ladders they carried. They were rickety constructions of light timber, held together by twine and hope. But they also had climbing ropes with steel barbed hooks at the end. All were thrown against the wall. And the enemy that yet lived, which was still the greater part of them, commenced to climb.

The men of Cardoroth worked speedily now, but with calm and efficiency. Gilhain gave no orders, nor did the captains along the wall. The soldiers knew what needed doing, and when, and they acted accordingly.

They used long poles to dislodge the ladders, sending the elugs screaming to death or broken bones below. Axes cut at ropes, though some of these were wound with wire also and that slowed their severing. Yet hundreds of the enemy hurtled to grim deaths, for it was a long climb.

Yet climb the enemy did, swarming up the wall until the forerunners clambered through some of the gaps at the top of the crenellated battlement.

The elugs slipped through, or jumped or leaped or rolled, but they came to their feet and wielded their curved blades with ferocity and desperation. For though they had attained the battlement, the greatest risk was now upon them. Many were cut and stabbed by sword as they reached the top. Those who survived this deadly greeting were few, and the mass of men atop the battlement pressed against them with grim determination.

But the elugs fought on. A trickle of their fellows joined them. There were now more elugs atop the wall than there had ever been before, and the enemy took hope from this. If they could but hold on a little while until more of their kind came, the wall might yet fall. And should that happen the city would swiftly follow.

The elugs fought with crazed desperation. The men hacked and slew with quiet determination. Blood slicked the stone. Screams rang out. The stench of death hung heavy over the walls. In the distance crows flapped on their perches in tall trees, croaking and sharpening their beaks. High overhead the Red Kites of Cardoroth, which lived off vermin and refuse, circled the airs.

In the enemy camp the war drums rose in sudden frenzy, and the whole host beat swords on shields and stamped their iron-shod boots. The din was maddening, and fear throbbed through the air.

Gilhain stepped forward and gave a signal. His standard-bearer lifted high his flag and the great carnyx horn sounded again. For just a moment every eye that could turned toward him.

The king drew his sword. It was the sword of his father, and his father's father. It leaped like a white flame from its sheath, but bright red sparks shimmered from its gem-encrusted pommel.

"The Cardurleth has never fallen," he cried. "Nor will it! Not while brave men hold its length. And you are as brave as any that defended the city during our long history. Teach these elugs what all their kind before them have learned: we do not yield!"

The men drove against the elugs with all their might. The elugs fought back, panic lending them ferocity, for should they fail to take the wall every one of them was dead.

For several long breaths Gilhain watched. He could not tell who would prevail, and he was ready to step forth and fight himself, for that would hearten the defenders. Yet if he did that now it would have less effect at some time in the future when the defenders might need it more.

He waited. Men died. Elugs died. The battlements roiled with the finely balanced potentials of victory and defeat.

Gilhain glanced at Aranloth. The lòhren stood, transfixed by the battle, his hands gripping his oaken staff, his eyes seeming to follow every slash and cut of a thousand blades. But he gave no sign of what he thought.

The decision was Gilhain's. He moved his right foot, preparing to step forward, but instinct told him to wait, and he listened to it.

The elugs pressed forward. They took the battlement inch by inch, but they did so in only a few places. In others, the men of Cardoroth held their own. New elugs scrambled up the ladders and climbing ropes, but many of these devices had been cut or destroyed the first time they were dislodged. There were much less now, and the newcomers were therefore fewer, and within a minute the men of Cardoroth pressed back. Soon no new elugs reached the battlement, for there was no way for them to pass through the ranks of their brethren, pushed right back against the stonework.

The men of Cardoroth were tired. Their sword strokes were slower, less powerful, and the elugs fought with the knowledge that this might be their last few moments walking in the world.

But the men outnumbered them, and though slowed by exhaustion, determination kept them on their feet. They continued to press their enemy, and in moments the tide turned. The elugs knew they had now lost and the fight went out of them. Resigned to death, they fell swiftly, their dark bodies littering the stone floor of the battlement, those that were not lifted and cast over the wall.

The last elug fell. A hush descended. The war drums came to a rumbling stop.

"We survive yet again," whispered Gilhain.

Aranloth let out a sigh beside him. "So it seems, though that was closer than I would have liked." His keen-eyed glance fell upon Gilhain. "You have nerves of ice. Few others in your position would have waited so long. But your own blade will yet be needed. Whether today, or tomorrow, or in a month. Keep it sharp!"

Gilhain grunted. "The blade is sharp, but the arm that wields it has lost its strength of old."

'Maybe so, but the mind that guides it is still strong and sure."

Gilhain watched as the men went to work. They moved quickly, for no one knew how long it would take for the next assault to come. But for the moment, the enemy remained subdued, and no sign of a further attack seemed imminent.

The wounded were removed first, taken below into the city to the care of the healers. Not that all of them would live. Many might though, and still have productive lives though maimed in body and mind. The dead were removed next. Elugs were tumbled over the wall, the men of Cardoroth taken away with solemnity. Then came the buckets of water to wash away the gore, and swiftly after that sawdust to soak up any moisture. The battlement was no place for a slippery surface where men could fall.

Gilhain kept his gaze on the enemy. He wanted to read what they would do next, for most of what he did as commander relied on discerning the intentions of the enemy. Yet he was perplexed at the moment. The opposing host had suffered a defeat, perhaps a great one, for they had worked themselves into a frenzy all night in order to try to win the fight today. They had lost, and yet

117

now was also the time to attack. The defenders on the wall were weary. Their spirits might be high, but if the enemy could not take the walls in a single assault they must show that they had the numbers to keep on coming back, even after a defeat. That would be the most demoralizing message of all, and yet no attack came.

"What are they doing?" Gilhain asked the lòhren.

Aranloth followed his gaze. "The unexpected," he said.

"What do you mean?"

"Look to the center of the host. There is movement there."

Gilhain did so. "All I can see are a few figures coming forward. It's not an attack."

"Not of arms," Aranloth answered.

"Then what? Sorcery? I see now that the figures are black-cloaked elùgroths."

"Perhaps," Aranloth said slowly. "I don't rule that out, but I think this is something else. We shall see soon."

They watched as the figures came to the front of the host. There were three elùgroths and three men of the Azan race.

The elùgroths clutched their wych-wood staffs, and the Azan stood meekly behind them. Yet what the purpose of the enemy was, no one knew.

The men on the walls watched keenly, and Gilhain kept an eye on the soldiers' reaction also, for so far the sorcerers had stayed back and let the elugs attack. The men were familiar with the chanting at night, the words of power that rolled through the enemy host intended to uplift the dark horde and at the same time weaken the determination of the defenders. They knew that a sorcerous attempt had been made on his life, but they must wonder even as did he, what would be next?

118

But of that, Gilhain could not even guess, and it disturbed him. Whatever it was, as Aranloth had said, it would be unexpected.

13. A Token of Death

Gilhain watched nervously, but he did not allow any of his inner feelings to show. He stood casually, his hands clasped behind his back, as if he surveyed nothing more than the scenery on a morning walk.

The elùgroths left the ranks of the host and came forward. Their strides were long and confident. The one in the middle held his wych-wood staff loosely in his left hand. Something small caught the sun in his right.

Gilhain stepped to the edge of the wall and leaned against it. Aranloth followed.

"What do they want?" Gilhain asked.

"They do not want anything. They come to tell us something, and it will not be good. Prepare yourself."

Gilhain did not move, but his heart sunk and his stomach churned.

The elùgroths drew closer, the three Azan that served them following close behind.

"The one in the middle is Khamdar," Aranloth said. "He is the leader of the elùgroths gathered here."

Gilhain studied him. He was very tall, and he strode with confidence, or perhaps arrogance. He showed no doubt and no fear at approaching the wall so closely. Gilhain considered ordering a hail of arrows, but that was not just, for these men had come to parley, however evil they were. More than that, he doubted they were vulnerable to arrow attack, or else they would not venture so close in the first place, and seeing such an attack fail would dishearten the men and rally the elugs. He waited, unmoving and patient.

The elùgroths came beneath the shadow of the wall, and there they stopped.

"Be wary," Aranloth hissed. "Khamdar is dangerous. Everywhere he goes he leaves death and woe behind him as other men leave trails in the snow."

Gilhain did not answer. There was nothing he could say.

In the shadow of the Cardurleth the sorcerers stirred. Khamdar muttered something to those beside him, and then he looked up.

Even from the ground below, Gilhain felt the force of his stare. The man's head was cowled, which shadowed his face, and though no eyes were visible, yet still Gilhain sensed their probing. And it was more than probing; it was a wave of malice that smote the wall and those upon it as a physical blow.

Some of the men took a step back. Some gripped their swords in trembling hands. Gilhain stood still and waited.

Khamdar raised his wych-wood staff. The dark wood was dull in the shadows, but the long-fingered hand that held it, pallid and blue-veined, was clearly visible. Gilhain reminded himself that the sorcerer was a man, whatever his age or powers – however he looked and acted. He was still a man.

"I come not to offer hope," Khamdar said.

His voice was slow and deep. It welled up to the battlement like a rising tide, and by some art of sorcery it carried far along the wall to either side.

"I come to take it away. Today, there will be no granting of mercy. We will not promise to let you live if you surrender. We will not depart, though you try to buy freedom with a hundred wagons laden with heavy gold."

Gilhain finally moved. He gave a nonchalant shrug.

"Tell us something new," he said, and by the power of Aranloth his words were also carried far across the wall and even to the enemy host.

"Since when do elug armies grant mercy? Since when did elùgroths become noble leaders? Try to kill us with blades or sorcery if you must, but don't be so stupid as to think that words will purchase what only blood and courage can buy."

There was a sharp hiss from one of the Azan men below, but the elùgroths showed no reaction.

Khamdar laughed into the sudden silence. It was a fell sound, like a wolf's howl born on a midnight wind, and Gilhain's blood ran cold. He wondered if his enemy was a man after all.

"So brave!" Khamdar cried. "Well, bravery is for those who possess hope. But the hopeless fall away and die. You shall see that my words are true, but first I would speak with the old man beside you. To him would I bring tidings of events beyond this wall."

Aranloth did not move, but his voice rang out.

"Speak then, Khamdar, lòhren that was. But we shall judge the truth of your words."

"Truth?" Khamdar answered. "You do not recognize truth when you see it. Through the ages you have blindly fought the long defeat. For there is no stopping my kind, or the power that we serve. Still, you try. And that is a noble, if foolish, thing. Yet nobler would it have been for you to die in one of the many battles that you have seen. But no, you endure while others fight and die, giving their lives for your cause. Is that not so?"

Aranloth remained still. "It is not, but speak on. I do not have all day to exchange insults with a renegade that deserted his friends. But tell me this – was it worth it? You betrayed the lòhrens in search of power. Have you found it? Or have you found only servitude instead?"

Khamdar snarled. "Betrayed! It was you who held me back!"

A wave of malice drove against the wall, and the anger in the sorcerer's voice throbbed through the air.

Khamdar was silent a moment, as though gathering scattered thoughts that he had lost.

"Ever you know how to use words to twist things," he said at length. "Was it not so with Brand?"

He paused, and Gilhain leaned closer against the wall.

"Ah," the elùgroth said, looking at him. "I see that the name is not unknown to you. Nor to me. For I have met Brand."

Khamdar turned to Aranloth again.

"Would you like to know, O mighty lòhren, what his last words were?"

Aranloth gripped tight his staff.

"You will speak, whether I will or no, so get to it."

"Very well. I have no wish to prolong your pain. I will tell you, but first, I think that perhaps all the men who so valiantly protect both king and lòhren should know what the last hope of Cardoroth was, how the city leaders devised it, and who they sent in their stead for its accomplishment. Who, in fact, faced dangers beyond them so that cowards might live a little while longer."

A hush fell over the wall, and Khamdar paused. His words were dripping with poison. They could fester among the men, and Gilhain knew he should say something. But he was overwhelmed. The enemy knew of Brand. They said he was dead, and that wrenched at him even more than he feared it would, but he straightened and took heart. Words were often easy to say – proof was harder.

Khamdar spoke again. His voice was slow and assured.

"We elùgroths possess great power," he said. "But there is an object that we use to enhance it. Your leaders," and here he pointed at Gilhain and Aranloth with his staff, "sought to break that power. They sent Brand, your precious Durlindrath, on a quest to do so. They sent him alone. One man against an army. That was so ... *brave* ... of them, was it not? But Brand is now dead, though he lived a long time, despite torture and torment. Yet with his dying breath he cursed both lòhren and king."

He turned again to Aranloth.

"Does that surprise you? It should not. You sent someone to complete a task that you dared not attempt yourself, and he died in your stead. What else did you expect?"

Aranloth gave no answer, but he leaned on his staff and bowed his head.

Gilhain spoke. "You have much to say, but I see no evidence that your words are anything more than dust on the wind."

Khamdar laughed again. "Dust on the wind? Then let the air bring you the proof you want!"

He drew back his arm, and though the wall was high, and Gilhain stood more than fifty feet above him, the elùgroth hurled an object with speed and accuracy. It flashed through the air, spinning and glittering as it wheeled.

It would have struck Gilhain even though he tried to leap back, but Aranloth was quicker than he looked, or perhaps had anticipated such a move. Either way, his staff struck the object down to clatter on the stone flagging at their feet. The lòhren bent down quickly to pick it up.

From the ramparts several archers loosed arrows. But no shaft reached the target below. With a dismissive wave of the wych-wood staff the arrows shattered in flight and fell whining in smoke and ruin.

"Halt!" cried Gilhain, holding up his hand to stop any further attack. "Don't fire."

The men fitted new arrows to their strings, but did not draw.

"This is a parley," Gilhain said, moving back to the edge of the wall. "But I suppose I shouldn't expect elùgroths to hold to the rules of civilization."

Khamdar looked up at him and grinned. The cowl fell back a little and there was a sudden flash of white teeth and also a high-cheeked but pale face.

"It was no attack – merely a returning of your own. But think on how I came to possess it? See! Aranloth already knows."

Gilhain turned to the lòhren. Aranloth stood there, his head bowed and his posture limp. Yet in one hand he held a knife, the very knife that Gilhain had given the previous night to Brand. He knew it by the sign of Halathgar that was on it. It had not brought Brand the luck he needed...

The elùgroth spoke again. His voice was cold.

"We know your purpose. We learned your plans. Your hope is lost, and the city will fall. The proof is in the lòhren's own hand."

The elùgroth turned on his heel and strode back toward the camp. It was a dismissive gesture, but one that his comrades did not imitate. They backed away carefully, keeping a close eye on the ramparts for any further arrow shot, but it was needless. Gilhain's command held firm, and the men did not draw their bows.

The lòhren staggered back from the rim of the wall. He looked as ancient as he was, and Gilhain's own heart sank in anguish. Their last hope was truly lost, and Brand, like a son to him, was gone with it.

The retreating elùgroths merged back into the host. Aranloth stood there, leaning on his staff as though it were all that held him upright.

"We tried," Gilhain said. "But Cardoroth will fall, sooner or later. And Brand will neither walk its streets nor return to the lands of the Duthenor. I wish now that we had not sent him."

Aranloth slowly straightened. He lifted up his head, and though his face did not alter, Gilhain saw that some great emotion flowed through him like a river, and the power that he veiled ran near the surface. Then it was gone, and the lòhren went back to normal, but he laughed and a look of merriness was in his eyes.

Gilhain stepped back another pace, but the lòhren raised a hand and stayed him.

"O king! Do not think I am mad. Grief has not broken me, though well it might have through the long years. If I seem other than you expect, it is because the situation is not what it seems. Khamdar is a *liar*. Thus he has ever been, but this is the happiest lie ever he told. Brand is not dead."

Gilhain looked at him. Then he looked at what the lòhren held in his hand.

"But he has given us the proof of his words. The knife is the token of death that we feared."

Aranloth shook his head. "No. It is not. You do not know Khamdar as I do. I said he was evil, and evil shows us what it is by its nature. If he had taken Brand, he first would have learned what he could from him, and then, in order to weaken us, he would have had him tortured and slain before the walls. And if Brand were killed when they tried to capture him, then Khamdar would have brought and then broken his body before us. That is his

126

nature, to inflict pain, both physical and emotional. You can be sure that Brand yet lives, and somewhere out there," the lòhren gestured widely with the knife in his hand, "he still strives to fulfill the quest."

Gilhain slowly reached out and took the knife. He studied it carefully. There was no doubt that it was the very same that he had given Brand. Yet it was a thing of luck, and suddenly, despite what the elùgroth would have him believe, he saw many ways that it might come into the possession of the enemy, and yet by luck Brand might have escaped their grasp.

He felt hope surge through his veins once more and looked up. Tears misted his vision and he felt ten years younger. Joy surged within him just as it had a few moments ago in the lòhren.

"But why then this act? Why pretend to believe the elùgroth?"

Aranloth grinned. "Let them think we are beaten. The soldiers on the wall know little of Brand or his quest. They trust rather to their own strength of arms. Let that continue. In the meantime, if the enemy thinks you broken, they will be less swift to try to kill you. That is to our advantage. Never let the enemy know what you are really thinking. You know that."

Gilhain grinned back at him.

"So I do. We'll turn this to our benefit, and I'll make them rue the day they tried to break me."

Aranloth sighed, and as swiftly as joy had shone from his face, it now faded.

"Alas, joy is always short lived. Brand yet lives, but I do not doubt that they know of him, that they have learned his purpose and hunt him. He is not dead, at least not yet, but neither will he know safety again for a long while."

127

Gilhain understood the truth of those words. And yet having felt despair only moments before, he would not allow it to overwhelm him again, no matter what the enemy said or did, no matter that hope was as tenuous as a fluttering heartbeat.

14. Forbidden Lore

Brand drew his sword. The hounds swam toward the little boat. For all their splashing and the froth of water about them, they came on in unnatural silence. But still they came on.

The girl rowed as swiftly as she could, but the shuffa was not a fast vessel. She would never outpace them.

Brand stood up, carefully keeping his balance by spreading his legs. He could not fight properly like this, but it was all he could do.

The shuffa began to spin to the side, taking him away from facing their enemy. The girl tried to right the boat, but all she could manage for the moment was keeping it at the same angle, yet still they drew away from the bank. It was now invisible, swathed in the thick fog.

For the first time one of the hounds made a noise. It was a deep howl, like that of a wolf's, but Brand heard words weaved through it, and it held something of the timbre of a human voice.

The other two hounds took up the howl, and the girl began to slow her rowing. In a moment, Brand saw why.

The craft was now in deeper water, and the hounds seemed to have come as far as they dared. They were not good swimmers, being heavy set, and their thick wet fur weighed them down. Great tufts stood out in places, while in others only pale skin showed.

The howling ended in vicious snarls, and the beasts turned back toward the shore. The girl did not stop rowing.

In the following moments they ventured further out into the lake. Shore and elugs and hounds were gone. He was alone with the girl in a world of water and thick fog.

It was eerily quiet, and she was obviously unsettled. Whatever the beasts were, they were not natural. They were a product of sorcery, and he thought it must be a great sorcery at that. But it did not bear thinking about too deeply, for however it was done he guessed that not just beasts were involved, but also men. In some manner the elùgroths had fused both together, and it was an abomination such as only they could conceive. He remembered Aranloth's words that even among elùgroths, Khamdar was the worst. If he did not believe it before, he did now.

The girl turned the boat southward. How she knew which direction was which, he did not know. But she told him so and he believed her.

They took turns at rowing. He found it cumbersome, but soon grew competent after her terse instructions. It was not that difficult, but neither was their rate of progress fast. Still, the enemy could not see or track them, and so far as he knew, they could not discover in what direction his quest lay. Only Aranloth and Gilhain knew that, and in them he trusted.

Only the distant sounds from shore kept them from straying too far out over the lake. He could not tell himself in which direction they were headed, but at least he knew they were not getting lost on the vast expanse of water. At first they heard elugs, but when the noise of their tramping through the brush and calls to one another faded, there was only the occasional hoot of an owl or yelp of a fox.

When the silvery dawn finally glimmered through the fog, they could dimly see the shore again and struck out toward it. As the light grew, Brand could see his companion better. Her eyes were green with flecks of brown. Or else they were brown with flecks of green. He could not tell which. And what he had taken for white lòhren robes were not. Rather, she wore a flowing tunic, all of pale gray and tied at her waist with a black belt.

He studied her closely now, for suspicion rose in him, and a terrible fear that he had made the most dreadful mistake – notwithstanding that he had not had any choice.

Her hair was long and ash-blonde, bound by a black ribbon. She gazed back at him with eyes that sparkled not just with intelligence but also secrets. But for all her fierce gaze she was even more beautiful than he had thought, though it was beauty of a high and remote kind.

With an insight that surprised him, he realized that few people ever got close enough to her to discover what she really thought or felt. She held everyone at a distance, even as she was doing with him.

She grew annoyed at his scrutiny, but before she could say anything he spoke.

"Are you not lonely? You know, independence is a fine thing, but sometimes it's nice to be able to lean on others when you most need it."

She gazed at him with such fierceness that he thought she was going to attack him, and Aranloth's diadem felt hot against the skin of his forehead.

"What business is it of yours?" she snapped.

"Oh, I know a thing or two of loneliness. I'm a Duthenor tribesman, the only of my kind in a great city with a recorded history stretching back into what my people think of as legend. My family is dead. And they did not die of old age. And what was theirs was stolen from them. Yes, I know a thing or two of loneliness. But if you're content so, then there is no need to speak of it."

131

"I'm content," she said, but for a moment it seemed to him that she drew a veil over her face, and yet he glimpsed a little of what lay behind it. And a flicker in her eyes gave the lie to her words, for he momentarily saw a yearning in them every bit as fierce as her independence.

He let the matter drop. They were getting close to the shore now, and he trained his attention on it.

"The enemy could be out there," he said. "We wouldn't know if they were swarming beyond the beach and in the trees."

The girl shrugged with nonchalance, as though what he said did not matter, or was wrong.

"Maybe," she replied. "But they can't know where we'll make land. Lake Alithorin is vast, and I'm pretty happy with our chances of avoiding them – at least for now."

"If they're not here, and I agree with you for the moment, they'll sooner or later find our tracks wherever we come to shore, and follow."

"That's a given," she said, flicking her hair impatiently. "And don't forget those beasts. I guess they'll have your scent, and the water won't put them off forever." She paused, and stared straight at him. "Are you scared? Do you wish to abandon your quest so soon, even though I'm babying you through it?"

That made him angry. She seemed one of the few people able to draw that emotion out of him with ease.

"You've helped me," he said with deliberate slowness, "and I thank you for it. But I don't take the names of scared or baby from anyone. Not from a warrior. Not from a lòhren. And not from you, who say you are a lòhren, but aren't."

He stood in the shuffa and drew his sword. "Now speak! Twice you have lied to me, which lòhrens don't

132

do. Your staff isn't broken. That was your first lie. And you said you were heading in the direction of the Angle. That was your second. Now, speak truly. Why were you waiting by the lake, and who are you?"

The girl glared, her eyes boring right through him, but he did not flinch. At length, she smiled, or at least bared her flashing white teeth.

"Well, the young kitten has claws after all. But are you not afraid? I have lòhrengai at my command that could blast you to a cinder." As she spoke, flame played across her fingertips, ready to leap at her will.

"I mistrust magic," he said without hesitation, "but I don't fear it. I've faced it before, from greater threats than you, and survived."

She eyed him again for a long while, and a frown creased her face.

"Maybe you have."

Her words were calm, but the air was charged with tension. Anything could happen at any moment, and he could not read her except for a sense of bafflement. Nor, he suspected, could she read him. They were opposites, as unalike from each other as possible, and that was dangerous.

They stared at each other, unmoving, while fate and destiny swirled around them like currents in the misty air. Then suddenly she smiled, and it was genuine this time, though flame still darted and danced at her fingertips.

"Very well. You're right, but you're wrong also. I was drawn to Lake Alithorin. Don't ask me why, I don't know. I found myself studying the battle, though I knew that wasn't what drew me. And I saw no way to get through the fortress to help anyway, and that confirmed my instincts. I was needed, but not for what was most obvious. A lòhren's feelings often work that way. A hunch, a momentary vision, a whim that turns out to be something more. So I waited, unable to help the city, but unable to go either. I didn't know for what I was called until I saw you flitting through the trees, and a merry chase you gave me until finally I caught up. I can say no more than that. I acted on instinct, and it has never yet let me down."

He thought about her response, but never lowered the point of his sword. What she said had the ring of truth, but it did not really answer his most pressing question.

"Why did you lie about your staff? It isn't broken, that much I know, and a lòhren without a staff ... isn't really a lòhren."

A shadow of remembered pain crossed her face.

"That isn't true. A lòhren doesn't need a staff. It just helps, and in the eyes of the people all across Alithoras it acts as a symbol. But the lòhrengai of a lòhren..."

She looked at him thoughtfully for a moment, and then changed what she was about to say. "All you need to know is this – I was a lòhren. I had a staff. And as you say, it wasn't broken. It was taken from me – taken away by the Lòhrenin, the council of lòhrens. Too deep I delved into forbidden lore. They thought I was turning down the paths of an elùgroth. At least so they feared." She gave a shrug. "Maybe they were right to stop me, maybe not. But no lòhren is the same as any other. Anyway, they would have expelled me from the order, but Aranloth persuaded them otherwise. They confiscated my staff, but they did not break it. For that, I owe him, and for other things beside. And I do not forget my debts. Had you killed him, you would not have seen this dawn. Yet still for five years they sent me away. Five long years, and only two have passed. When my punishment is ended, then I can return and they will judge me anew."

134

She said these last words with bitterness, and he glimpsed some of her great pride. And he understood also that she had no desire to tell him any of this, yet still, just as he had been forced to tell the truth before, so was she now. Fate or circumstance had caught them both in a tight grip. And just as he needed her help before, so now he knew that for some reason she would do anything to come with him to the Angle. But why?

She had not told him everything, but she had still told him much.

"And what of your second lie? You were not heading to the Angle or anywhere near it, until you knew that I was going there."

"That was no lie. It's true that I didn't intend to go there, but when you said that you would, then I knew that I must also. It is, as I said, what I've been waiting for. I didn't *know* what I was waiting for, or where I would end up going, but when you said that you must go there, and why – well, that was where I was going too. There was no lie in that."

She stared at him again, but this time it was not in anger, and when she spoke he felt that she was trying to tell him something different than what her words said.

"It's true that lòhrens don't lie. And maybe I've erred in telling you that my staff was broken. Maybe so, but a lòhren can weave greater deceptions by far, and yet still tell the truth."

He did not understand what she was getting at, but there were more important things to discuss.

"Tell me why you want to help," he asked. "You owe Aranloth, which I can understand. But why help *me*?"

"Because Aranloth would want me too. And I *do* owe him. But more is at stake than one city. All of Alithoras stands upon the brink. This is not the only battle. And there are other forces in the world besides swords…"

She had told him precious little. Then again, how much did she know and understand herself? A lòhren's intuition she had said. Perhaps he should just accept that, and her help. Certainly he needed it, but only if he could trust her.

Time was slipping away. He must be up and going, for the Angle was far away and the elugs and sorcerous beasts would find his trail sooner or later. The faster he moved now, the greater his lead would be, but on foot he could not count on keeping things that way.

The girl stared at him, assessing him even as he assessed her. The moments flitted by, and he knew he could not stand here talking all day until he learned and considered every detail of what was going on. He must either trust her, or not.

15. Troubled Sleep

Brand felt the weight of the sword in his hand. He also felt responsibility, and it was heavier. He and the girl faced each other, both ready to spring to defend themselves if necessary.

And yet both hesitated. Neither wanted a fight, that much was obvious. What Brand wanted, he knew in full. What she wanted, he knew only in part. And yet her words came back to him: she trusted in her instincts.

So must he. Whatever she was hiding, and he was certain that she was hiding more than one thing, he did not think she meant him harm. Or anyone else, for that matter, however abrasive her attitude.

Also, though he might part with her here if he chose to, she was obviously powerful, and would help him at need. And no greater need had he ever had, for to fail in this quest was to doom the king he served, and also Aranloth and the friends he had made. And an entire city.

What would Aranloth want him to do? Dare he risk taking this strange girl into the tombs with him? Had she even offered that? And what about revealing the charm Aranloth had taught him to protect himself once inside? He saw no way that he could keep that secret from her. Yet they were words that the lòhren had kept back even from Gilhain.

He had no answers, and he shrugged to himself. Sometimes, there *were* no answers. But he looked one last time into her eyes, and her gaze held his own unflinching.

He slowly sheathed his sword. "I'm Brand," he told her.

A moment longer she looked at him, and then the flame at her fingertips died away as she understood his choice.

"I'm Kareste," she answered. She held out her hand and he shook it. It was warm to touch as it had been before, although the fire was gone.

"We'd better move swiftly," she said.

They came to the shore in haste and hid the shuffa as best they could in some reeds. Brand doubted that he would ever see it again, yet he still looked around him and memorized the place. The future was dark, and unexpected need might drive him back here.

But it was likely the enemy would find it, if and when the beasts sniffed out their trail again.

Without any more words they headed off. Kareste led, setting a long loping pace that he could match, though it was still fast, and the day ahead of them long.

Swiftly the pine forest thickened around them again. Whatever sun rose in the east was hidden here. It remained a world that belonged to the night. The gray trunks of the trees were still – they seemed as statues in some ancient city. The fog was all about them, though not particularly thick. The needle-like leaves of the pines dripped moisture, slow but sure as the loping strides of the two runners, the only things that moved in the eerie shadow world.

On they went. Morning passed, if morning it was, and noon eventually came, revealed only by a lifting of the fog and the distant sounds of birds rather than an increase of light. Where they were it remained in perpetual dark, but the ground was soft with the needles of many years and the paths of some forest animal were clear. The running was good, and the walking better when they slowed to rest. For few could run all day without stopping. And even if they could, they would not be fit to fight should they need to if discovered by their enemies.

So time passed, and they spoke little, but they travelled with a greater sense of comradeship and understanding.

There were times when words were unnecessary, and this was one to Brand. He had made his decision, and he would not worry about her any longer. His mind was bent on one thing alone now: to put as much distance between him and his enemies as he could. And to this end she led him well, for she ran swift as a deer when need demanded but loped like a wolf with mile eating strides, hour after hour. She was fitter than he was, more used to running. Or else she sustained herself by the power of lòhrengai that she commanded, yet Aranloth had told him that lòhrens shunned such uses of the art, relying on it as only a last resort, and that was one of the things that separated them from elùgroths who used it without discrimination, heedless of the consequences in the pursuit of short term gain.

Without warning they burst from the shadows of the forest onto sunlit grass. Kareste slowed and came to a stop. He drew up beside her. The sun was blindingly bright above, and the grass seemed brilliant green. The sky was a cooler and deeper blue than he ever remembered. So it seemed to him to see these things for the first time after the long dark, and his spirit swelled within him.

"Evil cannot endure forever. Not in the face of this," he said.

She raised an eyebrow. "Spoken like a true Duthenor tribesman."

139

She did not say it with malice, but still he was taken aback.

"I haven't told you that I'm of the Duthenor. How did you know?"

She did not hesitate. "It's my job to know these things. You speak well, almost as a native of Cardoroth, but still I hear the slow tongue, deep and rolling of the Duthenor, in your every word."

"You've been among my people?"

"I've been many places in Alithoras. Even to the wild lands of the Duthenor and the ancient homelands beyond where once the Camar dwelt before they came east and founded realms."

"And how do things stand among the Duthenor? I have heard no news in years."

At this she gave him a strange look. "How long has it been?"

"I'm older than I seem," he answered. "It's been some while."

"Then know this. The Duthenor chieftain is not well liked. Yet the people have little choice but to obey him and suffer his rule. Other tribesmen, not of the Duthenor, support him. They are related, but are not like your people. They are warriors, fell and fierce, without pity or morals."

"Do the Duthenor not revolt?"

"That they have done. But the chieftain is as ruthless as the strangers he invited in to help him. It led only to blood and death. They endure his rule now, waiting for a time they believe will come."

"What time is that?"

"The time when the trueborn chieftain returns."

There was a pause. Brand did not speak, and she looked at him with eyes that seemed to read his every

140

secret. If he did not believe she was one of Aranloth's kind before, he believed it now.

"Perhaps the trueborn chieftain will one day return. If so, the Duthenor must yet wait a while. But it's good to hear tell of my people. And know this. They are patient. They *will* endure. But they do not forget. He who assumed the chieftainship by murder may sleep in the long hall that he stole, but he does not sleep well. Distrust and suspicion surround him during the day, fear assails him at night. For justice will prevail, and for every act of treason there is a price. He dreads that, and he'll one day learn that his fears are well founded."

Kareste gazed at him with the eyes of a lòhren. She knew much, guessed more, but revealed nothing of her thoughts by her expression.

They paused where they were for a while, resting in the last cover of the forest where its eaves gave way to the grasslands.

"We have a choice," she said, sitting down with her back to a tree. "The lands are wide and empty between here and the Angle. Our enemies roam them with freedom, though they are mostly concentrated around Cardoroth."

"There may be enemies ahead," he said. "But there are sure to be enemies behind, also."

She rested the back of her head against the tree trunk. "I've not forgotten them. And our journey must be on foot, which will make it hard to avoid them, either those before or those behind."

"What of the country that we have to traverse? What's it like?"

She closed her eyes. "The Great North Road, which is not that far away, is flat and smooth. It would speed our journey, at least the beginning of it, but it's impossible to hide there. The other way, direct across the land, will reduce the miles we must travel, but it'll be slower going for hills, woods and streams will hinder us. But those same things will also provide cover."

Brand made his decision quickly. "We should go that way," he said. "The land is our friend, in all its varied forms. An open road in the wild is no place to meet the beasts that come after us."

"No place is good for that," she said.

They did not linger long, but soon struck out again across the grass. Of the enemy, there was no sign, but still Brand felt vulnerable in the open. Yet there was no choice in what they did, and to wait until the cover of nightfall was more dangerous still.

The afternoon waned, and it grew dark. He was weary as he had rarely been before, and even Kareste showed signs of tiredness, she who seemed proof against danger, peril and exhaustion. But neither of them had slept for a long while, and many hard miles lay in their wake.

They sat beneath a lone pine that towered into the sky. It was, perhaps, the last remnant of a once larger forest that had grown around Lake Alithorin and shrunk over time through the damage of successive waves of migrating men. Or maybe it was the first thrust of the forest to conquer new lands and cover them with a mass of dark-leaved trees. He did not know, but the old needles that lay thick beneath it were a soft place to sit and rest.

They ate little and spoke less. But it was a comfortable silence, and it enabled him to think. Night crept from the dark band of the forest now far away, but it rolled ever more swiftly over the grasslands and soon swamped all in its vast blanket.

The stars sprang like sparks from a forge into the blackened sky, and he looked up at bright Halathgar. The two glittering points shone at him like seeking eyes. They looked down also on Cardoroth, and he wondered what was happening there. And lastly, he considered that they also gazed on the lands of the Duthenor far away.

What was happening to his own people? The Careth Nien, the Great River, offered them some protection against the hordes of elugs that had come into the north. The river was not easy to cross. He knew that better than most. And it would be harder for armies than a lone man, but still they were at risk. Now, more than ever, he wanted to be with them. But his task in these foreign lands was not yet done.

At length he fell into a deep sleep. He found rest in oblivion, and ease from his many cares and worries, but it did not last. They lit no fire and it grew cold. The leaves were not so soft as he had thought, and the roots of the tree formed hard ripples in the earth. He dreamed that they rose up and took hold of him, shaking him fiercely.

He stirred, coming to wakefulness with a wrench, and found that the roots were just where they should be, but that there *were* hands on him nonetheless, and they *did* shake him.

It was Kareste, and even in the dimness beneath the great tree he saw the expression on her face. It was one of great urgency.

"They come," she said.

And he knew what she meant, for even as she spoke the beasts that had hunted in silence through the forest, seeking to take their prey by stealth, now howled in frenetic glee as they followed a warm scent.

16. Called from the Otherworld

Brand leaped up, grabbed his pack and strapped it on. Without further delay, the two of them loped off.

"We need cover and height," she said.

Brand did not answer. She was right, but even as she spoke their boots trod ground that led them on a steeper grade. They did not see it so much as feel it, but they followed the rise in the land and hoped that somewhere ahead in the dark was cover.

This proved to be the case. As they ran, trees grew up about them. They were not pines this time, but rather some kind of shrubby evergreen. The cover was not great, and Brand felt in his heart anyway that their time of hiding was over. The time for fighting was near.

They reached the crest of the rise. It could hardly be called a hill, and the shrubby growth about them dispersed rather than grew denser. From their vantage they saw the black shadows of night spread out below them, yet the sky was gray and the stars fading even as they looked. He might yet see one last dawn, but after that, hope would dwindle swiftly.

Even as they looked behind them they saw five creatures race amid the trees. The noise of thrashing branches and the crashing of large animals through underbrush came to them loudly in the otherwise peaceful dark.

And then they heard once more the beasts give rise to their baying din. This time they did not howl. Instead, they voiced deep and bellowing barks.

Brand looked ahead at something that he had seen earlier. Boulders littered the crest of the rise. They would not help much, but they offered some advantage, and he would take what he could get at the moment. He did not need to say anything to Kareste. They both ran for them at the same moment.

They leaped onto the largest, clambering over its rough surface until they reached the top, though it was little more than six feet above ground level. Within moments the beasts raced across the grass toward them, tufty fur prickled in rage or excitement, red tongues lolling from slavering jaws.

The beasts drew close, snuffling and snarling as they circled the boulder. Not yet did they attempt to climb it or leap; they were wary, considering with an intelligence beyond animals what was to be done next.

Kareste hissed as she studied them.

"Foul summonings. Dredged from the darkest pits of sorcery. Yet sorcery is not the only power in the world."

Brand watched them closely also. Where skin showed, not covered by the bristly fur, the muscles beneath rippled with size and strength beyond any beast he had seen before. These things were not quite hounds, and they were not quite wolves. They looked back at him with an expression that unnerved him. He saw malice, and believed that his earlier fears were founded.

"Are these creatures part man?" he asked Kareste, not taking his eyes from their roving forms.

"Of course," she replied. "They're called from the otherworld, but held in place by the transformed bodies of men."

"The elùgroths sacrificed some of their own soldiers?"

She shrugged. "These are more valuable to them than any soldiers. The staff is their greatest concern, greater

145

even than taking Cardoroth. It wouldn't surprise me if one or more sorcerers came after the beasts. We're lucky that they ran ahead of the hunt, though the rest cannot be far behind. Men, elugs and elùgroths all."

Brand looked around. He saw nothing else but the hounds. These still circled below, biting and snapping and growling. Suddenly, one leaped high. It scrambled over rock, the great forepaws heaving its vast bulk upward like a man climbing a ladder.

Kareste did not hesitate. Flame, blue as the midnight sky, roared from her fingers and smashed into it.

The creature howled and dropped off the boulder, but it merely lumbered into the shadows and glared at her with bared lips. It did not die.

That was a shock to Brand. He did not expect her powers to obliterate the creatures instantly, but he saw clearly that they would not be enough. The beasts could be hurt by lòhrengai, but killing them all would take time. And of that they had little.

Even as the beast snarled at them from a safe distance, the others drew closer, studying the boulder and analyzing the situation for a better way to attack.

And in the distance, the new-risen sun shone golden light on the last thing Brand wanted to see. Azan riders. Light flared from their naked swords, and it flashed from spears and polished helms. Yet there were only six, and that gave him hope, and the spark of an idea.

He shivered, part in fear and part in excitement. Whatever was to be done must be done soon. Otherwise, more and more of the hunt would gather.

He looked at Kareste, tall and proud and calm on the top of the boulder.

"We need those horses," he said

She returned his gaze. "Yes we do. But are you mad? We have to worry about the hounds first. They're a greater threat than the riders."

"We can't delay. Others will likely soon come. Either hounds or elugs or elùgroths. We cannot wait any longer."

"Wait for what?" she asked.

But Brand did not answer.

17. Not for Nothing

Brand remembered the words of Aranloth. *The staff will help you.* He had no magic of his own, yet the staff did. His question was, how much did he trust the lòhren? For surely he could not attack the beasts with his blade. He would need more than that to survive against them.

Kareste still looked at him questioningly, unable to guess what he was about to do. He sheathed his blade, shook off his pack and smiled at her fiercely. The thrill of battle pumped in his veins. And then, without warning, he turned and leaped from the boulder into the very midst of the hounds.

The girl screamed. It was a sudden cry of shock and fear. It pierced the air and brought all eyes to her. All except for Brand's.

He landed lightly, even as the hounds turned toward him. He spun among them, smelling their fetid breath and hearing up close their throbbing growls. The very earth beneath his boots seemed to thrum to their deep-throated rumbling and the padding of their massive paws.

But he did not wait for them to attack. They were as shocked as Kareste had been, and that was the moment of opportunity he hoped for. Fortune favored the bold.

Aranloth's staff sang as he swung it. With all the strength of his will he brought it down upon the skull of the nearest beast. To his surprise, there was a flash of magic. It sputtered to life, and he felt a strange power tingle through his body and flare in the timber. After a faltering moment, as though of a kindled flame that might yet be snuffed out, it roared in a fury of fire that blazed like the sun, though the light was silver, shot through with blue.

He nearly dropped the staff. The hound leaped in pain and surprise. It landed, stumbling and disorientated. With a howl it thrashed in rage as fire caught in the great ruff of fur around its neck, sending curls of putrid smoke into the air.

The beast shambled away, howling and rolling in the grass to try to put out the flame that burned it. The other hounds held back, growling. A moment they studied him, uncertainty in their eyes.

That moment was all he needed. He was off, sprinting straight at the horsemen. He saw from their faces that they did not believe what he had just done. With luck, it would take them a few seconds to realize what he would do next.

All was caught in a net of confusion and surprise, and he was at the center of it. But the hounds, after their initial reticence, bounded after him. Brand feared they would reach him before he could accomplish his true aim, but just then he heard a wild yell from behind.

Kareste had left the safety of the boulder, and with the hounds before her, oblivious to what she did, she sprayed blasting fire among them.

He saw the streaking light flicker all through the air, heard the yelps of pain and noticed the pounding chase falter and grow disordered.

Before they grasped what was happening, Brand was among the horsemen. Their steeds were wild with fear, both from the nearing beasts and the sudden flame. They bucked and kicked and screamed with fright.

Some of the men lifted their swords, and the bright blades flashed as they swept toward him. But he was fleet of foot, and they must also try to control their mounts and avoid falling.

He blocked a vicious cut that came too near, but this time Aranloth's staff did not flare with lòhrengai. It seemed that only the sorcerous beasts triggered it, or something else entirely. But he needed no magic. He was better skilled at fighting than these warriors, and he knew exactly what he intended, whereas they were still in shock at being attacked in the most unlikely circumstances.

He waited for just the right moment when the weight of one of the horses shifted and the rider was fighting for balance, and then he struck with the point of his staff, thrusting the man from his saddle to land with a heavy thud. In a moment he had dislodged yet another rider.

He ducked beneath a wild slash, and then grabbed the loose reins of the nearest riderless horse and jumped into the saddle.

The mare bucked and kicked, but he held on. He realized that it was not trying to dislodge him. Rather, it lashed out in fear. For the hounds were among the riders now. Some aflame, but all maddened and confused. And all driven by their sorcerous instinct to attack.

The Azan men that he had pulled from their horses came to their feet, but they were too slow to realize their danger and react. The hounds were upon them, driven by pain and frenzy, and they pounced at what was nearest to them.

The Azan screamed. The hounds mauled them. Blood spurted and bones cracked. It was too much for the remaining Azan. They kicked their mounts into a gallop and fled.

Brand struggled with his horse, but he managed to direct it away from the hounds and toward the second riderless horse. This spun and kicked, catching one of the hounds that mauled the men. He heard a thud that could only mean cracked ribs, and then the second lot of reins was in his hand and he was off.

He galloped back toward the boulders. Kareste was running toward him, ash-blond hair trailing in her wake and green-brown eyes on fire. Smoke curled from a swathe of burnt grass at her feet, and one of the hounds lay there, dead. It was a blackened thing. Fire smoldered in the deep fur at the ruff of its neck, but it had been burnt away from the rest of its body. Everywhere bright red blood seeped from the charred skin.

Kareste grabbed the reins of the second horse and mounted. Behind him, Brand heard a gut wrenching scream and a vicious snarl. The Azan were dead, and the beasts would now turn back to their proper prey.

They wheeled the horses round to face their enemy. The hounds looked at them. Blood smeared their snouts. Their lips curled back and low snarls rumbled in their throats.

At the same moment, Kareste lifted her hands and Brand his staff. Lòhrengai sprang to life, streaking across the gap and smashing into the beasts. It knocked two of them off their feet, concentrated on one and drove it back, rolling and tumbling until it lodged against a low bush.

Leaves flared. Fur caught alight. A frenzied series of yelps turned into a suddenly human wail. With a final blast of lòhrengai both beast and shrub burst into billowing flames like a bonfire.

The other beasts stood their ground. Brand pointed the staff at them and spurred his horse forward. This was become too much for them, and they turned and fled, racing back down the slope and into the cover of the trees.

151

All was still now atop the slope except for the burning shrub and what lay beneath it.

Brand looked at Kareste. She returned his gaze. They were both silent. Sweat dripped from them, cold on their skin although the sun shone warmly from the clear blue sky.

At length, Kareste nudged her mount closer and spoke.

"Not for nothing did Aranloth choose you. And though you distrust magic, there is more to you than meets the eye. Mine at least. Aranloth, obviously, saw more clearly. But still ... you *are* mad."

He smiled at her again, filled with exuberance.

"Maybe so. But I'm alive, and if you want to stay that way – follow me!"

That his words were an echo of her own were bound to annoy her, but he did not care. She deserved that little rebuke, not that anything mattered now except that the quest might still be fulfilled.

He gathered up his pack and they sped off, both riders and mounts happy to leave the slope behind them. It stunk of sorcery, death and fear, and it would take many days of open air and bright sunlight to make it otherwise.

The long strides of the horses made easy work of the hill, which soon angled downward, and they pounded to its bottom and then raced away even faster on the level ground beyond.

Of the hunt, Brand did not yet see any sign. But it would regroup. Others would join and strengthen it. The pursuit would not falter, for the trail it must follow was clear and scent was no longer needed.

The beasts could be killed. That was heartening. So also was the fact that he and Kareste were now mounted. That would lengthen the chase, but he did not doubt that sooner or later their enemy would catch up with them. That did not matter so much, even if there were elùgroths next time, so long as he first obtained Shurilgar's staff and destroyed it. If he accomplished the quest, nothing else really mattered. He just hoped that Kareste had left him by that point. Alithoras was vast, and they would not pursue her if they found him first.

18. A Great Darkness

They rode warily but with great speed. The sun arced above them, bringing ever greater warmth and light to wash away some of the horror of their encounter with the beasts.

But Brand knew he would never forget the hounds that looked at him with the calculating eyes of a man. Worse, he guessed that it was not the last time that he would see them, or their kind.

He felt fear and determination in equal parts. Fear, because the creatures were made of evil and bent on his death. Determination, because such atrocities should not be allowed to walk Alithoras. The elùgroths and the dark powers at their command must be stopped. Fate had given him an opportunity to help with that, and it was more important than his personal goal among the Duthenor. And, in the end, what helped Cardoroth also helped his own people, even if they did not know what he was attempting, nor ever would learn of it.

They rode and rested and rode again. The day passed, and night came after with a shimmer of stars. Yet darkness did not stop them. On they went, oftentimes walking the horses to give them relief, at other times just urging them forward at a gentle trot. But ever they went on, striving toward their goal.

And *their* goal he now thought it, for though the danger and obligation to reach the tombs was his, Kareste had shared in the risk so far and become a companion rather than a stranger met along the way. She had stood by him when he needed it, and he would do the same for her. Loyalty was like trust, he thought: swiftly earned but impossible to regain once lost. But she had both his loyalty and his trust.

Brand studied her as they traveled, but she veiled herself and her thoughts. Not lightly did she give her own trust, and even less easily did she make friends. Yet the abrasiveness that was in her when they first met was gone. Something had made her angry then, perhaps that she helped the cause of the lòhrens even when they shunned her. But now the two of them were getting to know each other, and he did not think that she held anything against him any longer.

He scratched the skin of his forehead beneath Aranloth's diadem. The metal ornament was warm to touch, and he wondered for the first time what power it held. For it seemed to him that he had greater insight into Kareste's thoughts and motives than he would have expected. But he did not really believe that any lòhrengai could do that. Such intuition as he had came through his experiences, both the good and the bad. No artifact could substitute for that. Life must be lived, people known through both good and hard times to understand why they did what they did. No diadem could replace that, no matter if it was imbued with magic.

Well into the night they finally slept. And a deep slumber it was, for pursuit or no, hounds or not, they must rest. Yet they woke with the dawn and sped away again.

The lands they now travelled seemed strange to him. He had heard rumor of them, and had it described to him by Aranloth, but still the country was different from what he knew. There were few trees, and what hills there were marched far away and seemed bare rather than choked by tree and bush. He guessed it likely that he had become the best travelled of all the Duthenor that ever lived, for his feet had trod the eastern side of the Great River, led him up north to the verge of the northern mountains that lured him so, and now he rode south into lands beyond the dominion of Cardoroth. He supposed they were still Gilhain's lands, yet the king was far away, as were his soldiers, and if any people lived here they were brave homesteaders, recking little of kings and cities, and trusting in the hidden ways of forest, hill and valley to hold them safe from enemies.

"You haven't been here before?" Kareste asked him.

Brand shook his head. "Aranloth told me something of the area, but that's not the same."

"No, it's not. So in case we get separated, I'll tell you what I know."

She was silent for a moment, deciding best how to describe things. Then she pointed with her long right arm.

"Quite a few miles to our right is the Great North Road, made by the Halathrin long ago. It's still a good road, and it runs straight and true." She glanced at him. "You must have crossed it further north when you came to Cardoroth."

He nodded, and she continued. "The road drives deep into the south, much further than we'll go. It reaches to the crossings of the Carist Nien river, and even well beyond that to the Careth Nien, more than a hundred leagues away, nigh to the borders of the forest realm of the Halathrin. Also to the right, beyond the Great North Road, are the hills of Lòrenta. There stands the keep of the lòhrens – secure against enemies, sorcerous or otherwise, though few guard it. It isn't protected by swords, but by powers older and stronger than iron and steel."

She shifted in her saddle and swept an arm out to the left. "Some fifty miles that way lies the sea."

156

Of the sea, Brand had heard many stories. But he had never seen it. Vast it must be if Lake Alithorin was as a puddle beside it, as some in Cardoroth had told him. Yet pearls he had looked at once, on a necklace of his mother's, and they were said to come from it. And once a twisted shell which had come from some strange creature. His father had held it to his ear and told him that the strange sound he heard, the soft and undulating roar, was the sound that the great waters made as they surged and flowed. Well he remembered those words, though he was very young, and he wanted to see the truth of it.

Kareste went on with her description, and he listened, entranced by her every word.

"When we reach the Carist Nien, if not sooner, we must turn east and follow it in that direction, toward the sea. Thence we'll come at length to the Angle – the home in ancient days of an empire that crumbled to dust ere either Camar or Duthenor wandered out of the dark into the brighter lands of the east and founded chieftainships and after realms."

As she spoke, her words evoked the history and the wonder of the land, but he sensed also that forces were at work within it. The lòhrens and their allies on one hand, and the elùgroths, elugs and Azan on the other. Far to the south was the home of their enemies, beyond the Careth Nien, beyond green Galenthern, which was but a rumor to him, beyond the Graèglin Dennath mountains that tales of legend spoke of, and then, in a far country, Grothanon, whence the great powers of the enemy dwelt.

Of other cities that lay between he had heard some names: Faladir, Menetuin, Camarelon. But there were once other cities, fallen to the enemy, as also would Cardoroth if his quest did not succeeded. If it did, then perhaps they had a chance, for the wiles of the king were great, and many bold hearts wielded swords with hope and defiance.

They rode ever on. Kareste was often quiet beside him, withdrawn into some world of her own. What troubled her, he did not know. Perhaps what surely followed after them. Perhaps what lay ahead. Maybe something else entirely.

And then on other days she was suddenly happy, as though the sun burst through clouds on a rainy day. He was not sure what to make of her, but he was growing to like her better and better. Certainly, she was unlike the girls of his homeland, and unlike the girls of Cardoroth as well.

A great darkness lay behind her, and he guessed her life had not been easy. That she hid much, he knew, but he trusted her more and more. He supposed, thinking about things honestly, that it would seem to her that he also hid much. So he did, and she did not press him, so the least he could do was offer her the same grace.

But one day, when a gray veil of drizzle covered the land and she seemed talkative, he asked her a question. She would either respond or not, and he would not press her.

"You're not from Cardoroth," he said. "Where do you come from?"

She hesitated, deciding whether or not to answer him. She was, he guessed, coming to like him and more inclined to talk. So he hoped, but at the same time the thought was unsettling.

"Am I not from Cardoroth?" she answered. "Well, perhaps not, although I did live there once. But before that, *long* before that, some few people from that city sought out new lands, well away from the rule of the king – not the current king, and the trammeled ways of stone and gate and city streets. They trekked north, settling at last along the Alith Nien river that feeds Lake Alithorin. There they fished and tilled the fertile soils to either side of the river. It was a good life, but a hard one. But the fish were plentiful, and the harvests of grain and fruit were good. Thus also, dwelling where they did, they became skillful with boats – the crafting of them as well as the using of them. But there were hunters among them too, for meat was ever scarce even when the crops were good."

Her horse picked its way through some broken rocks and she gave it free reign to do so, absent-mindedly watching the ground as she spoke.

"And the hunters travelled far, seeking ever new lands where the game was less shy of men and the hunting that little bit easier. They strayed even under the shadow of the northern mountains, Auren Dennath as they're called in the Halathrin tongue, and some few followed ridges and dim forest paths, hunting higher and higher, ever nearer to the snow-mantled peaks."

He listened to her as she spoke, feeling once again that tremor of excitement that shivered his body when he heard the name of those mountains, Auren Dennath, the high lands that he had seen from a distance but never climbed. But he asked her no questions about them, fearing to interrupt, for she spoke so seldom of anything that mattered to her, and he felt also that what she said now touched on the darkness that lay behind her. Especially since he had wandered over the lands on either side of that river before coming to Cardoroth, and had never met any people nor seen sign of them.

"Fair they thought those mountains, and the hunting was good, so more and more of them went there. But after a time, none returned. So it happened that my people were discovered, for elugs dwelt there of ancient

159

days, though not in great numbers. Yet their roaming bands were enough. They gathered together one wet autumn, and falling upon our folk slew them – men, women and children. Only a handful lived. Of these, I was one. And I too would have died save for Aranloth." She shuddered. "I was very young. And very scared. Too young to remember much, and too scared to want to. But I'll never forget the fire and smoke and great lights, and Aranloth standing there, alone and unaided, defying a band of elugs. They retreated, and he scooped me up and took me to Lòrenta. There were none that I knew there, either young or old, for the few others who survived went to Cardoroth."

She paused for a moment, and when she went on her voice held a new note.

"But I didn't forget my past. Against the elugs I hold a grudge, for they took my childhood from me, and more. Yet Aranloth gave me a new life, and ever was I keen to learn the ways of power, for he trained me as a lòhren, and this I became. But whereas the others my age spent their time learning how to heal, and to offer counsel and succor to the needy, and power last, I turned in a different direction. Power I would have, and I would have it as swiftly, and as much of it as I could get, to defend against enemies."

Here then was the beginning of how she fell afoul of the Lòhrenin. He could not really blame her, and it comforted him that Aranloth had stood up for her, and in that lòhren's judgement he trusted completely.

Yet he noted that she said little of *what* powers she sought, and what she would do with them if gained, other than the vague comment of *defend against enemies*. That could mean just about anything.

Whatever else, he guessed that she had made good on that desire and acquired many skills, a few of which he

160

had seen. What exactly she intended to do with them, and what dark lore she had delved into that had forced the lòhrens to cast her out, even if only for a time, were other problems. But if problems they were, they were not to be solved now, if ever they could be.

19. Beyond the Reach of Thought

It felt to Gilhain that he now lived on the Cardurleth. He dared not leave it, for the attacks of the enemy did not let up. And he trusted to no other to organize the defense. Not that others were incompetent; there were many who could do the task, but the responsibility was his alone.

Aurellin, his wife, spent much time with him. Little love she had for battle, but her temperament was always calm, and though unskilled in arms herself she had a store of knowledge on warfare that would put a general to shame. He relied on her as much as them, if not more, but still so many decisions were his alone, and they weighed him down.

He was getting old now. His mind retained its agility, but his body constantly let him down. If he survived this, if Cardoroth survived this, he was reaching a point where he must either abdicate his throne or else hold on, old and infirm, while his enemies within the city, and perhaps those outside such as his half-brother, plotted against him. That would not help Cardoroth. But it was a problem that he must put aside, even though it weighed increasingly heavy upon him.

Aurellin was by his side, as usual, when the new day of battle began. He glanced at her but did not speak. As the years went by he found they conversed less, not because their love faltered, but because they knew each other so well. She smiled back at him, a weary attempt, and her eyes were shadowed, for she guessed at what he now thought. Their time together was drawing to an end.

She was younger than he, and they both wanted to spend what years were left away from war and trouble and the rule of a great city that would burden even a young man.

Aranloth was there too. The lòhren never seemed to rest. He had a kind word here for a wounded soldier, a helping hand there to those in need, and he remained ever a source of courage and humor when these things were required.

He was a better strategist than Gilhain was himself, but he never put himself forward, always offering humble advice, and allowing Gilhain to lead. For this much was true: Cardoroth had trust in their king. Even now, after so long a siege, they seemed little worried. They waited for some grand stroke of his that would break the enemy. Only he did not have one. What hope they had he had already placed in Brand.

He thought about the lòhren. He gave no commands, yet his influence was everywhere. Aurellin was here because she wanted to be, yet that was Aranloth's idea first. It was true that she did not wish to be parted from him. It was true that she also gave heart to the men, for she was much loved and respected. But Gilhain knew that Aranloth had encouraged her presence to help put his mind at rest. If his wife was away in the palace, he would always worry of some sorcerous attack that might be made against her. That would break him, but here at least, with Aranloth constantly by both their sides, he did not fear that, and he was free to think only of the daily attacks against the wall.

And though no further attacks had been made directly at him, still the sorcerous chanting during the night continued. But it was directed at the whole city. It was like a soul-sapping dirge: depressing, bleak and used with the elug chant to lower the morale of the defenders.

163

So things had been for a seemingly endless series of days, though in truth it was not that long. Yet today was different. They all sensed it, most especially Aranloth who had been uneasy since yesterday afternoon, and that tenseness grew over the long night.

Other lòhrens moved along the walls. Their white robes gleamed, and they shifted their staffs from hand to hand. It was a rare sign of nerves.

"What is it?" Gilhain asked, turning to his old friend.

Aranloth slowly shook his head as though coming back from somewhere far away.

"I don't know. *Something.* Something that the enemy hasn't tried before. This much I can say – there's a change in the air. I feel it. The other lòhrens feel it. Even some of the men sense it. But what it is … I don't know."

Gilhain knew what he meant. There was a brooding menace to the air like a storm in the distance: building, growing, massing – but not yet ready to break. But when it did break, and that felt inevitable, it would not be with wind and rain and hail.

He studied the dark host below. He cast his gaze around its perimeter. He considered its center, scrutinizing elugs, men and Lethrin with his experienced gaze. But he learned nothing.

For whatever reason, the enemy had also ceased the chanting. Normally that would be welcome, but just now he was not so sure. Nothing made sense today, and that worried him more than anything.

What was he missing? Was there something that he could do, or was the attack now moving beyond strength of arms and the courage of brave hearts to something that only lòhrens could defy?

The morning ran its course. As usual, the attacks began, but he knew they were half-hearted. The elugs were driven forward by their masters, climbing the walls in a dull stupor, knowing that they ran and climbed to their deaths. It was clear to both sides that those who sent them did not send enough, nor did they support them with archers or the beat of war drums.

The attacks were easily beaten off by the soldiers on the wall. Men laughed and joked. They leaned on their spears or the stonework, talking freely and enjoying this turn of events. It was better than the desperate fighting for life against a maddened enemy imbued by rage to kill. But that only fuelled Gilhain's unease all the more.

At noon, the enemy host grew quiet. No further sallies were made. Through its dark ranks paced a wedge of elùgroths. As a wave they came forward, the host parting for them, either in awe or fear for their lives.

Aranloth strained to look. And whether his sight was better than a normal man's, or he used some art of lòhrengai, he saw what Gilhain did not.

"Khamdar is not there."

They both guessed what that meant. "If he is not there," Gilhain said, "with his host at a time when they're obviously preparing for some great attack, then he has gone after Brand."

That scared him. If Brand was not dead, then soon he must face an enemy beyond his strength, for no man and few even among lòhrens could face an elùgroth, least of all one such as Khamdar.

"There's still hope," he said after a pause. "If Khamdar had caught and killed Brand, he would have returned to his host. His absence is, in a way, promising."

"Maybe," Aranloth said uncertainly. "But he might still be returning."

"That is so," Gilhain replied. "And yet if Brand still lives he must now be approaching the Angle and the last part of the quest. The staff is within his reach."

They said no more. The elùgroth wedge had stopped between the host and the wall. They sat, still dark statues as they seemed, their wych-wood staffs pointed at the Cardurleth.

The war drums began to beat again. The elug chant rose also, becoming one with them and they one with the words:

Ashrak ghùl skar! Skee ghùl ashrak!
Skee ghùl ashrak! Ashrak ghùl skar!

And then the elùgroths began to chant themselves. What words they uttered, Gilhain did not know. Yet their force reached out into the very air, stretched to the wall, sunk deep into the earth and soared into the heavens. The sun seemed darker. The air more chill. Elugs, drums, chanting and sorcery all worked to one dark purpose. That much he knew, but what it was he could not guess.

The air tingled. The sun dimmed further as though clouds veiled it, yet the sky was empty. A gusty wind came up from the south, tugging at banners, blowing dust in little whirlwinds and scattering dead leaves as though thrown by the hands of the enemy themselves, for there was spite in it, even if it did no damage.

Gilhain squinted against a slap of dust-filled air.

"What is it?" he asked again, hoping that this time Aranloth had an answer.

The lòhren did not reply at once. He stood straight and tall. If the wind and dust and driving leaves annoyed him, he showed no sign of it. His gaze remained fixed on the enemy as though nothing else in the world mattered. At that moment, it did not.

At length, Aranloth glanced back at him. It was strange to see him without diadem or staff, but one thing was unchanged. His eyes were those of a man who had seen tragedies unfold: the death of loved ones, the massacre of innocents and the fall of nations. Pain was in them, both remembered and expected.

"I do not know," he said hoarsely. "But it is something wicked beyond the reach of our thought."

20. Bright were our Swords

Brand and Kareste had long since turned eastward. They had reached, and now followed, the Carist Nien river. Somewhere ahead was the land that Aranloth called the Angle.

There was no sign of any pursuit, and he thought that strange. He glanced at Kareste, quiet as usual where she rode on his left.

"Do you think we've lost them?"

"Maybe. But there's another way to look at it. They may know where we go, and where Shurilgar's staff is secured. There's great power in it, and they will not allow it to be destroyed – if they can help it. Even better if they can obtain it for their own use. And no doubt it has many uses that neither Aranloth nor the elùgroths have considered…"

Brand did not like that new line of thought. "I don't see how they could know where we're going. And though elùgroths might set a trap, I don't think the hounds, intelligent as they are, would run ahead rather than pursue."

"That might be true, but don't forget the elùgroths created the hounds. They obey their commands, and no matter how keen the chase, if one of the masters was with them they would be held under their control."

That was likely enough, and the thought of the enemy being ahead of them was not a pleasant one. So it was that for the next several days they moved warily along the grassy trail they followed.

And trail it was, for even here in the wilds of Alithoras men had come and dwelt here, though there was no sign of them now. Yet their long-ago presence marked the land. The faint path they followed was only one such sign. Another was the presence of fruit trees. These had grown wild, the descendants of trees once cultivated but long since gone to seed. How long ago, Brand could not guess…

He took out and looked over the map that Aranloth had given him. It had seemed detailed in Cardoroth, but now it was scant of information.

It showed several entrances and exits to the tombs in case of need, but a particular path was marked in heavier outline: the one the lòhren had preferred. It was the shortest, and Brand had no desire to prolong his time underground.

The closer he got to the tombs the more real Aranloth's warnings became. There were things there that he had no wish to see and meet, yet if wishes were truths he would not be here, would never have come to Cardoroth and the chieftainship of his people would be his. Nor would his parents have been killed by an usurper.

Yet wishes were not truths, and as much as he wished that he could change things, doing so would now mean a loss to him. He would be a poorer person for never having met Aranloth or Gilhain, for dwelling in the great city of Cardoroth, nor, and the thought surprised him, would he have met Kareste.

The river to their right grew as the days passed. A mighty thing it was, yet still not so great as the Careth Nien, the great river of Alithoras. Yet this one was still too broad to cross, a massive sweep of water that drove all before it. And it gathered pace and hurried along its course now, for the land began to slope downward at a steeper angle.

One night came when the roar of the river was loud as they slept, and the next day they saw rocks in the water and furious white-foamed rapids.

"We are come close to the Angle now," Kareste said. And she had to talk loud to be heard over the toss and thrash of the waters.

The path was plainer here. In fact, he saw several paths, but they followed only one. This led down steeply now, but before it did Brand took one last look at the river. It surged ahead, spilling and floundering over a mighty waterfall in the distance. Waves crashed and foamed. Spray cascaded into the air, and through it all the sun shot rainbow rays that came and went, leaped and fell as swift as the water-mist of the river rose and swirled above the land.

Suddenly, Brand had a sense of how vast Alithoras was, how many treasures it contained. He had seen but a fraction of it, and a hunger woke in him to see more; to tread paths that no man before him had trod, to explore the valleys, to find his way through the green-lit forests, and most of all to climb the northern mountains, whatever their dangers and look down on the land that the Halathrin had named Alithoras – the silver land, the land that even the immortals thought fair.

With slow steps he followed Kareste down the rocky path. Cliffs formed to his right, blocking out his view of the river. A great gorge opened up on the left, steep and shear, a drop so deep that it made him dizzy, and on the other side were more cliffs.

On the rock faces he saw at last the mark of the people who had once dwelt in these lands. No wild fruit trees grew here. This was mightier. This had endured through the ages intact, not seeding and growing and

170

seeding again through the long ages, but enduring wind and rain and sun and cold, enduring time itself. And if time had marred what once was there, time also had draped over it a sense of awe. For what he saw was carved by men, by men that had once lived and breathed as he did now, but who had died, according to Aranloth, some ten thousand years before. Yet still what they made spoke to him now with the freshness of a spell cast just at this moment. He looked. He saw, and the power of the magic, the power of time itself, smote him.

They both stopped together. Side by side they looked across the gorge and at the great figures in the rock on the other side.

A series of giant carvings were there, hundreds of feet high. The elements had blunted and cracked the images, but from this distance that was nearly invisible. There were bands of laborers working in unison to harvest wheat with sickle-shaped blades before they threshed the chaff from the grain. Nearby stood massive stone querns, turned by oxen to make flour. Hunters with keen spears, stealthy and silent, left a village with their heads lowered, searching for the spoor of game animals. There were miners, long-handled picks and shovels in the meaty hands, smiths and masons, dancers and storytellers. And there were warriors also. These were hard looking men in leather armor with round shields and short swords. And then Brand's eye was drawn to the largest carving of them all. He saw at the end of the long procession what must have been a king and queen. They were stern and fearful to look upon, and there was an edge of cruelty in their stony glance. They wore no crowns; instead, great diadems encircled their brows, such as the one he wore upon his own head.

Brand had never seen anything like it before, and the age of it, the greatness of it, took his breath away. All that work must have taken decades, even hundreds of years, to carve into hard rock.

Neither he nor Kareste spoke. At length, with a simple glance, she led him on once more. They went down the rough path that looked out over sharp-rocked death below and timeless beauty beyond.

The path was steep, and as they descended the roar of the waterfall lessened greatly. After a while, they came to a kind of recess where the ledge widened. That was as far as they could go because a rock fall blocked the way.

Brand studied it. It was not recent, but it did not seem old either. Nor was it natural. Some battle had been fought here, for the cliff above the rock was blackened by fire. Not the fire of burning timber, for there was none on this rocky slope, but of lòhrengai or elùgai. His battles were not the only ones in Alithoras.

But the rock fall was not the major point of interest. To the right of the recess was a kind of statue, and beyond that a cave. It was his first sight of the entrance to the tombs, and his heart sank. Even he, unskilled and void of magic, could sense the powers that dwelt within. There was malice there, a hunger for life and a will to bring death and destruction. Whatever waited inside was not his friend, nor the friend of any living thing.

Kareste looked at the statue, and he went over. At once he saw that it was a monument of some kind, rather than a statue.

"It's quiet here," he said. "I don't like it."

"It is ever thus," she answered. "This is a dead land. But even so, I know what you mean. It seems even stiller than normal."

"You've been here before?"

"Once. Long ago, it seems now."

"Have you been inside?"

172

She laughed at that, but it was a grim laugh. "No. None go in there. It is death."

"Then why do you think of doing so now? You don't have to, you know. In fact, I would prefer it if you didn't. This is my quest, and my responsibility. You've helped me greatly, and whatever debt you owe to Aranloth is paid."

She ran a hand through her long hair. "No, it is not paid. It can never be paid."

"Why not? You've saved my life, even as Aranloth saved yours."

"Because of many things…" Her voice trailed away.

It was no answer. But he knew he would get nothing more.

He looked around him, thinking. The recess they stood on was a large half-moon shape, perhaps forty feet long and just as deep at its furthest point. In the center sat a squat and ugly stone, the thing he had taken for a statue. It was as tall as he, but somewhat wider. Each of its four faces was carved with unusual writing.

He peered at it closely. The marks were a series of slashes, dots, and half circles, evidently some kind of writing, but it differed greatly from anything he had seen before.

"What does it say?" he asked.

Kareste rested her hand against the stone. "As you guess, it's the writing of the Letharn. It's an ancient thing. But as for what it says, it's better that you don't know."

"Words can't hurt me,' he said. "Tell me what they say."

Kareste shrugged. "So you say, but do you know all the secrets of the world, all the powers that battle to and fro, of which men hear only distant rumor? No, you don't. And it's better that way. But see the cave, there is writing there if you would have me translate it, though that too is a dangerous thing."

21. I am Death

Brand looked into the shadows around the mouth of the cave. It was buttressed by slabs of stone, and the high lintel was inlaid with the same curious writing. He looked back at her, and though he did not ask it, she read his will.

"Very well," Kareste said. She walked close. He followed, and when they stood near the entrance she spoke again. Her words were slow and halting, for he saw that she must translate the ancient script with care. But her voice, unhurried as it was, seemed more like a chant than anything else:

Attend! … We who mastered the world … are become dust. We possessed the wealth of nations. Gold adorned our hands; priceless jewels our brows; bright were our swords. The world shuddered … when we marched! Now, our glory lies unheeded in the dark of the tomb. Servants … mutter secret words as they walk the hidden ways … Death and despair take all others!

She fell silent. A long time Brand considered the words. It was a warning, but warning or no he must go inside. He looked around. There was no sign of the hunt, which was just as well, for they could not take the horses in.

Kareste followed his lead when he finally moved and tied her reins to some jutting rocks after him. They did not look particularly secure, but it was the best place available.

"We won't be that long," he said.

Kareste grinned at him. "Or we'll stay in there for eternity – one or the other."

"You're a real laugh, you are," he said, but there was a smile, albeit nervous, on his own face.

"Neither of us will be laughing by the end," she warned.

Brand looked one last time up the rocky trail that they had come down. He saw nothing, and he heard nothing, but that only made him mistrust the unnatural quiet all the more.

He led the way into the cave. It was not long before he saw the first bones. They were ancient things, crumbling near to dust, and swords rested near them. He did not look closely.

The road led inward, but then swiftly dropped at a steep angle. This was the route that Aranloth had chosen, and Brand remembered the lòhren's description. He also ran the charm through his mind, but he saw as yet no reason to use it.

The mouth of the cave behind them was nothing more than a pale glow, but Kareste muttered some strange words and a mist rose from the floor near her feet. But it was no ordinary mist. It eddied and swirled and followed the two of them, going wherever they went and giving off a faint pulsing light.

The road was straight. Brand heard the faint slap of their boots, quiet as they tried to be. It took him some time to realize that there were other noises as well. There was a whispering presence somewhere in the dark with them.

He spoke Aranloth's charm, stumbling over it a little, used rather to hearing it in his mind than saying it out aloud.

Shapes reared up behind them, and he turned, but by the time he did so they had dispersed again, either

176

unwilling to be seen as yet or mollified by the charm, though he spoke it so softly that even Kareste would not have heard the words properly.

As they went ahead, slowly, cautiously, peering both before them and behind them, they saw that the tombs themselves had started. No longer was it a cave that they walked through, but a tunnel shaped by men, and in it, and the many smaller side passages that ran from it, the Letharn had laid men, women and children to their long rest.

Alcoves lined the sides of every passage, filled with bones and pottery and the implements of everyday life. All were ancient, seeming so fragile that they might break into dust at a careless breath, and yet Brand could not help wonder about them. Here were people who had once lived and breathed. They had once cooked meals and eaten. They had raised families, suffered sorrow and joy. They were the same as him no matter the vast gulf of time that separated them. And one day, regardless of whether or not he fulfilled this quest, or reached his other goals in life, he too would be bones and dust, memories on a forgotten breeze long ago blown across the world.

His thoughts were sobering and depressing – even immobilizing. Yet determination and stubbornness coursed through him in reaction. He might not know what had happened before he was born. He might not know what would happen after he died, as surely he would, but the time in between was his. And a long life or a short, it was *his* to make of it what he would.

He walked ahead more briskly, and he did not look to the sides.

"Touch nothing," he whispered to Kareste. "Touch nothing at all, for Aranloth warned me there is poison on

177

everything. Deadly poison – enough to kill you within moments."

"I haven't seen anything worth taking. But don't worry, I won't touch a thing."

"Remember that, and hold to it, for later there is wealth that you will never have seen. At least so Aranloth told me."

"Do you believe everything he says, always?"

It was a strange question, and he wondered why she asked it.

"I like many, but I trust few. Aranloth is one. The king of Cardoroth another. I would trust my life to either of them."

There was a pause. "Indeed you have, and I did not say it was a bad thing. But it may turn out differently than you expect."

"Doesn't it always?"

She did not answer, but he saw in the dim light the white flash of her grin.

The tombs changed as they went ahead. Brand's gaze was drawn against his will to look. And what he saw began to stun him.

Here were no ordinary tombs of laborers and peasants, as before. He saw piled gold and gems and artifacts of everyday life for the privileged, carved, decorated and inlaid with jewels. They were things of great craft: the harness of horses, combs of ivory, harps of polished timber, still strung; and there were lutes and drums and dresses and candleholders. He saw many things that the living used, but the dead needed not. And he saw the dead also. The preserved dead, dried and withered by time, but still with faces and arms and legs, uncorrupted because of some art of the Letharn.

He looked ahead again, for the dead fascinated him, but in that fascination was a trap. Something else was in the tombs with them, and he could afford no distraction.

If the thing, or things, with them was not dead, then neither were they alive. The figures that he had seen before began to press unseen at his mind, and he knew that the trial had not yet even begun.

He looked behind, but they were not there. He looked ahead, but he saw no sign of them. Yet he heard their whisperings in his mind and felt the cold touch of their unfathomable thoughts.

Eventually, he slowed, and then stopped. He had come to a place that Aranloth had told him about, but no description could prepare him.

There was a great crack in the rock. Through the fissure that ripped across the floor ahead of them there bubbled up the sound of rushing water. But it was faint as though coming from a great distance. Yet the way was not blocked, for over the gulf a slim bridge leaped, decorated and carved with strange figures at each end and graciously arched in the middle.

Strange lights shone upon it. Not from above, but from below, and they shifted and turned amid the dark, throwing up a shimmer onto the bridge. And a pillar stood before it, writing of gold-inlay glimmering from its black stone.

"What does it say?" he whispered.

Kareste peered at it for a moment. "It says, in the language of the Letharn, dead as they are themselves: *Harak kur likkil, harak ben luluck.* This I know, for Aranloth favored me with lore that not all lòhrens learn. Few know what those words mean now, and few spoke them even in the elder days when the iron-gripped rule of the Letharn rested heavily across wide realms. But once those words meant something, frightening even the

179

mighty ancients that often knew war but seldom fear. When they were uttered, so Aranloth told me, the strongest warrior would cringe, kings would bow their heads and queens would wail."

Brand looked at her, solemn and unflinching in the strange lights, and he did not look away.

She gazed back at him, perceiving that he was not afraid of words alone, and gave him the translation.

I am death. I will devour you.

Brand looked at her a moment longer. "Fitting words for such a place."

He turned back to the bridge and stepped upon it. It felt hollow beneath his feet, for the stone was not thick, and he pictured the yawning gap below. But he did not look.

They began to cross. The roaring of water in the deeps of the earth grew louder. A faint breeze played across his face, and the lights glimmered up into his eyes.

After a while he could resist no longer and looked over the edge. It was black down there, blacker than the midnight sky, and yet like the sky there were lights that sparked and shimmered. But unlike stars they moved and spun, wheeling and arcing amid the blackness.

"What are they?" he asked.

Kareste stared at them for a moment. "I don't know. Not even the lòhrens know all things. And if Aranloth knew, he never told me."

They went ahead. Reaching the other end of the bridge, they stepped out again onto the solid stone of the earth once more. Ahead, they saw now a crossroads.

The main path ran true and straight before them, disappearing swiftly into the dark. Two other ways, smaller and narrower, shot left and right.

Brand did not hesitate. "This way," he said, and he turned left as Aranloth had told him to do. But they did not get far. Almost immediately he looked back, his eyes drawn by some instinct that he did not understand, for he had heard no noise.

Upon the crest of the arched bridge he saw three figures. The strange lights from the fissure below them flared, shining now many times brighter. Brand looked, and he saw, but he did not believe what he beheld.

Three women stood there. Three beautiful women. They were naked. Long hair streamed from proudly held heads. They gazed at him with sharp eyes, eyes that could bore through greater dark than that gathered even here in the tombs. They wore no ornament, not even the least of rings. But in their long-fingered hands they each held wicked knives: curved, serrated, designed to rend with pain and then draw forth intestines when pulled out of a victim's body.

And then, beyond his understanding, beyond anything he could have anticipated, they began to sing. It was a sound so strange, so unexpected, and yet all the more beautiful because of that.

He listened, entranced. And as he did so the figures seemed to grow. Tall they stood, their long hair shimmering in the strange lights, and their keen eyes bent upon him as though fascinated. He gazed back, caught in their spell, but it was not one of magic. His will was free, and he could act as he chose, do what he wished. Nor did he forget Aranloth's warning about the power they possessed and their charge to protect the tombs.

And yet they were beautiful, and in that was a spell of its own; one that was stronger, deeper and more dangerous than any magic brought forth into the world of men since time began.

Kareste slapped him. It was a heavy blow, fueled by some desperate emotion.

181

"The words!" she yelled at him. "The charm!"

Brand reeled from the force of her fury, and he remembered his purpose here, for beauty or not, harakgar or not, still he must leave this place with Shurilgar's staff.

He straightened and spoke: *Har nere ferork. Skigg gar see!*

Many things happened as Aranloth's charm filled the tombs. The lights in the fissure spun and whirled in a frenzy. The three figures of the harakgar stiffened. The singing ceased, but not all sound, for now they hissed at him. Their long tongues writhed in their mouths like snakes, and their hair stood on end. The lights of the fissure suddenly winked out, and shadow took the bridge.

Silence fell, dismal after the singing, reminding him that he was far beneath the earth, and he felt the great dark closing in and also the weight of earth and rock and stone, and the very river that flowed high above it all out in the sunlight, the golden sunlight that he might never see again.

"Sorry," he said, turning to Kareste.

"Lead on!" she answered.

They went forward. Whether the harakgar were still there, or the charm had banished them, Brand did not know. But on they went and they were not followed. At least, not by anything that he saw or sensed, but having felt the presence of the harakgar once, he thought he would know if they were close, and they were not, but they were not far away either. Somewhere in the uneasy tombs they waited.

Ahead of them a vast chamber opened up. The mist beneath their feet that Kareste had called swelled and flowed and gave off a greater light to fill the space.

It was a grand place. Marble flagging lined the floor, and benches of the same stone were set in rows. Here was a place where people rested, and looking up at the walls Brand saw carvings that confirmed his thought. For he saw there a great procession of men and women.

They followed an ox-drawn cart, and their heads were low and tears streamed down their cheeks. It was a funerary procession, of that he had no doubt, and the mourners on the wall sat in such a place as he stood in now while robe-clad figures at the head of the cart performed some rite. That they spoke was clear, and he realized that in their mouths was the very same charm that he had uttered himself.

He said it again, for though there was no sense of danger, he had not felt one last time either. Immediately, the light seemed brighter, and the great chamber not so old and remote as the dimmer light had made it seem.

They walked to the center. The noise of their steps was loud, echoing from the vaulted roof high above, no matter how softly they paced. Here was another crossroads.

Brand thought, reaching back to what Aranloth had told him about this place. Kareste remained silent by his side.

If she was surprised that he did not take any of the paths, but instead headed for a carving on the left wall, she did not show it.

They came to a halt before the wall. Here were many carvings in bas-relief. Brand studied them, seeing even the grooves here and there of a chisel. It was a strange thing to see. The art looked as though it was made yesterday, yet it was crafted in a time older even than legend. The Letharn were myth, and yet it seemed that even the myths of Alithoras were real. It was a sobering thought, because it made him question all that he knew

183

and caused him to wonder what other powers existed in the land that might yet have survived, and of which he knew nothing.

But the carvings held his attention. They stood out from the wall, giving things a look of reality as though the people there might step out of the stone and talk to him.

But he soon found the particular carving Aranloth had told him of. It was a man, tall and athletic, a spear raised in his right hand, ready to throw.

Brand reached out. His hand touched the cold surface, and then he applied force. Not a great deal, but not a light amount either. He pushed the spear, as though to propel it along the path chosen by the hurler. And the spear moved.

There was no grinding sound. Nor a click or any other noise. The spear just moved, and when it did a thin split appeared in the very wall that they looked at.

The split grew, and then there was a sound of movement, of stone rolling on stone, but it was a faint thing, barely a whisper.

Ahead of them was now a door. It was not large, and they had to duck to go through, but it was wide enough for them to pass ahead with ease.

Brand went first. Kareste's misty light followed him, and then she came herself.

Almost immediately there was a set of stairs. Of what stone they were made, Brand did not know. But it was black as the darkness around them, and there was no ornamentation.

They descended slowly. The stairs went on and on, and his legs began to ache from the repeated stepping.

At length, the stairs brought them to a narrow corridor. And though it was narrow it was decorated as the stairs were not. The flagstones and walls were of white marble, milky smooth with yellowish swirls. There were no tombs, but there was gold. There was gold everywhere, inlaid on the walls and floor, even in the ceiling above.

Brand wondered if it was poisoned like the other treasures. He thought not, for otherwise people could not walk here, but he had no intention of trying to take anything. The staff was his only concern.

Without warning the gold glimmered and sparkled. Suddenly three beasts stood at the end of the corridor. They were not wolves, though they looked like wolves. Nor were they the sorcerous beasts of the elùgroths that hunted him.

Brand knew what they were. They were the harakgar, taken another form as Aranloth had warned they could. And if they were beautiful before, they were hideous now.

The beast-harakgar began to snarl. White teeth flashed. Red tongues lolled. Saliva dripped to the floor.

"How did the things hunting us get in here?" hissed Kareste.

"No," he answered. "These are not the sendings of the Elùgroths. These are the harakgar. Their form changes, but the feel of their presence does not."

He saw that she gave him a peculiar look.

"Didn't Aranloth tell you that they can take any form?" he asked.

"Yes, I suppose he did, but I still didn't see the difference as swiftly as you."

She gazed at him once more with those green-brown eyes as though he were something strange, but he had no time to think about it.

The harakgar began to pad along the bridge, and he voiced Aranloth's charm one again. *Har nere ferork. Skigg gar skee.*

185

The beasts cocked their heads and looked at him, ears pricked.

Har nere ferork. Skigg gar skee, he said again, louder.

The light in the passageway flickered. The beasts stood unmoving. Yet the stone about their feet no longer seemed solid. Instead, it rippled like water and the harakgar sank into it, their long ears the last thing to disappear.

Brand moved ahead. Kareste came with him. They passed over the spot where the beasts had stood, but there was no sign of them, nor any sense of their presence nearby.

Kareste trod warily, but he walked over the stone with confidence. Soon a new noise began. It was a dull tinkling that gradually became louder. They glanced at each other but did not speak. Neither of them knew what it was.

Eventually they came to another chamber. It was a great dome. Beaten gold plated the walls. The floors were flagged with colored mosaics. Strange symbols swirled in endless shapes and patterns beneath their boots.

From the center of the dome a column of water rushed and whispered, falling from on high in a direct line.

The water did not gather inside a basin. Rather, it gushed into a gold-rimmed hole in the ground. Before the streaming water a throne was set. Ringing it in a half circle were thirteen lesser thrones. Or perhaps they were only grand chairs, signifying some high station, but not the highest. They were tall backed and oddly shaped. Once, maybe, they had been cushioned, but if so that material had long since turned into a fine dust that lay thick on the seats. And the seats were of gold and the backs of ivory swirled with silver.

Brand looked up. High above, the ceiling was black; not the black of darkness, for Kareste's light reached there, but the black of some dark stone. It was, perhaps, jet. But it was not stone alone. Glittering from the black dome were thousands of lights that winked and shimmered. It looked like a replica of the starry sky, and so it was, for he soon saw many constellations that he knew, including bright Halathgar. But it was not stars that shone upon him, reflecting Kareste's light, but a vast treasure of jewels and gems. And a pale moon hung there also, a silver crescent worth a king's ransom.

"What *is* this place?" Kareste whispered, and the gem-stars seemed to shimmer and tremble at the sound of her voice.

"Where the ancient priests met," he answered. "So much Aranloth told me. But he said nothing of the wealth."

Kareste looked around. "There are thirteen chairs," she said. "That's a number favored by elùgroths. The Lòhrenin is a council of twelve."

She stepped closer to one of the chairs, but was careful not to touch it. He saw that they were of a strange design, both the seat and the backs being triangular in shape.

And he saw also what he had not noticed earlier: there was writing on the backs in the strange script of the Letharn.

"What does it say?" he asked.

Kareste peered for several moments, shifting her gaze from one seat to another.

"They're names, I think. I see Ubrik and Fikril. I see Dilik and Barak-bar. I see…" here she paused for a long while as she studied the thirteenth. There was an expression on her high-cheeked face that Brand could not read.

187

"Here also I see the name of Harlak," she said at last and turned to him, her eyes widened by awe. "That translates to 'noble might' from the tongue of the Letharn, even as Aranloth has the same meaning in the speech of the Halathrin."

She said no more. And though Brand now understood the strange emotion that ran through her, he saw something else.

On another seat, even as the lòhren told him it would be, he saw the object of his quest. It rested on the third chair from the left, wrapped in tattered cloth, but the dark end of a shattered staff stuck out. He knew what it was.

Kareste looked also, and she studied the writing on that chair also.

"Here the name translates as 'midnight star,' which is what Shurilgar means."

Brand reached out slowly. The cloth fell to dust at his touch, and beneath lay a black wych-wood staff. Well he knew it, for he had seen the other half.

He picked it up, feeling a strange thrill at its touch that was more than excitement.

But he had no time to reflect on what he sensed, for many things now happened at once.

He felt suddenly dizzy as though he were in two places at once, and a force of malice struck him as a blow. The thing was not as Aranloth's staff, an artifact imbued with power: this talisman took it to a far higher level. Magic swirled and flowed and oozed from it with raw power. A great black stream shot up his arm, into his body, and up to his head. Aranloth's diadem flared, and as swift as he had felt dizzy, now he was clear headed again.

A moment he had to choose, to accept the power and let it flow into him, to join with him. Or to reject it utterly.

And one other thing he knew. The black staff was broken, yet he felt its other half now with great clarity. It throbbed and pulsed far away to the north. He sensed even the elùgroths that touched it, that worked some great sorcery. And they sensed him. Their power was immense, and unified, yet something else lay behind it. Some force, far, far more remote, far greater than they, yet it sustained them. Away over countless leagues and beyond many plains and rivers and mountains a mind stirred: vast, imponderable, drenched in ancient enmity. It guided and uplifted the others.

Brand withdrew. He pulled his mind away from the staff, from all that it showed him. Black fire flared, then subsided. The staff was cold in his hand and dark again. The senses he had were lost.

He turned, and saw that Kareste was looking at him as though he were the strangest thing in the tombs. It was not for the first time. He was about to speak, but then he saw what was behind her.

"The harakgar!" he yelled.

She spun to look. Lòhrengai trailed from her fingers even as she moved. But she halted in shock, seeing what he saw.

In the column of water were the three figures. Like serpents they seemed, writhing and twisting among each other as the water poured over them. But they had faces, the same high-cheeked and beautiful faces that he had seen before.

The harakgar hissed, the noise blending with the sound of the water, and then the creatures slid out of the column. Their entwined coils looped over the flagging, wetting it as they undulated.

With a final sharp hiss they separated. Suddenly, the three of them reared, now part serpent and part woman. In their hands they held high the serrated knives, and they attacked.

22. Out of Dim Legend

There was no time for thought. Brand leaped to meet them, stepping between the creatures and Kareste who seemed transfixed. He held both staffs upraised in defense. And then he yelled the charm.

The serpents hissed. They slid and coiled and arched before him, tongues angrily flicking the air.

He chanted louder, and from behind him the girl also spoke. Having heard and learned the words, she added her voice to his.

What Aranloth would say to that, Brand did not know, yet the serpents reluctantly slid back into the column of water. There they twined among themselves as they rode and swam the current, plummeting out of sight.

He ceased chanting. So did Kareste. Yet they both knew the charm was losing its force, or else having touched some item bestowed in the tombs, the power of the harakgar was increased.

Kareste faced him. "Twice now you have saved me. That puts me in your debt, for once only have I saved you."

"We need not speak of debt, you and I," Brand answered. "They say that adversity bonds people together. But adversity or no, I like you anyway. But if you would repay me, one thing alone I ask."

"What's that?"

"Tell me the truth. Now, once and for all. And swiftly. There's more going on you said when we first met than a battle for Cardoroth. I gave those words less heed than I should have, for just now I felt ... something when I picked up the broken staff. And a name, maybe, I could put to it. One out of dim legend."

She eyed him without speaking, but at length she sighed.

"Very well. I'll tell you what I know, and more maybe of what I guess. We have little time. The harakgar will allow us small respite, yet while we rest, without trying to take the staff away, they will endure our presence the better, I think. And rest we must, for when we go they'll not hold back their power. Rather, I think it will increase the closer we get to the outside world."

They sat down on the mosaicked flagging before the ancient chairs. Strange they would have looked, in that ancient and domed room, where once great councils and ceremonies were held. But to them, in their tiredness, a seat was a seat and they dared not sit on the chairs.

"I know what it was that you felt in the staff," Kareste said. "Or rather through it. Others, though deeper steeped in lore and power, have felt the same thing. You should not feel it. But the broken staff, and Aranloth's staff, and the diadem open your mind to these forces. Still, you sense more than you should. And with each passing day the more do I think that Aranloth chose you well. Though you're a warrior, the staff of a lòhren is not so ill-suited to you as I thought at first."

He grew agitated, and she held up a hand. "Now, I'll answer you. Yes, there's more going on. The history of these lands is enough to tell you that ever we are at war with the south; the elugs, the Azan and other creatures besides that dwell there. They have attacked and harried the north since before the founding of Cardoroth and the other Camar cities. They are our enemies, for they would overrun this land. But cast your mind back to a

192

time of legend before even ancient history. Of that, what can you say?"

"Little," he answered. "Only what every child learns in stories. That the exodus of the Halathrin brought them to our lands in pursuit of a great evil. And greater evil followed. A Shadowed Lord rose – master of the elùgroths. And war raged over the lands. Yet that great lord was thrown down at the last, though his designs and plans and minions live after him in the elùgroths."

"Thus the legends tell us," she said. "And they speak truly…"

"And yet?"

"And yet for long ages the lòhrens and the Halathrin dreaded that while this power was defeated, it was not wholly destroyed. One day, they feared, he would rise again, and gathering darkness about him start once more to complete what he had not finished in ages past."

"*Elùdrath*," he whispered. The shadows of the cavern flitted, and he felt that even the dead in the tombs all around listened to his hoarse voice.

"Yes. And you have sensed him now as others have before you, though they be greater in power."

"Very well, then," he said briskly. "All the more reason to destroy this thing. Maybe so shall Cardoroth survive, though clearly other battles will come."

He made to stand, but she raised her hand again.

"Wait," she said. "There's one thing more."

"What?"

"This only. Before the elùgroths came to Cardoroth with war, they escaped from Halathar, the forest realm of the Halathrin. Much evil they did there, but the greatest was this – somewhere in the hills of Lòrenta they loosed a great sorcery. Contrived of the half of Shurilgar's staff that they possess, they created beasts as you have seen at Lake Alithorin. But even as those hounds were made of men, these others were bound to Alithoras by Halathrin forms. Immortals of great power. They roam now in the hills, twisted by sorcery, driven by the evil that possesses them to prowl and kill and slay. And lòhrengai avails little against them, for the blood of the immortals is stronger, more enduring, surer than that of men or elug. This is an evil in itself that cannot be borne, and yet also it threatens the lòhrens. And therefore all Alithoras."

Brand brooded on the news that she gave and wondered why she had not mentioned it before. He did not like it. The dark sorcery sickened him, yet he saw no way to help, no matter how much he wanted to.

"What can I do about that?" he asked. His answer was curter than he meant, for being powerless annoyed him.

"You? You can do nothing. But me ... that is a different question. I have the skill to undo the sorcery and free the immortals thus caught from torment. So I think, at least."

"Then you should not be helping me. Help them instead."

"Ahh..." she sighed. "There it is. In helping you, I *am* helping them. For ultimately, there is only one way to undo the sorcery. Perhaps I alone of all the lòhrens could achieve it. But I cannot do it with lòhrengai. The dark spell can only be undone with the same power that brought it into being. To free them, I need Shurilgar's staff."

She looked away. There was a long silence, profound within the tombs. Only the streaming column of water made any noise.

Brand stood, and she looked up at him from where she sat. There was much that he could read in her face, and much that was still hidden.

"We'll speak of this later," he said.

194

"Will you give me the staff?" she insisted.

"Truly, I don't know. For to do so would betray Aranloth's hope in me, and the king's. And perhaps allow an entire people to be murdered. Yet would they not want this other sorcery, this abomination, undone? I cannot say. And I won't decide here in the dark. When I feel the light on my face and breathe fresh air once more, and when the listening ears of the long-dead are not about me, then will I speak of it again."

"So be it," Kareste said.

Without another word they left the great chamber. But even as they took the first steps he felt the growing pressure of the harakgar on his mind. He realized that now they were roused. The charm had worked before, but whether it would hold off their waxing fury he did not know.

He spoke the words that Aranloth had given him at nearly every step, but still the pressure grew until the dead air of the tombs seemed to spark with malicious life.

They made it back to the bridge before the harakgar attacked, despite his constant voicing of the charm. But this time they dropped from the air above.

Brand spun and thrust Aranloth's staff at the nearest one. She flew on black wings, graceful as a swan, and her long hair trailed behind her in the wind of her descent.

Silver flame burst from the staff, and the shock of the impact drove him to his knees. The harakgar twisted to the side, for a moment looking less graceful, and then she rose above the bridge again.

Next to him a spray of lòhren-fire struck the other two. They screeched and hissed, fluttering higher to join their companion.

Brand and Kareste began to move across the bridge. They made it to the other side, and though Brand repeated the charm, this time the harakgar did not go away. They hovered in the high shadows, and the deep lights in the chasm far below spun wildly.

The two of them ran. As best they could they watched behind them. The harakgar followed, gliding down and then running swiftly on long legs, their wings gone but their shadowy hair still trailing behind them.

The clamor of the chase was loud. Surely no such noise had been heard here in the dark amid the dead in all the endless years of their rest. Brand had a sudden and stabbing fear – the dead would begin to wake. He tried to put the thought from his mind, but the pounding of his boots seemed to drive the fear through his body, and the echo of the chase ran ahead of them all, stirring other strange noises to life.

Behind, the harakgar screeched and leaped. He lifted Aranloth's staff, fighting off all three. No fire burst from it this time. The creatures bashed it from his grip before he was ready. The weight of them knocked him down, and even as his head struck the ground he heard the clatter of the falling staff somewhere away to his right.

He tried to raise Shurilgar's broken staff, but the harakgar were upon him. They weighed on him like stone statues come to life, and the strength of them was beyond any man. They pinned him, their hot breath beat upon him like wild beasts, and their long hair billowed and rolled in choking masses over his face.

But half blinded as he was, he saw the serrated knives rise as one. He made a last effort to throw the creatures off, but one hand caught him by the throat and squeezed like the death-grip that it was.

Then suddenly he was blinded by light. A great roar filled his ears. The harakgar screeched. He saw lòhrengai take their arms, melting flesh from bone.

196

The screams filled his ears and suddenly the weight was off him. He gasped for breath, struggled to grab Aranloth's staff and used it to prop himself up.

Kareste stood between him and the three harakgar. She screamed in her own turn, but it was in fury rather than pain. Back the harakgar ran, disappearing into the tunnel behind them, swallowed by the dark.

The two of them looked at each other. He felt the slow drip of blood along his arms, but he did not think he was badly hurt. His neck ached, and he realized that even without the knives the harakgar were close to killing him. A moment longer and they would have broken his neck.

Kareste had fared better, yet she had used so much of her power that she now seemed exhausted. They moved ahead, neither having the strength to run or even speak.

On they went, near-dead things themselves, ignoring the alcoves and the bodies and the treasures that lay to either side. Fresh air and light were the treasures they sought.

And ahead, tantalizingly close, was the dim outline of the cave entrance. But something shuffled toward them, silhouetted by the pale light of the outside world.

Brand and Kareste went forward to meet this new challenge, but their strength had not recovered. They needed rest, but that they would not have unless they broke out of the tombs.

The figures ahead drew near. There were three, but they were not the harakgar; at least, if they were, they had taken yet another form. For what approached now were warriors. Tall they stood, proud and stern. White tunics gleamed and their silver-helmed faces shone with a pale light. Golden hair spilled over their shoulders. Their eyes were keen, and in their hands they held bright swords.

197

He recognized the design of both helm and sword. He wore something similar on his own head, and carried something alike at his side.

On came the warriors, now stalking toward them with a grace that no man could match.

"Halathrin!" Kareste whispered fiercely.

"Yes and no," he replied. "Remember the skeletons we saw as we came in? These are they – Halathrin, but long dead. The harakgar have raised them, put upon them the guise they wore in life."

Kareste looked at him, and he saw the fear in her eyes. But he had no words. That same fear was in his own, and she saw it.

Close as they were to escape, this last battle seemed too much. How could they kill the already dead?

There was no more time to think. The lead warrior drove at him with a gleaming blade. Brand stepped aside, deflecting it with Aranloth's staff, but the warrior was quicker than any he had fought before. Straightaway the white-clad attacker turned and thrust his blade again.

Brand retreated. Beside him, Kareste did likewise. Fire lashed out from her fingers. It lit the tunnel with a sizzle of light and heat, but when it subsided the warriors were still there, advancing upon them, driving them deeper into the tombs.

"The staff!" Kareste called. "Give me Shurilgar's staff!"

He stepped back another pace, caught in fear and uncertainty. Dare he give it to her? Did he trust her? Would it be destroyed, or would Cardoroth fall instead?"

"The staff!" she screamed again.

Brand hardened his resolve. Cardoroth must not fall. He stopped his backward movement. The Halathrin looked at him, eyes as keen as swords, but their real blades flickered with a pale light as though a fire burned within them.

He took a firm grip on Aranloth's staff. Thrice he struck it down upon the stone. The Halathrin did not move. The tombs waited until the slow echoes died away. And then Brand shouted in a clear voice.

Har nere ferork. Skigg gar skee!

And as he voiced the charm he summoned the last of his strength. He thought nothing of the blades and battle and the warfare that he knew. He drew on some deeper part of his mind that was waking, though he did not want to admit it, and from his inner self a fire sprang. It leaped from him into Aranloth's staff, and there it burned, hot as the sun, before it rushed out in a stream from its tip.

The Halathrin that were harakgar staggered back. Their long hair burned. Their green eyes caught fire and sizzled. They reeled away, and as they did he reached out, seeking for the remnant of whatever had once been their own, for that part of them that was not the harakgar.

He glimpsed a brief vision of faraway lands. There were trees and light and singing and beauty. As though some door suddenly opened, what was left of the Halathrin fled away. Their form fell from the harakgar, and there the three sisters stood again, naked, pressed back against the wall, but already he saw their hair begin to grow back, and the light come once more into their eyes.

"Run!" he yelled.

Kareste was with him. They sped up the last part of the tunnel. Darkness rolled behind them, gathering pace like a storm about to break, and then they were out of the cave, sprawling to the ground into the light and beyond the reach of their attackers.

199

A dark wind shrieked behind them, whistling at the entrance of the cave, but it swiftly faltered.

"We have it!" Brand said. 'The quest is ours!"

He staggered to his feet, looking for Kareste, feeling the glory of the sun. He saw instead something that stole the joy from his heart and flooded his mind with despair.

The horses remained where they had been left, but beyond stood Khamdar. He towered above Brand, who was a big man himself, and the elùgroth looked down upon him with cold eyes. There was also a band of elugs, scimitars drawn and three hounds, tongues dripping sweat, and a low growl in their throats.

Brand sensed Kareste moving close to him. She was spent, as was he, and their enemies ringed them. The only place to retreat was into the tombs, and he hoped never to go in there again. Better to face death in the sun than in the dark.

Khamdar spoke, and his voice was quiet, yet full of confidence.

"Long was the chase, but the hunt is over. Now you shall learn what it means to defy an elùgroth. It is a lesson few need teaching, and of those who do, none live to beg for mercy."

Brand did not answer. He still struggled to breathe. But next to him, Kareste spoke softly.

"Give it to me," she said.

Brand knew what she meant. He did not know what powers she could draw from Shurilgar's staff, but he knew that it would aid her.

"Give it to me!" she said more fiercely. "It's our only hope."

Brand hesitated. While he stood there in doubt, the elùgroth flicked his cold gaze between them.

"Wise are you to mistrust," he said. "For she commands great power – even without the staff. But with it – with it, she could be a great one. Great among elùgroths." He turned to her, his dark eyes black pits. "Is it not so? I sense the power of elùgai in you. Though blended with the taint of lòhrengai."

He turned back to Brand with a fierce smile. "Yes. Give her the staff. It will be the final step in her transformation. And well would she wield it."

Brand swayed and the world spun around him. He felt the truth in what the elùgroth said. Yet was it the whole truth?

201

Thus ends *Raging Swords*. The Durlindrath trilogy continues in book two, *Defiant Swords*, where Brand learns more of the threat to Alithoras and faces his greatest challenge yet.

Sign up below and be the first to hear about new book releases, see previews and learn of upcoming discounts. http://eepurl.com/Rswv1

Visit my website at www.homeofhighfantasy.com

Encyclopedic Glossary

Note: the glossary of each book in this series is individualized for that book alone. Additionally, there is often historical material provided in its entries for people, artifacts and events that are not included in the main text.

Many races dwell in Alithoras. All have their own language, and though sometimes related to one another, the changes sparked by migration, isolation and various influences often render these tongues unintelligible to each other.

The ascendancy of Halathrin culture, combined with their widespread efforts to secure and maintain allies against elug incursions, has made their language the primary means of communication between diverse peoples.

For instance, a soldier of Cardoroth addressing a ship's captain from Camarelon would speak Halathrin, or a simplified version of it, even though their native speeches stem from the same ancestral language.

This glossary contains a range of names and terms. Many are of Halathrin origin, and their meaning is provided. The remainder derive from native tongues and are obscure, so meanings are only given intermittently.

Some variation exists within the Halathrin language, chiefly between the regions of Halathar and Alonin. The most obvious example is the latter's preference for a "dh" spelling instead of "th".

Often, Camar names and Halathrin elements are combined. This is especially so for the aristocracy. No other tribes had such long-term friendship with the Halathrin, and though in this relationship they lost some of their natural culture, they gained nobility and knowledge in return.

List of abbreviations:

Azn. Azan

Cam. Camar

Chg. Cheng

Comb. Combined

Cor. Corrupted form

Duth. Duthenor

Esg. Esgallien

Hal. Halathrin

Leth. Letharn

Prn. Pronounced

Alithoras: *Hal.* "Silver land." The Halathrin name for the continent they settled after the exodus. Refers to the extensive river and lake systems they found and their appreciation of the beauty of the land.

Alith Nien: *Hal.* "Silver river." Has its source in the mountainous lands of Auren Dennath and empties into Lake Alithorin.

Anast Dennath: *Hal.* "Stone mountains." Mountain range in northern Alithoras. Contiguous with Auren Dennath and location of the Dweorhrealm.

Angle: The land hemmed in by the Carist Nien and Erenian rivers, especially the area in proximity to their divergence.

Arach Neben: *Hal.* "West gate." The great wall surrounding Cardoroth has four gates. Each is named after a cardinal direction, and each also carries a token to represent a celestial object. Arach Neben bears a steel ornament of the Morning Star.

Aranloth: *Hal.* "Noble might." A lòhren.

Aurellin: *Cor. Hal.* The first element means blue. The second appears to be native Camar. Queen of Cardoroth and wife to Gilhain.

Auren Dennath: *Comb. Duth.* and *Hal. Prn.* Our-ren dennath. "Blue mountains." Mountain range in northern Alithoras. Contiguous with Anast Dennath.

Azan: *Azn.* Desert dwelling people. Their nobility often serve as leaders of elug armies. They are a prideful race, often haughty and domineering, but they also adhere to a strict code of honor.

Barak-bar: *Leth.* A long-dead priest who served in ancient times within the tombs of the Letharn.

Brand: A Duthenor tribesman. Currently serving King Gilhain as his Durlindrath.

Camar: *Cam. Prn.* Kay-mar. A race of interrelated tribes that migrated in two main stages. The first brought them to the vicinity of Halathar; in the second, they separated and established cities along a broad sweep of eastern Alithoras.

Camarelon: *Cam. Prn.* Kam-arelon. A port city and capital of a Camar tribe. It was founded before Cardoroth as the waves of migrating people settled the more southerly lands first. Each new migration tended northward. It is perhaps the most representative of a traditional Camar realm.

Carangar: *Hal.* "Car - red, angar - outcrop of rock or something prominent that juts from the surface of the land or another object." A Durlin.

Cardoroth: *Cor. Hal. Comb. Cam.* A Camar city, often called Red Cardoroth. Some say this alludes to the red granite commonly used in the construction of its buildings, others that it refers to a prophecy of destruction.

Cardurleth: *Hal.* "Car - red, dur - steadfast, leth - stone." The great wall that surrounds Cardoroth. Established soon after the city's founding and constructed with red granite. It looks displeasing to the eye, but the people of the city love it nonetheless. They believe it impregnable and say that no enemy shall ever breach it – except by treachery.

Careth Nien: *Hal. Prn.* Kareth nyen. "Great river." Largest river in Alithoras. Has its source in the mountains of Anast Dennath and runs southeast across the land before emptying into the sea. It was over this river (which sometimes freezes along its northern stretches) that the Camar and other tribes migrated into the eastern lands. Much later, Brand came to the city of Cardoroth by one of these ancient migratory routes.

Carist Nien: *Hal.* "Ice river." A river of northern Alithoras that has its source in the hills of Lòrenta.

Carnhaina: First element native *Cam.* Second *Hal.* "Heroine." An ancient queen of Cardoroth. Revered as a saviour of her people, but to some degree also feared, for she possessed powers of magic. Hated to this day by elùgroths, because she overthrew their power unexpectedly at a time when their dark influence was rising.

Carnyx horn: The sacred horn of the Camar tribes. An instrument of brass, man high with a mouth fashioned in the likeness of a fierce animal, often a boar or bear. Winded in battle and designed to intimidate the foe with its otherworldly sound. Some believe it invokes supernatural aid.

Chapterhouse: Special halls set aside in the palace of Cardoroth for the private meetings, teachings and military training of the Durlin.

Crenel: The vertical gap on a battlement between merlons. The merlon offers protection, the crenel an opening through which missiles are fired.

Dilik: A long-dead priest who served in ancient times within the tombs of the Letharn.

Drùghoth: *Hal.* First element - black. Second element - that which hastens, races or glides. More commonly called a sending.

Durlin: *Hal.* "The steadfast." The original Durlin were the seven sons of the first king of Cardoroth. They guarded him against all enemies, of which there were many, and three died to protect him. Their tradition continued throughout Cardoroth's history, suspended only once, and briefly, some four hundred years ago when it was discovered that three members were secretly in the service of elùgroths. These were imprisoned, but committed suicide while waiting for the king's trial to commence. It is rumored that the king himself provided them with the knives that they used. It is said that he felt sorry for them and gave them this way out to avoid the shame a trial would bring to their families.

Durlin creed: These are the native Camar words, long remembered and much honored, uttered by the first Durlin to die while he defended his father, and king, from attack. Tum del conar – El dar tum! Death or infamy – I choose death!

Durlindrath: *Hal.* "Lord of the steadfast." The title given to the leader of the Durlin.

Duthenor: *Duth. Prn.* Dooth-en-or. "The people." A single tribe, or sometimes a group of tribes melded into a larger people at times of war or disaster, who generally live a rustic and peaceful lifestyle. They are raisers of cattle and herders of sheep. However, when need demands they are fierce warriors – men and women alike.

Elugs: *Hal.* "That which creeps in shadows." A cruel and superstitious race that inhabits the southern lands, especially the Graèglin Dennath.

Elùdrath: *Hal. Prn.* Eloo-drath. "Shadowed lord." A sorcerer. First and greatest among elùgroths. Believed to be dead or defeated.

Elùgai: *Hal. Prn.* Eloo-guy. "Shadowed force." The sorcery of an elùgroth.

Elùgroth: *Hal. Prn.* Eloo-groth. "Shadowed horror." A sorcerer. They often take names in the Halathrin tongue in mockery of the lòhren's practice to do so.

Elu-haraken: *Hal.* "The shadowed wars." Long ago battles in a time that is become myth to the Camar tribes.

Erenian River: A river in northern Alithoras. Some say its name derives from a corruption of the Halathrin word "nien," meaning river. Others dispute this and postulate the word derives from a pre-exodus name adopted by the Camar tribes after they settled the east of Alithoras.

Exodus: The arrival of the Halathrin into Alithoras from an outside land. They came by ship and beached north of Anast Dennath.

Faladir: A city founded by a Camar tribe.

Fikril: A long-dead priest who served in ancient times within the tombs of the Letharn.

Foresight: Premonition of the future. Can occur at random as a single image or as a longer sequence of events. Can also be deliberately sought by entering the realm between life and death where the spirit is released from the body to travel through space and time. To achieve this, the body must be brought to the very threshold of death. The first method is uncontrollable and rare. The second exceedingly rare but controllable for those with the skill and willingness to endure the danger.

Free Cities: A group of cooperative city states that pool military resources to defend themselves against attack. Founded prior to Cardoroth. Initially ruled by kings and queens, now by a senate.

Galenthern: *Hal*. "Green flat." Southern plains bounded by the Careth Nien and the Graèglin Dennath mountain range.

Gernlik: *Cam*. A Durlin.

Gilhain: *Comb. Cam & Hal*. First element unknown, second "hero." King of Cardoroth. Husband to Aurellin.

Graèglin Dennath: *Hal. Prn*. Greg-lin dennath. "Mountains of ash." Chain of mountains in southern Alithoras. The landscape is one of jagged stone and boulder, relieved only by gaping fissures from which plumes of ashen smoke ascend, thus leading to its name. Believed to be impassable because of the danger of poisonous air flowing from cracks, and the ground unexpectedly giving way, swallowing any who dare to tread its forbidden paths. In other places swathes of molten stone run in rivers down its slopes.

Great North Road: An ancient construction of the Halathrin. Built at a time when they had settlements in the northern reaches of Alithoras. Warriors traveled swiftly from north to south in order to aid the main population who dwelt in Halathar when they faced attack from the south.

Grothanon: *Hal.* "Horror desert." The flat salt plains south of the Graèglin Dennath.

Halathar: *Hal.* "Dwelling place of the people of Halath." The forest realm of the Halathrin.

Halathgar: *Hal.* "Bright star." Actually a constellation. Also known as the Lost Huntress.

Halathrin: *Hal.* "People of Halath." A race named after a mighty lord who led an exodus of his people to the continent of Alithoras in pursuit of justice, having sworn to redress a great evil. They are human, though of fairer form, greater skill and higher culture. They possess an inherent unity of body, mind and spirit enabling insight and endurance beyond other races of Alithoras. Reported to be immortal, but killed in great numbers during their conflicts with the evil they seek to destroy. Those conflicts are collectively known as the elù-haraken: the Shadowed Wars.

Harakgar: *Leth.* The three sisters. Creatures of magic brought into being by the lore of the Letharn. Their purpose is to protect the tombs of their creators from robbery.

Harlak: *Leth.* An ancient name of Aranloth.

Harath Neben: *Hal.* "North gate." This gate bears a token of two massive emeralds that represent the constellation of Halathgar. The gate is also known as "Hunter's Gate," for the north road out of the city leads to wild lands full of game.

Immortals: See Halathrin.

Kareste: A mysterious girl who helps Brand. She possess potent magic.

Khamdar: An elùgroth. Leader of the host the besieges Cardoroth.

Lake Alithorin: *Hal.* "Silver lake." A lake of northern Alithoras.

Letharn: *Hal.* "Stone raisers. Builders." A race of people that in antiquity ruled much of Alithoras. Only traces of their civilization remain.

Lethrin: *Hal.* "Stone people." Creatures of the Graèglin Dennath. Renowned for their size and strength. Tunnelers and miners.

Lòhren: *Hal. Prn.* Ler-ren. "Knowledge giver – a counsellor." Other terms used by various nations include wizard, druid and sage.

Lòhren-fire: A defensive manifestation of lòhrengai. The color of the flame varies according to the skill and temperament of the lòhren.

Lòhrengai: *Hal. Prn.* Ler-ren-guy. "Lòhren force." Enchantment, spell or use of arcane power. A manipulation and transformation of the natural energy inherent in all things. Each use takes something from the user. Likewise, some part of the transformed energy infuses them. Lòhrens use it sparingly, elùgroths indiscriminately.

Lòhrenin: *Hal. Prn.* Ler-ren-in. "Council of lòhrens."

Lòrenta: *Hal. Prn.* Ler-rent-a. "Hills of knowledge." Uplands in northern Alithoras in which the stronghold of the lòhrens is established.

Lornach: A Durlin. Friend to Brand and often called by his nickname of "Shorty."

Lost Huntress: See Halathgar.

Magic: Supernatural power. See lòhrengai and elùgai.

Menetuin: A city on the east coast of Alithoras. Founded by the Camar.

Merlon: The vertical stonework on a battlement between crenels. The merlon offers protection, the crenel a gap through which missiles are fired.

Otherworld: Camar term for a mingling of half-remembered history, myth and the spirit world.

Sellic Neben: *Hal.* "East gate." This gate bears a representation, crafted of silver and pearl, of the moon rising over the sea.

Sending: See Drùghoth.

Shadowed Lord: See Elùdrath.

Shazrahad: The Azan who commands an elug army, or serves as a lieutenant of an elùgroth.

Shuffa: A type of boat. Small, fast and ideal for travel by river. Favored by the villagers who dwell along the Careth Nien, and based on a design originating from ancient times when the Letharn fished the two rivers of the Angle. The same name is used in Cardoroth for a different kind of boat, slower and of a different shape. It's unclear which version is closer to the original design.

Shurilgar: *Hal.* "Midnight star." An elùgroth. Also called the betrayer of nations.

Sorcerer: See Elùgroth.

Sorcery: See elùgai.

Surcoat: An outer garment. Often worn over chain mail. The Durlin surcoat is unadorned white.

Taingern: *Cam.* A Durlin. Friend to Brand.

Tombs of the Letharn: The ancient burial place of the Letharn people. All members of the population, throughout the course of their long civilization, were laid to rest here. It was believed that to be interred elsewhere was to condemn the spirit to a true death, rather than an afterlife. The dead were preserved, and returned even from the far reaches of the empire. This was withheld from perpetrators of treason and heinous crimes. These were buried in special cemeteries near the river. Petty criminals were afforded an opportunity to redeem their place in the tombs on payment of a fine determined by the head-priest.

Ubrik: A long-dead priest who served in ancient times within the tombs of the Letharn.

Unlach Neben: *Hal.* "South gate." This gate bears a representation of the sun, crafted of gold, beating down upon a desert land. Said by some to signify the homeland of the elugs, whence the gold of the sun was obtained by an adventurer of old.

War drums: Drums of the elug tribes. Used especially in times of war or ceremony. Rumored to carry hidden messages in their beat and also to invoke sorcery.

Wizard: See lòhren.

Wych-wood: A general description for a range of supple and springy timbers. Some hardy varieties are prevalent on the poisonous slopes of the Graèglin Dennath mountain range and are favored by elùgroths as instruments of sorcery.

DEFIANT SWORDS
BOOK TWO OF THE DURLINDRATH TRILOGY

Robert Ryan

1. Brave Fool

Brand was at a loss. His enemies had him in a trap, and there was no way out. And yet, if he had the courage, there *was* a way. But it would take daring of a kind that did not involve swords or magic.

Khamdar stood tall and still. His pallid hands rested loose and confident on his wych-wood staff. He gave no hint of outward aggression, and yet a wave of malice, strong as a flood, flowed from him like a physical thing. Brand had heard of this before. It was said that the mere presence of one of the great sorcerers was enough to unman brave warriors. He believed it. And yet there was something in him that did not like to be pushed. The greater his fear became the stronger that thing inside him grew.

He felt the weight of the broken staff of Shurilgar in his hand. His whole purpose in retrieving it from the tombs was to destroy it, and thereby destroy its other half that was used by the enemy in their siege of Cardoroth. Anything less was a failure.

Yet Kareste looked at him, pleading silently, for she alone could use Shurilgar's staff with hope of defeating Khamdar.

The sorcerer, a brooding shadow, watched with malicious fascination. Dare he give it to her?

It was a good question, for it was now plain that Kareste had her own agenda, and if he gave her the staff he may never again have the chance to destroy it. If so, Cardoroth was doomed, and perhaps the whole land also, for he sensed that she teetered on the edge of becoming a sorceress. Khamdar had not lied when he claimed that.

One other choice Brand had, and he pondered it swiftly. He could take the staff back into the tombs and leave it there. He might survive the harakgar, the dark guardians of that shadow-haunted world, long enough to drop it into some bottomless chasm, for now that Kareste knew the charm that kept the harakgar at bay, she could retrieve it otherwise. Doing so, he might live, for as long as he did not attempt to take the staff out of the tombs the harakgar would probably not kill him. And there were other exits than the one he now stood before that would allow him to escape Khamdar.

But if he did any of that, Cardoroth would certainly fall, and likely Kareste also. His mistrust of her would surely push her closer to the enemies of the land.

He made his choice. There was no way to know if it was right, otherwise it would not have been so hard.

The ring of enemies behind Khamdar did not wait with the sorcerer's stillness. The Azan warriors gazed with hatred, their eyes dark slits, their hands tightly clenched about sword hilts. The elugs milled uncertainly, their iron-shod boots scraping the stone of the high ledge as they shuffled impatiently. From the beasts, the hounds born of dark sorcery, a low growl throbbed, deep and rumbling as though the earth moved and tumbled masses of stone into the abyss behind them.

Brand took a slow step back, and then another. All eyes watched him, even Kareste's, whose face showed at first surprise and then swift disappointment. She guessed his choice: he would not give her the broken remnant of Shurilgar's staff – instead he would return into the tombs of the Letharn behind him, preferring to dare its dangers rather than trust her with it.

218

He took another step and hoped that his instincts were right. Kareste studied him, understanding all that had just passed through his mind, or thinking that she did, for her face was stricken. The sight of her anguish stabbed him in the heart.

But she was wrong. The enemy now focused on him, which was what he intended, and they had forgotten her. With a sudden but sure motion he threw the staff to her. The black wood glinted, and its jagged ends of broken timber caught the light like flashing daggers.

Her eyes widened, but still her hand reached out, swift and sure as his own movement had been, and plucked the staff from the air.

Even as she did so, Brand voiced the Durlin creed.

Death or infamy! he yelled.

His voice rang clear and loud in challenge, but he did not wait for any answer. Instead, he leapt forward and struck out, aiming for Khamdar. If he destroyed their leader those who followed might falter. So he hoped, for no matter his skill at arms he could not defeat them all. He could not even defeat Khamdar alone, but his attempt might give Kareste the time she needed to decide what she was going to do – if she had not already fallen to the lure of dark sorcery.

But Brand did not use his skill at arms. He sensed that Khamdar was beyond such attacks, warded by arcane power. Instead, he drew on the newfound, unwanted, but desperately needed strength of magic that he had discovered within himself.

Blue-white flame spurted to life and ran along the oaken staff that Aranloth had given him. It flared and fluttered, then streaked toward the sorcerer.

Khamdar, poised and sure of himself, made a smooth motion with his own dark staff and waved Brand's attack aside without effort, diverting it harmlessly into the chasm that ran behind him.

Brand tried again, but even as he summoned flame Khamdar knocked the staff from his hand. It clattered over the stone as it fell, and Brand stood unprotected before the sorcerer.

At that moment he felt the full power of Khamdar, of one of the great elùgroths, and it chilled the blood in his veins. Fear surged through him, overwhelming dread that drove into him and urged him to run, to run anywhere to escape, even over the ledge and into the abyss, for surely such terror could not be endured.

He tore his gaze from the sorcerer and looked at Kareste. Her hands gripped tight the broken staff of Shurilgar, but she had not moved. Her face seemed strange, as though she summoned some great power, but he saw no sign of any spell. He did not understand what she was doing, but he saw no indication that she made any move to help him.

He gritted his teeth and planted his feet firmly on the ground. He was not going to run anywhere, no matter the shadow of madness that the sorcerer cast over him. If he must die, he would die fighting.

Khamdar laughed softly. He seemed perfectly at ease, confident that he could kill his prey whenever he chose, no matter that it tried to fight back.

Brand trembled. Despite the cloud of horror that deepened over him, that drained both strength and will, he slowly drew his sword.

The sorcerer grew still. His laughter ceased, and Brand drew assurance from the fact that his enemy seemed surprised.

The Halathrin-forged blade glittered and flickered in Brand's hand. A cold light seemed to shine within it.

Brand shook off a little of the fear that clung to him like a fog.

"You can kill," he said slowly to the elùgroth, "but you cannot win."

Brand was surprised at the steadiness of his voice, and his final choice was made, as he always made it: live or die; win or lose – he would fight.

He took a pace forward, and it required an enormous effort. Yet in doing so it freed him, for the fear that gripped him fell suddenly away, and despair and mad terror vanished with it. All that was left was a soaring will to defy the person who would oppress him, and in that moment, life and death, his quest, and the fate of Alithoras itself were all forgotten. There was only one thought, and that was to resist his enemy.

A shadow of doubt crossed the elùgroth's features, and his fingers flexed uncertainly on his wych-wood staff. Brand understood intuitively that it had been many long years since anyone had dared to challenge him. But whatever misgivings the sorcerer had, he swiftly stifled them, or else confidence in his unassailable might rose once more to the surface. He smiled, and then stepped forward himself.

An unexpected roaring filled Brand's ears. If it was some attack of sorcery, he did not understand it. But judging from how the elùgroth tilted his own head to listen, it was a surprise to him also.

And then suddenly Brand felt rough hands on him from behind. Kareste was there; he knew her by the flick of ash-blond hair that he saw from the corner of his eye. With a strength that he scarcely believed, she spun him around toward the cave and threw him to the ground. Taken by surprise and unprepared, he fell hard and tumbled awkwardly across the ancient stone ledge.

221

He had made a mistake – the greatest of his life. Kareste would side with the enemies of Alithoras, perhaps even rejoin the two halves of Shurilgar's staff, and the woe that would come of that was unthinkable, yet he must think of it, for it would be his fault.

A voice cracked at him like a whip. "Back, you fool! Back!"

It was Kareste. Her eyes were wild, and immense strain showed on her face. He staggered to his feet near the entrance to the tombs.

Kareste leaped back to join him, the broken staff of Shurilgar raised high. A moment Khamdar paused, uncertain of what was happening.

The roaring grew louder. Brand stood next to Kareste. He held his sword before him but was unsure where to face or what to do. From just behind he felt the stale breath of the tombs, and he sensed the harakgar stir within the tunnels that they guarded. A shiver ran up his spine, and the hair on the back of his neck prickled.

Khamdar made to move forward. The band that he led followed in his wake. But in midstride the sorcerer paused once more. This time he looked up, a wary expression on his face. The roar grew unbearably loud. A thrum ran through the ground.

Without warning Khamdar turned and fled through the ranks of his own followers. An Azan warrior, not quick enough to get out of his way, was blasted by crimson flame and propelled to the side in smoke and screams. At that moment white froth flew through the air above. It was followed by a spray of water and then a flood that tumbled and roared and raced in an avalanche of fury.

Kareste had called forth water from the river that ran above the tombs and drawn it to the ledge. The band of enemies screamed and panicked. Yet before they could move Brand saw many swept away over the ledge and into the abyss. Moments later all were lost from sight in the mighty torrent that gathered pace, sweeping rocks and smashing boulders before it.

Water-spray lashed Brand's face. The ledge before him trembled, and he was sure that some was taken away. He feared that Kareste had called too much water and that the whole platform of stone might crash and topple into the abyss, and they might yet be forced back into the caves, if even that was safe from collapse.

2. Evil must be Fought

The ledge groaned and the water roared. Rocks and boulders tumbled over the precipice, tearing and ripping away at the lip as though it were mere cloth. Yet as quickly as the water came, the great flood ceased.

Brand looked for any sign of their enemies. His searching gaze first took in the ruined edge of the platform, broken and tattered along its length, and then closer in where rubble and deep layers of silt had settled. Water trickled across the surface in little streams, draining into the abyss.

The ancient stone marker remained as it had for years beyond count, though its inscribed sides now glistened darkly with moisture. All these things he saw, but of the hunters who had pursued them from Cardoroth to the tombs of the Letharn, there was no sign.

Brand shivered, for the air was chill. It was as though the enemies who had stood there just moments ago had never existed. The force of Kareste's magic had swept them into oblivion. He had seen her use power before this, but not to such a catastrophic end. Her claim was true: she could use Shurilgar's staff. And though that had just now saved them, yet also its lure would draw her very soul into jeopardy.

He sat down on the stone, exhausted and uncaring of the wet surface. Kareste remained standing, gazing out into the abyss. There was an expression on her face that might have been elation, but there were times when he could not read her, and this was one. What she was thinking, he could not even guess, but certainly she gripped the black staff hard, as though she would never let it go, and that worried him.

After a while her fingers relaxed, and she glanced down at him.

"Don't think that they're all gone," she said. "We'll have trouble from them yet, before the end."

Brand looked out toward the chasm. "Surely nothing could survive that."

Kareste closed her eyes. "I no longer sense Khamdar, but that doesn't mean he's dead. He may have reached safety. Or, even if swept away by the flood, he might have survived it. Elùgroths are hard to kill. Harder than lòhrens, for they use their power all the time to ward themselves against the chances of the world."

Brand groaned and stood. It seemed that every muscle in his body ached, and even sheathing his sword hurt him.

He walked past the horses, huddled and scared near the wall, and gave them some reassuring words and a rub along their withers to help steady them. As he did so, he noticed that the rockfall that had once blocked the downward route along the ledge was gone: the flood had cleared it away, yet the stone cliff above remained blackened where the fire of some previous battle scorched it.

Brand moved cautiously to the broken edge and looked into the abyss. Kareste joined him. They gazed in silence, for below them was a scene of death. The bodies of their enemies were at the bottom of the gorge. Some floated, tugged back and forth in the ebb and flow of the receding floodwaters. Others, the tattered remnants of creatures that once walked, lay sprawled and broken on hard rocks.

"Better them than us," Kareste said.

225

Brand did not answer. Her comment was true, and yet it was not a sentiment that he would have voiced himself.

They stepped back from the ledge. "They're not all there," she said. "Perhaps some escaped, or maybe we just can't see all of the bodies. The rest may be obscured by water or swept away."

"There's no way to know for sure," he said. "Yet I admit that I'd feel more at ease if we'd seen Khamdar down there."

"He was quick to flee, sensing what was coming before the others. And he is warded also. He may be injured. Or he may be dead, but I doubt it."

"He's definitely not easy to kill," Brand said.

She raised an eyebrow. "Nor are you. That much I've learned for myself, though Aranloth evidently knew it before me."

Brand looked at her, drawn as always to her green-gold eyes, but unsure how well he knew her, if he knew her at all. And yet the risk he had just taken, enormous as it was, had paid off. They were safe, at least for the moment.

"What now?" he asked.

Kareste gazed back at him, her face masking the many things that she must have felt.

"First," she said, "Tell me why you gave me the staff. I didn't think you would."

Brand shrugged. "Honestly, I'm not sure myself. But what has been done to the Halathrin is a great evil. It cannot go unchallenged – it must be fought."

"So too must the siege of Cardoroth, but that continues. Yet you gave me the staff, and you must know that it occurs to me to keep it."

Brand shrugged again, but gave no answer.

She kept looking at him, her gaze intense. "You *trusted* me to give it back, but I don't know why."

"I pick my friends carefully," he answered. "And my quests also. If we stick together, we might both yet live. And may the king forgive me, but I agree that the Halathrin, entrapped by sorcery as they are, must be freed. How can I decide to help only Cardoroth or to help only the Halathrin? It's in our power to attempt both, but it's a heavy burden to stand here knowing that my first quest is achieved – that I could destroy Shurilgar's staff and save Cardoroth – and yet not do it."

Kareste continued to look at him, and though her face showed nothing, he guessed at the turmoil that battled across her mind.

Her face did not change, but suddenly she held out the staff to him.

"We all pick our friends carefully. Or at least we try to."

For just a moment some great emotion welled to the surface, and her face flushed. But then she pushed it down and became the perfect picture of a lòhren again: calm, poised and tranquil.

"Take it," she said. "Khamdar was wrong. I'm no elùgroth, though I feel the lure of elùgai."

The staff shimmered darkly between them. He saw how hard it was for her to return it, though she nearly hid that from him. And he admired that she had the strength to offer it back, for surely if she kept it great power was at her command.

He saw also, more clearly than she, that her final choice of Light or Shadow, of lòhrengai or elùgai, was not yet made. From the moment that he took the staff from her, she would yearn for it. From the moment it was destroyed, which he still planned to do as swiftly as the Halathrin were freed, she would regret her choice.

227

The blush of great power was on her, and its lure was strong, but so too was the freshness of her gratitude for his trust in her. But those opposing forces would wax and wane over time, the first growing stronger and the second receding.

She was not ready to make her choice, and to force the issue now might be to jeopardize her soul. For once a person walked beneath the Shadow it was near impossible to turn around again. But if she could do it, it must be done in her own time and of her own will.

Yet still he hesitated amid a wave of doubt, for if he did not take the staff now and destroy it, then the risk to Cardoroth would grow, and with it the peril to the rest of Alithoras.

What would Aranloth want him to do? The knowledge that there were Halathrin, caught by foul sorcery and turned into beasts that roamed the world at the will of elùgroths, would tear at the lòhren's heart. And that the elùgroths did this, Khamdar chief among them, was not just a matter of spite or malice. There was a plan behind it.

He made his final choice. Even Cardoroth was a small thing compared to the fate of Alithoras. But he felt alone, for he was making decisions that even lòhrens and kings would find hard.

Aranloth had warned him that at all costs the staff must be destroyed as soon as it was brought from the tombs. Otherwise, it was at risk of being obtained by the enemy, and the damage they could cause with it was incalculable. But he must take up the burden of choice – there was no one else to do so.

He shook his head.

"Keep it," he said. "We go to the hills of Lòrenta to free the Halathrin, or to try to. But we must go there swiftly and destroy the staff when our quest is done."

Kareste looked at him strangely, and then slowly lowered her hand. She gripped the staff fiercely.

"I thought you would take it," she said.

He flashed a grin at her.

"So did I. But my choice is made, may the king forgive me, and it's behind me now. All that matters is to get to Lòrenta quickly, but I fear that Khamdar waits for us above. He, and any of the band that survived with him."

"That may be," she said. "But another way, an old way has opened."

She pointed to where the rockfall had been cleared away. The downward path, though steep and narrow, seemed passable. "Taking it we can avoid Khamdar, for a time, but it will take us longer to get to Lòrenta. If we go that way it will take us into the Angle and we must cross rivers. And no doubt we will meet other dangers that we don't foresee."

"The new way might be safer," he said. "But the old way – back the way we came – will be swifter. And we're in need of haste."

"But however fast we get there," she answered, "we must still get there. The slower way offers a better chance of that. And not all the hunt was gathered here with Khamdar. We'll surely meet with the rest if we go back that way."

Brand sighed. "The delay chafes me, but what you say is true. We'll take our chances on the new road."

They mounted and looked around one last time. Brand would not be sorry to leave here. He still felt the presence of the harakgar, furious but muted within the tombs, and he knew he was lucky to have escaped.

The path ran steeply. The rockfall was gone, blasted away by the force of water that had flowed down the ledge like a river, but the stone was wet and treacherous, and it was no place to slip; the abyss opened to their left like a yawning mouth.

Kareste went first, leading her horse by hand. Brand did not like the Angle at all; everything that he had seen so far stank of death. Yet he wondered if it had always been like that. The great carvings on the cliff opposite the chasm told him that there was more to the Letharn than he had seen so far.

They continued downward, moving with caution. Kareste paused often, as though probing with some secret sense the state of the stone beneath their feet.

"It's perfectly safe," she said.

Brand was less sure. "Then why are you being so careful?"

She grinned at him but gave no answer.

Nothing, and no one, followed them, but the roar of the waterfalls, of the mighty river pouring down the escarpment just ahead of them, grew louder every moment.

As they went Brand studied the view. The Angle was visible between the two silver bands of river that bordered it. It was a green and lush land that swelled into a smooth-sloped hill toward its middle, but it was far away and hard to see properly. There were, perhaps, buildings on that rise, covering its crest and stretching down its long sides. If so, they were decrepit, barely more than rubble, but it was hard to tell though Brand strained his eyes. No doubt, if they were buildings rather than masses of broken and toppled boulders, they were the remnant of the city, or at least one of the cities, of the Letharn.

They neared the bottom of the ledge. There was water in the chasm below them, much closer now and still running from the flood Kareste had summoned. The broken body of an elug was caught between some upward thrusting rocks. Its head lolled at an unnatural angle, and flies gathered at its vacant eyes and open mouth.

Brand looked away. He took no joy in death, even of those who would kill him. But his thoughts soon turned to what lay ahead.

To their right was the face of the great escarpment, and over this thundered a mighty waterfall nearly a quarter of a mile wide. He had never seen anything like it.

Beyond, he saw the two rivers more clearly, for amid all the roar and spray of water this was the place where one river became two. Thus had the area earned the name of the Angle. But just before the Angle began, there was an island. A bridge spanned the first river and led to it, and then a second bridge spanned the next and led to other lands.

They rode ahead. Spray from the waterfall drove at them, and the horses became skittish. They crossed the first bridge and made the island. Water churned all around. Wind howled above, whipped up by the cascade of white water that smashed into stones, frothing and foaming.

Beneath the waterfall was a lake. From this sprang the two rivers. But the lake was not still and peaceful as was Lake Alithorin. Rather, it roiled and tossed in ceaseless motion.

They came to the second bridge. It was of ancient stone, pitted and marked by uncounted years, but it still had something of its original grace.

They crossed and worked their way through rocks and scree when they came to the other side. Brand was not sure there was a path, but Kareste seemed to have at least an idea of where she was going. Soon, a faded track became visible. It climbed the escarpment, winding to and fro. The horses slipped on loose rock and steep banks, sending sheets of scree sliding and clattering behind them, but they made progress, albeit slowly.

Eventually, they came to the top of the escarpment once more, but now on the opposite side of the river. Night was drawing on. It had been a long day, and they were exhausted.

To their right, some distance away, was a building. Brand saw it clearly, though clouds of fog rolled up at times from the falls. Ahead, the river flowed past, tree-lined and peaceful compared to what it became when it tumbled over the escarpment.

The building was of stone. It was an ancient thing, seeming lonely and deserted. It held something of the same grace as the bridges below. They did not ride past too closely, but Brand saw that it was constructed of granite blocks, each one at least as long and as high as a man. Its gray sides were dirtied by long years of fog, causing moss and lichen to grow thickly, and yet the building, the closer they approached it, gave off a feeling of awe. It had many strange windows, triangular slits in the stone.

The building itself was also shaped as a triangle, and massive entrances, triangular as well, stood open at each of its three sides. If there were any doors originally, they were long gone.

"What is it?" Brand asked.

"I don't know, but I sense danger there. Or somewhere beyond it."

Brand agreed, and as the sun set they left the escarpment and the strange building behind. There was something about it that disturbed him. Perhaps it was a feeling that beyond it waited the harakgar, though how he knew that, he could not be sure.

Night drew on swiftly, and the rush of the river dropped now to a smooth and steady flow, a faint and pleasant gurgle in the background.

They stopped to camp. They could go no further though all the hounds of the elùgroths were on their trail and an army of elugs to keep them company. But the land about them was still and peaceful, void of any obvious threat. Brand liked it. Yet it was still too dangerous to light a fire. Their enemies could be anywhere about, whether there was any sign of them or not. But neither was it cold, and no fire was needed.

They ate a simple and quick meal. And though they had not eaten in what seemed a very long time, they were not hungry.

Beside them was a small wood. Moths flew from it, and bats followed, wheeling and darting through the night. The stars were not bright; a haze filled the high airs and low clouds scudded, but they were not many and Brand did not think it would rain.

He liked woods, but he liked better being able to see and hear far into the distance. If their enemies came, he would have noticed from where they rested. And though he knew they should take turns to sleep, it was out of the question. No sooner had they finished eating than they lay down on the green grass, lush near the river, and sought the rest that only sleep could bring.

Yet for all Brand's tiredness, he slept poorly. Many times he woke. Once, sometime after midnight, a noise alerted him. A long while he listened, hearing a scuffling sound somewhere away in the dark, but it was only some small creature that sought worms or beetles on the verge of the wood.

The bats were gone. The clouds had disappeared, and the stars shone bright. It was cooler also, for a breeze played over the grassland and carried the nighttime scent of the river with it.

For a long while he did not get back to sleep, and he thought as he lay there, tossing and turning as the stars blinked at him and the creature wandered away in search of other food.

His thoughts turned at first to Kareste. He had been right to trust her, to give her the staff. Yet she was at risk, for the power in the talisman would call to her, but how else could she make her choice of Light or Shadow unless it was offered to her?

And when her moment came, as come it must, he intended to be there. Perhaps he could make a difference, as he saw now that Aranloth had tried to do when the other lòhrens would have had her expelled from their order.

At length, his thoughts turned to where they had shied away from all through the day. But now, in the deep night, where a man's troubles always rose to the surface of his mind, he could avoid it no longer. Aranloth had misled him. There was no real power in his staff. Brand knew that now. He realized also that Kareste had known the same thing from the moment they had first met, and had not meddled in Aranloth's affairs by stating it directly, though she had hinted at it.

Aranloth's staff was different to Shurilgar's. The broken staff was a relic, infused of old with enormous power, but with the lòhren's there was only the memory of enchantments worked through it, the bare traces of things that once were.

What power Brand had summoned had come from within himself. The thing that he most mistrusted in all the world was a part of him, inside him, at his very core. But why had Aranloth not told him that?

234

He felt a flicker of doubt at the lòhren's motives. And though what Aranloth had said could not be called a lie, it was bordering on it as close as was possible. He shrugged his misgivings aside, for he trusted Aranloth, and trust was easily eaten away by doubt. He would not doubt him, and he would not doubt Kareste either. They each had reasons for what they did, though it occurred to him with unexpected clarity that so too did Khamdar. In the sorcerer's own mind he was doing the right thing.

It was a startling realization, and it did not make Brand comfortable.

3. From Another World

Gilhain did not know what was happening, but he knew this much: Aranloth was right. Something was approaching; something wicked beyond the reach of thought.

The black-cloaked elùgroths sat in their wedge before the wall. Their wych-wood staffs pointed menacingly at the Cardurleth, and the rising chant of their spell smoked through the sorcery-laden air.

Beyond the wedge was the enemy host, and its multitudinous voice rose also in some eerie union with the invocation of the elùgroths, lending them power.

A wind blew, dry and hot, and then suddenly it changed. In what way, Gilhain could not be sure. It now smelled of moisture, or mold, or the decaying leaves of a forest that was thicker than any that grew near Cardoroth. But it was more than that.

"It comes!" hissed Aranloth.

Gilhain was sick to the pit of his stomach. He felt a great evil. It washed over him as did nausea to an ill man, in ever-greater waves that took him deeper into misery. Something was coming, and its arrival was inevitable. He could do nothing but wait.

He did not speak. Aranloth did not move. Soldiers waited all along the wall, and Gilhain knew that each and every one of them felt just as he.

The sun dimmed. The sky grew dark. The wind dropped, but the smell in the air intensified. It was putrid. He knew now that his guess was right. It was of a forest. A wet forest. A forest layered deep by centuries of rotted leaves and mildew.

There was a growing sound also. It was an eerie thing, something over and above the world that surrounded him; he heard rain. Not just any rain – and certainly not the gentle nighttime rain that usually fell over Cardoroth, but a torrential downpour. It was a sound of watery fury, a sound that thrummed and boomed and lashed like a hundred storms gathering together and drawing near.

Gilhain looked around, confused. He did not know what was happening, nor did he understand why it grew suddenly hot. But hot it was, and more humid than he had ever felt before. The very earth before the Cardurleth began to steam.

Wisps of vapor rose sluggishly from the trampled earth. The gray tendrils twined about each other, swirling and undulating. His eyes followed them upward for a moment, and when he looked down again, he saw that the earth was gone. Where the ground had been, the same ground that he had known all his life and trod uncounted times, there was now a gaping void.

He saw at once that it was not quite empty. It seemed to be a valley, even if it had no place in Cardoroth. And within he saw a vague outline of steep banks, wind-lashed trees and cascading water.

But none of those things held his attention. Something else filled his vision, drew his gaze even though the horror of it was repellent.

A shape rose amid the steam. It flowed and writhed, but it was a thing of substance and not vapor. And it was massive.

He knew what it was, but his mind refused to accept what his eyes saw. It rose higher, reaching up and out of the void and into the air of Cardoroth.

237

"What is it?" he whispered to the lòhren. "How have they created such a sorcerous beast?"

Aranloth answered through gritted teeth. "This is not made of sorcery. Rather, it is called forth by the dark power of Shurilgar's staff. It is a beast, a real beast, but drawn from the otherworld, summoned from some dark pit of horror. It is a serpent, but one such as has never hunted any dim-lit forest of Alithoras."

Gilhain shook his head. "No. It can't be. No serpent ever grew so big."

"Not on *this* earth," Aranloth answered.

Up the serpent rose, swaying back and forth, yet ever its eyes, slitted pits darker even than the hollow from which it emerged, fixed on the Cardurleth – or those standing upon it.

"How shall we fight it?" whispered Gilhain.

"Nay," the lòhren said. "Men must fight men, and lòhrens must oppose dark sorcery. This task falls to my kind. It is for this that we came."

He stepped close to the edge of the battlement, a figure robed in white and clothed in determination, but a small and frail thing compared to what it faced.

Aranloth raised his arms, and all along the wall a dozen other lòhrens, apparently waiting for some such signal, lifted high their staffs.

The serpent rose higher still, and its shadow fell over the Cardurleth. It looked down upon the lòhrens and soldiers. Slime dripped from its pale belly. The scales that formed its skin were large and smooth, shimmering luminously from beneath but gleaming darkly along its top. Near its midsection was a massive bulge; the remains of what it had last eaten.

The chanting of the elugs reached a new height of frenetic madness. The drums beat wildly. But the spell of the elùgroths soared above all else, and yet gathered all in and drew it into its own power, shaping it to its own dark will.

On the battlement, all was still and no sound was made. Men flinched when the shadow of the serpent touched them, but they made no cry of fear. Though terror menaced them, they held their ground; the longer the siege endured, the greater their defiance grew.

Gilhain gave a signal. Perhaps this attack was beyond mortal strength, but that did not mean the soldiers could not attempt to fight anyway. No one should just meekly await their fate.

A carnyx horn sounded at the king's gesture, and its deep-throated voice sent a command to every captain along the wall. And they in turn gave their own commands.

Within moments the air was dense with arrows – the red-flighted arrows for which Cardoroth was famous. They whistled as they flew, blazing through the air like a spray of blood. But when they struck the massive serpent they shattered or glanced away. Some few stuck, but they did not penetrate the thick scales into the softer flesh beneath. The creature ignored the attack, swaying ever higher.

The next volley of arrows flew. These were better aimed, seeking the two places that were likely more vulnerable: where the great angular head joined the body, and the eyes.

Arrows stuck thickly in the skin at its neck, but they had no effect there. Those that struck the eyes seemed to trouble it, and it rose higher with a jerk, but then two great inner-lids, thick and leathery, came across from the sides. These offered protection, but seemingly no hindrance to its sight.

A ripple of movement ran through those on the battlement. Gilhain looked, but he did not at first see the cause, though he noticed a change. The men stepped back, but not in retreat.

It was only when the lòhrens took a pace forward that he realized the time for another type of attack had come. They would soon see if lòhrengai proved more effective than steel-headed shafts.

In unison the lòhrens raised their staffs. Aranloth reached forth with his hands. Lòhren-fire flared. A light, brilliant and flashing, sprang into being, dazzling and shimmering with its varied colors: silver, white, green, blue and many hues beside.

The lòhrengai struck the serpent, and the air all about it wavered with heat. Those who watched turned their heads away from the stabbing brightness. A moment later there was a crack as of thunder; it rolled and boomed, drowning out the drums of the enemy and their chanting. For long moments the noise throbbed, sending shivers through the rampart and deep into the earth. Light and thunder roiled over Cardoroth, and then slowly receded.

Gilhain lifted his gaze, but the serpent was still there.

"How is it *possible*?" he muttered.

Unaffected, the creature swayed higher. The arrows that had prickled its skin were now burnt away, and their ashes drifted like black snow through the air. The slime on its belly steamed, but the monstrous thing was unharmed, oblivious to the mighty power unleashed upon it.

Gilhain struggled to think of something to do, but he, the supposed strategist, the war-leader with a thousand tricks, was powerless and void of ideas. Truly, Aranloth was right. The serpent was from another world, for powers that would destroy a thing born of this earth were as nothing to it.

Aranloth looked ancient and weary, but he spoke with unexpected determination in the face of what had just happened.

"Long has been my battle against the Shadow," he said. "Mayhap it is ended, and Cardoroth with it. And yet know this, O king, the lòhrens will fight, no matter that they lose."

Gilhain knew it. He felt it in his bones. He looked around and sensed the same in the soldiers all along the wall. They would fight. Every one of them would carry their blades until the end. But if lòhrengai had not harmed the creature summoned to break them, nor swift-flighted arrows shot from strong bows, then swords would not either, no matter how defiant.

"The great dark is coming," he answered slowly. "Yet now I feel better about sending Brand on his quest. He at least has a hope of life, and it may be a long time before the same darkness overshadows him."

4. A Haunted Man

Brand grappled with the thought of the power that was in him. He wanted no part of it, and vowed at some point during the night not to ever use it again. Lòhrengai was for lòhrens, and he was a warrior. Besides, he mistrusted it for good reason. Magic changed the wielder. It used them even as they used it. For a lòhren less so than an elùgroth, because they invoked the art only at need, but that was beside the point. He wanted to stay just as he was.

Aranloth knew. He knew the dangers better than any, and he had known that hidden away somewhere inside Brand that power lurked. At least he guessed it. But Brand did not really blame him for saying nothing. Just as he himself knew that Kareste faced a great choice, and that such choices must be discovered and faced by the person, in their own time. Pressure from outside only got in the way.

Dawn came after a long night. Brand's choices were made, though he supposed they would yet be tested. But he thought no more of magic or problems or the dark corners of a man's soul. Instead, he reveled in the new day.

The sun shone bright and clear. The sky was a glorious blue, and the grass was green beneath the hooves of the horses as they got underway. Afar, he heard the gurgle and rush of the river, and closer to hand the calls of many types of birds that he had never heard before. But he could not see them, for they came from within the many small woods that dotted the landscape.

The horses travelled quickly. It was good country in which to ride, the earth being soft and the way clear of obstacles. All should be well, Brand thought, and yet Kareste was withdrawn and thoughtful.

He considered her as they rode. At first, he guessed her state of mind was because of Shurilgar's staff. After some while though, he realized that was not the case. He began to feel something himself, something which she had sensed earlier than he: a mood of unease that lay over the land despite the beautiful day. It was not strong. It was, in fact, barely there. But he had learned to trust his instincts, and now that they sensed this thing there was no doubt in his mind.

He caught her glance and they slowed the horses to a walk.

"What is it?" he asked.

"You sense it also? I thought it was just me."

"No," he answered. "There's something … not right. At first I didn't notice because the weather is so fine and this is a fair land. But there's something else going on."

Kareste gazed behind them. "Khamdar?"

"It could be," Brand said, following her gaze. "But there's no sign of any pursuit."

"Whatever it is, it's unsettling," Kareste said. She turned her gaze back to the front with an air of determination, and they continued on.

Now that their misgivings were in the open, their unease grew. It was like a shadow over the whole land, though they rode in bright sunlight.

They did not push the horses too hard. It was a long way to Lòrenta, and it was wise to keep them in good health and with a reserve of speed should it be needed. To tire them out now was to leave nothing available if they were pressed hard by a pursuit later.

Every moment that passed seemed like an eternity to Brand, but he pushed such thinking aside. To rush now might be a mistake, and he knew that although they did not hasten unduly, they were still making excellent time. Cardoroth could not endure forever, but he trusted in the king and the brave hearts of the city's people to hold out until the last. And by then, well, by then his own troubles would be sorted, one way or the other.

To their left was another wood. It was small, perhaps only a patch of five to ten acres, but it seemed green and lush as did everything in this land. He realized as they neared that no birdcalls came from it. But it was not silent.

Drifting through the sunlit air was music: high, wild, and laden with grief. It was a flute, that much Brand knew, but he had never heard such a tune before, and goosebumps stood out on his skin.

They came to a halt. "Who lives in these lands?" he asked.

Kareste frowned. "None that I know of. But Alithoras is large, and many people from the south are on the move. Maybe some have come here to escape trouble."

"If so, they'll be disappointed."

She looked at him, her eyes giving away nothing of her thoughts, but there was a catch in her voice.

"When people are desperate, even disappointment can be an improvement on their situation."

Brand did not answer. Kareste had suffered in her life, even more than he, so he took her at her word. He did not know what it would be like to lose his family as young as she had, and to be taken to some strange place among just as strange a people. At least he had stayed in his own land, moving from family to family, hiding spot to hiding spot, but always among his own kind who

244

protected and taught him while the usurper of his father's chieftainship hunted for him.

Brand sighed. The past was a part of him, and he could not shake it any more than Kareste could distance herself from her own. But now he must force himself to think of only the present.

"Could it be a trap?"

Kareste shrugged. "Maybe, but I don't think so. It's not something that Khamdar seems likely to do, but there are other perils in the world beside elùgroths."

Brand made up his mind. "I would meet the person who could create such music."

"Curiosity is a dangerous thing," she said. "You like the music, but you may not like the maker. And it *may* be a trap, for all that I know."

"That's true, but it may also be a chance to hear news. We're wandering in a foreign land, and information helps. There could be elug armies on the move for all that we know."

She shrugged. "Very well. But be ready – for anything."

"Being ready is easy. It's making good choices that's hard."

She raised an eyebrow at him as though considering his words in a range of contexts, but did not speak.

They moved ahead. The wood was a little bigger than Brand had thought, but it was still small. Not so small that it could not hide an army of elugs if it came to that, but he did not really believe that to be the case. Khamdar must still be behind them somewhere, if he was even alive at all. And any enemy from the south was likely to be gathered around Cardoroth or one of the other cities along the coast of Alithoras. There was nothing for them here in the wild lands.

When the two riders entered the woods the light turned yellow-green. There were mostly oak trees about them, and the shade soon grew thicker. But it was a young wood, not so dense and dark as what Brand was used to.

They moved quietly, and with caution. But for all that they did not make any noise, the music died almost as soon as they rode beneath the leaf canopy, and it did not start again.

There was a path of sorts, though it veered at strange angles that no animal would make. But Brand was little skilled at tracking, and he was not sure of this. But however the path was made, he followed it, for it led to the center of the wood, and that was where the music had come from. So much he realized before it ceased. But whether the maker would still be there when they arrived was another matter.

A breeze whispered in the high leaves of the oaks, but it was still and peaceful amid the dark trunks and spreading boughs. The smell of the earth, deep and rich, was strong in the air and Brand liked it. It reminded him of the scent of new-ploughed soil, and not for the first time he missed his childhood home where once he had lived and toiled honestly, helping to raise livestock and crops for those who hid and protected him.

His past, his broken childhood, seemed a long time ago now. And yet it was not. But much had happened since then, and he had been forced to grow in strength and wisdom more quickly than he should have. Now, instead of crops, he harvested only death. Many were the enemies that he had left behind him. Sometimes, he wished for a simpler life. But then he would never have met Gilhain or Aranloth … or Kareste.

It was a mistake to allow his mind to continue wandering, and he focused his attention once more on

246

the present. They neared the center of the wood. There was smoke in the air, the sweet-sharp odor that was a camper's friend. But not all campsites were friendly.

Brand brought his horse to a stop and looked around. He immediately saw the faint flicker of firelight from a glade a little ahead. The trees closed around it; the path passed to its side, but within the circle of trunks was a clearing: green-grassed and shining in the sun.

"Be careful," Kareste whispered.

He nodded, and urged his mount forward. The trunks were close, but not so close that a horse could not pass between them. On the inside, the light was brighter and the blue sky gleamed above.

It was a beautiful little glade, quiet and peaceful. The fire burned merrily in the middle, and to its side over a bed of black-red coals was a spitted hare, nearly roasted through. Behind that a magnificent black mare stood. She remained still, but occasionally an ear twitched or her tail lashed to dislodge flies. Against an ancient tree stump, thick but near-rotted by age, leaned a flute of black walnut, trimmed in gold. But of the flute's owner, the mare's rider and the fire's maker, there was no sign.

"Whoever it is has good taste in horses," Brand said.

There was a noise to the left of the glade and a man stepped from behind a tree trunk.

"There are few things in life better than a fast horse and sweet music," he said.

The man was tall and grim. He was also armed. He held a sword, finely crafted, in his hand, and he looked to Brand's trained eye like he knew how to use it, but he made no threatening move.

Brand thought quickly. He did not blame the stranger for drawing his blade in such a situation, but he did not draw his own. Instead, he ignored the naked steel. That would send a signal that he did not wish to fight, but also that he was not scared.

"To that," he answered, "I can only agree. But I would add this to it – a trusted sword ready to one hand, and a tankard of beer in the other."

The other man laughed. It was a deep and rich sound, but he did not lower his sword.

"You're a man after my own heart," he said.

Kareste sniffed loudly. "Enough of this. If I hear either of you say that the only other thing you need is a beautiful girl by your side, there's going to be trouble."

"My dear," the man said in his rich voice, "a beautiful girl is *always* trouble."

Kareste tossed her hair and glared at him. The man pretended not to notice and gazed back, a slightly impudent smile on his face.

Brand liked him. But then he felt an unexpected pang of jealousy. He did not know where it came from, and he did not like it.

The man looked from one of them to the other. With a nonchalant shrug, he lowered his sword.

"You're not one of my enemies," he said.

"Nor are you one of ours, I think," Brand answered calmly.

The man sheathed his blade. "But there's trouble nonetheless, and for once it's not of a kind that beautiful women bring." He ignored Kareste completely as he spoke, and she bit her lip, forcing herself not to react to his teasing.

He gazed at them a little longer. "But this you already know."

Brand nodded slowly, unsure of what to say, and thinking it best to say as little as possible.

"There are enemies behind us. Dangerous enemies. But we don't know for sure if they're still on our trail."

"I see," the man said. "Well, you seem able to look after yourselves; that much is obvious. So too is the fact that you tell me nothing that I couldn't already guess by your attitude. But that is no matter."

He turned to Kareste and gave a well-practiced bow. "My name is Bragga Mor."

Kareste sniffed again as a sign of irritation, though whether to the man as a person, or to his shrewd guesses, Brand did not know.

He gave the stranger their true names – there was no reason not to. In the pause that followed, he asked a question.

"Where are you from?" He had thought it a simple question, but Bragga Mor seemed suddenly to lose a little of his poise.

"It doesn't matter. I'm nothing but a vagabond wanderer now, and far I've travelled, and many things I've seen."

Brand was not going to press him on his home city. There was some darkness there, that much was obvious, but that the man had travelled was interesting.

"What have you seen?" he asked. "What passes in Alithoras?"

"Many things," Bragga Mor replied tiredly. "The enemy is now in the northlands. There are raging bands about, but, at least as I hear it, most are concentrated around Cardoroth. A vast army besieges that city." He gave Brand a questioning look, and Brand nodded without speaking. Bragga Mor seemed to need little else by way of confirmation. He was clever, and had already guessed where Brand had come from, and no doubt many more things besides.

The stranger continued. "There's rumor of dark deeds in the west. The eastern realms are nervous, knowing that trial of war may soon come to them, though as yet I

249

have not heard that anywhere is attacked save Cardoroth. At least, that was the last I heard, but my news is old, for the wild lands call me now, and the works of men that do not last only haunt me. I avoid them."

Brand felt again that some darkness lay behind this man, and he was making his own guesses. But a sharp hiss from Kareste distracted him.

"Something comes!" she said.

Brand drew his sword and remained quiet, but into the silence Bragga Mor spoke.

"Of course," he said, turning to Kareste, "as you knew it must." He faced Brand again. "The very air sings with unease, and the beautiful girl knows why."

5. It Calls to the Dark

The two men looked at Kareste; one with apparent knowledge, and the other in surprise.

Kareste merely shrugged. "I did not know – I only guessed."

"But now you know that your guess is right," Bragga Mor said.

"They usually are," she answered. "But more to the point, how do *you* know?"

"Oh, I've seen a thing or two. Yes I have. More than I would like. Things to burn a man's vision and haunt his dreams. I know power when I see it – lòhrengai, elùgai and even ùhrengai, the force that forms and substances the world and from which both light and shadow spring."

"Is someone going to tell me what's going on?" Brand asked.

Kareste nudged her mount toward him. "Shurilgar's staff is a powerful thing. It calls. It calls to the Shadow, and the Shadow hears. I don't just mean the enemies that have hunted us, nor just Khamdar, if he still lives. I mean the dark things that dwell in Alithoras – the evil that lives in deep valleys, or lurks in the marshes, or haunts the forests and roams the lonely hills. The evil that hides; in short, all the shadowy creatures that have hated people since people first learned to kindle fire and keep the dark at bay."

"What does all that *mean*?" Brand asked.

"It means," replied Bragga Mor, "that you're in trouble. As the girl says, something comes. I have seen it.

Or rather, I have seen *her*. A witch she is. I spotted her walking the starlit grasslands last night. To be sure, she is not one of the great ones, but she is still mighty powerful. And," he pointed at the broken half of Shurilgar's staff, "she would have more – more of what *that* can give to her."

Kareste did not seem disturbed. "How do you know that she isn't one of the great ones?"

"I've seen one of them," he said. His voice trailed away and his gaze became distant.

Brand had heard enough. "It's time to go," he said, "And quickly."

Bragga Mor looked at him sharply. The past obviously troubled him, but he could give his attention to the present swiftly enough if he chose to.

"No. You cannot flee her. You must stay and fight, if it comes to that. Better to face her now than at some point in the future when you may be less able."

Brand thought quickly. There was something to what Bragga Mor said. Who knew what the future held? And if the witch joined forces with Khamdar, then the situation would become much worse.

"Will you fight with us?" Brand asked. He knew nothing of this stranger, and the man had no reason to help. But there was something about him…

"Or," Kareste cut in, "Will you fight with the witch?"

Brand had not thought of that as a possibility, but immediately on her words he wondered if his own instincts were wrong.

Bragga Mor looked at her and smiled. "That, we shall see."

Brand cocked his head and listened. A change had come over the wood. He could not quite name what it was, but it seemed as though even the leaves at the tops of the trees were hushed, and the trunks were still like an army of wary men that silently watched an approaching messenger, unafraid of him, but fearing the import of his tidings.

The witch came. One moment she was not there, though her presence filled the wood, and then she was among them, seeming to coalesce from the shadows at the fringe of the clearing into flesh and blood that stepped upon the grass.

Brand was ready. He maneuvered his mount to face her, but he did not put his back to Bragga Mor.

She that had come was light-footed, for her steps quickly took her to the middle of the glade, but she moved without haste or sign of threat. And it was a strange thing to see how she elegantly walked, for judging by her appearance, it seemed to Brand that she should have hobbled.

The witch was old. Her skin hung on her in wrinkled folds that swung as she moved. Her hair, a mess of long gray strands and wisps of white, fell over her narrow shoulders and down her hunched back. Her nose, long and hooked, jutted forward like a bird's beak. Above it, glaring like a hawk's, her eyes held each of their own in turn. There was no sign of frailty there, despite her decrepit body and her ancient, ugly face.

She raised an arm. The tattered remnants of robes fell back, revealing more withered skin. A crooked finger, dirty-nailed and swollen at the joints, pointed at Kareste.

"I know what it is that you carry," she said.

Her voice confused Brand. It was smooth and clear and beautiful: the voice of a woman in the flower of her youth.

Though the voice surprised him, he perceived instinctively that her power resided in it. It was a voice to command, to persuade, to inspire trust. Most of all, it was a voice that could carry and enhance spells. And

253

spells he would be wary of, for she had come to take Shurilgar's staff, and she would not be idle in pursuing that goal.

Her words to Kareste were not loud, but they seemed to fill the clearing and to echo strangely up and down the shadowy aisles of tree trunks.

Kareste quivered with emotion. "Stay back, hag. Or die."

Brand looked on silently. Bragga Mor did not move. Surprisingly, the witch showed no anger. She gazed at Kareste calmly, her hawk-like eyes gleaming with humor.

"By that," she replied, "you mean 'don't try to take the staff, or I'll fight to the death to keep it.' Has it already got such a strong hold on you?"

Kareste stiffened, but the witch went on speaking. "You are young in your power. I am old. Old as the hills and wily as the ancient beasts that roam them, seldom seen by man. I have many names. Hag is one. Slithrest, Netherwall and Angrod are others. Those names were old before even the Halathrin strode ashore to this land."

The witch straightened, and a hard edge of threat came into her voice. "But they named me Durletha – enduring as stone. And that should be a warning to you, for I have seen frost break mountains into plains and flat plains themselves raised into high mountains. I have seen the great sea, black and terrible beyond the reach of your thought, climb the shore and sweep all before it. I will be here when it comes again. I have seen the bright Halathrin, proud and stern and aloof. I watched unmoved as they came, and I looked on uncaring as they dwindled. I saw the Letharn rise before them, whose lands you are passing through, whose lands you would still be passing through though you rode for weeks, and I saw them fall. And before them were the Kirsch, whom men have forgotten. So, foolish girl, will you contend with me?"

It was Brand who answered. "She is not alone."

Durletha turned her fierce eyes upon him. "Ah. You speak at last. You are younger than she, but perhaps wiser." The witch frowned for a moment, assessing him. "Yes, I see it now. There is no give in you. You will fight for her. But will you *die* for her?"

"No one needs to die today," he said.

She paused, continuing to look at him intently. "But death follows you, does it not?" she said after a moment. "Everywhere you go. Even in Red Cardoroth, that will fall in blood and flame. And who protects you? You think you protect the king, but the king is protecting you, else you would be dying with him even as we speak."

Brand showed nothing of what he felt at those words. Durletha seemed to know far too much about what was happening. That she had some measure of Sight was evident, but that did not mean she was not lying.

Her gaze did not leave him, but her haggard face broke into a grin and she clapped her hands.

"Yes, you're wiser than your companion. She shall surely fall at the end, but you, you might yet stand tall. Yes, even without me you could command armies, wear a crown and conquer wide realms. But with *me* at your side, we could rule all of Alithoras. The petty lòhrens and the shadow in the south would fight each other for the crumbs under our table. Yes, it could be so."

Brand raised his eyebrows but did not speak. He had heard this kind of thing before from those with the Sight, but not from one so old and decrepit – not from one who would make him her paramour.

"And you are polite, too. But I have more pleasing forms than this!"

255

The forest remained still, but birds now sang in the dappled sunlight. A sweet breeze blew, carrying the scent of earth, leaf and flower, and some exotic perfume that he could not name.

"I am not of the Light," she said softly. "But neither am I of the Shadow."

"Are you not?"

"No. But I can be anything between them!"

The sun now seemed dazzling bright in the clearing. Bright beams shot amid the trees and Brand raised a hand to shield his eyes.

As quick as the stabbing light came it disappeared. When it was gone, the witch stood just where she had been, but she was transformed.

Durletha was now young, and it seemed to Brand that it was no spell but her true form. Her hair was long, flowing in golden locks that shimmered like burnished metal. Her skin was smooth and unblemished, seeming to glow with health and beauty. Nor did she stand bent and hump-backed, but tall and proud. She gazed at him with a cool look, a look of utter confidence, but yet from the same hawk-like eyes as before.

And with a shimmer she changed again. This time she appeared as Kareste, but it was a Kareste that he had never seen before. In form, the likeness was identical, but there was a sweet smile on her lips, and a grace in the way she stood that spoke of gentleness and care, not of a strong sword arm and a sharp tongue. This time also her eyes had changed: they were green-gold, and they laughed at him with a carefree joy.

"I can be anything you want," the witch said. "Anything." And her voice was Kareste's, but it contained a promise of intimacy that he had never heard in it before.

"I can be anything you want, and the world will be ruled by your sword, and by your will."

Brand hesitated, and then he grinned back at her boyishly. She had made a mistake. She spoke of realms and armies and swords. She spoke of war and conquest and rule, but she made no mention of the staff he bore or of the power that was in him, and that told him what she most feared and least wished him to consider.

He gripped Aranloth's staff tightly. It was warm to his hand. He felt the residue of lòhrengai within it. That force called to him, and he felt it all around him also.

The forces that formed and substanced the world were everywhere, and he was becoming more sensitive to them. He knew now that he could summon them, transform them, use them. That ability was in him, but in bringing those forces into himself they would change him even as he changed them.

And each time he used such power he would become more adept. He would sense the call more strongly. Each step he took down that road was a step that he could never retrace. Once followed, there was no turning back from the path ahead. And in following it, it would alter him forever, and perhaps not for the best.

Dare he try to use such power one last time? And what of his vow? Could he so easily break it, even if need drove him? They were hard questions, and he had no answers. But at the same time he sensed that the choice was before him. The witch had made it so, and she had no fear of his sword. That much was clear.

There was little time left. That Durletha would try to claim the staff was obvious. It was equally obvious that she must not have it. To that end, he would fight. But how?

She did not fear his sword. To what extent she feared lòhrengai, he could not tell. But she was far more skilled

257

in such things than he. If he used it, she would defeat him easily. And yet there was Kareste also. She would fight, and between the two of them they might defeat her. But if he joined Kareste in that, he would become what he did not wish, what he least trusted.

Still he stood, undecided, and the brief moments flitted by. Soon the witch would realize that her attempt to persuade him had failed, and then she would attack.

But he was caught in a dilemma that he could not solve. And a new thought struck him as a blow, and disabled him.

Why should he not embrace his new-found power?

6. An Iron-hard Will

The great serpent rose higher, a massive thing that even those in distant parts of Cardoroth could see. People ran into the streets; some screamed, others remained deathly quiet, watching.

Gilhain, atop the battlement, was one who watched in silence. The creature's coils flowed and undulated, ascending from the vast pit without end.

It towered above the Cardurleth, blotting out the sun. But it did not strike. Gilhain realized that it would not attack that way; it would not rend with its great fangs or use poison. It had some other means to visit destruction upon them.

The creature's lower portions began to slide along the rampart. It covered hundreds of feet of stonework, grinding and smashing against the merlons, sending them tumbling down in ruin to the earth below.

Though the coils were thicker than the trunk of an ancient oak, the soldiers attacked. Their blades did nothing. Some of them, getting too close, were crushed by a sudden heave of the serpent. The stones ran red with blood.

With its slow haste, the serpent continued, oblivious to the hundreds of men that attacked it like a swarm of ants.

A stench filled the air, and Gilhain and his wife gagged at the putrid smell. Slime dripped down the stone. Aranloth stood close by, unaffected. His head was down, either in acceptance of an opponent beyond his ability to fight, or else in deep thought.

"May fate show us mercy," whispered Aurellin.

The great loops of the serpent began to constrict. They closed slowly, but surely. Stone popped. Sprays of dust and loose gravel filled the air. Cracks appeared, not just in merlons but lower down. A deep grinding noise thrummed through the air and pulsated up through the stone into Gilhain's feet.

He took Aurellin's hand in his own. "It will bring down the Cardurleth," he said softly.

"And let in the horde," she answered.

They watched in terrible fascination as a white-robed lòhren, near the head of the beast, made a desperate move. Her black hair spilled out behind her as she ran. Swift she moved, but the creature paid no heed. And then she was upon it, thrusting her staff into its mouth.

Purple-blue lòhrengai flared. Men with axes raced behind her, attacking in unison. They hewed with mighty swings at the neck, as near as they dared approach the flame.

The creature made no sound, but a ripple ran through it. Suddenly, it threw up coils of its long body. They crashed into the men and sent them sprawling, axes clattering from lifeless hands. Some few crawled away, broken bones slowing them, but they escaped.

The lòhren was not so lucky. Bravely she stayed where she was, lòhrengai flaring from her staff until she dropped to her knees, exhausted. But the great jaws of the beast snapped shut around her.

She screamed. Blood sprayed. Bones snapped with a crack audible even to Gilhain. Her staff fell from her writhing arms. The creature then spat her out, its massive jaws agape, and the ruined body of the lòhren fell, tumbling across the rampart and down the other side into the city streets.

Wider still the jaws opened, and the beast vomited the lòhrengai back out. It seemed unharmed.

The screaming of the city folk was a sound such as Gilhain had never heard before, nor ever wanted to hear again. It was primal fear given voice, unfettered by thought or hope or restraint. Other cities had heard it, other cities that had fallen before the enemy. But they had not fallen without a fight; they had not gone willingly under the shadow, and nor would Gilhain.

Without word or gesture or haste, the king drew his sword. He stepped forward to attack, and men followed him. It was no longer about hope of victory; it was about fighting an enemy, about never surrendering to an opponent. Blades would not work. Lòhrengai would not work. But that did not mean he would not try to the last, and there was a victory in that worth more than life. It *was* life, for nothing else mattered in the end.

The great sword of the king hacked and slashed. The soldiers near him did the same. Yet for all their effort they were like men hewing at a mighty oak with paper axes: the scales of the serpent were too thick and the blows were as nothing.

The massive coils of the serpent rose above the king. The queen now leaped to his side, stabbing with a knife, and the shadow of the creature fell over them. Whether by accident, the intelligence of the creature, or the design of the elùgroths who had summoned it, the coils crashed down seeking to crush them both.

But the Durlin were there. In a last great effort they flung themselves forward, some to attack the creature with pikes, others to pull back the king and queen to safety. Some died beneath the toppling coils, crushed and broken, but the king and queen were saved, the pikes holding back the weight of the monster for just a moment before they slipped away beneath its vast bulk.

More stone popped, and powdery dust filled the air. Rubble fell. The foundations of the Cardurleth shook. The coils gripped ever tighter, yet no one fled.

Gilhain stumbled back. This was it. This was the fall of Cardoroth. He was powerless to stop it, and the prophecy of old, the foretelling of destruction that had come down through the long years was correct: the city would fall in red fire and blood.

Cold fear stabbed him. Despair smothered him. His own life would soon end also, and that of his wife. Ruin would take them all.

He held out a hand to Aurellin, and she took it. They did not speak. No words were necessary. All that mattered was that they would be together when the end came.

He drew his gaze away from the person he loved most in the world, and looked to Aranloth. He would say goodbye to one of his great friends. But the lòhren did not look at him. Instead, he strode forth.

Aranloth lifted his arms high, and there was a look of such determination on his face that the king's heart skipped a beat. The lòhren would not yield. His was a will beyond a normal man's; a will honed and strengthened by forgotten ages. He was like a force of nature, and his heart's beat was one with the life of the land that he had wandered for years beyond count.

The lòhren spoke no word. He gave no sign. And yet every other lòhren along the rampart instantly looked at him. Something passed between them, between the students and the master. If it were possible, the expression on his face of iron-hard will strengthened further. It was a will that had seen ages of men come and pass. He was a thing of the land itself – old as the hills, bearing a burden of time and change even as did they.

262

And he had learned a thing or two in that time. He had survived.

Gilhain watched, awed and puzzled. What would the man he dared to call a friend do?

7. The Flicking Wings of a Hawk

"You cannot tempt me," Brand said. "I want neither realms nor armies. I want nothing you offer. Stand aside. You have no claim on the staff."

The witch smiled at him sweetly. Her glance was long and keen and intimate. With a sudden stab he knew that he wished to see that same look on the real Kareste.

"Begone!" he said.

She tossed her ash-blond hair. "In life you often get what you don't want, though few say no to realms or armies – or even magic."

It disturbed Brand how much she knew of him, how much she read from his mind. Some things were easy to guess, but others were not. Hers was a peculiar magic, but all magics had strengths and weaknesses. He would discover her weakness in due course, and to that end he did not mind talking. It would give him time.

She smiled at him. It was a smile for him alone as though no one else in the world mattered.

"I know what it is that you most want. A simple thing it is too. You wish to inherit what should have been yours – the chieftainship of the Duthenor. You already wear the helm on your head, and the sword of your forefathers is always by your side. But an usurper rules in your place, supported by men from other tribes, and he will not be easy to dislodge. Yet it would be a small thing for me to accomplish. For you, I could do it. I could do it with ease. And you should know this, also. The usurper will one day be usurped himself. The wild men that he has brought in will turn on him, and in the end they will rule the Duthenor. And they will be harsh masters."

Brand was troubled, and this time he could not disguise it. Not that it would be worth the effort to try; Durletha seemed to know more about him than he did himself. Worse, she seemed to know his very thoughts.

"Begone!" he said again. "Temptation will not sway me, and fate will be what it will be."

For the first time, the witch showed displeasure. And in that Brand took hope, for it seemed to him the only reason she had to be displeased was that her offers were rejected. Yet, if she truly knew his innermost thoughts, she would have known from the beginning that it would be so. He was loyal, if nothing else, and Gilhain, and now Kareste, were his friends. No force on earth, and no temptation, would cause him to break trust with them.

Durletha hissed. It was a frightful sound, and it was all the stranger to now see open hatred on the mask of Kareste's face. That hurt him, even though he knew it was not her. Suddenly, he realized that he could hear that same hiss in the tops of the trees all around them, and then he understood that all the while that she had been talking her voice was also reflected in the wood. The sound of it was in the hollows of tree trunks, in the whispering of leaves, in the slow creak and mutter of tree roots. It was in the bubbling of water in a rill somewhere further into the wood and out of sight, and it was even in the slow seeping of water though the earth.

He understood now what had troubled him all along about her voice, for there was power in it, and all the while that she spoke it was gathering itself, building, forming some spell, and only at the last did his instincts perceive it. At the last, and perhaps too late.

There was a sudden noise. It was shrill. From all around them it came, and Brand understood even as it drove into his ears, turning, twisting, piercing like a hot needle, what it was. All the sound for miles had been turned into a weapon by the witch. Her magic had taken it, transformed it, compressed it into a single thing and sent it tunnelling into their ears. It was unbearable.

Kareste fell off her horse, yet she managed to hold onto Shurilgar's staff. Brand could not think. He was dizzy, and the pain drove him like a madness. He wanted to act, to do something to relieve it, but it only grew and scattered his thoughts to the wind.

All the while he heard the voice of the witch beyond the shrill sound that speared into him. She chanted, and though he did not understand the words, he perceived that her power was growing as the need for subterfuge was gone. Soon, she would kill them.

Brand struggled to control his mount. The idea came to him to ride the witch down, but he floundered in a sea of pain and confusion. It took him some moments to realize that the horse's reins were no longer in his hand but had fallen and trailed between its legs.

Durletha's chanting rose to a higher pitch. If it were possible, the pain redoubled. Brand's vision swam, and he knew that there were only moments left before he fell from the horse as had Kareste.

And then he heard another sound. Faint at first, but something different from the high-pitched daggers in his ears. It was Bragga Mor's flute. As it had been earlier, so was it now: beautiful, sweet, haunting.

The chanting of the witch faltered for just a moment. She seemed perplexed by how to take this new sound up into her attack. In that moment Kareste regained her feet. She staggered up, but she did not attack with her sword or try to summon power from Shurilgar's staff.

266

Brand, his newfound senses growing day by day, dimly perceived her mind reach out, and her own power become one with the music of the flute.

He was staggered by the shadowy sense of what she was doing. With skill and precision her power became one with the music, and swift as thought took hold of it and transformed it into a kind of shield. It veiled them from the witch's attack, not nullifying it completely, but subduing it so that it was no more than an unpleasant noise.

He realized that though his sensitivity to lòhrengai was growing, he had only the same skill in the craft as a young boy picking up a sword for the first time. It had taken him years of hard practice to acquire the skill to be bodyguard to the king, and that same effort awaited him if ever he wished to become proficient with the power that was in him.

He shut down that line of thinking. It was yet another way the magic inside him tempted him to its use, for to learn a skill was a challenge, and the harder something was to achieve the more Brand set his mind to attain it.

All sound in the wood now seemed muffled, yet still Brand heard the witch shriek. Whether it was in anger or pain, he did not know, but he sensed her frustration and knew instinctively that the danger had not passed. She would not give up on claiming the staff, and a new attack was imminent.

As soon as Brand had that thought he knew that he must attack to forestall her. But driven by need rather than considered reason, his body reacted with an instinct of its own, or at least the magic that was in him did.

Without thinking he raised Aranloth's staff. Fire burst from it; a hot wild stream that roared to life and leaped at the witch like a living thing.

He rode toward her, forgetting his sword and concentrating only on the flame.

Kareste moved also. No flame came from Shurilgar's staff, but it was raised in threat. It was a threat that Durletha saw and understood. She understood also that her attack had failed. Temptation had not worked, nor surprise. And she did not like it.

The witch hissed again. Her left arm she held up as a shield, and by the power that was in her she rebuffed Brand's flame. A small thing for her to do, and easily could she turn it aside and launch her own assault upon him. But for this Kareste waited, for in that moment she would strike herself, and the witch would be open to a greater attack, directed by skill and strength.

"Begone!" Kareste yelled, taking up Brand's words.

The witch looked at them, poised amid the flame, beaten, but not defeated.

"This is not over," she said. "It will never be over until that staff is in my hands, and then the other half after it. Old as the hills I am, and I have patience. I'll watch you fall yet, and it will be all the sweeter."

With a toss of her ash-blond hair she fixed Brand with a look of hatred, and he wished never to see such a look again, for it was Kareste, Kareste as she would be if she fell to the Shadow and refused to destroy the staff at the end. It was the way she would look at him if they fought, and fight they must, no matter that it was the last thing he wanted, if that came to pass. For he saw now more clearly than ever before, understood so much better Aranloth's warning, that for the sake of Alithoras the staff must be destroyed. Otherwise, the evil in the world would constantly seek it.

One moment the witch was before them, her ash-blond hair tossing, and then she was gone. In her place were the flicking wings of a hawk and a fierce cry from its hooked beak. The pale underwings flashed. Feathers beat the air and swift as an arrow it drove, talons outstretched, at Brand's face.

He ducked, but not quick enough. Talons ripped and clawed, seeking for his eyes, yet his head was now bent low and the shrieking attack struck only the helm of the Duthenor.

There was a flash of silver light, and then the hawk shot upward into the air and was gone.

Brand and Kareste looked at each other. They did not speak. The only sound they heard was the playing of the flute.

They turned to Bragga Mor. Tears ran down his face, and the music, up close as they were to it now, filled them with sadness and a sense of longing for something forever beyond reach. It had saved them, but it was heartbreaking, and Brand felt the outside edges of a sorrow greater than any he had ever known. It was a grief that this stranger endured every day.

Bragga Mor ceased playing, and he looked at them with eyes sadder even than the music.

8. What Hope for Cardoroth?

Aranloth stood still. His hands were raised, and only the sleeves of his robe moved, fluttering in the northerly breeze. Gilhain felt the same air on his face.

For a moment, the stench of the serpent was gone. The air was sweet once more, sweeping down from the north, from the mountains that Gilhain had never seen nor now ever would. He even fancied that he smelled the scent of pinewoods and snow – crisp and fresh.

He heard a grinding noise and more stone popped to dust under the enormous pressure exerted by the serpent's tightening coils. The odor of stone overpowered whatever else Gilhain smelled, for it was driven into his face by the north wind which gusted stronger, moment by moment.

With the wind came cold. Either that, or the shadow of death that fell over the wall blotted out all warmth and drained the air of life.

The wind now blew with genuine force, whistling through the crenels and moaning along the sides of the merlons. All the while, the lòhrens stood unmoving.

Gilhain felt something on his cheek. At first, he thought it was crumbled stone from the battlement, and then he knew that it was sleet.

The wind suddenly died. Yet it remained cold, strangely cold given how hot it was before. So cold that Gilhain noticed with amazement that white frost began to settle in patches over the stonework of the Cardurleth.

He looked about him. The soldiers were shivering, and a great shudder ran through his own body. He looked at the blade of his sword. It glittered with ice.

Gilhain whipped his head around in astonishment. Even the serpent was coated by a layer of rime: the slime that dripped from its belly was now turned to a dirty white crust.

And the serpent did nothing to shake off its icy coat. It lay, twisted and sluggish, over the Cardurleth. The coils no longer tightened. The dust of crumbled stone no longer filled the air.

Nothing moved in the icy stillness, not until a sudden sign from Lornach to a few of the Durlin. They leaped across the rampart and closed the short distance between themselves and the serpent in the flicker of an eye. They hacked with their swords, but these were still useless. Then Lornach seized a long spear from a nearby soldier, and Taingern joined him.

Together the two men positioned the spear beneath the creature's pale belly. And then they drove it upward with slow precision. The air from their lungs billowed out in a silvery mist about them, and the spear, driven with their combined strength, guided by four hands, penetrated the thick skin.

The serpent moved with a spasm. Cold or no, sluggish or not, it felt pain for the first time and lifted its body away from it.

A great coil rose. The belly shone pale beneath. Blood dripped from the spear wound, turning to dark ice as it spattered the stone.

The two men did not relent. They followed the creature, continuing to push the spear upward by clambering atop the merlons.

With another great heave the coil lifted high above them. The spear was taken beyond their reach, and they tumbled from the merlons back onto the rampart. The coil rose higher, the spear sticking from it, and then with a twist and thrash the loop of the serpent's body dropped once more.

More merlons burst. Men were crushed. The two Durlin scrabbled away from the rubble, and the serpent shuddered, raising up the coil with a jerk more sudden than the first, for its efforts had only driven the spear deep; the full six foot length of it now pierced the creature.

It thrashed. Coils rose and fell all along the Cardurleth. For a moment it hung there, roiling in pain, but then the extremity of its anguish drove it to twist too far. With a final undulation of its whole body, it lost its grip on the battlement and fell.

Down the massive creature plummeted. It thrashed as it went, and when it landed it sent a tremor through the earth and the battlement shook. There in the dust it writhed. A long time it would take to die, but Gilhain had no doubt that it would. Somehow, Cardoroth was saved.

On unsteady legs the king walked over and looked down. The creature churned violently in its death pangs. Blood streamed from its wound. He looked along the battlement. The men were in shock, but quickly they began to clean the rampart of bodies and broken stone. The lòhrens all along the Cardurleth leaned on their staffs.

He turned toward Aranloth, but did not see him at first. Then, some way from the broken edge of the rampart, he spotted him, collapsed to the ground.

He raced over. From afar he heard the groaning of the enemy horde, and also the pain-filled screech of elùgroths. When he came to Aranloth the old man's eyes flickered open, and the lòhren spoke, his voice soft but grim.

"Thus do they pay for their sorcery," he said. "They linked themselves to the serpent to bring it here and keep it in this world. And as it dies, so too do the weakest among them."

Aranloth spoke no more. His eyes blinked strangely, and then closed. Gilhain looked at him, dread creeping though his veins even though he had thought that after the serpent nothing could scare him again. But dread was worse than fear – dread spoke of human tragedy and loss that was irrevocable, but yet to come.

The king bent down and felt for a pulse. He could not find one, but he had little skill with such matters. The Durlin had more.

He looked up to call one over, but Taingern was already striding toward him. The Durlin kneeled. With deft movements he felt at Aranloth's wrist and neck.

Gilhain knew that he should have seen this coming. The lòhrens had no prop as did the elùgroths. For them, there was no artifact such as Shurilgar's staff. What they did, they did by the power that was in them, and by the strength of their will and the courage of their hearts. And Aranloth, oldest and greatest among them, he who had given most for the longest, had perhaps finally given too much.

Gilhain felt suddenly cold.

"Well?" he asked.

Taingern did not look at him, did not remove his intent gaze from the lòhren.

"I don't know. I thought I felt a pulse, but then it was gone. Sometimes, it's hard to find."

Gilhain did not quite believe that. The Durlin had some skill in healing. It was necessary, for they might have to help someone before a proper healer could

273

arrive. There were times when battlefield medicine, the treatments given to a wounded man while the blood spurted from him, later made the difference between life and death. At other times, if not done correctly, the man was dead before help arrived at all.

Gilhain bit his lip. Yet, he saw that Taingern had not stopped feeling for a pulse, and that surely must be a good thing.

The king remained where he was. He took the lòhren's hand, the hand of his old friend. But beyond friendship there was this also – the fate of the city was bound to him. Without Aranloth to lead them, the other lòhrens were no match for the elùgroths. What hope for Cardoroth without him?

9. The Shadow is Rising

The sad music of Bragga Mor trailed away.

"Who *are* you?" Kareste asked.

"I'm a bard," he replied, "A wanderer. A man without a home."

Brand felt sorry for him. He guessed his origin, and if he was right, there was reason for the man's sadness. He sensed also that he had no wish to talk about it.

"Where will you go now?" he asked. "You've made an enemy of the witch."

"She would not be the first. Yet, in this case, I'm in no danger. It's the staff she wants, and if the stories I know about it are true, I can see why. She will follow you and not me. Though I would not care to cross paths with her in the future." The man sighed. "I'll continue to wander, going wherever my horse takes me."

They did not spend long with Bragga Mor. He invited them to eat with him, and they did, enjoying the roasted hare. In return, they gave him some small supply of dried fruit and nuts. Their own provisions were getting low, and Brand knew that soon he must begin to hunt or forage. That would not be easy, and worse, it would take time. And time was something they had little of.

"Know this," Bragga Mor said when they parted. "The Shadow is rising, but ever men contend with it. Even as it is here, so too is it in other places. It never conquers unopposed."

With those words he mounted his steed and rode slowly away. Brand did not think they would meet again, which was a pity: he liked him. Yet the ways of fate and fortune were mysterious, and he sensed, for no reason that he could see at all, but with confident certainty nonetheless, that Bragga Mor had a vital part to play in the future of Alithoras.

"What chance brought him to us?" Kareste asked.

"Who knows, but it was a good chance, if chance it was."

They mounted and rode out of the wood. There was no sign of Durletha, but she would be about somewhere. She would attack them again, Brand knew. Or, more disturbingly, she would set a trap for them. He must be on his guard.

They kept the river close by on their right as they travelled. Day by day it kept them company, for its constant gurgle and splash was like a familiar companion. But they did not approach it too closely. Its banks were lined by trees, and Brand preferred to stay in the open where no ambush could be set.

The weather was good; the grass was green and the sky a brilliant blue. Each day was such a day as made Brand glad to be alive, for Alithoras was a beautiful land and he could never see too much of it.

Where they travelled now was much like his homeland, only here it was empty of people, and the lack of ploughed fields and livestock seemed peculiar. But there was no lack of wildlife, and some of it was strange to him. But he heard often the familiar sounds of *nudaluk* birds, and hares and foxes were everywhere. He saw no deer though, but feed was plentiful at the moment. In winter, they would be drawn closer to the better pastures on the river flats.

They stopped to camp one evening as dusk fell. It crept over the land, and it brought peace with it, as it always did. This was Brand's favorite time of day, and

276

there were few things better than working hard through the daylight hours, and then laying down tools of an evening to enjoy the peace and quiet and to contemplate the day's achievements. But that was a farmer's life, not a warrior's, and he saw no way that he would ever obtain those simple pleasures that he longed for again.

They set up their camp with practiced efficiency, each performing tasks by established routine, and then they sat down and talked.

Brand enjoyed these fireside conversations with her. During the day they were always in haste and their minds were on finding a safe path forward. Also, she only seemed to truly come alive in the evening. She was not a morning person as was he, and she seemed to respond to starlight and night better than sun and blue skies.

Smoke curled lazily upward, soon lost in the dark heavens. The burning timber shimmered with warmth. Coals formed, red-hot gledes that glimmered like precious jewels. There was a pop, and then a spray of sparks, and he realized, quite suddenly, quite unexpectedly, that he was smitten by her. No sparkle of any jewel was as precious to him as a fleeting glance from her eyes.

The realization took his breath away. He could imagine the rest of his life with her. It was not hard to do so. But with a sinking feeling he understood also that she had no such desire. She was caught up in her own troubles at the moment, always deep in thought and of divided mind. She felt for the Halathrin entrapped by sorcery, and a part of her wanted to fight to free them. But another part was lured by the power in Shurilgar's staff. And how much of the former was a dissimilitude of the latter, either her own or of the power in the staff?

He did not know which part of her was the strongest. And there was a darkness in her past, too. She had never openly said as much, but she sought power not just for the sake of it, not just to protect herself, but to take revenge on elugs. Elugs had killed her family and destroyed the life she once knew. And Shurilgar's staff offered a means to wreak dreadful havoc upon them. She had no time for him, and she might yet fall to the Shadow. If that happened she would be lost to him forever, and he felt suddenly cold to the marrow of his bones. But he must give her the freedom to choose, for without temptation there was no certainty of choice. Only the first made the second real.

The smoke curled into the starry night, otherworldly and elusive. All his hopes rode on the whims of a fate that he could not see, just as invisible currents of air took the smoke.

He hoped the king could forgive him, if he was even still alive. But life was one risk after another, one choice piled on top of endless decisions, and if he risked Cardoroth he did so for good reason. Khamdar was right: Kareste had it in her to be great. If she turned to the Light, she could give Alithoras hope. At least, he wished so, just as he hoped that those he respected most in the world would see things the way he saw them. But he was no longer sure if his judgement was sound. Emotion clouded it.

He looked at Kareste and found that she was looking at him.

"Are we doing the right thing?" he asked. "Have I the right to jeopardize a whole city?"

Kareste seemed taken aback by the question. "I don't know," she said at length. "Who is to say what's right or wrong? But I know this much at least – I'm most wary of anyone who *does* have all the answers."

Brand suddenly grinned. "You're dead right there."

The fire popped and cracked. Kareste looked at him, one side of her face lit up by the flames, the other in shadow.

"Why so philosophical?" she asked.

"Aren't I always?" he replied.

She raised an eyebrow. "Actually, most men claim to be, at least when they're talking to girls, but few are. You're one of the few."

He gave a little bow from where he sat, but did not answer.

"So," she said. "While you're in this mood, what's the meaning of life?"

It was his turn to be taken aback. "You might be better off asking Aranloth that. He's lived more of it than I have."

"True. Maybe I *will* ask him one day, but just now I'm asking you."

He looked into the fire. It was dying down to embers. It would not last, and suddenly it occurred to him that nothing ever did. His time with Kareste would come to an end one day, just as this conversation would. The only difference was the time it took. But time was a strange thing. The past was hazy, the future clouded. The only time that counted was the here and now. It was a somewhat depressing thought, and then he thought that even depression and joy were transient.

He smiled sadly. "I don't know the meaning of life. I'm not sure that there *is* one – unless we choose one for ourselves."

"And what have you chosen?"

"To give rather than to take. To enjoy a cold drink after a hard day's work. To follow it with a fine meal, preferably cooked with food I've grown myself. And to see the flashing smile of a girl I like. Most of all, to be kind. There's not enough kindness in the world."

She looked at him a long time. "Many would call that simplistic."

"I'm a simple man."

She grinned at him suddenly. "Then you've fooled me."

"What do *you* think?" he asked. "What's the meaning of life?"

She looked away. "I don't know, but I'll think on what you've said."

10. If only Chance Allowed...

The seconds slipped by. Each one seemed to Gilhain as an hour, but at length Taingern paused in his search for a pulse. The Durlin held two fingers steadily against Aranloth's throat.

"Well?" the king asked.

"There's a heartbeat," Taingern replied. "It's weak, but it's there."

Relief washed through Gilhain, but he shut it down. Whatever ailed Aranloth was so serious as to bring him near to death. And he might still die without proper help. This was no time for emotion, but one for action.

He stood and strode to the nearest soldier. "Quickly!" he said. "Go and fetch the healer Arell. Make sure it's her – not any other will do."

The soldier saluted and ran off.

The king moved back to Aranloth. The Durlin had appropriated a stretcher – there were many being brought up to the wall now to take the dead or injured back into the city. They had laid Aranloth upon it.

"Good," the king said. "But we'll wait here. I've sent for Arell, and she'll know where to find us. I won't trust him to the other healers."

He did not wait for a reply. Quickly, he signaled another soldier over.

"Go to the stone mason's guild. They have their headquarters near the palace. Do you know the building?"

"Yes, my Lord."

"Tell whoever's there that I want their three best experts to meet me here. And I want them as soon as possible. We must make repairs to the wall. Run!"

The soldier did not salute but sprinted away.

Gilhain turned to yet another soldier. "You," he said. "Get me a lòhren."

The soldier glanced at where Aranloth lay on the stretcher.

"Right away, sir."

It was not long before Arell came. She moved without seeming haste, yet her eyes took everything in at a glance and in a moment she knelt beside the lòhren and examined him.

She took the lòhren's pulse at the wrist as had Taingern, only she seemed to take three at slightly different locations. She then took the throat pulse in the same place as had Taingern, but she surprised Gilhain when she removed one of Aranloth's boots and took a pulse at his foot.

She did not give any indication of her thoughts, and Gilhain did not interrupt her. For a moment she pressed her palm over the lòhren's chest, though what she was doing was hard to guess. Then she placed her fingers on his earlobe and gave a sharp squeeze. Aranloth seemed to shrink away from the pain, but he raised no hand to try to brush away the cause. If this worried her she gave no sign, unless it was a slight frown that had not been there before.

She checked his eyes next, tilting his head back and forth to let in more or less light.

During the course of her examination another lòhren arrived. This was a seemingly young man, though it was hard to tell with lòhrens. He wore the same white robes as them all, but his hair was shoulder length and blond. What his nationality was Gilhain could not guess, but he was calm, even after seeing his master lying unconscious on a stretcher.

Arell finished her examination and stood. She spoke to the king, but her gaze strayed to the lòhren.

"He's near to death," she said. "Very near, though I can find no injuries. He may have had a stroke, but the signs in his pulses don't indicate that. My king, I don't know what ails him."

Gilhain thought about that. Healers never admitted that they did not know what was wrong. It was, he thought, her way of saying that not only did she not know what was wrong, but that she knew of no treatment to keep him alive. That was something that must be faced, and given the state of the siege, she knew he must prepare for it.

She looked at the young lòhren. "I don't know of any medical cause for his collapse, but perhaps it has more to do with magic?"

The lòhren gave a slight nod. "If it helps, I can tell you this much. Likely, he expended too much power and exhausted himself. To use lòhrengai takes a great mental effort – it's hard like physical work. And just as a man can work too hard and collapse, so it is with lòhrengai. He has taxed his mind beyond its endurance. Worse, he does not have his staff, which grounds his mind to this world. Now, it may roam other worlds, or other realms beside the physical. It is caught out of time, neither here, nor really anywhere else, though I cannot be sure of the latter."

"And how do lòhrens treat this?"

The young man shook his head. "There's no treatment. We're taught never to let it happen in the first place, unless we're prepared to die. I've never seen this before, but I've heard of it. He might live, or he might die. There's nothing to be done." He paused, showing the first sign of nerves. "I wish there were…"

Arell thought for some moments before she addressed Gilhain again.

"I may be able to keep him alive for a while, at least his body. That may give his spirit, if you believe in such things, time to return."

The young lòhren shook his head. "Without his spirit, the body will wither and die swiftly. At least, so our lore of such things says. Aranloth would know more…"

There was a pause. The king eventually forced himself to ask the question that he did not wish to ask.

"So nothing can be done to save him?"

Arell did not speak. Nor the young lòhren. They had no answers. In truth, Gilhain knew, not all questions had an answer. It was a bitter truth of life.

He dismissed the lòhren, who walked slowly back toward his white-robed comrades. There was no one left but him and Arell.

"Take him to the palace," Gilhain said. "In you I trust, for once you brought me back from the dead. But I'll tell you the truth now. I don't expect any miracles from you – I know you'll do everything you can. If he dies, it won't be through a lack of your trying. But know this: if he *does* die, Cardoroth is unprotected. The elùgroths will be too strong for us."

Arell looked him straight in the eye. "Can we not hold against the enemy?"

Gilhain returned her gaze. "You told me the truth about Aranloth before. Now, I'll tell you the truth about our situation. We cannot hold for long against either the elùgroths or the horde. The rumors that you have heard are true. We sent Brand on a quest. It's the one true hope for Cardoroth. If he fails, we will fall, sooner or later. But know this, the elùgroth lied. Brand is not dead;

at least we don't think so. And hope for Cardoroth lives so long as he does."

Surprisingly, Arell laughed. "I never believed Brand was dead. Many in the city do, but not me. I *know* him. He's hard to kill. If anyone can find a way to succeed in whatever task you set him, it's him."

She called for some soldiers and got them to lift up Aranloth's stretcher. Quickly she gave them instructions on where to go, and she followed after them, a thoughtful but determined expression on her face.

Aurellin came to the king's side. "Will he live?" she asked, straight to the point as she usually was.

Gilhain bowed his head. He made no attempt to hide his feelings from her.

"No," he answered. "Arell will do what she can, but she cannot do the impossible. Neither she nor the young lòhren offered any hope. Aranloth gave too deeply of his power to save us, and he will now pay the price, as he must have known he would."

Aurellin put her arm around him. "Aranloth seldom got the respect he deserved. Always he put his life at risk for others. And if the legends are true, he's been doing that for many lives of men. I've often wondered what drives him, for surely something in his past must do so."

Her gaze followed the departing healer, and then she shook her head. "But it's too early to speak yet of death. Once, Arell saved your own life, and there was then less hope than there is now for the lòhren."

"That's true. But she had Brand with her then. Now, she's alone."

"Perhaps," Aurellin said. "But then again, it was not Brand who effected your cure. She did that herself, and Brand merely saved her from the same assassin that tried to kill you."

He smiled sadly. "Ever the optimist, aren't you?"

"There's no other way to live. Though I suppose some try."

"Well, if you still have hope, then so do I."

She took his hand. "Hope is good, but it can be cheated too. From the moment Brand and Arell met, I thought they were meant for each other. But nothing ever came of it."

Gilhain grinned for just a moment. "Maybe not. But then again he reached out to her and had her teach the Durlin basic healing skills. They've spent much time together, though most of it was hidden away in the Durlin chapterhouse."

"That, I didn't know. Well, perhaps there's hope for them after all."

"Brand has wandering feet though," he said. "There's something in him that wants to explore, to go where he's never been before. I'm not sure if he'll ever settle down."

She pursed her lips. "Maybe. But I don't believe it for a second. He wants to see the land as you said, but he wants more to settle down with a girl. He'd put aside his sword, his fame, all his training and ambition; he'd put aside everything to start a farm – and a family, if only chance allowed…"

Gilhain scratched his chin. "You mean if I set him free of my service."

"That too."

"And what of the Duthenor? Do you think, now that he's grown into a man, that he'll leave the usurper to continue ruling his people unchallenged?"

Her eyes narrowed. "No. You're right there." She paused. "But I see better why nothing has happened yet between him and Arell. I was sure it would, but if so, he would not leave her here while he went home. Nor would he lead her into danger. That explains much, very much indeed. But freeing the Duthenor from tyranny is

286

one thing; ruling them himself is another. He might attempt the first, and if successful, forgo the second. In fact, I think he would. He has no wish to rule others."

"A very interesting observation," Gilhain said thoughtfully. "One that I've also made myself."

Aurellin looked at him sharply. Likely enough, she knew exactly what he was thinking. She usually did.

11. Magic, not Medicine

Arell had time to think as she followed the stretcher-bearers toward the palace. In the distance, the elug war drums began to rumble to slow life once more. She was sick of them. She was sick of many things, but she endured. And endurance had always served her well.

Her beginnings were humble. Her prospects had been poor. And she was too strong willed, too ambitious, to merely use her looks to attract a husband of wealth. Not that she disdained the girls she grew up with who used wiles to attract a partner of influence. The idea had occurred to her too, but something else drove her. She had a thirst for knowledge, and marriage and children would not satisfy her. Not completely, anyway.

That thirst for knowledge took a special form – a desire to understand the human body, to cure illness, to slow aging, to make people's lives better. It was a worthy goal. But a goal, at least in Cardoroth, reserved as the special province of men.

She learned and studied under bearded old healers, never more than a servant to them, never having any real hope of being more than their pretty flunky. But she kept her mouth shut and her eyes open – and learned – and endured. Until one day Brand exposed her master as a fraud and propelled her into the light. For she had learned her lessons well through long years of servitude, and he had given her the chance to save the king's life.

It was a kingly gift, for Brand had earned enemies that day. The bearded old man knew other bearded old men, and they talked and plotted and schemed against him.

But he was Brand, and he smiled at them when he saw them, but he did not turn his back on them.

Now, she wore the white smock of a healer herself, the only female in Cardoroth to do so. Though many still called her a witch behind her back, even those who begged her to heal them when they were sick, she had prosperity and fame. But not respect. Then again, the king respected her, and the queen, and the Durlin. And there was always Brand. There was *always* him. The esteem of a few like that was worth more than the veneration of the masses.

She followed the stretcher-bearers to the palace and the chambers of healing situated within its east wing. These rooms were shared by several healers, those old men she despised so much, but medications and equipment were close to hand.

The rooms could be noisy, for the king paid the healers to see not just to palace staff but every morning and every evening they opened the doors to the poor. And the poor were many, and often in need of treatment.

Barok was there, though he was not busy. He paid her little attention though, until he saw who was on the stretcher. His eyes widened at that, and she could see his mind working and knew where it would take him.

She went into a room. It was empty, containing little more than a bed. What she wished most for was a door though, but there were none anywhere in the chambers of healing. Had there been one, she would have closed and barred it.

Barok followed her inside, as she knew he would. He was in charge of these rooms, and the only healer left because all others now served in rooms close to the Cardurleth. He was going to try to take over, for to heal

Aranloth would win him praise, and praise meant fame and money.

"Gently," she instructed the soldiers as they began to transfer the lòhren from the stretcher to the bed.

"You've done well to bring him here," Barok said.

She raised an eyebrow and shot him a flinty look with the other eye. It was no easy thing to do, and it usually had the desired effect. But Barok had seen an opportunity and he would not be so easily put off.

He ignored her and made ready to commence an examination.

"Out!" Arell said with intense force, but still quietly. "I didn't bring him here so that you could squint at him and pretend you had an idea of what was going on. Out!"

Barok turned. He gave her his own look. It was one of superiority. His pale hands, nearly as white as the smock he wore, were clasped in front of him. He peered down at her, eyes cold as they studied her from above his long beard. It was a look that she had seen him use on troublesome patients, but it had no effect on her.

"Out!" she repeated.

"Don't you think someone of Aranloth's stature deserves treatment from one of Cardoroth's finest healers?" He looked at her, leaving no doubt in his expression that he did not consider her worthy of the task.

Arell had had enough. "The king placed him in my care, and I'll do what can be done." She spoke quietly, her voice filled with icy determination, and it carried an edge of threat. "Speak with the king – if you dare interrupt him while the city teeters on the edge of destruction. If he places Aranloth in your care, so be it. But while we argue, the lòhren's life slips away. Now

290

stand aside, for I'll not tolerate any further delay. Don't interrupt me again except at the king's word."

She made to move past him, but Barok blocked her path.

"I'm in charge here. I'll treat the lòhren. I don't know what the king said, but there are ways of making such pronouncements officially, and I've seen no paperwork nor heard from any messenger. *You* can go and get leave from the king to treat the lòhren. Until then, I'll do what needs doing."

Arell wanted to slap him, but that would not be enough. He was too thick headed for that to work, and time was running out. Instead, she made one swift move and drew a knife from her boot.

The blade gleamed wickedly between them, and she would use it if she had to. If Aranloth died, the city would fall.

Barok looked at her in astonishment, but what he was going to say, she would never know.

Taingern strode past her and before Barok even realized what was happening the Durlin had grabbed him in a headlock and manhandled him out the door. When they were in the corridor, he threw him to the floor.

"Fool!" he said. "That's your message from the king. "And if you step inside this room again, I'll kill you. Cardoroth needs the lòhren, but it doesn't need *you.*"

The Durlin drew his sword to emphasize the point.

Barok scrambled to his feet. This was more than he expected, more even than Arell expected; but it proved the point that Cardoroth was on the edge.

The healer fled, and his dignity went with him, but Arell was already moving to Aranloth as the sound of Barok's retreat pounded away into the distance. Faintly, she heard him yell when he reached somewhere he considered safe: *this is beyond her — the lòhren will die, or worse, she'll kill him with ineptitude.*

She spared Taingern a brief look of thanks as she sheathed her knife.

"Pay him no heed," the Durlin said. "Not for nothing are you the king's own healer. Not for nothing did Brand recruit you to train the Durlin. And not for nothing does Brand speak highly of you."

She gave a little bow. "May I prove your confidence in me."

Once more she examined the lòhren. He was no better, and she knew with the certainty of natural instinct and honed skill combined that no art of medicine could bring him back. They needed magic for that, but it seemed not even the lòhrens themselves could achieve such a thing. If it was possible, perhaps only the greatest lòhren of them all knew how, but he lay silent and dying on the bed before her.

She sat and thought. There were medicines that might make his heart beat faster, for it was slow now, so slow as to be pumping blood at half the rate that it should. No wonder that his pulse was hard to take. But those medicines were no cure. They would buy some time, but time for what?

Taingern sat near her. He did not speak, did not ask questions that would interrupt her flow of thought. She appreciated that. He was a thoughtful and kind man, notwithstanding his earlier violence.

But the more she thought the deeper she sunk in a pool of despair. It swallowed her up, drowned her in hopelessness. It was not enough to prolong Aranloth's life for a day or two. It was not *enough!*

She stood and looked out the window. The city stretched out before her. Her city, and it would fall. Of that, there was no doubt.

Brand was out there beyond it, somewhere in the vast land of Alithoras. He gave her hope. They must endure; they must survive the enemy for as long as they could to give him the time to do what he must do. And only Aranloth had the power to stem the dark tide of sorcery the elùgroths would throw against them. The other lòhrens would fight, and they would die. Against the might of the enemy they would not stand long without their leader.

She must *think*. Medicine was of no avail. Perhaps magic would help, but there was no magic in the city except for the lòhrens, and they had admitted they knew of no way to bring Aranloth's spirit back to his body. But if magic had freed it from the bonds of the flesh, then magic could summon it back. That was only logical. But if not the magic of the lòhrens, then whose?

There were witches in Cardoroth. But they had no real magic, at least so she believed. Their talent lay more in foresight and prophecy. It was too far to go to Lòrenta for more help; Aranloth would be dead before such a journey even began, not to mention that an army barred the way, and the lòhrens left in Lòrenta probably knew no more than the ones here.

Barok's words haunted her. This was beyond her skill. Aranloth *would* die. It made her feel no better that he would die no matter who cared for him. The other healers would fuss and meddle. They would draw blood and prescribe herbs and potions. None of it would work.

She had done what could be done. It was a simple thing. She had positioned him on pillows so that he half sat in the bed. That allowed him to breathe a little better. Soon, she might give him a medicine that would make his heart beat faster. But that put strain on it also, and it came with risks. There was nothing else to be done, and she must face defeat.

293

She looked through the glass window. They were on a lower floor of the palace, but they still had a good view. There were many houses out there. All along the streets were homes where she had healed people. They were everywhere, all the way to the Tower of Halathgar and beyond.

Her mind wandered, and then it focused on the tower. It was distant, but it stood tall and strange. It was a great landmark in the city, the tower of the Witch Queen. The tower of Carnhaina, who had once ruled in Cardoroth. *She* had power. Power beyond an ordinary lòhren. Power enough to rival Aranloth himself. And there were stories of what the queen had done with that power. Arell had read of them in medical textbooks.

That gave her pause for thought. Carnhaina was a battle queen, not a healer. And yet there was a story of some healing that she had done. A distinct image of the book's cover came to Arell, and fragments of the story with it.

She bit her lip and looked at Taingern. There was another story, a story that Brand himself had told her of Carnhaina, though she was long dead and become dust.

"The Forgotten Queen," she whispered. "Carnhaina."

That was all she said, but Taingern's face paled. She read fear in his expression, or perhaps awe, and it was confirmation that Brand's story was true; not that she doubted him, but it was a wild story, a story to frighten even brave men. It was also a story that just now gave her hope. And even if it was a wild hope, desperate and no doubt dangerous, it was still *hope*.

"Let no one into the room!" she said.

She raced away. The corridors were empty, though there were patients in some of the rooms. She saw no sign of Barok, and it was just as well for him. The knife

294

was still in her boot, and she would use it if he got in her way.

She sped up a flight of stairs, taking them two at a time, and then spun around a corner and flung open a door.

Inside was the library of the healers. She knew each book, though there were hundreds. She had read them all, studied them, committed their knowledge to her memory. Much was false, proven wrong by her own experiments, but much was true and valuable.

She headed straight for the book she sought. It was old. Its cover was black, faded to gray. Gold script covered it, and the sign of Halathgar was there as well, the constellation that the Forgotten Queen had taken for her seal.

Arell raced back. She had an idea, but the book would give her the confirmation that she needed. But even if her memory was correct, the look on Taingern's face when she mentioned Carnhaina gave her pause for thought. And, given the story Brand had told her, well it might.

12. Blood Calls to Blood

Arell returned to the room. Even in so little time the fear that Aranloth had already died near paralyzed her.

She stopped running when she neared the entrance. Haste was not a good look for a healer; it inspired a sense of panic, and that was not what patients, or anybody else, ever needed.

She methodically checked the lòhren's pulse again when she returned, and she hid her relief that he still lived as much as she hid her fear that he had died.

"What've you got there?" Taingern asked, gesturing at the book.

"It's old," she replied. "It must have been copied several times, for the language, while stilted, is modern."

She sat down and opened it. For one brief moment she looked at him, noted that his face still seemed pale, and then she put her head down and flicked through the pages.

"It was written in the court of Queen Carnhaina. The author, one Karappe, was a great healer, responsible for many of the treatises that we still use today – but this is more a memoire of his queen's accomplishments."

"That's not a Camar name."

"No. He was a foreigner. "The queen rescued him from a battlefield somewhere when he was a child. He thought of her as a mother, and in a strange kind of way that was exactly what she was to him."

She paused, flicking carefully through the pages. The earlier parts dealt with Carnhaina's ascension to the throne, and then her first battles. She skipped those chapters, seeking one of the last ones where the queen was old. Old, of course, was a relative term. The events in the book had occurred near on a thousand years ago.

She nearly held her breath when she found the chapter that she wanted.

"This is it. It's a little story, one of many the healer tells about Carnhaina. But all his stories serve a purpose."

She paused, and then began to read out a sentence here or there to give Taingern the gist of events.

So it came to pass that the lòhren Gavnor, the least of the lòhrens in Queen Carnhaina's court, attempted to Spirit Walk.

She read on, swiftly passing by much else that was interesting.

At length, the bonds of the flesh were broken; his spirit soared. He saw what was, and what yet may be, and he reported to his queen ... but the enemy discovered him. Thus was he assailed. Pursued by those of greater might, he fled. Chased incessantly, he retreated into the uttermost darkness. There, he lost his enemies. They dared not follow. Yet, in saving himself, he therefore was lost also. Too far he strayed. Too weak was become the link between body and spirit. On the brink his life hovered...

Arell read on. It was clear to her that the healer was reporting things that he did not fully understand, yet it was the essence of his story that counted, not the details.

Gavnor was a favorite of the queen. She desired his service, and not even death would she let prevent it. At great risk to herself...

"Some of this just doesn't make sense," Arell said.

Blood calls to blood she proclaimed. And Gavnor was related to her through her father's line ... Her face was set. No doubt she showed. With a swift motion she cut herself. The small blade, marked with the Sign of Halathgar, cut with ease. Sharp it was. Her palm seemed uninjured, and then her royal blood sprang forth. She that was queen bled like a commoner, but no common act it was: rather it was a deed of nobility ... Red her blood was, and

297

bright, and her Court muttered in astonishment and averted their gazes. She laughed at them, her deep-throated laugh filled with disdain and courage and defiance. She that was as a Queen of the World cared nothing for their petty opinions. Gavnor was of her blood, and she would save him if it could be done.

"There is more like that. Karappe cared little for her court, it seems, though his love of her is plain.

Queen Carnhaina spoke, her voice haughty and prideful as ever. To Gavnor she called, her great utterances ringing through the uttermost dark … And Gavnor, hearing and obeying, came back into the light. Thus did the queen recall her servant; thus did blood call to blood.

"There's more, but that's all that counts."

Taingern looked at her stonily. He knew what she intended, and he did not like it. Yet he did not try to talk her out of it.

"Speak, Taingern. Am I mad, or is there some hope, however slim, in this?"

He sighed. "As Brand obviously told you, we met her once. Her spirit at least. We saved her tomb from a sorcerer. Of that, I'll not speak. But to try to summon her, to summon her by asking the king to spill his own blood, well, that is doubly bold."

"But do you think it'll work? I have here the very words that Carnhaina spoke, and Gilhain is of her line. Blood calls to blood."

"Maybe. But the king has no magic. Then again, I don't think anybody could compel her – with or without magic. If she comes, she'll come of her own choice, and judging from my past experience, anything is possible. But she is not the sort that likes to be summoned, even if it's only an attempt…"

"I'm a healer, Taingern. It's a chance I'm willing to take. It's the *only* chance we have."

The Durlin ran a hand through his hair. "There's a flaw in your plan though, as well you know."

"Yes, I know. The king is of her blood. But Aranloth is not of hers. She may not be able to recall his spirit as she did long ago for her servant. Yet Aranloth is not just any lòhren. And the queen, even in death, has power."

Taingern closed his eyes. What he was remembering, and he obviously *was* remembering something, etched an expression of awe over all his features.

"Yes, she has power. Even in death, she has power. But she's not like Gilhain. They share the same blood, but she is ... she is the *Witch Queen*."

13. The Ancient Past

Gilhain did not expect a let up in the battle. Nor was there one. The horde came again, hurling itself against the Cardurleth, spending its life at the command of the enemy leadership.

And the enemy leadership spent life cheaply. But the horde seemed near endless; no matter how many died, more were sent against the wall. Yet for this much Gilhain could be grateful: there had not as yet been any further sorcerous attacks. Elùgroths had died when their summoning had been destroyed.

He looked down over the battlement. The serpent was still there, twitching now and then in its long death. The enemy must clamber over it when they came to attack, and the reminder of the failure of one of their great hopes would sap their morale. Yet in time the stench of it as it decayed would rise up to the defending soldiers, and it would add yet one more thing to the many that they must endure.

Yet they *would* endure. Pride swelled his heart and tears glistened unexpectedly in his eyes. Everything had been thrown at the defenders, steel and sorcery both, and they still defied the enemy. Live or die, save Cardoroth or fall with it into oblivion, they had earned a place in the history of Alithoras. Their story would be told as long as free people remained in the land.

During lulls the stonemasons worked on the battlement. There were many of them, and soldiers helped also. Bit by bit the Cardurleth took shape again. The merlons were necessary: they offered protection to

300

the archers and soldiers both. Men had died because of their lack, but what the serpent had broken men now repaired. And a will seemed to be growing among them, a spirit that he had never seen before. Nor would he have, for Cardoroth had never been pressed this hard in his lifetime, or for many long generations before.

He saw on the faces of the men a certainty of future death, but he also saw a look of determination. Death would not claim them one week, one day, one hour, nor even one moment sooner than it must. They would fight without stint and bring as many of the enemy with them into oblivion as they could.

Gilhain contemplated the opposing host. The sorcerers who led it must be tired. But so too were the lòhrens. And Aranloth was gone. It was only now that the old man could no longer be seen, leaning on his staff and calmly watching the enemy, that Gilhain realized how much he had leaned on him. He was the king's staff, the crutch for the whole city. And Gilhain missed him.

He felt the small soft hand of his wife slip into his own. She always knew what he was thinking.

They did not speak, but stood watching the enemy as the elug war drums slowed to a near stop, and then began a different beat.

Aurellin tilted her head. "What does *that* mean?"

"I don't know," Gilhain said. "Aranloth would. And I miss him."

"We all miss him. But if he's not here to tell us, then we'll discover it in due course ourselves."

They did not have to wait too long. Within a few moments Aurellin coolly drew the short sword that she had taken to wearing at her side.

"They'll now use what they always hold back – the lethrin."

Gilhain saw straightaway that she was right. The lethrin began to march to the fore of the host. They strode in unison; their towering seven-foot frames dwarfed the elugs. The iron maces they carried were held over their right shoulder, and the precious stones on their black uniforms glinted.

In silence the lethrin strode, singing no marching song nor chanting any war cry, but the stomp of their boots rose up toward the defenders, and it seemed that the ground reverberated with their menacing approach. Fear came before them in a wave, for these were the troops that had taken cities in the past; these were the creatures whose hide-like skin defied edged weapons; these were the shadow-spawned soldiers who slew in silence and made no cry even in death.

They came before the Cardurleth. A hail of arrow shafts greeted them. They bore no shields and wore only silvered mail vests, for they needed little defense. Instead, they now held their maces before them and flicked arrows away with deft movements; too deft for their size, but in these creatures great strength and athletic grace were combined: Gilhain knew that and feared it.

Yet he knew also their weaknesses. Legend spoke of them. Aranloth had discussed it with him. Fire and axes could bring them down.

He gave a signal. Men brought forth vats of oil, stored at the back of the battlement. These they got ready to pour over the wall, and archers prepared special arrows that would be tied with oil-soaked cloth and set afire.

The lethrin ceased their march. They stood ready beneath the wall, but they held no ladders. These were being brought up swiftly behind them now by elugs, and with these ladder-carriers came other elugs. They held wide shields constructed of some sort of metal, though they were thin and easily borne.

This was something new, and Gilhain's mind raced. Swiftly he considered these new things, double the width of a normal shield, and discovered their purpose. They were not foolproof, but they would offer a greater chance to the lethrin climbing the wall. That was where they had often been defeated in the past, for their numbers were never great and by killing them by fire as they climbed the axemen waiting for them would not be overwhelmed. But now this would not work, for the shields would deflect the oil. And it would take many axemen to kill each lethrin.

"We're at risk of being overrun," Gilhain said.

"What's to be done?" Aurellin asked.

"I'm working on it."

At that moment the lethrin did what they had never done before. They raised their heads and in seemingly one voice yelled a single word: *Kardoch!*

Gilhain did not know what it meant. But it filled him with a growing worry. It set the lethrin loose like an arrow sped from a bow and they commenced to run toward the wall. And he still had no plan.

The lethrin were silent once more. Their great strides took them to the base of the Cardurleth, and there, elugs scampering about them, they commenced to climb the ladders brought by their comrades. Up each ladder first went an elug, and each of these lifted one of the strange shields above them. They climbed swiftly for all that they were encumbered, and Gilhain knew they had special straps to help hold the shields to one arm and that also they had spent much time training the maneuver. That could be a good thing, for if they were repelled their morale would sink low. The serpent was destroyed, and if their special surprise method to take the city failed, they would be disheartened.

But Gilhain must first make that happen. And at last he knew what he was going to do. If the oil was of no use thrown over the battlement, he must use it at the top of the Cardurleth itself.

He quickly gave orders and they were carried out all down the defenses to each side.

The lethrin climbed. Up the ladders they came, their long arms hauling them with speed. Their black tunics, trimmed with precious stones, gleamed and sparkled. Their silvered chain mail vests, which left their arms free, glinted. In their mighty hands, though they climbed, they still held their enormous maces.

The defenders were not idle while the lethrin climbed. Some shot arrows or dropped rocks, but these had little effect. Most were repelled by the lead elug on each ladder that held the strange shields. Anything that slipped past them was shrugged aside by the lethrin like an ox merely flicking its ears in annoyance at a fly. But other men carried out a task of greater importance. They ran oil in a line along the entire length of the Cardurleth assailed by the enemy. When they were done, they stepped back.

Gilhain waited. To fire it too soon was to allow the lethrin a warning. To fire it too late was to risk them passing over the lip of the battlement and beyond before the flames took hold.

He gave a signal. A lone horn blew, and men with torches ran forward and dropped them by the score in the oil. Everyone leapt back.

"Now, have hope!" Gilhain said to Aurellin.

The lethrin neared. The shield-bearing elugs came first. Over the rampart they came, and fear came with them for they knew their job was done and that they

304

would die. Yet they were surprised that the defenders had backed away.

Momentarily, hope showed on their faces. Then grim fear again as the flames took to the oil. But the elugs had nowhere to go. The lethrin surged up behind them, forcing them to leap forward like sparkling wine from an uncorked bottle.

The elugs spilled out on the battlement. Flame took them. They screamed. Some tried to jump back over the battlement to end the pain, but the lethrin still drove them forward. There was no retreat that way.

Yet the lethrin paused themselves. They saw the flame, and they feared it. While they paused, men shot at them from only a few feet away with their longbows. Neither their toughened hide nor their chainmail vests were entirely proof against attack at such close range. Some died, but those still coming up from behind pushed them ahead even as these had pushed the elugs.

They jumped through the flames. Their black tunics caught alight. But their great maces rose in their hands and they charged at the defenders.

Gilhain assessed his men. They remained resolute, and pride surged in him. The enemy had thrown everything at them, yet still they held firm. And they held again against the rush of lethrin that now threatened to swamp them.

The lethrin crashed into them, maces swinging, using their size and weight to try to smash all opposition away. But the men fought doggedly, ducking, weaving, avoiding blows and distracting the enemy as best they could while axemen worked their trade.

The axes did little damage, but here and there a lethrin fell. When that happened, they were not allowed up again. It was a grim business.

The battle hung in the balance. The lethrin fought silently. The men fought determinedly. There was no give in either, and yet the fire had not been without effect. It played a small part in the initial rush, but oil splashed up from boots onto skin and clothes. It caught and burned, and it did not go out.

The lethrin began to waver, yet they had driven the men back and soon the enemy would order another charge. If a new wave of attackers reached the wall, the fight would be lost.

Gilhain gave the signal that he had waited for patiently. It was now or never, and it would raise morale and speed the fight, or they were all doomed. He turned to the man behind him, his horn-bearer, who held one of the great carnyx horns. He would lead all the horn-blowers, and all down the line they would blow, perhaps a hundred of them.

The first low note sounded, and the others came to life with it. It was a sound out of the deep reaches of the past, out of the age of heroes. The horns were man high, tall as the tall men who bore them, but they held them up until the brass mouths voiced their unearthly moan twelve feet in the air.

And so unearthly was the slow growing din that thrummed and boomed and bellowed like a wild beast that goosebumps stood out on Gilhain's skin. Here was the same sound that rang in the ears of his ancestors as they fought to survive and eventually found realms. Here was the sound that laid their kings to rest since before Cardoroth was even built, back in the dim days when the Camar dwelled nigh to the lands of the Halathrin, back into even dimmer days before that when they lived on the green plains and in the dark forests west of Halathar.

And the defenders stirred to it. It roiled through their blood. It gave strength to their arms and courage to their

306

hearts. Their axes bit harder. Their eyes burned with the spirit inside them. They fell, but they got up again. They were wounded, but they fought heedless of their injuries. They saw death press at them, but they stared it down.

And the lethrin faltered. This was courage that they had seldom met, and the fire still burned wherever the oil touched them. Their attack wavered, and then for the first time in the history of Alithoras they turned and fled. And the jeers of the defenders went after them.

The enemy horde moaned. Their drums ceased to beat and Gilhain yelled in a high, clear voice. *Cardoroth*!

14. A High Price

For Brand the days passed in a strange blend of ease and tension.

He enjoyed riding with Kareste, but he did not appreciate the feeling of pursuit. Without doubt, the witch was around. If she was as old as she claimed, she would have learned patience if nothing else. He often felt that pinprick tightening of skin on his back that crawled to the top of his scalp – that uneasy sensation of being watched. She was around, and she was waiting, and she would bide her time.

He was confident however that she would not try anything for a while. She did not disturb them, and she made no overt threat. But her presence was a palpable, if remote thing, and he did not like it. It took away from the sense of comradeship that he had with Kareste: that it was just the two of them alone in the wild and beautiful lands of Alithoras.

It was still a peaceful time though, all the more so for the fact that trouble lay ahead. He wanted it to last, to continue and to allow his bond with her to grow, but it would *not* last. Durletha would make another attempt on the staff. Khamdar was likely enough still alive. And ahead of them lay a trial to try to free the Halathrin warriors transformed into fell beasts by dark sorcery.

Each of these things was a challenge on its own that might test them to their limits and defeat them. Together, just surviving seemed an unreachable goal. And behind them all lay Cardoroth and Brand's quest to save it. It felt as though the sky had filled with an ocean of dark water that was about to inundate him forever and draw him into its blackness.

Brand shrugged to himself as he rode. His mistake was to think of these things all together, but in truth they must be broken down and faced one step at a time. Even the greatest challenges could be tackled that way. And right now the only step he needed to concern himself with was finding the Great North Road and the ford that led across the Carist Nien and back into the north of Alithoras.

The river was close by on the right. The long green grass nearby bent low at the touch of a warm wind, and perspiration beaded his face. The river, beyond the band of trees that lined its bank, was a silver ribbon. Long they had followed it, yet they had seen neither its source nor its end. Alithoras was vast, and even Brand, who had seen more than most, realized that what he had seen so far was like a single sand grain on the shores of Lake Alithorin.

"We're getting close," Kareste said.

"How far do you think the witch will follow us?"

Kareste flicked the end of her reins at a fly that kept trying to land on her hand.

"What do *you* think?"

"Well, I guess I know the answer. But I was hoping you'd prove me wrong."

She grinned at him, catching his little barb. "I can be a bit like that."

In truth, he had no hope at all that Durletha would ever give up, but he knew so little about her.

"Is she really as old as she claimed?"

Kareste frowned. "I'm not sure. I don't really know much about her, but there's mention of her in the lore of the lòhrens."

She seemed to consider this as she rode, reaching back in thought or memory to something learned long ago.

"She probably told the truth about her age, but there are others beside her. She's not the only creature of magic that wanders Alithoras, or abides in remote and secret places. There are many powers besides lòhrens and elùgroths, some older and some younger. Some are aligned to the Light, and some to the Shadow, but most stay hidden and pursue their own goals. Some are quite strange, but they do us no harm."

"The world is a strange place," he said.

"Truly," she agreed. She became thoughtful then, and after a few moments chanted softly:

> *Many things lie*
> *Beneath the sky*
> *Beyond the ken*
> *Of mortal men.*

Brand looked at her quizzically.

"It's an old rhyme of lòhren lore," she explained. "There are many such snatches of verse, and there's truth embedded in them."

Not long after they came to the Great North Road. Brand still thought about what she had said of the other powers in Alithoras, and he wondered yet again what her final allegiance would be, to the Light or to the Shadow. He did not really believe in anything in between. And then he began to question himself as he had done ever since they escaped the tombs of the Letharn: was he right not to try to talk to her and influence her decision?

As always, he came to the same conclusion – it was better not to. His best option was to lead by example, if he could. Actions spoke louder than words, and people had a habit of doing the opposite of whatever someone tried to talk them into.

They neared the ford where the road crossed the river. The sun-bleached sky was pale, yet he saw a speck wheeling far away and high up. He had the feeling it was a hawk, that it was Durletha, though of that he could not be sure. It was nothing more than intuition. But Kareste had become subdued, and he guessed that she sensed the same thing that he did.

The rush and gurgle of the ford was loud.

"I'm not sure that I want to cross here," he said.

"Nor I. Yet there's nowhere else."

That was true, but it did not mean that he had to like it.

They moved ahead warily. Here, the trees that usually banded the river gave way to deep drifts of sand and to coarse gravel. And there were boulders and hollowed out pits where rushing water had gouged the ground. It was all in the open, and yet there were many places that people could hide.

The mighty river was wide here, so wide that the far bank seemed a long way away, and yet the frothy water flowed and bubbled as though the riverbed were only a foot or so below its sun-glinting surface. But closer than the far bank, perhaps half way across, was a little island of sand and driftwood. The Great North Road ran straight and true, and there were signs of it even on the island.

Brand was in no hurry. He waited and watched, and Kareste did the same beside him. His feeling of unease grew, though he saw no sign of anything disturbing.

The silence built. The only sound was that of the river, and far away the high-pitched call of the wheeling hawk. Insects flickered through the humid air, drawn to the water, and a fish leaped high and quick in search of a meal, and then dropped back with a splash into the river.

Eventually, there was movement. A man emerged from behind one of the boulders halfway down the slope to the river's edge.

The man was scar-faced and grim. He was tall, his black hair long and lank. His clothes seemed strange, a patchwork of items gathered here and there, none of them clean. A sword was belted at his side, and there was a lump here and there in his clothing where other weapons were likely hidden. Beneath thick brows his eyes were narrow and dark. Brand read meanness there, or worse, but the man tried to mask his natural features with a pretense of friendliness.

"Well met, fellow travelers."

Brand inclined his head slightly, but he did not take his eyes off the man.

"Hello," he said in a voice that was friendly but not especially encouraging of further conversation.

"Where are you going?"

"Just passing through," Brand answered. He was attempting to be as short as he possibly could without being rude. He did not wish to start anything here, but he knew that the choice of that was not likely going to be his.

The man showed a flicker of irritation, but he soon covered it. His strategy, and Brand *knew* it was a strategy, was to lull suspicion by friendly talk. He was not alone. Others remained hidden, and there was going to be trouble.

"Perhaps you have some food to share with someone who hasn't eaten in days?" The man said awkwardly. He had been forced to come to the point more quickly than he wished.

312

Brand had seen the starved and the hungry before. Faces came to him out of the past, before he had come to Cardoroth. This man was neither of those things. Still, generosity was never a bad thing, and he would do whatever could be done to avoid a fight.

"A little," he answered, with a quick warning look to Kareste. "We're willing to share what we have."

"Then come down by the river," Scarface said. "It's cool near the water."

There was a pause, and Brand made no move. "Come up and join us."

Scarface did not answer. There was a longer pause this time, and his expression slowly changed. The pretense of friendliness dropped away as he realized that he had not fooled the two travelers.

"Come out, boys," he said over his shoulder. "They're on to us. Not that it'll help them."

Men came out of their hiding spots. Some were concealed in the declivities; some behind boulders. Several even emerged from the water. They would have been set there as a last resort in case the riders sped through before any trap could be properly sprung.

Brand noted that some of the men *did* indeed look hungry. But not Scarface, nor those who came to stand closest to him. Some were well armed and dressed, but he was pleased that none carried bows.

Scarface spoke when his men had gathered around him.

"It's food we want, but we'll take everything else as well." His grin turned to a leer when he looked at Kareste.

Brand wondered what the man would think if he knew of the massive diamond that was stashed away in one of his saddlebags. It was a kingly gift from Gilhain; and a gift that Brand had no intention of losing to the

313

likes of Scarface and his men. Yet he and Kareste must cross the ford.

In the silence that ensued, Scarface spoke again. "Most especially, I like your helm and sword."

Brand looked at him coolly. When he answered, his voice was neutral. He did not wish to provoke anything here if it could be avoided.

"Both those items come at a high price."

Scarface laughed. "I have men enough to help me pay. More than enough."

Brand studied them with a casual glance. "No, you don't."

15. It will be a Long Night

The carnyx horns sang their unearthly song. It ran through Gilhain's blood and made him feel young again. The retreat of the enemy buoyed him, and he held Aurellin's hand. It was good to be alive, and though there could be no such thing as winning the war against an enemy that overpowered them, no one and nobody could take away this victory, no matter that it would be short lived.

He felt a sense of overwhelming love. Aurellin's hand in his felt warm and soft, and it was a bridge for the love that existed between them. They needed no words, no glance, and in truth did not even need to hold hands to express their feeling for each other. Gilhain felt it in the very air around him just by her presence, and he knew that she felt the same. But it was still nice to hold hands.

"They'll come again. And soon," she said softly.

"I know," he answered. "I would do the same in their position. They cannot let their troops ponder the defeat of the lethrin for long – that would sap morale. They must now throw everything they can against us to distract their own from defeat, and to show us that no matter how many times we throw them back, they'll come again. By doing that they'll sap our own morale."

Aurellin nodded. "But is it possible to undermine the morale of an army that already acknowledges its ultimate defeat, and fights anyway?"

Gilhain considered that. It was a good question. While he thought, he saw the first movements of the enemy.

315

"That, we shall soon see," he replied.

Aurellin did not answer. She watched as did he, as did all the defenders, while a great wave of elugs came from the horde and surged toward the wall. Fear came before them, and among them were some of the lethrin who still lived, shamed by their earlier retreat and eager to regain their prestige as invincible warriors. But the defenders now knew that they were not, and fighting was always played out in the mind before ever a blow landed.

The enemy crashed against the wall. The war drums thrashed. Up the elugs climbed; down were cast rocks and spears, and swift were the hissing arrows of the archers dispensed.

On came the enemy. Ladders were toppled. Climbing ropes were severed. But still they came in a seething mass, intent on reaching the top and destroying all that Gilhain loved.

The enemy crested the Cardurleth like a flood. Driven by sorcery or fear, compelled by their masters, they would not retreat this time. Either they were killed, or all would fall beneath their onslaught.

The men met them. Sword crashed against sword. Cries filled the air. Red blood flowed, and the glint of weapons flashed like a thousand wicked suns.

The great maces of the lethrin smashed all before them, but they were few and the elugs many. Yet the many filled the gaps the few provided, and together they pushed back the defenders, inch by inch.

There was no respite. There was no mercy. Even in the long course of the siege there had never been a fight as this: desperate beyond desperation, filled with a vicious kill or be killed attitude that made all else that had gone before it seem as a game.

The enemy seemed possessed, and well they might be. Gilhain wished that Aranloth were here, but he was not.

316

A quick glance along the Cardurleth showed that the lòhrens held back. If this fight was going to be won by the defenders, force of arms and courage of heart alone would achieve it.

The noise was deafening. Cries of fear and pain melded with the clash of blades and the tramp of boots. Over and above that the elug war drums vied with the carnyx horns. The din of it all together was hideous.

But the horror before Gilhain's eyes was worse. The stone was thick with gore. There seemed to be so much that it looked like the heavens had opened and rained blood. And through it were severed limbs and dead bodies and the innards of men and elugs spilled into the bright sunlight. The slaughterhouse of the Cardurleth was grotesque.

But the smell that assaulted his nose was perhaps even worse. He retched. The stench was near overpowering, and battle-hardened though he was, he had not experienced its like before.

Yet beside him Aurellin looked on, her face a mask that hid her feelings. He *knew* she felt as he did, but there was steel in her. And whatever she felt she kept it in one part of her mind and allowed another to assess the battle dispassionately. And so must he.

Things hung in the balance. No battle could long continue at this ferocity. One side must soon gain the advantage. And the defenders were being pushed back. More and more elugs came to the wall, and when one fell, two took its place. Yet the lethrin, now few in number, were not immune to death. They fell and died, though it took many men to bring them down. While the men did this, the elugs gathered about them in their turn and killed them.

Gilhain wondered what he could do next. Had the time come to wield his own blade? Could he rally the defenders by joining the fray? Yet there was risk in that, for the enemy would be drawn to him like moths to a flame: if they killed him the heart would go out of the defense.

He fingered the hilt of his sword. Then Aurellin put a hand on his shoulder.

"Wait," she mouthed, for her voice would not carry above the screaming mayhem of battle.

He followed her gaze, for though her hand was on his shoulder she did not look at him.

A large man caught his eye. He was part of a group that surged forward against the enemy. But the group was soon hammered down by the broad sweeps of a lethrin mace and the quick stabs of elugs that darted in and out, swords flashing, in their massive companion's wake.

But the man had not fallen. Alone now, and nearly as massive as the lethrin, he strode forward, his eyes bent on his great adversary with grim determination.

Gilhain did not know who the man was. He was just an ordinary soldier. But there was an air to his movements, in the intent look on his face, that signaled that something extraordinary was about to happen, and the hair prickled all the way up the back of the king's neck.

The man threw down his blade. It rang against the stones and shattered. Hundreds of eyes turned to him, and hundreds more when his mighty voice boomed out.

"Fight me!" the big man called, and his challenge rose above the mad din of the battle.

The elugs darted in to kill him, but he shrugged them aside, his mail protecting him from the worst of their blows.

He went straight for the lethrin. The lethrin raised high his mace. As a thunderbolt it fell, hurtling through

318

the air, but the big man was quicker than he looked. With a slight move, only just enough, he stepped to the side. The mace smashed into the stone and sent chips flying, but the big man was moving again.

Incredibly, the lone soldier reached out with his meaty hands and grappled with the lethrin. One hand pinned the arm that held the mace, the other gripped the creature's throat like a vice.

There the two of them stood and strained against each other. The elugs began to land blows against the man, but he ignored them. And then an archer let fly arrows that sang through the air and stuck in several elug throats in the space of two heartbeats.

The elugs hunkered down. The man and the lethrin continued their struggle alone. The great creature tried to raise his mace, but the man held his arm pinned with a strength that Gilhain did not think a man could possess. All the while the breathing of the creature grew labored, and what air it could get whistled in loud rasping gulps down its throat.

The lethrin hammered his other arm against the man, smashing his fist into head and body, but the helmet and mail offered some protection, and grimly the man endured the blows. Soon the lethrin turned instead to trying to prize away the death grip from his throat, but nothing loosed it.

Eventually, the lethrin dropped the mace. He could not bring it to bear, but by letting go of its great weight he now had a better chance to lift up his pinned arm. This he did, slowly but surely, reaching up to try to break the grip that suffocated him.

But the man, not quite able to match strength for strength, was not done yet. He swiftly changed his grip, letting go of both throat and arm, and then in one swift motion he shuffled closer and took the lethrin in a bear hug.

There the two combatants stood. The man tightened his grip. The lethrin rained mighty blows upon him with both fists. Bright blood ran from beneath the soldier's helmet, and then the helm flew loose from his head revealing a shock of red hair and a battered face, swollen and cut.

The two of them staggered back and forth beneath the strain of the forces they brought to bear.

"Watch!" hissed Aurellin.

Gilhain could not have taken his eyes off the scene even if he had wanted to, but he felt the first inkling of an idea of what would happen next, just as had she, and time seemed to slow.

The lethrin drove the man back a step, but the man was not beaten. As he retreated he sunk his weight lower, and then, incredibly, beyond the anticipation of all but a few, he heaved the lethrin off the ground.

There he stood a moment, his legs near buckling under enormous strain. The battle all around had ceased and it seemed as though the struggle between the opposing masses was now centered on the two combatants alone.

And then the man staggered forward, still holding the lethrin above the ground, ignoring the blows landed upon him by the desperate creature.

He tottered forward, his grip unbreakable, and drove the lethrin into a section of the battlement wall that was not yet repaired.

The lethrin ceased his useless striking and took the man in a headlock. For just a moment, as the creature's arms moved, Gilhain glimpsed the beaten face of the soldier. It was a bloody mess, and the flesh around the

320

eyes had swollen so much that Gilhain doubted the man could even see any more.

There the soldier stood for several long moments. The stonework crumbled. A crack ran through it, and all the while the man not only held the lethrin up, but also continued to drive forward with his failing strength.

With a final heave the man pushed the lethrin through the crumbling wall. He knew what would happen. He knew, and the lethrin soon realized it. The massive creature screamed, perhaps the first of his normally silent kind to voice terror atop the walls of a besieged city.

Slowly, surely, inexorably they tumbled over together, locked in their embrace. The man was silent. The fear-filled bellow of the lethrin invoked a sense of sympathy – even among the defenders. But Gilhain's thoughts were mostly of the brave soldier, now slipped from sight. Who was he? Was he married? Where had such courage come from?

But Gilhain knew the battle hung in the balance, and he had no time for sentimentality. The soldier had chosen his own time to die, now Gilhain must use that sacrifice to save his people a little longer, for he saw now how it could be done.

The battle had come to a standstill. Men, elugs and lethrin stood in shock. Gilhain was the first to act. He signaled quickly for the carnyx horns to start again – they had fallen silent. But without waiting he leaped toward the enemy taking all by surprise, even the Durlin who stood near.

His great sword swung. Blood flowed. Elugs died, and he cried *Cardoroth!* at every stroke of his blade. The defenders saw their king smite the enemy, and they followed suit. Courage swelled their hearts, and dismay fell upon their opponents. They could not believe what they had just witnessed, and they could not rally.

The defenders drove into them. They pushed them back. The windrows of dead and dying lay thick on the battlement; the living were caught between a plunging death behind them and a storm of flashing blades ahead of them.

The king was not alone. Aurellin was with him, her own short sword slicing and stabbing, and around them, trying their best to protect them, were the Durlin.

The white surcoats of the Durlin were stained with blood. But none of it was theirs. They slew with skill and speed that astonished even Gilhain, and the enemy fled before them, fighting among themselves to find the ropes and climb down the battlement to safety.

But the ropes were few, and elugs were climbing up them from below. None escaped that way. The swords of the defenders cut them down until none were left save those starting to climb, and these began to turn and flee.

Gilhain looked along the Cardurleth. It was the same elsewhere. The enemy had been routed once more, and yet it had come at a price.

Men hurled the dead bodies of the elugs over the wall. They piled down below, burying the serpent. Gilhain wondered if the enemy intended to build a ramp of their own dead in order to reach the top of the wall. They had the numbers to do it. But in any civilized war, if there was such a thing, the besieging army would take away their dead at prearranged times without fear of being shot by arrows. But the enemy had made no such request of Gilhain. Rather, their leadership preferred to use the stench as a weapon, hoping to make the defenders uncomfortable, no matter that it did the same to their own soldiers and provided a breeding ground for disease.

But the enemy dead were not the only ones. Brave soldiers of Cardoroth had died also – by the hundreds. There were too many to be taken away all at once, and the dead lay there, their eyes vacant, and in their exhaustion the defenders who yet lived sat down beside them. At times it was hard to tell who was alive and who was dead. And though they had just now won a great victory, it could not go on like this indefinitely. Cardoroth was a big city, but it could not match the enemy soldier for soldier. They must not take so many losses in the future.

All the while the wild carnyx horns had been blowing. If they were eerie before, they were more so now in the sudden silence after the enemy's retreat. Now, however, the horns took up a new note. It was only a subtle difference, but there was in it a hint of victory. And well the army deserved it; they had fought for it and it was pleasing to see the enemy, a disorganized mass, heads low, officers barking orders, faces sullen and most of all – the hateful elug war drums gone quiet.

The enemy host was at its lowest ebb yet. Had he the numbers, Gilhain would have ordered a sortie, for there was no better time than now to strike.

He sighed. He did not have the numbers. Instead, he must simply watch as the enemy regrouped and then came back at them again. But at least the defenders would have that same time as a respite.

He leaned on his bloody sword, Aurellin standing near. There was still a fierce look on her face, and after all these years she still surprised him. There was steel in her; that he had always known, but it was a thing of the mind and not of the body. At least so he had thought. Yet she had propelled herself into the fray and wielded her blade with ferocity. She had no great skill, yet she had killed, and the sight of her fighting beside their king had lent strength to the defenders.

There was a noise in the silence behind him. Taingern had returned. His face was grim, though whether because of what he saw atop the Cardurleth or for news of Aranloth, Gilhain did not know.

"You look tired," Taingern said.

Gilhain cleaned his sword on a rag. "It's been a long day."

Taingern looked him in the eye. "I'm sorry, my King, but it will be a long night also."

Gilhain sheathed the blade. "How so?"

"Arell has discovered a way to attempt a healing of Aranloth."

"What way is that?"

Taingern's gaze did not falter. "You won't like it."

16. The Forgotten Queen

They were atop the tower, the Tower of Halathgar, the Witch Queen's tower, and Gilhain felt uneasy.

The attacking horde had withdrawn to lick its wounds when dusk fell. Their campfires sprang to light, the vast host gathering in and enveloping itself in its pain.

They were unnaturally quiet, for their great attack of sorcery had been foiled – the serpent lay dead, or still dying, and the great charge of the lethrin had been repulsed. Yet the leadership, both sorcerers and shazrahads, those strange men from the south, would work through the night. Tomorrow, the host would attack again. And if their confidence had diminished, it would grow again over time. In a day, or a week, the enemy would be ravening for blood once more.

But for a time, Gilhain could put that concern aside. For a few brief hours something else would hold his attention. And though there were no armies up here at the summit of the tower, though there would be no fighting, what was about to happen was just as important as any battle played out on the Cardurleth. Possibly more so.

It was dark. Yet the crows in the trees croaked and flapped their wings. Perhaps the men holding flaming torches disturbed them. Perhaps it was something else.

Gilhain looked out over the parapet. He could see little of the park where the trees grew; shadows lay thick over it like drifts of black fog. Like fog, the shadows moved too. Or something within them did, but it was too far away and too dark to see.

Further away he saw the torch-lit city, for here at the top of this tower he was high, high enough to feel a cool breeze blowing against the cold sweat that slicked the skin of his face. There was no breeze down below.

He heard a muffled curse. "Careful," Arell said to the Durlin who carried Aranloth's stretcher.

It had been hard work to get the stretcher all the way up the stairs, for there were few people here. Gilhain wanted it that way, and all that he allowed were the Durlin, himself, Aurellin and of course Arell. They all spoke in hushed tones. Some knew what was to be attempted up here, but even those who did not sensed that something strange and unusual was in the air.

Gilhain smiled to himself. Strange and unusual did not even begin to cover it. Carnhaina, better known as the Witch Queen, sometimes called the Forgotten Queen, was his foremother. Near on a thousand years had passed since her rule of Cardoroth, and though the general population had forgotten her except for a few strange stories and ballads that were told late at night in inns, his family had not. She was venerated by all of his line, and every subsequent king or queen of Cardoroth had lived in her shadow, for she had achieved great things. And now, more than ever, he felt unworthy of his heritage, for it seemed likely enough that the city would fall despite his best efforts. And it was not remembered that Carnhaina was forgiving.

Gilhain glanced over at the sarcophagus that held her remains. Few knew that this was her resting place, here in her tower atop its parapet, beneath the light of the constellation of bright Halathgar. He fingered the hilt of the knife he carried, the same one that he had given to Brand, the same one that the elùgroth had hurled at him. It was marked with the constellation, marked with the queen's sign.

326

He looked at Aranloth on the stretcher. His face was gray, and he was near death. The crows flapped raucously in the trees. Taingern was somber and distant.

Taingern. He was a man who had been here before, and he had an idea of what to expect, assuming that anything at all would happen. Gilhain had been here himself; there were certain rituals involved in the coronation of a king, and though that was long ago he remembered it well. Yet the queen had never appeared to him. But she *had* appeared to Brand and Taingern, had summoned their help to thwart a sorcerer who would rob her tomb. Would she appear now? Was there merit to Arell's wild scheme? Was there truth in the dim legend that had come down from his forefathers that Carnhaina, even in death, guarded the city and that she would return in its darkest hour? He would soon find out, but what he knew of her, what he had learned from Brand, made him wonder if he wanted her to appear at all.

He steeled himself. He must do this for Aranloth's sake. And for Cardoroth as well, whatever his personal fears.

"It's time," Aurellin whispered in his ear.

Gilhain stirred. He saw that Arell was looking at him. The stretcher was laid out next to the sarcophagus. The Durlin had stepped away.

Gilhain walked forward. He gave a sign and Taingern used a metal bar to lever, ever so carefully, the stone lid off the casket.

Stone grinded on stone. The crows flapped and cawed, some taking clumsily to the air to circle the tower.

It seemed to take forever, but eventually Taingern was done and the lid was moved half off. There he stopped, and the king noted that the Durlin did not look inside.

Gilhain hesitated, and Arell came to his side. She must have sensed what he would keep hidden. "There's no other way," she said.

He nodded and suppressed his fear. *That* he could overcome, but the thought that Carnhaina may hold him responsible for the looming fall of her city was something that he could not suppress. And well she might hold him so, and such a rebuke might break him.

He drew the knife. Her knife. The blade that had come down through long generations to him.

He stepped closer to the sarcophagus. The breeze died, and the crows grew still. Stars glittered overhead with a cold light. He looked over the stone edge and gazed within.

He saw bones; pale in the starlight, broken and fragmented. The flesh of the queen's body, laid to rest in antiquity, had decayed to dust. The skull, white and stark, glared back at him; under its dislodged jaw rested a torc, its twisted gold gleaming bright. Jewels and coins and rings and treasures of a lost age winked at him, colder than the stars.

"Hear me," Gilhain said. His voice was a croak, and the words seemed empty high up at the top of the tower, almost as though the dark night all around swallowed them.

"Hear me!" he said, suddenly loud. "I, Gilhain, King of Cardoroth, have come. I, who am descended from thy line, seek audience. I, Gilhain, summon thee!"

With a deft move he held up the palm of his left hand and sliced with the blade in his right. He did it quickly, else he knew he would have trouble to do it at all.

He felt nothing, but the blade was sharp and in a moment his bright blood flew. It spattered over the bones and the skull. Then the pain began. It stung, and

328

then it ached, and then it sent a stabbing pain through him. He ignored it.

"Hear me, Carnhaina! Hear me, my Queen! I summon thee. Blood calls to blood. Come, for Cardoroth needs you. Hear me, and come!"

He ceased speaking. It was deathly quiet. Nothing happened. The pain in his palm grew. It throbbed. He felt it like a creeping thing that gripped his hand and squeezed, and then it moved up his arm and to his whole body until he trembled in agony.

The crows in the park now clamored madly, and the cold breeze fluttered to life once more. The dust at the bottom of the sarcophagus, that once had been living flesh, seethed. An ethereal shape formed and rose in a swirl of color and Gilhain and Arell stumbled back.

The vision of a woman stood tall and stately before them. She gazed at those atop the tower, her eyes terrible and stern. They were blue, a deep and cold shade that Gilhain had never seen before, but her skin was pale and freckled, and her unbound hair shone like spilled blood. Wild curls, thick and lustrous, ran down the length of her back and shimmered at the touch of the night-dark air.

She was a massive figure, heavy-boned, thick-limbed and large-jawed. The gold torc he had seen in the sarcophagus gleamed brilliantly about her neck, and about her body was cast a cloak of many colors. In her right hand she grasped an iron-headed spear as though ready to strike.

Her cold stare bored into Gilhain. "Who dares wake me?"

Gilhain bowed. As king, he bowed to none, but he could not help himself, such was the awe that mantled her.

"I, Gilhain, King of Cardoroth, Lord of the Camar, Ruler of the North—"

329

"Halt!" the queen commanded. "I know you and have heard those titles before. Once I bore them, and others beside. But when you are dust you will learn how empty they are. Speak! Why have you dared to disturb me?"

Gilhain grew in confidence. He had not summoned her, he had not the power. But she had come anyway, and she sought to hide the fact that it had been willingly. Thus he believed that it was possible that she might help.

"Cardoroth is in great need. A host besieges us—"

"This I know. I am dead, but I am not stupid."

Gilhain was unprepared for this. That Carnhaina had been a difficult woman in life, he knew. But how to deal with her, how to deal with a long-dead spirit and try to negotiate her help, was beyond even his wide experience. Still, he straightened and spoke with directness.

"The city will fall. Elugs we can, perhaps, withstand. But not sorcerers. Lòhrens we have on the walls, but the greatest of them lies dying beside you. His spirit is sped from his body, and I would have you call him back. Without his aid, Cardoroth is lost."

Carnhaina did not look at Aranloth. She knew he was there. She knew why they had come. She knew each of them atop the tower and read their innermost hearts. She exchanged a brief look with Taingern, and a smile flashed from her eyes, and then in an instant she was stern again.

Her glance fell on Gilhain once more and he shivered.

"Plans rarely run true," she said. "You see the death of Aranloth as your greatest problem, but what if I told you that Brand has obtained the second half of Shurilgar's staff? What if I told you that he has not destroyed it, and now the Shadow comes for him? All now stands in jeopardy, and even if Aranloth lived he could not help the greater cause."

That hit Gilhain as a blow, but he did not hesitate to answer.

"Maybe so, yet still could he help Cardoroth, and I would have it so!"

She raised an eyebrow at him, and he did not think she was dissatisfied with his answer. For the first time she looked at the lòhren, and her face was unreadable.

Surprisingly, it was Arell who spoke. "Why hasn't Brand destroyed the staff? He wouldn't betray us, so there's some reason you haven't said."

The queen's glance fell on the healer, but Arell returned the cool gaze without flinching.

"He seeks now to save a soul. One soul while a city of people is on the brink. Once, I would have called such an act wrong. Now, I do not know. But I will tell you this – he seeks to save the soul of a girl. He travels with her. Does that upset you?"

Arell did not answer, and Carnhaina spoke into the silence.

"Yes it does. You see much, but I see more. You cannot hide your thoughts from me. You would be with him in her stead. And truly, that might be better for Alithoras. But not even the dead see all ends."

Carnhaina dropped her gaze down to the stretcher and looked at Aranloth again. The breeze gusted and flared her hair in a shimmer of red, but the queen gave no sign that she felt it.

"Have you considered," she said, turning back to Gilhain, "that of all who ever lived, Aranloth has most need to die – to leave toil and struggle and sorrow beyond endurance behind? Anyway, it is of no matter. I cannot recall him."

Gilhain was dismayed. It must have showed on his face, for his foremother looked at him and raised an eyebrow.

331

"This surely you knew? He is too far gone. The blood of kin recalled me, but the lòhren is not related. Blood alone is not enough. It would take more, much more than blood for me to even attempt it."

A cold feeling settled in the pit of Gilhain's stomach. Aurellin tensed beside him.

"What *would* it take?" The words were a dry whisper in his throat.

"When blood does not suffice, a life might avail. But not any life. It must be the sacrifice of a king."

Gilhain did not move. He had known that was coming, as had Aurellin. And both of them knew what his answer would be. She said nothing and did not try to dissuade him. She merely put her hand in his and squeezed. It was such a small movement, but he felt a world of love in the gesture, and it was all he could do to stifle the tears ready to spring to his eyes.

There was utter silence. He gave Aurellin's hand a squeeze of his own, and then reluctantly let go and took a pace forward. He did not speak, but turned around the knife he still held in his hand and offered it to Carnhaina, hilt first.

The queen looked at it curiously. And then she laughed. Gilhain wondered if she was not a little mad. She made no move to take the blade, but suddenly she stood taller and the smile left her face. Terrible and stern she seemed. Her fingers gripped tight the spear shaft that she held in her right hand. She looked up at the sky, and Gilhain knew she was looking at Halathgar, that constellation of two bright points whose semblance she must have seen on the knife. He guessed it was his imagination, but it seemed to him that the light of the real stars glittered in her eyes and sparked off the iron-tipped spear.

A moment she stood like that, and he did not move. The Durlin, however, stepped closer. With a glance at Taingern he stilled them. His life, for the possibility of Aranloth's, was a good exchange.

A wispy cloud dimmed the starlight, and a shadow passed over the top of the tower. He blinked, and when he looked at Carnhaina again he found that she was gazing at him, and her face was unreadable.

"You are a fit king," she said. "Thus do you pass the test. Put the knife away and watch, for I am Carnhaina, and once the world trembled at my power!"

The queen leaned forward, and she reached through the stone of her sarcophagus as though it were not there. With the tip of the spear she pricked the lòhren's flesh twice. Two bright spots of blood blossomed on his robes near his heart.

The air grew chill. Cold starlight glittered on the blood-wetted spear-point. It gleamed on Carnhaina's torc. Her eyes grew fierce, and her meaty hands wrapped around the ash-wood shaft.

"Aranloth!" called the queen. "Hear me, lòhren. Hear me, priest of the Letharn who are gone. Hear me, prince of the race who are no more. Hear me, and come!"

Thus she stood, spear in hand, and her eyes flashed with power. Yet Aranloth did not move. The blood darkened on his robes, and the queen hissed.

She raised her arms high, and the star-shadow of the spear leapt from the parapet and into the night. "Come!" she commanded, and even Gilhain, who possessed no magic, felt the force of her will. It thrummed through the tower and reached out, out into the night, out over all the land and into an oblivion so vast that he recoiled from the sense of it.

But Carnhaina did not recoil. She was one with it. Her voice filled it, and her mind encompassed it, seeking the spirit of the one she called.

Gilhain shook his head. This was more than he expected, perhaps even more than what Carnhaina herself had expected. He had been willing to give his life to recall the lòhren, but now he wondered if any force on earth had that power.

17. The Head of the Snake

Brand did not move. But at a signal from Scarface his men drew their weapons and spread out. The situation was clear: the trap of the bandits had failed, but likewise the two travelers were mounted; they could retreat at any time – unless there was some reason they must cross the ford. And obviously they still intended to, otherwise they would already have turned and galloped away.

Scarface smiled, and Brand felt a sudden wave of intense dislike for the man. Yet he pushed it down. There might still be a chance of getting through this without a fight.

"There are only two of us," Brand said. "But we're mounted. If it comes to a fight, blood will be shed. And some of it will be yours. That is certain. But if it's food you want, we're willing to share what we have. No blood need be spilled. No harm need be done to anyone."

Scarface smirked at him. "The more you talk, the more I know that you need to cross. I don't know why. Perhaps there are other men after you, though I had thought the wild lands south of the river empty of people. But all that really matters is that you want to cross, and you will need to pay to do so."

Brand spoke calmly. "There will be a price paid by you as well. But there—"

"Enough!" Scarface yelled. "Turn and flee. Otherwise, lay down your sword and helm. And leave your horse behind. That way, if you're so concerned about our welfare, you can avoid bloodshed. We promise to let you walk away, free and with your life, but the girl will stay with us."

Brand looked at them all coolly. He knew their type, but there was some darker shadow on them. Something drove them, and his glance flicked to the dot that wheeled in the sky. He understood what was happening, and though these bandits were murderers, he did not doubt that the will of the witch was also on them. There was no way forward without a fight. Men might die, but he must avoid that at all costs. He must show mercy and use his skill only as a last resort. The eyes of all these men were on him, but so too was the silent gaze of Kareste. He must show her that there were better ways than violence, that the darkness in the hearts of men did not always prevail.

He did not speak to Scarface, but to his men. "This is no way to live," he said, "to waylay travelers and accost women. If your leader doesn't see sense, then get yourself a new leader. You can have food for free, but everything else will cost you blood, and some will die. Is it worth it?"

The men did not answer. They looked at him darkly, and once again he felt the will of the witch at work. Without her, without Scarface among them, these men might have seen reason.

"You have your answer," Scarface said.

Brand had tried reason. Now, he would try threat.

"It's not too late to back away. Leave now while you can. I can fight. I can fight well, and I wear armor and wield a sword the likes of which you have never seen."

He drew his blade. The pattern-welded steel shimmered in the bright light, and he heard several gasps. These men would not have seen a Halathrin-forged blade before, but they still recognized it.

336

"I'm no ordinary warrior. I have skill beyond anything you have encountered. If you come against me I will kill you, each and every one. I do not say this to boast. I say it to save your lives. Stand aside and let us pass, and live another day."

A few of the men wavered, but not enough. Many looked to Scarface, but he stood there, sure of himself, hatred burning in his eyes. The band made no move to part.

Brand dismounted and handed his reins to Kareste. She looked at him strangely, but said nothing.

The Halathrin blade gleamed in his right hand, and he placed Aranloth's staff on the ground with his left.

"Even yet, it's not too late," he said. "I'll fight your leader, one on one, and you'll see that it's better just to let us pass. There need be no more blood shed than that."

Scarface laughed. "The only blood to be shed will be your own."

Brand looked at him coldly. "That's easy to say, surrounded by your men. Step away from them and face me."

Brand was trying his hardest to keep things just between him and Scarface. The leader was the head of the snake, and if he was killed the rest would lose heart. But Scarface knew it too. He spat contemptuously, and with an abrupt gesture signaled his men forward.

Kareste spoke for the first time. "Kill them, Brand. You've tried everything else, now kill them all."

The men paid her no heed, but her words made Brand tremble. They were cold. Colder than he had ever heard her speak before, and he knew that he must still try to avoid bloodshed. He must do something special here, but it would come at great risk.

337

Brand smiled at the men who stepped slowly toward him. They followed their orders, but they were in no hurry. It gave him time to reach into his saddlebag and pull out the diamond Gilhain had given him. He casually dropped it on the ground at his feet. It shone and sparkled, and the men stood still, their shocked silence absolute.

But Kareste was not so quiet. A gasp escaped her lips, for she had travelled far with him and never knew that he carried such a great treasure.

Now was the moment to act, and Brand timed it to perfection. He waited for the nearest man to blink before he moved. It was the smallest of advantages, so small that an ordinary warrior could not make it work for him. But he was Brand of the Duthenor, and his skill had been honed since childhood and ripened by his service as bodyguard to a much-threatened king.

One moment he stood there, the sword held loosely in his hand, and the next he sprang forward and bridged the gap quicker than the thought or reflex of his opponent. He could have killed him before the man even realized what was happening, but he did not. Instead, he struck with the flat of his blade, cracking it into the other man's hand. Bones broke, and the bandit's rusty sword fell from his shattered hand as he fell backward.

Brand did not hesitate. He wheeled among the outlaws, spinning and leaping. The sword flashed, but it never drew blood. At times he struck with a fist into an opponent's neck, sending them to the ground gasping for air. At other times he kicked, low and swift, striking at groin or knee.

Men fell around him. One toppled and groaned after another kick, and Brand knew that man would never father children. Swords flashed at him, but they only cut the air where he had been. Once, a blade glanced off his helm. There was a ringing noise and a flash of pale light as though sparks flew, but then he felled the man with a blow to his temple from the pommel of his Halathrin sword.

Six men were disabled, felled or falling to the ground before the other six could rally. The initial surprise of Brand's attack was gone, and now the bandits tried to circle him.

For the first time, steel rang on steel as he parried blows. He slipped among them, swifter than they, but one blade against many. Yet the Halathrin blade was of a quality so far beyond the others that when it struck them, they shattered. Steel shards flew. Daggers were drawn, and they drove through the air, but Brand's mail shirt protected him.

Yet still he began to bleed. Several times he had been cut on wrist and arm. But several more men lay on the ground, knocked out by the pommel of Brand's sword. Momentum was with him, and fear pumped through the remaining bandits who still stood upright. They backed away.

Brand knew he must now make a choice. Scarface, never having joined in the fight, backed away with his men. But if he was left alone, left free to continue as he had started, other travelers, less prepared than Brand had been, would die. Brand did not lower his sword. Should he kill Scarface? If he did, the band would probably fall apart and go their separate ways. But what effect would killing him have on Kareste?

But Scarface was not yet done. He tried surprise as Brand had done. The retreat was only an act, for he drew a dagger and flung it with all his might. It spun through the air, wheeling and glinting, but it did not strike its target.

Brand was already moving. The knife whooshed through the air, but he was a little to its side and moving forward. Before Scarface could react the Halathrin blade slid into him, drove deep, and then came out the man's back.

Scarface tensed. Blood gushed from his mouth and then he collapsed. Quickly, Brand tried to withdraw his sword, but it did not come out as easily as it had gone in. Scarface fell dead to the ground. Brand jerked and twisted his sword free. The others had a moment to attack him during this vulnerability, but they did not move. Shock marked their faces.

Brand looked down at the man he had killed. He had not wanted to do it, but he would not have the deaths of innocent travelers on his conscience. Better the death of a murderer.

Brand glanced at Kareste. She was still mounted, but her sword was drawn, and it dripped blood. A man lay beneath it, dead also, his limp hand open near the great diamond.

Kareste dismounted. She stepped over the body and picked up the jewel. For a moment she studied it, and then she tossed it to Brand.

He caught it. And his movement frightened the bandits that still stood, and they fled, hurrying downriver.

"You're full of surprises," Kareste said. "And just when I thought I was getting to know you." Her eyes glittered as she studied him, but Brand could not read her expression.

"Time to go," he said.

They mounted and rode into the shallow water of the ford. Behind them several men staggered up, but they seemed frozen in place by awe, and they made no move to follow.

The horses splashed through the water, and it frothed and foamed about their legs. After a while they clambered up onto the little island in the middle of the river, and then plunged into the water again.

Eventually, they made the far bank. The road started once more, a smooth and wide surface, turfed and slightly sloped to run water from the center to the sides.

They trotted forward. Brand studied the land ahead, and then the sky. He saw nothing to alarm him. Even the hawk was gone.

As they rode he sensed Kareste's eyes on him. Probably, she guessed why he had not killed the men and what he was trying to do.

"You can fight," she said eventually. "That much I already knew, but you still managed to surprise me anyway."

Brand shrugged. Most of the people who knew how well he could fight were dead.

Kareste did not take her eyes off him. "But you should have killed them – killed them all. I would have."

Brand did not answer. He rode slightly ahead, and he felt her eyes burning into his back.

18. Hope for the Hopeless

"Come!" commanded Carnhaina, and Arell felt the force of her will. It lashed her like a whip, so strong was it, yet it was not even directed at her.

Arell tore her eyes away from the queen. Her concern was for her patient. Aranloth remained still, yet to her expert gaze he looked different. There was more color in his skin, at least as best as she could tell by the shifting lights of torch and star. But more than that, she saw the rise and fall of his chest as he breathed: faster, deeper, more lifelike than before.

"Come!" commanded Carnhaina, and the spirit of Aranloth heard her call and followed her voice. Suddenly, he tensed where he lay on the stretcher; the blood seeped anew from the two wounds on his chest, and his eyes flicked open, wild, uncertain, unknowing of where he was or how he got there.

Arell knelt down and put her hand to his hot brow. She soothed him, and though she saw that he was back from the near-dead, she saw also that he was weak, terribly weak.

She spared a quick glance at Carnhaina, but the queen was already fading. The arm that held the spear seemed insubstantial as it slowly fell. Her eyes were closed. The starlight seemed dim and the torches gutted. In the flickering air the motes of dust that had formed her figure drifted apart and settled slowly into the sarcophagus once more.

The great queen was gone, but Aranloth was back. And yet, a voice, imperious and commanding as always, rang out as though the very stone atop the tower spoke:

Aranloth is returned, but the hope of Cardoroth, as always it has done, rests with Brand. Remember!

Gilhain surveyed the enemy. From the rampart that had withstood the seething masses of darkness, he looked out into a bright morning.

The enemy remained. Fear remained. The knowledge of likely defeat remained. And yet there was hope too. For Aranloth, pale and sickly, yet alive, stood near him. Or rather, he leaned against the stone of the battlement in view of the enemy.

Aranloth had placed himself there. Without speaking he had come with the dawn. What his thoughts were, Gilhain did not know, but he knew this much at least; even in his weakened state the lòhren's mind was still sharp. The enemy would see him, and whatever spies the enemy had, whatever means of gathering news that they relied on, they would have heard of his collapse and hoped for his death. When the sun had come up, they had all seen that their hope was cheated.

Gilhain moved to stand beside him. "He's still out there, somewhere," he said.

Aranloth knew that he meant Brand. The lòhren's tired eyes looked into his own.

"Do you fear that he has betrayed Cardoroth? That he has betrayed our trust in him?"

Gilhain slowly shook his head. "No, I don't believe that. But I can't help but wonder what he's doing and what he's thinking. If what Carnhaina said is true, and Arell must have told you of it, he recovered the second half of Shurilgar's staff, and he escaped the tombs of the Letharn. Yet the staff is not destroyed, and Cardoroth is

343

sorely pressed. What if the sorcerers commence another attack? You're very frail, my old friend."

Aranloth looked anxious. "There are many chances in the world, for good or for ill. Something has happened. More is going on than we know, and I wish I knew what it was. But I know this much at least. I trust Brand, and I gave him my staff, and I gave him my diadem. Those things are symbols, but with my trust in him I gave him power also, the power embodied by those symbols. He now represents the lòhrens, and he must make choices even as a lòhren, and the fate of Alithoras has become his concern, not just Cardoroth, no matter how much he loves us."

Gilhain thought about that. There was evidently more going on than he knew. He had thought that lending Brand the staff and diadem was just a practical means of giving him some power to fight off enemies. It appeared to be more than that though, but in just what way he could not quite see.

Aurellin joined their conversation. "Brand is not as others," she said. "Whatever he does, he does for us, and perhaps now also for others too. But I will continue to trust in him, to hope in him, as I have done before."

Her words struck a chord with Gilhain. That was how he felt, even though after what Carnhaina had said, he should have been riddled with doubt.

Lornach interrupted his musings. "Look over there," the Durlin said.

Gilhain followed his gaze. He saw nothing at first, but taking his eyes off the closer northward fields and looking in the distance, he saw what the sharp eyes of the little man had noticed before anyone else: a dust cloud.

They watched in silence. Soon other men along the wall noticed it too, but there was nothing anyone could

344

do but wait and continue to watch. That it was caused by riders was obvious, and a great many of them too, but who they were and what they were doing was beyond any guess.

The cloud deepened. The riders drew closer, and there was an occasional flash of metal and color. As they approached, Gilhain estimated their numbers. He took it to be a large group, perhaps a thousand strong.

"Is it an attack on the enemy?" Lornach asked. "Or reinforcements for them?"

Gilhain was beginning to understand. "No," he answered. "It's not either of those things. Most especially, it's not an attack. Look at the horde. They have set up no defense, moved no troops to face the riders."

"Then what is it?" Lornach asked. "And what difference can a mere thousand riders make?"

Gilhain did not answer. Nor did Aranloth speak, though by the look on his face he had guessed the same answer that Gilhain knew in his heart.

"It depends on who leads them," Aurellin said.

Lornach pulled at an earlobe, trying to figure it out. While he thought, the column drew closer.

"They're not Azan," he said. "Nor are the horses the alar breed of the south. These are northerners, that much is now obvious. But if not Azan, then who?"

They continued to watch. The elug war drums muttered away, sending a different message from normal; it was not a battle beat. And this was proven as the horde opened its ranks and allowed the column through.

The men on the walls were watching also, and this made them uneasy. It was bad enough that the enemy received reinforcements, however small the number in the greater scheme of things, but it was worse that they

345

were men, and northerners also. It was not something that they could comprehend.

There was much movement in the camp below. Messengers were sent, riders went back and forth, and the horde itself was excited by some news that rippled through it.

"We could have done without this," Gilhain said.

Lornach shrugged. "It's still only a thousand odd men."

"But look at the horde. They have news to consider, something different to think about, and likely enough a reason for better hope. All those things are taking their minds off their recent defeats sooner than would otherwise have happened. The timing is bad for us." Gilhain straightened his shoulders as though mentally preparing himself for something yet to come. "But it is what it is, and we'll deal with it as we've dealt with everything else."

A little while later a small group of riders emerged from the ranks of the enemy. They wore bright colors, and the harness of their horses glittered. They were proud men, sitting astride their mounts as though they owned the very land and all that they could see.

At the head of the group rode one man, aloof and prouder even than his companions. On his head he wore a winged helm, a Halathrin helm, for no others gleamed as did they, or bore the mark of such craftsmanship. But Cardoroth had seen its like before. It seemed to some that it was Brand returned, but others said nay. Brand's helm was horned.

The man's mail coat shimmered in the light. No cheap thing was it either, and there were few in the realm who wore armor to match it. Likewise, his sword was a precious thing. Light flashed from the diamonds and precious stones set at its pommel. Yet he bore the look

346

of a man who could fight, and the sword was not just for ceremony.

They approached, proud and haughty. No flag of truce they raised, deeming it beneath them, yet no arrow sped from bow nor jeering word from mouth to rebuke them.

Just behind the lead rider was a second man. His face was pockmarked, his long black hair held bound by a thick ring of beaten gold. And he carried a staff with a banner wrapped around it.

They came to a stop near the wall. The lead rider did not turn, but he made a flicking gesture to the man immediately behind him. The rider undid a leather thong that held the banner wrapped tight in its position. When it was untied, he held high the staff and shook free the cloth.

All the men along the Cardurleth saw it. The Durlin saw it, and Lornach saw it and finally understood. It was a well-known banner: on a sable background was threaded a gold eagle, one taloned claw lifted and raking at an invisible enemy, its great wings half stretched out.

"The royal banner!" hissed Lornach, and he looked sharply at the king.

"Indeed," Gilhain said. "None should dare to unfurl it except at my order, and none do – except one."

"Hvargil," muttered the queen.

Gilhain had been ready for this. He knew it would come one day, guessed even when he first saw the column of riders who it was that led them. But it was still a shock, not that he should be any longer shocked at what his younger half-brother did. It was not the first time that he had consorted with the enemy. His capacity for treachery knew no equal, unless it was the extent of his lust for the throne of Cardoroth.

Hvargil reached up slowly and removed his helm, tucking it under his arm in a gesture that reminded Gilhain of their father. The horse seemed restless beneath him, but with a squeeze of his legs he guided it a few steps forward. The other riders stayed where they were.

"Hail, half-brother, and well met," Hvargil called.

Gilhain raised an eyebrow. "Hail, brother. But our meeting would perhaps have been better if you brought better company."

Hvargil glanced back at the elug host and shrugged. "A means to an end," he replied.

"Exactly," Gilhain answered. "But which of you is the means and which the end?"

Hvargil laughed. "You're very witty for a man who knows the answer to your own question. The only end we need speak of is your reign over Cardoroth. It draws to a conclusion soon. And your life with it."

"Perhaps," Gilhain answered. "Certainly, we're outnumbered. But then again, things started off that way, and yet we're still here. If I were a betting man, I'd stake all I owned on it staying that way. Why don't you change sides, while you still can?"

The horse beneath his brother moved restlessly, but Hvargil betrayed no sign of nerves.

"Oh, I don't think so. I grant you this, you've held on well, I'll not deny it. But we both know that time will wear you down. I've made the right bet, and I'll stick with it."

Gilhain shrugged. "It's your head. As I recall, you made the same bet on a battlefield not so long ago. And against the odds Cardoroth won, despite your treachery."

Hvargil showed a flicker of displeasure, but he covered it swiftly.

"You were lucky that day. Ninety nine times out of a hundred you would have lost."

Gilhain smiled. "I'm a lucky king."

"And I'll be a long reigning one."

"Is that what they promised you? Do you really think they'll just give you the crown if the city falls and leave you to play kings and queens by yourself?"

"What a way with words you have. But actions speak louder than words. Consider this." He drew his sword and held the helm up high in the other hand. "You know what these are. They're Halathrin forged. The helm alone is worth more than any crown in any kingdom of men. And the sword is priceless. These they have given me in token of riches to come. And they *will* come, for the leader of this host rewards well those who serve him loyally."

The sword and helm glittered and sparkled. Gilhain knew their worth, and their rarity.

"I've seen their like before. But the man who bore them impressed me more than any such possessions. You can dress a pony up with ribbons, but you can't turn it into a warhorse."

"More words of wisdom. But where is your precious Brand now? Alive? Dead? Fled back into the wild lands from whence he came?"

Gilhain did not answer straight away. The first option was his hope, the last his fear. But Aranloth spoke for the first time.

"You know where Brand has gone, and what his quest is. Your elùgroth masters will have revealed that to you, at least if you're as high in their confidence as you think. But I grow bored of this banter. Speak your message, for surely they put one in your mouth, and then return to them."

349

"Bored?" Hvargil said. "You've come back from near death only to be bored the next day? Perhaps you should have considered staying dead." He placed the helm back on his head and sheathed the sword. "You see, old man, I'm very well informed indeed."

"But still you don't name Brand's quest, for I know elùgroths better than you, and they will not have told you of their fear."

Hvargil gripped tight his horse's reins. "The elùgroths fear *nothing*."

"How little you know them," Aranloth said. "But speak. Deliver your message and begone."

Hvargil seemed supremely confident. He did not speak to Gilhain or Aranloth, but rather to the men atop the wall, knowing that those who could not hear his words would hear them second hand soon enough.

"I know your numbers – the living and the wounded and the dead. I know where your food is stockpiled, and how much is left, and I know which wells in the city have run dry and which still supply good water. I know that Aranloth was healed last night by the spirit of Carnhaina, she who once ruled this realm but now is dead."

He paused for a moment, the hover of a smile on his mouth.

"That came as a surprise. The elùgroths did not like it, but the world turns in strange ways, and many things happen beyond the ken of mortal men. So indeed Aranloth taught me himself when I was a young lad, only as high as his knee and fascinated by the stories he used to tell. But that was long ago, and times change, for cities as much as for men. Carnhaina was a great queen, but her time is long since passed. These are our days now. It's our turn to shine and grow and flourish beneath the sun. It's now time to befriend the south, to help each other, to put an end to the long years of strife and war and fear. We can make that happen. Can you see it? Can your mind encompass how good it would be? The truth is, if you follow Gilhain, you will die. If you follow me, you will live to see the future you just pictured. Follow me, and prosper! That is your choice. Put down your weapons. Put aside the stories you have heard of the south. They're lies. Come! Join me, and put an end to fear and the shadow of death. Come now, what do you say?"

Hvargil ceased speaking. He looked up at the Cardurleth, his gaze serene, his posture confident. He looked every bit a king, and a glorious king at that, and the royal banner fluttered proudly beside him.

There was a stir all along the wall. Gilhain remained as he was. He did not answer Hvargil himself. To speak now was to try to take the choice away from the men, and that would be a mistake. He could almost see Hvargil's chagrin that he avoided that trap. And yet, all along the wall, men spoke to one another. A ripple ran through them, for hope to the hopeless was a powerful gift.

19. The Great North Road

For the next two days Brand and Kareste rode at a fast pace. And they found that the Great North Road was good for riding. It may have been built in ancient times when the Halathrin dwelled in the north of the land as well as their more southerly forest realm of Halathar, but when the immortals built something, it lasted. The turf was green and springy, the path straight, and the gentle slope to left and right from the middle ensured the ground was never wet.

Brand knew there was danger in staying on the road. It was in the open. It was a place that may be watched. And it was a place where any of their enemies would know exactly where they came from, where they were going and how long it would take them to get there. But the speed it enabled was a necessity.

The two days of hard riding had seen them travel far though, and for the moment, in safety. And having done that, they could now veer away from the road and head west. Lòrenta lay in that direction, and the final destination of their quest. The Halathrin that had been trapped in the form of beasts roamed those hills, and when they reached them, well, Brand did not like to think too far ahead.

The riding was harder now. It was still grassland, but there were many obstacles in the form of rough ground, little creeks and gullies, and an increasing feeling of riding uphill.

Lòrenta was close. The hills themselves were visible, wild and gorse covered. And even in the middle of the day many were capped by cloud or fog.

They spoke little as they travelled. Kareste wrestled with something in her own mind, and it seemed at times that she had nearly forgotten that he was there. The days of peace and comradeship that he had enjoyed were gone, and he wondered if he would ever feel their like again.

Another two days passed. The weather was cold and overcast, but it did not rain. Ever they climbed upward, and though the river was now to their west, the ground oftentimes became boggy. Between that, and the upward slope, their speed reduced greatly.

"We're in the foothills now," Kareste said. "We must be prepared, for the Halathrin become beasts may roam this far."

It was more than Kareste had said all day, and Brand took the opportunity to ask a question. He wanted to know more about what they faced.

"What should I expect of these creatures?" he asked. "And if necessity demands it, how best can they be fought?"

She did not look at him as she answered, her gaze roving the lands ahead of them as they rode, but at least she did answer, even if her voice was quiet and her manner brusque.

"There are about twenty of them. They're strong. And they're fast, being in the shape of wolves, though bigger."

"So they're much like the sendings that the elùgroths set on my trail near Cardoroth?"

She shook her head. "Not really. They might look similar at a distance, but they're near impossible to kill. These are Halathrin changed by sorcery. They're strong, fast, intelligent and graceful beyond any wild animal. Almost you can see the Halathrin that is in them, and the Halathrin are immortal. These creatures would be hard to kill, and no lòhren would *want* to knowing who was trapped inside the sorcerous form that shaped them. The elùgroths knew what they were doing when they conceived their plan."

"But why create them at all? What's their purpose, for surely the lòhrens are safe within the walls of their keep."

"Their purpose is to hinder the lòhrens from coming and going. They would not try to kill the beasts, even if they could, for they would kill the Halathrin inside them. And they have no way to reverse the sorcery, as do I with Shurilgar's staff. But more than that, I think they did it out of spite. The elùgroths have no greater enemy than lòhrens and, at least in the past, the Halathrin. To subject them both to this abomination, one to endure it, one to see it, would be a satisfaction to them."

"How did the elùgroths achieve it? The Halathrin are mighty warriors, and it's said that even their warriors have skill with magic."

"The Halathrin band pursued the elùgroths after they stole the half of Shurilgar's staff that they guarded. It may be that they were deliberately allowed to do so, to lure them away from their home and toward Lòrenta. It may be that the elùgroths conceived of that part of the plan from the beginning. Yet one way or the other, they were led into these hills. Khamdar made sure of that."

"But if Khamdar went to Cardoroth from here after transforming the Halathrin, they had the staff right from the start of the siege?"

"Of course."

"Then why didn't they use it from the beginning?"

"I think they held it in reserve. Perhaps they wished to study it more before they used it. It cannot be used without effects, that much is certain, and they will have discovered so after they used it first in Lòrenta."

Brand wondered what effect it would have on her, but he did not raise that point.

"How do you know all this?" he asked.

"Because I was there. It wasn't that far from where we are now. The elùgroths came through with the Halathrin pursuit close behind. I followed, and I saw things that I wish I had not."

"Why were you even here in the first place? The lòhrens suspended you from their order."

She shrugged. "Maybe I yearned for what I didn't have. I don't know. The hills of Lòrenta have a way of getting under your skin, and this place is home to me. It looks desolate, but there are many beauties here for those with the eyes to see them."

He did not press her on the point. In truth, he did not have to. He knew better than most what it was like to lose a home, and to yearn for it.

He glanced around. The hills marched away from him, rising higher and expanding. They *were* desolate, covered in dried grasses and gorse, wreathed in mists and barren of farms, livestock and cultivation. Lòrenta was a wild and remote place, a place of great loneliness. But he thought he might like it too if he explored it.

The damp path they followed curved around a small stand of white-barked birches. It was the first stand of many, for it seemed nearly the only tree that grew on or near the hills.

"What now?" he asked.

"What else?" she replied. "We find the beasts – or they find us first. That's much more likely. And then I try to reverse the spell the elùgroths used. It won't be easy, even with the other half of Shurilgar's staff."

"Can you do it?"

"You have a lot of questions today, don't you?"

"Answering a question with a question of your own isn't much of an answer," he said with a tight grin.

"If I had a better reply, I would've offered you that instead."

20. By Ancient Right

Hvargil's words hung in the air. Gilhain remained silent. Yet after a while a soldier gave his own answer. He did not yell, but his slow reply was loud enough to be heard by many. And there was an emotion in his voice that made men listen.

"I lost friends the day you betrayed us on the battlefield, Hvargil. I'll not bow to you."

There was silence again, but another soldier spoke into it from further along the wall.

"I lost a brother that day," he said. "When he was younger I taught him how to use a sword. It didn't protect him from an elug arrow in the neck, though. If not for your treachery, the enemy might have been defeated before that arrow was ever shot." He paused, and then added. "I'll not bow to you, either."

A third soldier called out, his voice ragged and harsh. "I lost five of my friends that day. Men that I grew up with. Men that I knew all my life. They didn't have to die. They'd still be here if not for you, so as far as I'm concerned I'd rather bury you upside down in a cesspit than bow to you."

The men seemed suddenly unleashed. They jeered by the hundreds, and then by the thousands. One voice rose above them all. "Half-brother, and half-wit!"

This caused a ripple of laughter, and the chant was taken up and cast into Hvargil's teeth.

Gilhain suppressed a smile. He had never had any reason to worry. But the vehemence of the men's reaction surprised him. It must also have surprised

Hvargil, but he endured it unflinching and with no hint of his feelings showing.

The chant eventually died away and Gilhain spoke at last.

"You have your answer, Hvargil. Now go."

"Not just yet, Gilhain."

Hvargil drew himself up. He looked proud, every inch a king, and there was something to admire in the strength of his will, for to look like that after the jeering of the soldiers was more than most could manage.

"I have an answer to one question," he said. "So be it. A king does not rule by the will of the people, he takes the people and bends them to his own. That you will all learn, at least those who live. But this is my second question." He turned directly to Gilhain and looked up at him with an expressionless face. "Will you honor the customs of our ancestors?"

Gilhain felt a shadow of fear at those words. The question was not idle, but he could not see its purpose, and that worried him.

"What customs?" he asked.

"That is a poor answer. Either you do, or you do not. But I'll make it easy for you to reply, for by your answer the people shall know you." He gazed once more along the Cardurleth, seeming to make eye contact with all who stood there. "We are of the Camar. We trace our heritage back to long before Cardoroth was even founded. Our ways, our customs, our rights are ancient. There once was a right of challenge for the kingship of our people, a right of challenge by combat. It ensured that no weakling, and no coward, ever sat on the throne. That law still exists, and I invoke it."

Things made sense to Gilhain now, but this was tricky ground, and he must answer carefully.

358

"Maybe," he said. "But it has not been invoked in the history of Cardoroth. If ever it was used, it goes back to a time before we lived in cities. It may have been invoked then, if legends can be believed, but things have changed since then. So what if you won the kingship that way? I'm an older man by far than you. Beating me in combat would prove only that you're younger. It would not make you a better king nor make the people accept you. It would achieve nothing."

Hvargil looked at him smugly. "And yet it is my right. Will you deny it?"

Gilhain thought hard. There was a trap in this, and Aranloth leaned slightly toward him and spoke softly.

"Beware," the lòhren said.

"What does he hope to achieve?" Gilhain asked quietly.

"Not the kingship, for as you say the people would not accept him. I think you can take this at face value. He wants to kill you, either in combat or through foul means. That would be a great blow to the morale of our defense. I cannot guarantee your safety from sorcery if you accept the challenge and go out into the field."

Gilhain considered that. "But if I don't accept, that will undermine morale."

"So it would, and certainly the enemy always tries to paint us as cowards, but it would not impact morale as much. No one would really expect you to fight him. There's a twenty year age difference."

For the first time in a long while Gilhain wished he were young again. He had accepted old age, but at times like this his mind wanted to make promises his body could not keep.

"I don't like to suggest this," Gilhain whispered. "But there might be another option beside accept or decline. I'm an old man – under the ancient customs that

Hvargil's invoking I'm allowed a champion to fight for me."

"That's true, but whoever you chose as champion would face the same dangers, and there would still be a loss of morale if he was beaten."

"But to refuse is to allow them an uncontested victory, and they would try to build on it. It's morale that holds this defense together, as much as, perhaps even more so, than swords."

To that, Aranloth gave a slight nod, but he did not answer.

Gilhain straightened, but what he was going to say to Hvargil was forestalled.

"I'll do it," Lornach offered. The Durlin was close by, although Gilhain had not thought him close enough to hear what was said.

"I'll do it, and I'll do it gladly. I lost friends on that same battlefield the other soldiers mentioned. I have my own grudge against your brother."

Gilhain looked at him earnestly. Brand knew how to choose his men, for the Durlin were loyal even beyond the normal for handpicked troops.

"I need you to guard me," Gilhain answered.

Lornach shook his head. "Even as Brand is still guarding you, albeit in a different way through pursuing his quest, so too must I. I'm short, but I can fight. And if it comes to it, it would not be the first time that I've faced sorcery. I feel it in my bones – I was born for this fight."

Gilhain bit his lip. It was not like him to be indecisive, and he became aware that all the men on the wall now waited on whatever answer he would give to the challenge.

"What do you think, Aranloth?"

The lòhren did not answer. Instead, his eyes seemed to gaze into the distance as though he was trying to peer into the shadow-shrouded future. What he saw there, if anything at all, Gilhain did not know. Aranloth gave no sign.

And yet, within the space of a handful of heartbeats the lòhren looked back at him sharply.

21. Impending Doom

Aranloth spoke. "I cannot see the future. I'm weak, and foresight comes and goes to rhythms of its own. The choice, O king, is a hard one. I discern the potential for great harm, but also the chance of great good. It hangs in the balance."

Gilhain thought about that for a moment and then raised an eyebrow.

"They say a lòhren's advice can be two edged. Now I know what they mean."

"Advice is a serious business, my King. It's easy to give, but harder to get right." The old man sighed. "But since you press me, I'll add this. I cannot foresee the outcome of a fight between Lornach and Hvargil, and without that I can offer nothing that you don't already know. And yet, Brand chose the Durlin. He chose all of them, and whatever twist of fate made him who and what he is, made him someone to whom you would entrust the fate of the kingdom, may well also touch those he chose to surround himself with. Luck gathers luck unto itself."

Gilhain considered that. He was not sure if it added anything to the lòhren's previous comment, but time to decide ran out on him.

"Gilhain!" his half-brother called. "Enough of this! Will you gossip and talk all day like an old washerwoman with her cronies? Fate waits for no man. Decide, and be done with it!"

Gilhain grinned at him "I'm in no hurry, Hvargil. There's nowhere pressing I have to go, and fate, like death, comes when you least expect it. So you will discover when you're older – if fate is kinder to you than you deserve. But as it happens, I've made my choice."

Shorty wore the white surcoat and armor of the Durlin. He looked resplendent, as they all did in the uniform. But he did not feel like it, nor did he care to be. They all insisted on calling him Lornach now, even Brand when they were not alone, but he had been Shorty all his life, and there was an attitude that went with his true self even if it did not match his true name. He did not give a damn for wealth or position or influence. What excited him was adventure, and that was something that he felt now. Adventure, risk and exhilaration all coursed through his veins. He felt alive.

He was outside the Arach Neben, the west gate of the Cardurleth. The steel emblem that decorated it, the representation of the Morning Star, was the last thing that he saw before he turned to face the horde. The entire mass of the enemy, and the single man that for just a moment embodied it – Hvargil, was before him.

Nothing stood between him and the great mass of foes who would like to tear him to pieces, and never had he felt more alive.

But they would not tear him to pieces. At least not just yet. And he would do his best to ensure that Hvargil did not either, for the king had agreed to make him his champion, and he therefore represented, at least for a little while, the entire city of Cardoroth.

He felt *alive*, and he intended to stay that way.

The Durlin never wore any special ornament or insignia, but for this occasion Aranloth had tied about his waist a cloth belt in the colors of the king, and the Eagle of Cardoroth was blazoned upon it. It felt strange to wear it, for none but the king were allowed to bear that emblem on their person, and even Aranloth, who had watched him all the while with tired eyes, had given him a strange look at the end.

Hvargil strode to meet him. The small band that had come with the traitor to the wall withdrew. The two men faced each other between the city wall and the dark mass of the elug horde.

"You?" the man who would rule Cardoroth said. "You're the king's champion? Why don't you come back when you're full grown?"

Shorty grinned at him. "I'm short, *my King*, he said sarcastically, but I'm not stupid. You're trying to upset me so that I fight rashly, and that means that you're scared. And well should you be, for you know nothing of me, but I know all about you."

"Well, I know this much. You've learned a few Durlin tricks, for just now you're trying to insinuate doubt into my mind. But enough of these games. Let our blades speak."

Hvargil donned his helm that he had carried under his arm. It looked to Shorty much like Brand's, only it was perhaps more beautiful, for the wings on it flicked back like a graceful hawk in flight. But the horns on Brand's spoke of mad battle and a will of adamantine determination that would never falter.

And then Hvargil drew his sword with a flourish. It nearly seemed to leap from the sheath of its own accord, and the pattern-welded blade shimmered and caught the light from jewels and precious stones on the hilt and threw it into the air like a mist of light. Shorty had a sudden sense of what it would be like to face Brand in battle, and it was not a good feeling.

But it was not Brand before him. It was an enemy. An enemy of Cardoroth, and someone that Shorty despised. He held his own grudge against this man, and he would

364

now seek to repay him for past treachery. Justice called for no less.

And he who stood before him did not have Brand's quiet but strong presence. Nor was the sword the same. Brand's was plainer, for this was covered in strange runes of victory. Shorty had seen their like before, though he could not remember where. But he realized that the runes were an addition made well after the sword's ancient forging, and probably ordered by Hvargil himself. No, he was not like Brand at all.

Shorty donned his own helm. It was unadorned, but of good quality. Yet no helm would protect him from a full-blooded blow of a Halathrin blade. Skill alone would see him through this situation, if anything could, and not armor.

He drew his sword. It did not ring as it came from the sheath. It did not glitter as though cold flame burned inside it. It was not pattern-welded nor marked by runes of power. Yet it was well made, and he kept it sharp. And though it had none of the long history of a Halathrin blade that was forged before the Camar migrated west, it had a history for *him*, for he had used it since he was little more than a boy, and before that it had belonged to his father. There were thousands like it in the city, but it was *his*, and he knew the feel of it in his hands with surpassing familiarity.

Hvargil gave the customary bow before a duel. He bent at the waist, but not low, and the point of his sword touched the ground. That was an insult, and though Shorty was not of the nobility he knew it. A dirty blade was more likely to lead to infection, and it was a mark of disrespect.

Shorty gave his own bow. He kept the point of his sword low, but it did not touch the ground. He bowed his head also, as was the custom. But he dropped it a

365

little lower than he was supposed to, and he squeezed his eyes into slits.

Hvargil did not surprise him. The man-who-would-be-king straightened and flicked dirt up and into Shorty's face. It was intended to blind him, and so it might have if not for his precautions.

Shorty kept his head low and sunk into a fighting crouch. The dirt flew about his face and some pebbles rang against his helm, but it did not affect him.

Hvargil was poised to attack, but he saw that his trick was of no avail and did not move in.

"A low ploy," Shorty said. "But further proof that you're scared. If you really believed in your superiority you wouldn't bother with the like."

Hvargil grunted. "And nor would you with your continued, but nevertheless futile, efforts to seed doubt into my mind."

They began to circle each other. Hvargil moved with grace and balance. Shorty stayed lower and moved less.

Hvargil struck the first blow. His blade flicked out, and it was met by Shorty's. Steel on steel rang through the air like the one-off peal of a small bell. And then they separated once more. It was nothing more than a first test, and yet they both learned much from that single touch.

Shorty knew Hvargil had a reputation as a great fighter. Yet still a shiver of fear ran through him. He now knew that reputation was well founded, for his opponent was incredibly quick and also strong. It was not a common combination. And to make matters worse, Hvargil had the greater reach. Yet Shorty was used to fighting taller men, and he had his ways to deal with that. He began to wonder if they would be enough though.

Gilhain leaned on the battlement, his hands gripping tight the stone. "Lornach is outmatched," he whispered.

Taingern answered him. "That man has been outmatched all his life, but he's still alive. His is a heart that does not give up."

Aranloth did not speak, and Gilhain turned to him for an opinion.

"What do you think?"

A long while the lòhren took to answer and it seemed as though a great weariness was on him, or perhaps he was in some sort of trance. But at length he replied.

"I do not see what you see. I perceive from afar the elùgroths. They sit together, their minds bent upon the battle. They are near the elug war drums. Those drums beat. Sorcery joins the sound, twines with it, yet it is subtle and I do not see its purpose. I see Hvargil, full of pride, but also of doubt. He has cast all he has in a desperate gamble by joining the elùgroths and making this challenge. He is desperate and deadly dangerous. Lornach is fearful. But he knows in his bones that live or die this fight buys time, if nothing else. It buys time for Brand, and every hour that we survive is another hour in which Brand may yet prevail. And he senses something else. He senses it in the air, even as do I. *Sorcery.*"

Shorty felt sweat run down his back. His arms ached and his wrists were sore. But he was untouched by his opponent's blade. And yet Hvargil was also untouched. They circled and fought and delivered blows and retreated. All to no advantage. Not yet. But it could not go on like this. One of them must soon land a blow.

His hands were clammy. He had a sense of impending doom, and that was not like him at all. But he fought on, the sound of steel on steel ringing through the air and the thrum of the blows running up his arm.

Suddenly, he saw a gap in Hvargil's defense. He made to strike, but even as his weight shifted he heard the war drums of the elugs change beat and it seemed as though the very earth beneath his feet buckled.

Instead of striking a blow he staggered sideways, struggling to keep upright. Hvargil had no such problem. His eyes gleamed within the shadow of the helm and he seized his opportunity to attack.

The Halathrin blade darted like a tongue of lightening. Shorty saw it come. He tried to withdraw, but he merely stumbled further, and yet it was that which saved him. For instead of taking the blow to his neck, the glittering edge missed that death mark. Yet still it caught him a glancing blow on the arm.

He leapt back. The sword fell from his grip, and red blood dripped down his fingers. Pain stung him, sharp and deep.

Shorty stepped further away from his opponent. He drew his knife, but he knew that he was a dead man. Not from his wounded arm: that would need many stitches, but from lack of a real weapon. Hvargil stood between him and his sword, and the sword was his only chance at life.

There was only one thing that he could try. He must somehow distract his opponent and retrieve his weapon. But Hvargil looked at him with cold, unblinking eyes. He was not a man to give such chances, and he stalked forward now, confident and poised.

Shorty saw no reason to draw things out. He flung the last weapon he had. The knife spun through the air. It was no defense against a sword, but in this way he might be able to use it to throw his opponent off balance for just long enough to get passed him and reach his blade.

368

Hvargil saw the blade coming. Whether his reflexes were excellent, or he guessed the move in advance, Shorty did not know. But his enemy merely lowered his head and the knife struck sparks off the helm and clattered away. Hvargil barely moved, and there was not one chance in a thousand of getting past him. Shorty did not even try.

"Ready to die, little man?" Hvargil asked.

Aranloth stiffened. "Too late I understand the foul sorcery," he said.

"Can you help him with lòhrengai?" Gilhain asked.

"No," the lòhren answered. "It takes time to do something like what the sorcerers did, and anything more obvious would only work against us in the end. Lornach is on his own."

"Then he is doomed," Gilhain said. "A weaponless man cannot beat the likes of Hvargil."

Taingern, standing close but not taking his eyes off the battle, spoke.

"A Durlin is never weaponless," he said.

Shorty looked for some sort of an opening, for anything. But Hvargil gave him nothing. Worse, he had decided out of spite to move backward and pick up Shorty's own sword. That was his best opportunity to attack, but Hvargil was waiting for him to do it. Shorty could feel his expectation, and let the moment pass because of it.

Hvargil flung the blade far behind him. Shorty had the strange feeling that he would never again hold the familiar hilt in his hand, the same hilt that his father had gripped. A slow anger began to burn inside him.

Hvargil advanced. Shorty retreated. It occurred to him that he could run back to the gate, but that was not in him. He could also beg for mercy, but that was not in him either. Nor did he think it would be granted. Hvargil did not understand the concept of mercy.

Shorty took some deep breaths. He was thinking the wrong way, and he knew it. He must accept his death, if so it must be, but he would not die without one last attempt, no matter how desperate the plan seemed, to win this fight.

22. We Hunt

Brand and Kareste did not have to seek the beasts that the twisted sorcery of Khamdar had unleashed upon the world. The Halathrin transformed into beasts found them.

The two travelers had entered the foothills of Lòrenta. Those hills now climbed about them, but where Brand and Kareste rode along low paths between rocky ledges and creeks, following some ancient trail, the ground was damp, or more often even boggy.

As they penetrated deeper into the wild lands of hill and moor, the temperature dropped and thick fogs clung to the earth like a blanket thrown over a bed.

But the fog was not warm and comforting; it hung cold and clammy in the air, making it hard to see or to hear. And it hid things. Creatures roamed unseen, but the evidence of their existence was left in the moist earth the next morning, for the trail was marked ahead of them as well as behind them. Brand was no tracker, and he did not know how to read the signs, but something was drawn to them, though he did not think it was the beasts. If so, he guessed they would have attacked.

They moved now up and along the ridges, sometimes dropping back into dark hollows before the trail took them high again, but up or down they ever moved toward the center of the hills.

The silence of the wild land grew about them, and there was little to be seen in grass or sky or tree. Yet Brand knew there was wildlife here, he just did not have the skill or knowledge to observe it. Yet for all its remoteness, it was the kind of place that he would love to explore.

They camped one night beside a tarn. The dark water was still, so still as to seem as glass. Weeping willows grew about it, their drooping branches and long leaves overhanging the shadowy water.

In the trees were crows. The birds flapped near silently, stretching their wings and cawing in subdued fashion. They croaked and called and squawked, but the noise they made was quiet, or else the moisture-laden air deadened it.

All through the night the birds muttered to themselves, and no other sound was to be heard in all the world.

The next morning dawned, but the sun was little more than a white haze in the fog-shrouded east. The crows stayed where they were, and they became still and silent, looking about them with tilted heads and beady eyes.

Brand and Kareste ate a cold breakfast. They could find no dry timber for a fire.

Kareste was anxious, her green-gold eyes studying their surrounds. At length, she stood.

"Something comes," she whispered.

Brand stood also, his restless hand fondling his sword hilt.

"What is it?"

She concentrated. Her fingers twitched absently on the broken half of Shurilgar's staff.

"The sorcery that I must undo. My greatest test."

Brand felt a chill run through his bones. *No. Not your greatest test. But that will follow swiftly after.*

He heard nothing except the slow drip of moisture from the long willow leaves. And then, ever so faintly, he heard the padding of paws along dark trails somewhere in the nearby birch wood. The fog seemed to grow heavier. The white haze of the sun darkened.

"They bring it with them," Kareste whispered.

"The fog? How is that possible? They're now only beasts."

"They are what I told you earlier – creatures from the otherworld. They have their own powers, but they are bound to this earth not by men or elugs, but by the immortal Halathrin. That strengthens them, makes them different from anything you have seen before. They have powers of body and mind, and some of magic, as you would call it. Expect nothing of them. Be prepared for anything.

Brand was not sure what to make of her words, except that he did not like them.

Not long after, the creatures came into view. They were shy, but they made no real attempt to stay concealed. Kareste had been right about them: they were not like the hounds that had pursued him near Lake Alithorin. These beasts, although large and muscular, had no tufted fur or bare patches of skin. They were long limbed and sleek, and their coats were a glorious white, bright as the full moon.

There was fog all through the hills, but these creatures certainly did seem to bring their own with them. Wherever they paced, a silvery shimmer fell about them. They were sleek, graceful, beautiful. And they were otherworldly. That much he could see at a glance.

The beasts padded closer, their long legs delicately covering the ground, their paws sure footed. They seemed as dancers, their movements more fluid and natural than anything he had ever seen, and yet their every movement had a purpose. Not only did they draw closer, but they spread out and formed a half-moon ring about the two travelers.

Brand and Kareste backed away toward the picketed horses near the edge of the tarn. When the first wolf growled, it sent a shiver up his spine. For all the grace and beauty of the beast, the sound that came from it was hideous, all the worse for being unexpected. Its fangs were long and sharp, and its red tongue lolled from the rictus of its lips.

Several of the other beasts howled in response. One howled so loud and so pitifully that Brand wished he had never heard such a sound. It stood before him, shimmering silvery light all about it, and as though the light were fog that swirled and eddied, it seemed to rise higher on some invisible updraft of air.

But it was not air or fog. It was the beast itself. And when the swirling movement ceased, the beast was gone. What stood before him in its place was a Halathrin girl.

The girl seemed young, though she was an immortal and had perhaps walked the world since before the Camar had wandered out of the dim west as savages. Or she had been on the earth less than a score of years – he could not tell.

But he knew that she was beautiful. Her arms and body were covered by white samite. A soft hood was pulled up over her head, yet the shimmer from it paled beside the white-gold of her hair that spilled and escaped the confines of the cloth. Her eyes, above high cheek bones, were bright and keen, seeming one moment green and the next blue.

He stared at her, unable to take his gaze from the perfection of her skin or the nobility of her features. There was wisdom in her gaze, and pain. And both were deeper than the comprehension of his mind. But he saw anxiety there also, and anguish that tore at her soul however hard she strove not to show it.

When the girl spoke, she spoke in the language of the Halathrin. He knew it. He heard her words and understood them. It was the language of travelers all across the wide lands of Alithoras. And yet he had never heard it spoken like this. It seemed to him that anything he had heard before was like a blind man trying to describe how a day of high summer felt. But with her it was as though the warm sun shone and the green grass was soft beneath his feet and he could gaze through air so clear that he could see the red tongue of a bird gathering nectar from a flower across the other side of a valley. Summer was her very presence, and he felt it on his face and breathed it in with every breath.

"Forgive us," she said. And those simple words seemed to carry more meaning than a thousand words spoken by anybody else.

Tears from her bright eyes rolled down her high cheeks, but she made no move to wipe them away.

"We hunt. We must hunt. It is what we are made to do, and the devils inside drive us. We—"

The silver shimmer about her turned and twisted, suddenly becoming black. She raised her head and let out a tortured scream, and then she seemed to collapse to the ground. But she was gone, and the beast that Brand had seen first stood in the same place, its red tongue lolling.

He let out a long breath. His doubts were gone. The fate of the Halathrin was worse than death, for they understood what was happening to them but could do nothing to prevent it. Cardoroth might fall, might already have fallen, but Gilhain and Aranloth could not hold it against him that he came here to put an end to this. Kareste had been right.

But could she achieve what she had come here to do? And on what did she wait? For she stood silent and unmoving.

Brand did not know what would happen next, but it was the one thing he did not expect just at that moment.

There was a sudden flash of wings. A hawk darted through the air and screeched. The beasts looked at it. Kareste looked at it, and Brand looked at it with a racing heart.

It landed, seeming to spear into the earth with a thump, but even before the wings ceased beating Durletha sprang up from the ground.

The witch stood between the two travelers and the beasts. She had taken the form of the old hag that Brand had first met her as, but her eyes were keen and bright.

Brand's heart raced even more, and it seemed that he could not stop it. A sudden fear overwhelmed him, and sweat coated his palms.

Now, of all times, the witch reappeared, and it was not by accident. This was not just a test of Kareste's power, but also a choosing of Light or Shadow, and Brand dreaded what evil the witch might be able to work in the midst of all that.

23. A Man is Judged by his Deeds

Shorty was prepared to die. He had put up a good fight, and whatever else happened he had bought some time for Brand. Every hour counted. Every hour Cardoroth survived was an extra hour his friend had to save them.

With a thrust of his jaw Shorty stopped his slow retreat. He might die today, but he had no intention of making it easy for Hvargil.

The traitor to the realm, who would be its king, advanced. He smiled coldly, but in truth he had nothing to be happy about. Whatever arrangement he had with the elùgroths now, he did not guess how quickly it would dissolve later. Lust for dominion had driven him and blinded his sharp mind to what it would be like to rule under the hand of the elùgroths. Promises would come easily to them now, but their words would be less than dust and ash if the winds of fortune blew victory their way.

"Time to die, little man. Did I not warn you? You should have fled when you could."

Shorty made no answer, but his eyes glinted with hatred.

Hvargil grinned at him.

"Will you pit bare hands against a Halathrin blade?"

Shorty did not hesitate.

"If I must."

Hvargil looked at him, still advancing very slowly, but it seemed that a shadow of doubt was on him, and he grasped at an idea that suddenly crossed his mind.

377

"Perhaps I'll show you mercy. Run. Run back to the gate now, and I'll let you live. Your life for the sacrifice of some pride. It's a fair exchange, wouldn't you say?"

Shorty made no move, and Hvargil slowed his advance even more.

"Maybe when I rule the city I was born to lead, eldest of the royal line that I am, I will need my own Durlin. If you survive the fall of the city, seek me out. This much I'll say, for a king always rewards valor – you have fought bravely."

Shorty thought, and he thought quickly. Not about serving Hvargil, he would never do that, but about why the offer of mercy was made. There was only one reason, and a lot of little things came together to serve it. Hvargil always wished to show himself worthy of being a king, to show himself as reasonable and to present himself as an alternative to Gilhain. He, by contrast to the real king, could afford to show mercy, whereas Gilhain, constrained by necessity, could only ask men to serve and die. By drawing attention to these things Hvargil hoped to undermine the will of the defenders to fight.

Shorty knew what he had to do. He had to fight to the last, fight against all odds, and come out victorious. It was a near impossible task, but it would dismay Hvargil and defeat the purpose of the whole challenge. Hvargil had guessed from the beginning that Gilhain would send a champion.

But Shorty smiled to himself. He liked a challenge. It made him feel alive. And looking at things in that light he realized that even dying, so long as he faced it with courage, would work in favor of bolstering the hearts of the defenders.

Shorty did what should never be done in a fight. He turned his back on the enemy. But he felt safe, at least

378

for a few moments. Hvargil could not stab him in the back before all the defenders who looked on. That would only harden their resolve to fight.

Slowly, Shorty pointed to the battlement where the king stood, and he bowed to him long and deep. When he straightened, he loosed the cloth tied about his waist that bore the king's emblem, and he held it high.

Slowly, with a tight grin on his face, he turned to face Hvargil.

The man-who-would-be-king watched him. His jaw was clenched.

"A man is judged by his deeds," Shorty said, "and not by his height. And a king is judged by his loyalty to the people he rules. Kill me, traitor, if you can. But your gamble is already lost. In the eyes of those who defend Cardoroth, I will die as a hero, and they will oppose you, and those you serve, all the more."

Hvargil did not answer. But his face was a twisted thing beneath the beautiful helm, and he unleashed a furious attack.

Shorty retreated once again. As he stepped back he zigzagged randomly, making it hard for Hvargil to reach him. Agility combated brute strength, and it gave him time. But only so much. The Halathrin blade whirred through the air, always near and getting nearer.

So near the blade came that Shorty was indeed cut several times on his arms and hands. They were only nicks, and yet the white surcoat of the Durlin became blotched red with his blood.

Finally, Shorty saw his opportunity. Hvargil made yet another thrust, but this one was just a fraction too far.

It was not just for show that Shorty had taken the cloth belt of the king from his waist. He used it now, looping it around the blade, the fabric catching and tightening about the jeweled hilt.

379

With a great heave, using all his strength but applying it in one swift jerk, he pulled the blade from Hvargil's grip.

But he was not done. Even as the sword tumbled through the air he bounded forward and rammed his helm against the head of Hvargil. The other man was not ready for it. There was a mighty thump, for the blow hit Hvargil under the jaw and drove upward. His neck could not turn to diminish the force of the strike.

Hvargil staggered back. He was dazed, yet even so he drew a dagger. Shorty kicked it out of his hand. And then he unleashed his anger. For this was a man who had cost Cardoroth dearly.

With speed and agility he punched and kicked and struck a whirlwind of hammering blows at his opponent. Hvargil reeled away, and as he half turned Shorty managed to reef the helm from his head.

Drawn to that now vulnerable target that he had exposed, Shorty found renewed strength and struck with fury until Hvargil's face was cut and bleeding in many places.

Amazingly, Hvargil kept to his feet, trying to fight back. But a great right hook eventually caught him clean on the side of his head. His knees buckled. His legs gave beneath him like a felled tree, and he toppled to the ground.

Shorty stepped back a few paces and retrieved the Halathrin blade. It felt strange in his hand, but he walked forward again, discarding his own helm and placing the Halathrin wrought helmet on his own head. There he stood above Hvargil, the sword levelled at him as the other man tried to get up.

Anger flushed through Shorty again. His hand trembled, but he could not kill an unarmed man. He stepped away, and bent down to pick up the king's cloth that lay in the dirt. With a flourish, he held the belt high. From the Cardurleth came a roar. And then it doubled, thundering down from the wall and rolling across the field. He had won.

But even so, it was not yet over. The enemy war drums beat loud. There was a sudden rush of elugs. A thousand of them raced across the field. Shorty stared at them.

Hvargil staggered up and swayed before him, and then he bent over and vomited. Somewhere behind him lay Shorty's own sword, the sword of his father, and he knew he would never hold that familiar hilt in his hand again.

Shorty turned and ran. There was no shame in doing so now. But the gate would never be opened in time, and even if that were possible, the defenders could not do it anyway. They could not risk the enemy seizing it, and holding it open long enough for the great horde behind to enter.

Shorty knew he would be torn to shreds, and no sortie would come out of the gate to save him. They could not risk that for one man, nor could he blame them.

He nearly ran anyway, for the instinct to live, if even only for a few moments longer, was strong. But instead, he bowed once more to the king.

When he straightened, he faced the onrushing enemy, raised his sword high, and planted his feet firmly on the ground.

Gilhain looked down with horror on the scene far below.

"Do something!" he said to Aranloth.

It was not a command. It was not a suggestion. There was an element of begging in his voice, and he did not care who heard it.

But the lòhren was already moving.

One of Aranloth's arms swept slowly out before him, palm down. Then, just as slowly, he turned the palm upward.

There was strain on his pale face, for whatever he did taxed him; it taxed him more than a man who was newly come back from near death should be taxed, but he did it unflinchingly. And he did it with a slow determination, the same slow determination and inhuman patience that had enabled him to face situations such as this before, to withhold his power until just that moment of maximum effect.

Gilhain looked at the racing elugs. They streamed across the ground like a river that had flooded its banks, and they raised their swords, yelling and cavorting as they sped, each one trying to be the first to reach their victim.

Gilhain looked at his champion. Shorty stood still as a standing stone, a stone that had been planted there for millennia. His sword was up, but his head was down. There was something in his posture that told Gilhain the man was not scared of death, and yet all the same he was filled with overwhelming sadness. For the end of his life was come, and he knew not what, if anything, would follow.

And then, transforming that sad scene, a wall of flame spurted from the ground. It leaped and danced and grew.

Shorty slowly straightened. The flame stood between him and the enemy. He hesitated a moment, but no more than that, and then he turned and began to walk back to the gate.

382

He did not hurry, and he took the time to point his sword at Aranloth upon the battlement. It might have been a salute. Or a thank you. Or a sign of respect, but whatever it was, it was a solemn gesture, and the lòhren returned it just as slowly, the flames dancing higher as his arm moved.

"Thank you," Gilhain said quietly. "If ever a man deserved to live, it's him."

24. I Must Drink my Fill

Brand did not take a backward step. He drew his sword, but he knew that battle could not get him out of this. What he needed was time, but no man ever had enough of that.

Already he sensed Kareste begin to focus her will next to him. Her head was bowed, and her hands held tight Shurilgar's staff.

The witch spoke. "Now is the time, Brand of the Duthenor. Choose death, or choose … something else."

"My choice was made long ago," he answered.

"Then you will die."

"Perhaps. But I doubt it."

She studied him. "So confident? It's a trait of the young, though I won't say you have no reason for it. But you have less now than usual, surrounded on all sides by enemies that overpower you."

"Not surrounded."

"Ha! You speak of Kareste, and you would buy her time for the enchantment she begins. But what enchantment? To free poor Halathrin souls? So much I discern that she has told you. And truly, it could only be done with one of the halves of Shurilgar's broken staff. And yet, brave fool, have you not thought what else could be done with the broken half she carries now? What she does even as we speak?"

Brand offered no answer.

"I will tell you, brave fool. She holds in her hands the same power by which the beasts were made. By it they can be released … or they can be *controlled*. She could make them her own creatures and be a force in the world, and with the staff in her possession it would just be the beginning."

He looked at Kareste. She now lifted her gaze upward. Her face was expressionless. Her ash-blond hair shimmered like the beasts. Her green-gold eyes glittered, filled with incalculable power. She looked resplendent, beautiful beyond words, but distant and terrible as implacable fate.

She did not look at him. She did not look at the witch. The wolf-beasts howled and the crows danced madly within the willows.

"Kill her now!" cried Durletha. "Or all that follows, the great Shadow that will spread across the land, will be your fault. Kill her now, while her mind is deep within her enchantment, or be condemned by all who loved and trusted you."

Brand gritted his teeth. No man could make such choices, and yet he caught a glimpse of the long life of Aranloth, the many such choices he must have made, and appreciated anew what he had given of himself for the protection of the land. And he appreciated also what a burden it was.

He shifted his grip on the Halathrin blade. It glittered blue-white beside the dark waters of the tarn that he was backed up against.

His gaze went to the witch. And then to Kareste once more. He had though the choice to be made was hers, had thought that she must choose either Light or Shadow. That was certainly true, but he must also choose, and the world had suddenly become far less clear-cut than he had thought.

Beyond the ever-present but rarely seen extremes of Light and Shadow was the place that men must live. And what might be a dark deed to one was an act of heroism to another.

He did not know what to do, but after a moment he straightened.

A bitter brew you have mixed for me," he said to the witch. "But I came to the table when I agreed to this quest, and now I must drink my fill, for good or for ill."

She looked at him with hard eyes, and he thought that he detected a mixture of frustration and surprise in them. There was, perhaps, even admiration.

"Truly, you have a devil inside you. There's just no give. Do you know what you could achieve if only you set yourself free of constraints?"

Brand shrugged. He was happy to talk. It gave time to Kareste.

"There's no devil inside me. I'm just a simple man trying to do the right things for the people I love."

"Love will get you killed."

"And so might hate. Or greed. Or ambition. Or, for that matter, cowardice. And anyway, perhaps it's better to die trying to do right, than to live knowing you've done wrong. What do you think?"

The witch let out a long breath and gave a slight shrug of her bony shoulders.

"I think that you are not a simple man at all. But it does not matter what I think, anymore. Events have come to a head. I will have the staff now, even if I must kill you, for others come for it, and I *will* have it. It is easier to take it from her now than to wait and try to take it from them later."

Brand shifted slightly so that he stood between Kareste and the witch.

"For all your words, you still do not attack. I think you would prefer the beasts to do your work for you. But they make no move. They sense Kareste's enchantment building, sense that she will set them free. Or can you not feel that?"

The witch turned slightly and her gaze darted to the beasts.

Brand had no idea if what he had said was true, but it sent a shiver of doubt through her, and it gave him the opportunity he was looking for.

Surprise was his friend, and he needed all the help he could get, for once Durletha turned on him, which she was about to do, he would be outmatched.

He had held the sword before him, but it was with Aranloth's staff that he attacked. He did not doubt that he had to use it, to draw on the power that was in him, for without his protection Kareste would die and the Halathrin would be trapped forever. He would deal with the consequences later.

Bright flame, blue-white, shot from the tip of the staff. It enveloped the witch, knocked her down and sent the beasts scattering to get away from her.

A moment she rolled on the ground, and then she was up, her eyes blazing. Her hand darted forward, fingers spread. Green flame dripped from them, and then it shot in a shimmering spray at Kareste.

Brand knew the attack was directed at her, even though he stood in the way, he felt it in the driving force of the flame; it struck him, but it mostly sought to get passed him.

He felt the heat of the attack, and the grass at his feet withered and blackened. Yet a blue-white nimbus had sprung up about his body, summoned by some reflex of his mind to protect him, and it expanded and shrank, stifling the green flame.

But the witch was not done. She raised her other hand and sent a second stream of fire at him.

Brand felt the force of it envelop him. The nimbus flickered, and he sank to his knees as though burdened with a weight beyond his strength to carry.

The green flames darkened, turning near black. He felt ever greater heat from them, and the blackened grass at his feet disappeared in smoke while the very earth itself began to seethe and bubble.

Brand thought of Cardoroth. He thought of Gilhain and Aranloth, of Shorty and Taingern. He thought of Arell.

He lifted his head. His eyes blazed. There was a free and reckless surge in his spirit. It was something that he had felt a few times before: the darker the hour, the greater the light within him shone. So it felt now. He staggered to his feet, and then he took a pace toward Durletha. And then another one. He found that with each step his strength seemed to grow.

Durletha looked at him, her eyes wide. The green flame sputtered and died.

"There *is* a devil in you," she said.

Brand took another pace forward, his staff held high in one hand, his sword in the other.

Durletha shook her head. "You make it hard for me to kill you, but courage is no match for skill. Of the first you have an abundance, of the latter—"

She did not finish that sentence. Instead, she made a quick gesture with her left hand. The fog that was all about them shuddered, and then like an arrow shot from a bow, it darted at Brand. As a wall it struck him, but it was no longer insubstantial.

The fog roiled and bubbled about him. It was become heavy as water, though it did not fall to the ground. Instead, it pressed in on him, forcing its way into his mouth and ears and eyes. He clenched his jaw and

388

squeezed his eyes shut, but the water still drove into his nose.

He coughed and spluttered, lifting his arms to try to protect his face. He staggered toward Durletha, but she stepped nimbly away from him.

He could not breathe. Soon, he would choke and pass out. And then he was likely to drown, for already he felt the first specks of water in his lungs. That made him cough, but the moment he opened his mouth to do so, water forced its way in there, too.

He did what he did not wish to do: turn his back on Durletha. It left him even more vulnerable, and it did not stop the water as he thought it might. It followed him wherever he went, like someone with a pillow relentlessly trying to smother him.

He opened his eyes. The water rushed at them, yet through the rush he could still see a little of what was going on.

Kareste had not moved. She stood as she had done, but dark forces swirled around her. It was something that he sensed more than saw, and whatever she was doing occupied her completely. She could not help him, even if she wanted too. More, he sensed those dark forces reaching out to the beasts. She was binding them to her, joining with them, or the otherworldly power within them, and his heart sank.

Durletha may have been right in what she claimed before. Or not. Brand had no time to think, to get a true feel for what Kareste was doing. There was little time left for him, and he must soon discover a way out of the witch's trap, or die. Instinct had saved him the first time, but now, if he was to save himself again, he must draw on some knowledge or skill.

He fell to his knees. Not because he was quite incapacitated yet, but because it would assure Durletha that her attack was working. That might encourage her to just keep on going as she was. He did not need a knife in the back as well.

Out of the corner of his eye he saw some of the beasts. They howled, heads lifted up, snouts pointing to the sky, but he could hear nothing except the rush of water in his ears.

At least they were not attacking. Even if Kareste was binding them to her, it was helping him just at the moment. For if they attacked him now there was nothing he could do about it.

Blue-white fire still sputtered on Aranloth's staff. And where the rushing water touched it wisps of steam rose into the air. He stared at it, and then, dimly, an idea came to him.

He coughed and spluttered, feeling water reach his lungs, and with it a cold rush of heart-pounding panic. Yet he drew his will together and concentrated. It was harder than it had been before, much harder, for it was not instinctive. Yet the blue-white nimbus sprang to life about him once more.

This time he did not use it as a shield. Nor did he attack with it. Instead, he joined his thought with the water that surrounded him, and the lòhrengai he had summoned followed wherever his thought went.

Nothing happened. But he was not done. Having joined his lòhrengai with the witchery, he began to will the blue-white nimbus to grow hot. And hot it grew.

Steam sizzled through the air. Immediately he felt a lessening of the pressure of the water. He opened his eyes, stood, and faced Durletha.

He could not see her properly for all the steam and fog and light that surrounded him. But he saw enough to bring confidence to him. Her face showed surprise. She had thought him beaten, and he was not beaten. He stood taller.

The last of the water evaporated into the air. Still, he coughed, and each breath he drew felt as fire. Yet he looked at her with determination in his eyes, and he sensed her chagrin.

"Well," she said. "Aren't you just full of surprises? But I have the skill to play this game all day. Do you?"

He grinned at her. "Perhaps you do. But I know now that mine is the greater strength. Leave now, while you can. Give up the staff – it is not for you. It is a thing of the past, and it has no place in the world of today. Its evil *will* be destroyed."

"No," she said. "I'll have it. Though I don't see why you would try to stop me. What difference does it make to you if she has it," the witch pointed to Kareste, "or me? In either case, it will *never* be destroyed."

"But it will," he said. "The difference is this – I trust her. *She* will destroy it. And you never would."

"Fool!" Durletha hissed. "No one can wield such sorcerous power as she now does and not succumb to it. The staff will own her, if it does not already. Had you ever met its maker, had you ever met Shurilgar, you would know how great he was, and how strong his will. And his will lingers in the staff."

Brand winked at her. It was a gesture so out of place that it surprised her. And his following words threw her off balance even more.

"You know much, and you guess more. But you do not know all. When first I came to Cardoroth I met Shurilgar, or the spirit of him that haunted the dark woods of Lake Alithorin after his death. He turned his will upon me, and I survived. I defeated him, and set him wailing away in the dark. I do not fear him, and I fear you less. And as for Kareste—"

391

He ceased speaking and struck. All the while that he had been talking he had heard the crows caw and flap in the willows by the tarn. He took that sound and drew it together with his will, sending it as a spear at her.

Durletha flung up a haggard old arm, the rags she wore billowing with the sudden movement. But she moved with speed and confidence that bellied her looks. The driven sound struck her, sending her reeling back, but a shield of green flickered to life around her arm, and then she steadied herself and smiled at him. Her grin was gap-toothed. Her hooked nose twitched, and then she flung his own attack back at him.

But he was ready. With a wave of his sword, now flickering blue-white with lòhrengai, he knocked it to the side. The blade rang with a strange sound, and then he advanced.

Both sword and staff flickered with lòhrengai. She retreated. The beasts howled behind her. They trembled and shook and bit at their own tails. Whatever magic Kareste was working on them was having an effect, and he saw a glint of desperation in Durletha's eyes. She stopped her backward pacing.

Brand felt her thoughts reach out, out to somewhere behind him. He sensed the darkness of the deep tarn. Or did he sense *her* sensing the darkness of the tarn? Lòhrengai was a tangled web, but he had no chance to untangle it now.

Shadows flocked about him with a thousand wings. He perceived that her mind had taken the willow leaves and the black water and transformed them into this attack, this thing that pummeled and struck at him like a host of hawks, their wing-beats fierce slaps of shadow that shattered light into fragments and sent them spinning away until there was nothing but dark.

It was darker than the deepest cave. It was blacker than a moonless midwinter night. It was more shadowy than the dim flicker of long lost memories, and as memories could be lost, so too he began to lose a sense of where he was and what he was doing.

The will of the witch was on him – strong, soothing, blotting out all of the world except her own smothering thoughts. And she thought of death, and the long dark peace of the tomb.

As though from afar Brand heard the howl of a wolf. It brought back a fleeting image of Kareste, alone and imbued with eldritch power. Was she bending the beasts to her will, her first step in becoming a force of darkness on the earth? Or was she reaching out to them, becoming one with them so that she might break the sorcery that bound them?

Why should he care? The thought was overpowering. It was so much easier to drift back down into darkness. *But he did care.*

And because he cared, he fought. He struggled up as though he were at the bottom of the dark tarn itself, launching himself toward the surface. But he could not get there. That, he knew instinctively. No matter how hard he tried, he would never reach freedom. But if not that way, then how?

His mind drifted, and he saw many things. He saw the face of the usurper who now ruled the Duthenor, saw his father and mother holding hands, saw them dead, saw the moonlit night where he swore vengeance and struck fear through the usurper.

He saw his coming to Cardoroth, and Shorty and Taingern. And he saw Arell: quick-witted, skilled, quiet, brimming with compassion that she kept hidden. He saw Gilhain and Aurellin. He had learned from them all.

And he saw Aranloth. Older than the others, burdened by years beyond count and responsibilities so heavy that few men would have the will to bear them, and to endure their bearing, down through uncounted centuries. And he saw him atop the Cardurleth, sending his spirit into the elùgroth tent, worried that perhaps the task he had set himself would kill him and his soul be lost. He heard his words in the hollow dark that pressed about him. *Use your sword and prick my flesh, even to the point of drawing blood. That strengthens the tie between spirit and body, and should pull me back.*

Brand now knew what to do. Even as he thought of it he felt the hilt of the sword in his hand. It felt like a tongue of flame, and when he brought it to bear against his leg it whipped him with fire.

His eyes sprang open. The dark was gone. The world rushed upon him, brilliant and full of light and sound and life.

He stepped toward the witch. The sword in his hand burned, for he could fill it with lòhrengai just as easily as the staff.

Durletha looked at him. Surprise and fear was on her face. She began to shimmer, her arms lifting up, and he knew she was changing form.

Brand ran her through. The sword passed into her flesh as though nothing was there. The blade flared. Fire surged. Her arms dropped, and her body grew limp. It was heavy now, and it seemed to fall from the blade. She collapsed to the ground. Once she blinked, her hand reaching out to him. And then she who had endured as long, or perhaps even longer than Aranloth, died.

The Halathrin-that-were-wolves howled. The crows in the willows beat their wings in madness.

Brand reached down and with his palm closed Durletha's eyes. He had not wanted to kill her. But he killed her because he had to. Not just to save himself, or for Kareste, or for Cardoroth. But for all Alithoras.

He sensed now why he had the power that he did. He sensed that it came, as all power ultimately did, from the land, from whence he was born and to where he would one day return. He perceived his responsibilities and purpose, and did not know whether to shrink from them or embrace them. The second he was fearful to do, for it would change his life beyond the grasp of his imagination.

At least, he could not embrace it yet.

He turned to Kareste. The spell she wrought was at its peak. Shurilgar's broken staff was like a rent in reality. It was a thing of power, not truly belonging to this world, and it bridged the gap between this world and others. Nor did it belong to this time. It reached back into the distant past, sustaining itself on enchantments that were made long ago, and yet had not died with their maker. Shurilgar was gone, but his will lived on.

Force roiled through Kareste. Her ash-blond hair trailed in the wind, though no air moved. She shivered. And then she groaned. He could see that she was in agony. Or perhaps it was ecstasy. He could not be sure what she felt.

Suddenly, she stiffened. A wordless cry burst from her lips. She lowered the staff, and the power from it flickered and subsided.

The beasts howled again, and when he turned to look at them he saw that they were beasts no more. A score of Halathrin stood around him. There was anguish on their faces such as he had never seen.

There was a cry behind him, and he turned again. Kareste had fallen to her knees. Her head shook from side to side and she convulsed, her eyes rolling in her head, and then went still.

395

He ran to her. He turned his back to the Halathrin and ran. Kareste needed him, if it was not already too late. She needed him, and he would be there for her. Though what she would do if she recovered, he did not know.

Still less did he know what he would do if she died.

Thus ends *Defiant Swords*. The Durlindrath trilogy continues in *Victorious Swords*, where Brand learns more of the threat to Alithoras and faces his greatest challenge yet.

Sign up below and be the first to hear about new book releases, see previews and learn of upcoming discounts. http://eepurl.com/Rswv1

Visit my website at www.homeofhighfantasy.com

Encyclopedic Glossary

Note: the glossary of each book in this series is individualized for that book alone. Additionally, there is often historical material provided in its entries for people, artifacts and events that are not included in the main text.

Many races dwell in Alithoras. All have their own language, and though sometimes related to one another, the changes sparked by migration, isolation and various influences often render these tongues unintelligible to each other.

The ascendancy of Halathrin culture, combined with their widespread efforts to secure and maintain allies against elug incursions, has made their language the primary means of communication between diverse peoples.

For instance, a soldier of Cardoroth addressing a ship's captain from Camarelon would speak Halathrin, or a simplified version of it, even though their native speeches stem from the same ancestral language.

This glossary contains a range of names and terms. Many are of Halathrin origin, and their meaning is provided. The remainder derive from native tongues and are obscure, so meanings are only given intermittently.

Some variation exists within the Halathrin language, chiefly between the regions of Halathar and Alonin. The most obvious example is the latter's preference for a "dh" spelling instead of "th".

Often, Camar names and Halathrin elements are combined. This is especially so for the aristocracy. No other tribes had such long-term friendship with the Halathrin, and though in this relationship they lost some of their natural culture, they gained nobility and knowledge in return.

List of abbreviations:

Azn. Azan

Cam. Camar

Chg. Cheng

Comb. Combined

Cor. Corrupted form

Duth. Duthenor

Esg. Esgallien

Hal. Halathrin

Leth. Letharn

Prn. Pronounced

Age of heroes: A period of Camar history that has become mythical. Many tales are told of this time. Some are true, others are not. And yet, even the false ones usually contain elements of historical fact. Many were the heroes that walked abroad during this time, and they are remembered still, and honoured still, by the Camar people. The old days are looked back on with pride, and the descendants of many heroes yet walk the streets of Cardoroth, though they be unaware of their heritage and the accomplishments of their forefathers.

Alar: *Azn.* A strain of horses raised in the southern deserts of Alithoras. Bred for endurance, but capable of bursts of speed. Most valued possession of the Azan people, who measure wealth and status by their number. In their culture, where a person on foot is likely to die between water sources, horse-theft is punished by torture and death.

Alithoras: *Hal.* "Silver land." The Halathrin name for the continent they settled after the exodus. Refers to the extensive river and lake systems they found and their appreciation of the beauty of the land.

Alith Nien: *Hal.* "Silver river." Has its source in the mountainous lands of Auren Dennath and empties into Lake Alithorin.

Anast Dennath: *Hal.* "Stone mountains." Mountain range in northern Alithoras. Contiguous with Auren Dennath and location of the Dweorhrealm.

Angle: The land hemmed in by the Carist Nien and Erenian rivers, especially the area in proximity to their divergence.

Angrod: One of the ancient names of the witch better known in present times as Durletha.

Arach Neben: *Hal.* "West gate." The great wall surrounding Cardoroth has four gates. Each is named after a cardinal direction, and each also carries a token to represent a celestial object. Arach Neben bears a steel ornament of the Morning Star.

Aranloth: *Hal.* "Noble might." A lòhren.

Arell: A name formerly common among the Camar people, but currently out of favor in Cardoroth. Its etymology is obscure, though it is speculated that it derives from the Halathrin stems "aran" and "ell" meaning noble and slender. Ell, in the Halathrin tongue, also refers to any type of timber that is pliable, for instance, hazel. This is cognate with our word wych-wood, meaning timber that is supple and pliable. As elùgroths use wych-wood staffs as instruments of sorcery, it is sometimes supposed that their name derives from this stem, rather than elù (shadowed). This is a viable philological theory. Nevertheless, as a matter of historical fact, it is wrong.

Aurellin: *Cor. Hal.* The first element means blue. The second appears to be native Camar. Queen of Cardoroth and wife to Gilhain.

Auren Dennath: *Comb. Duth.* and *Hal. Prn.* Our-ren dennath. "Blue mountains." Mountain range in northern Alithoras. Contiguous with Anast Dennath.

Azan: *Azn.* Desert dwelling people. Their nobility often serve as leaders of elug armies. They are a prideful race, often haughty and domineering, but they also adhere to a strict code of honor.

401

Barok: A healer in Cardoroth. A man held in high regard by the profession he represents. Distantly related to the king on his mother's side. It is believed by some that he obtained his position as chief physician via political influence. Others argue that, his family being wealthy, they bribed the king's chancellor in order to obtain the favored position for one of their own. Be that as it may, it is well known in Gilhain's court that the king dislikes him. This likely stems from an older cause, however. In his youth, the king required stitches. Barok inserted them, but miscalculated the date of their removal. The process, undertaken many days later than it should have been, was painful. Gilhain still bears the scars on his arm, not just of the initial cut, but also the faint point marks where the string was pulled from his flesh.

Brand: A Duthenor tribesman. Currently serving King Gilhain as his Durlindrath. However, by birth, he is the rightful chieftain of the Duthenor people. However, an usurper overthrew his father, killing him and his wife. Brand, only a youth at the time, swore an oath of vengeance. That oath sleeps, but it is not forgotten, either by Brand or the usurper. The usurper sought to have him killed also, but without success.

Bragga Mor: *Cam.* A great poet and storyteller from the city of Esgallien. He traces his ancestry back to the days when one of his forefathers served Conhain, that realm's first king, as both bodyguard and court bard. It is said that Bragga Mor is similarly skilled in both music and in sword play.

Camar: *Cam. Prn.* Kay-mar. A race of interrelated tribes that migrated in two main stages. The first brought them

402

to the vicinity of Halathar; in the second, they separated and established cities along a broad sweep of eastern Alithoras.

Camarelon: *Cam. Prn.* Kam-arelon. A port city and capital of a Camar tribe. It was founded before Cardoroth as the waves of migrating people settled the more southerly lands first. Each new migration tended northward. It is perhaps the most representative of a traditional Camar realm.

Carangar: *Hal.* "Car – red, angar – outcrop of rock or something prominent that juts from the surface of the land or another object." A Durlin.

Cardoroth: *Cor. Hal. Comb. Cam.* A Camar city, often called Red Cardoroth. Some say this alludes to the red granite commonly used in the construction of its buildings, others that it refers to a prophecy of destruction.

Cardurleth: *Hal.* "Car – red, dur – steadfast, leth – stone." The great wall that surrounds Cardoroth. Established soon after the city's founding and constructed with red granite. It looks displeasing to the eye, but the people of the city love it nonetheless. They believe it impregnable and say that no enemy shall ever breach it – except by treachery.

Careth Nien: *Hal. Prn.* Kareth nyen. "Great river." Largest river in Alithoras. Has its source in the mountains of Anast Dennath and runs southeast across the land before emptying into the sea. It was over this river (which sometimes freezes along its northern stretches) that the Camar and other tribes migrated into

403

the eastern lands. Much later, Brand came to the city of Cardoroth by one of these ancient migratory routes.

Carist Nien: *Hal.* "Ice river." A river of northern Alithoras that has its source in the hills of Lòrenta.

Carnhaina: First element native *Cam*. Second *Hal.* "Heroine." An ancient queen of Cardoroth. Revered as a saviour of her people, but to some degree also feared, for she possessed powers of magic. Hated to this day by elùgroths, because she overthrew their power unexpectedly at a time when their dark influence was rising. According to dim legend, kept alive mostly within the royal family of Cardoroth, she guards the city even in death and will return in its darkest hour.

Carnyx horn: The sacred horn of the Camar tribes. An instrument of brass, man high with a mouth fashioned in the likeness of a fierce animal, often a boar or bear. Winded in battle and designed to intimidate the foe with its otherworldly sound. Some believe it invokes supernatural aid.

Chapterhouse: Special halls set aside in the palace of Cardoroth for the private meetings, teachings and military training of the Durlin.

Crenel: The vertical gap on a battlement between merlons. The merlon offers protection, the crenel an opening through which missiles are fired.

Drùghoth: *Hal.* First element – black. Second element – that which hastens, races or glides. More commonly called a sending.

Durletha: *Hal.* "She who is as enduring as stone." A witch of Alithoras whose birth was before even the rise of the ancient, but now forgotten, Letharn empire.

Durlin: *Hal.* "The steadfast." The original Durlin were the seven sons of the first king of Cardoroth. They guarded him against all enemies, of which there were many, and three died to protect him. Their tradition continued throughout Cardoroth's history, suspended only once, and briefly, some four hundred years ago when it was discovered that three members were secretly in the service of elùgroths. These were imprisoned, but committed suicide while waiting for the king's trial to commence. It is rumored that the king himself provided them with the knives that they used. It is said that he felt sorry for them and gave them this way out to avoid the shame a trial would bring to their families.

Durlin creed: These are the native Camar words, long remembered and much honored, uttered by the first Durlin to die while he defended his father, and king, from attack. Tum del conar – El dar tum! Death or infamy – I choose death!

Durlindrath: *Hal.* "Lord of the steadfast." The title given to the leader of the Durlin.

Duthenor: *Duth. Prn.* Dooth-en-or. "The people." A single tribe, or sometimes a group of tribes melded into a larger people at times of war or disaster, who generally live a rustic and peaceful lifestyle. They are raisers of cattle and herders of sheep. However, when need demands they are fierce warriors – men and women alike.

405

Elugs: *Hal.* "That which creeps in shadows." A cruel and superstitious race that inhabits the southern lands, especially the Graèglin Dennath.

Elùdrath: *Hal. Prn.* Eloo-drath. "Shadowed lord." A sorcerer. First and greatest among elùgroths. Believed to be dead or defeated.

Elùgai: *Hal. Prn.* Eloo-guy. "Shadowed force." The sorcery of an elùgroth.

Elùgroth: *Hal. Prn.* Eloo-groth. "Shadowed horror." A sorcerer. They often take names in the Halathrin tongue in mockery of the lòhren's practice to do so.

Elu-haraken: *Hal.* "The shadowed wars." Long ago battles in a time that is become myth to the Camar tribes.

Erenian River: A river in northern Alithoras. Some say its name derives from a corruption of the Halathrin word "nien," meaning river. Others dispute this and postulate the word derives from a pre-exodus name adopted by the Camar tribes after they settled the east of Alithoras.

Exodus: The arrival of the Halathrin into Alithoras from an outside land. They came by ship and beached north of Anast Dennath.

Faladir: A city founded by a Camar tribe.

Foresight: Premonition of the future. Can occur at random as a single image or as a longer sequence of events. Can also be deliberately sought by entering the realm between life and death where the spirit is released from the body to travel through space and time. To achieve this, the body must be brought to the very threshold of death. The first method is uncontrollable and rare. The second exceedingly rare but controllable for those with the skill and willingness to endure the danger.

Forgotten Queen (the): An epithet for Queen Carnhaina.

Free Cities: A group of cooperative city states that pool military resources to defend themselves against attack. Founded prior to Cardoroth. Initially ruled by kings and queens, now by a senate.

Galenthern: *Hal.* "Green flat." Southern plains bounded by the Careth Nien and the Graèglin Dennath mountain range.

Gavnor: A lòhren of Queen Carnhaina's ancient court. Driven by desperate need he attempted to Spirit Walk, though he did not have sufficient skill. He saw deeply into what was, and what yet may be. But he was assailed. He had neither the skill to attempt to defend himself, nor to return to his body. He was lost in the void, from whence none had ever returned. Yet Carnhaina recalled him, revealing herself as a great power, greater than most lòhrens or elùgroths. But Gavnor was changed by the experience. He withdrew from the court, renounced his stature among the lòhren order, and wandered the land as a lover of nature. It is said that his power was increased, and he may well yet still live. But none have seen him for long centuries.

Gernlik: *Cam.* A Durlin.

Gilhain: *Comb. Cam & Hal.* First element unknown, second "hero." King of Cardoroth. Husband to Aurellin.

Graèglin Dennath: *Hal. Prn.* Greg-lin dennath. "Mountains of ash." Chain of mountains in southern Alithoras. The landscape is one of jagged stone and boulder, relieved only by gaping fissures from which plumes of ashen smoke ascend, thus leading to its name. Believed to be impassable because of the danger of poisonous air flowing from cracks, and the ground unexpectedly giving way, swallowing any who dare to tread its forbidden paths. In other places swathes of molten stone run in rivers down its slopes.

Great North Road: An ancient construction of the Halathrin. Built at a time when they had settlements in the northern reaches of Alithoras. Warriors traveled swiftly from north to south in order to aid the main population who dwelt in Halathar when they faced attack from the south.

Grothanon: *Hal.* "Horror desert." The flat salt plains south of the Graèglin Dennath.

Halathar: *Hal.* "Dwelling place of the people of Halath." The forest realm of the Halathrin.

Halathgar: *Hal.* "Bright star." Actually a constellation. Also known as the Lost Huntress.

Halathrin: *Hal.* "People of Halath." A race named after a mighty lord who led an exodus of his people to the continent of Alithoras in pursuit of justice, having sworn to redress a great evil. They are human, though of fairer form, greater skill and higher culture. They possess an inherent unity of body, mind and spirit enabling insight and endurance beyond other races of Alithoras. Reported to be immortal, but killed in great numbers during their conflicts with the evil they seek to destroy. Those conflicts are collectively known as the elù-haraken: the Shadowed Wars.

Harakgar: *Leth.* The three sisters. Creatures of magic brought into being by the lore of the Letharn. Their purpose is to protect the tombs of their creators from robbery.

Harlak: *Leth.* An ancient name of Aranloth.

Harath Neben: *Hal.* "North gate." This gate bears a token of two massive emeralds that represent the constellation of Halathgar. The gate is also known as "Hunter's Gate," for the north road out of the city leads to wild lands full of game.

Hvargil: Prince of Cardoroth. Younger son of Carangil, king of Cardoroth. Exiled by Carangil for treason after it was discovered he plotted with elùgroths to assassinate his older half-brother, Gilhain, and prevent him from one day ascending to the throne. He gathered a band about him in exile of outlaws and discontents. Most came from Cardoroth but others were drawn from Camarelon.

Immortals: See Halathrin.

Karappe: A great healer of antiquity. Responsible for many of the medical treatises still used today among the Camar peoples. He lived to 109 years of age, and remained sprightly well past his hundredth birthday.

Famous for recommending two mugs of beer, or one glass of wine, a day as good for health.

Kareste: A mysterious girl who helps Brand. She possess potent magic.

Kardoch: A hero of ancient lethrin society. Revered by them, and at times worshipped by them. It is believed that the elùgroths stamp out the latter practice. They have no room in their rule for reverence of anything save their own power, and the power that they ultimately serve themselves.

Khamdar: An elùgroth. Leader of the host the besieges Cardoroth.

Kirsch: A race of men who established a mighty empire across Alithoras. Yet they predated even the Letharn and nearly all knowledge of them is lost forever.

Lake Alithorin: *Hal.* "Silver lake." A lake of northern Alithoras.

Letharn: *Hal.* "Stone raisers. Builders." A race of people that in antiquity ruled much of Alithoras. Only traces of their civilization remain.

Lethrin: *Hal.* "Stone people." Creatures of the Graèglin Dennath. Renowned for their size and strength. Tunnelers and miners.

Lòhren: *Hal. Prn.* Ler-ren. "Knowledge giver – a counsellor." Other terms used by various nations include wizard, druid and sage.

Lòhren-fire: A defensive manifestation of lòhrengai. The color of the flame varies according to the skill and temperament of the lòhren.

Lòhrengai: *Hal. Prn.* Ler-ren-guy. "Lòhren force." Enchantment, spell or use of arcane power. A manipulation and transformation of the natural energy inherent in all things. Each use takes something from the user. Likewise, some part of the transformed energy infuses them. Lòhrens use it sparingly, elùgroths indiscriminately.

Lòhrenin: *Hal. Prn.* Ler-ren-in. "Council of lòhrens."

Lòrenta: *Hal. Prn.* Ler-rent-a. "Hills of knowledge." Uplands in northern Alithoras in which the stronghold of the lòhrens is established.

Lornach: A Durlin. Friend to Brand and often called by his nickname of "Shorty."

Lost Huntress: See Halathgar.

Magic: Supernatural power. See lòhrengai and elùgai.

Menetuin: A city on the east coast of Alithoras. Founded by the Camar.

Merlon: The vertical stonework on a battlement between crenels. The merlon offers protection, the crenel a gap through which missiles are fired.

Netherwall: One of the ancient names of the witch better known in present times as Durletha.

Nudaluk: *Cam.* A bird of the woodpecker family.

Otherworld: Camar term for a mingling of half-remembered history, myth and the spirit world.

Red-fletched arrows: Cardoroth is famed for having great archers, and the greatest of them always use the red feathers of the Cara-hak turkey for their fletching. The bird is revered by them as a creature of luck, and it is considered ill fortune to shoot one. But many a farmer or hungry hunter does so, and the feathers are never wasted. But a wide variety of feathers are used from different bird species for arrow making, though all are dyed red before use.

Sellic Neben: *Hal.* "East gate." This gate bears a representation, crafted of silver and pearl, of the moon rising over the sea.

Sending: See Drùghoth.

Shadowed Lord: See Elùdrath.

Shazrahad: The Azan who commands an elug army, or serves as a lieutenant of an elùgroth.

Shorty: See Lornach.

Shuffa: A type of boat. Small, fast and ideal for travel by river. Favored by the villagers who dwell along the Careth Nien, and based on a design originating from ancient times when the Letharn fished the two rivers of the Angle. The same name is used in Cardoroth for a different kind of boat, slower and of a different shape. It's unclear which version is closer to the original design.

Shurilgar: *Hal.* "Midnight star." An elùgroth. Also called the betrayer of nations.

Sight: The ability to discern the intentions and even thoughts of another person. Not reliable, and yet effective at times.

Slithrest: One of the ancient names of the witch better known in present times as Durletha.

Spirit walk: Similar in process to foresight. It is deliberately sought by entering the realm between life and death where the spirit is released from the body to travel through space. To achieve this, the body must be brought to the very threshold of death. This is exceedingly dangerous and only attempted by those of paramount skill.

Sorcerer: See Elùgroth.

Sorcery: See elùgai.

Surcoat: An outer garment. Often worn over chain mail. The Durlin surcoat is unadorned white.

Taingern: *Cam.* A Durlin. Friend to Brand.

Tombs of the Letharn: The ancient burial place of the Letharn people. All members of the population, throughout the course of their long civilization, were laid to rest here. It was believed that to be interred elsewhere was to condemn the spirit to a true death, rather than an afterlife. The dead were preserved, and returned even from the far reaches of the empire. This was withheld from perpetrators of treason and heinous crimes. These were buried in special cemeteries near the river. Petty criminals were afforded an opportunity to redeem their place in the tombs on payment of a fine determined by the head-priest.

Tower of Halathgar: In life, the place of study of Queen Carnhaina. In death, her resting place. Somewhat unusually, her sarcophagus rests on the tower's parapet beneath the stars.

Unlach Neben: *Hal.* "South gate." This gate bears a representation of the sun, crafted of gold, beating down upon a desert land. Said by some to signify the homeland of the elugs, whence the gold of the sun was obtained by an adventurer of old.

War drums: Drums of the elug tribes. Used especially in times of war or ceremony. Rumored to carry hidden messages in their beat and also to invoke sorcery.

Wizard: See lòhren.

Wych-wood: A general description for a range of supple and springy timbers. Some hardy varieties are prevalent on the poisonous slopes of the Graèglin Dennath mountain range and are favored by elùgroths as instruments of sorcery.

VICTORIOUS SWORDS
BOOK THREE OF THE DURLINDRATH TRILOGY

Robert Ryan

1. Two Futures

Brand, his heart thrashing, ran to Kareste. Pain showed on her every feature, and tears of anguish glistened on her pale cheeks. She had fallen, and he went to help, as he knew he always would.

She trembled at his touch, but she was alive. And that thought nearly overwhelmed him, for he did not know what he would do if she died.

Her eyes, once green-gold, flickered open. There was now a shadow in them, and it was one of more than pain. The sorcery that she had invoked, the power that had run through her, had been beyond her strength to bear. But she *had* borne it, and such an act based on willpower alone, disregarding the weakness of the flesh, would have consequences.

He sensed the sorcery of the staff. Shurilgar's staff. A thing of ancient power beyond comprehension. The remnant of its unleashing still charged the air. Its lingering force was everywhere. And he saw it even in her eyes. What had her use of it cost her?

She shuddered violently, and then stilled. With her eyes half lidded, she spoke in a ragged whisper.

"You turn your back on the beasts?"

"You need me," he replied, "and I'm here."

She opened her eyes wider. "Foolish boy. But it's well for you," she added, "that I kept to my word."

She struggled to sit up a little higher. He helped her, and then she spoke more strongly.

"Behold! The Halathrin are free!"

416

For the first time, he turned to look. And what he saw amazed him.

They stood there, free of the forms of the beasts that had trapped them. They were gathered in a group, and a faint shimmer of white light was about them. Some were golden haired, but most had hair of a strange silver-white. It was more than blond. And the shimmer about them seemed as though the light of the full moon had been caught and refined, and it spilled from them in the same way that mist rose from the surface of a lake.

They were mostly men, but there were several women among them. One of these was the first that he had seen a little while ago. She looked back over her shoulder at him, but did not speak.

He turned to Kareste again. "Are you alright?"

She shifted position, trying to get comfortable. "I don't know. I feel strange."

He put his arm around her, helping her to sit upright. Shurilgar's staff lay on the ground between them. They both saw it, but neither of them said anything.

"I'll get you some water," he offered.

He walked over to the horses. There, he retrieved a waterbag and brought it back. He helped her hold it in her trembling hands while she drank.

When she was done, she gazed at him silently. He still saw pain in her eyes, and anguish. There was uncertainty too, and then, as though she cast a veil over her face, it was all gone. The lòhren inscrutability had returned, and she showed nothing of how she felt. So it always was with her. She hid her emotions out of habit, and he only caught glimpses at unguarded moments. Now, it seemed, she wished to hide them more than ever.

The staff remained between them, the unspoken question of what they each wanted to do with it hung in

417

the air. And they both ignored it for the moment. Neither of them was ready to raise that subject.

There was a stir behind them. The Halathrin appeared to have come to a decision about something, and the girl he had seen before came over to him. He saw relief on her face.

It was no surprise that she also seemed buoyant with a great joy. She was freed from the sorcery that had trapped her in the form of a beast. But then he remembered that Kareste had said the beasts were real as well, that the Halathrin had been joined *to* them.

His gaze darted around, and it quickly found what he sought. There were some twenty bodies beyond the Halathrin, back near the trees. They were misshapen things, twisted and fur clad, and he could only see them dimly. He was glad of that. But even as he watched, their dark forms faded into greasy smoke that drifted sluggishly away.

The girl stood before him. "Who are you?" she asked.

"My name's Brand. I'm bodyguard to the king of Cardoroth."

She looked with her clear-sighted gaze into his eyes, and then slowly shook her head.

"Nay, gentle Brand. That's merely your name and one of your tasks. It's not who you are."

He felt uncomfortable, for he had a sense that her mind perceived more of him than his could of her. She looked at him, but she saw more than was visible to the eye.

"Then, lady, who am I?"

She shook her head once more and there was a little shimmer of light as though a candle wavered in an otherwise unfelt breeze.

"Much I could say, but I will say naught. It is for you to discover, and the discovering will shape you. I dare not interfere."

"I've had many foretell my future," he answered. "Some with accuracy, but not yet has one with foresight *not* told me what they saw, accurate or otherwise."

"Foresight?" she said, with a little tilt of her head. "I don't know what you mean. I cannot see the future. I have not that power, else the elùgroth would not have caught me in his sorcery."

She shuddered, and a darkness dimmed her beautiful features.

"I see only the present," she continued, "but mayhap I see it clearly, and the present casts a shadow forward in time. You don't need to see the full length of a late afternoon tree-shadow to know the tree's shape – the living thing itself tells you that."

Brand did not understand, but he had no opportunity to question her because the other Halathrin were coming over.

They gave graceful bows, but did not speak. It seemed the girl was their spokesperson. She gave him her own little curtsey, and then straightened.

"My name is Harlinlanloth."

She turned her gaze away from Brand, and he saw a flicker of doubt in her eyes.

"Who is the girl that freed us? I would speak with her."

"Kareste," Brand answered. He turned around to look at his companion. She seemed to be recovering, but only a very little. It would take her days, perhaps weeks, to recuperate fully.

The girl curtseyed once again. It was a deft movement of sublime grace.

"You chose wisely," she said.

419

Brand could not decide if her voice was like velvet or steel.

Kareste answered, her own voice weak but edged with a curt tone that he knew well.

"How so?"

"If you had used the power of the staff for domination, to turn us into your slaves and to usurp the control of the elùgroths with your own, the power within the staff would instead own you. You mastered temptation, and therefore mastered the staff, at least this once. But the question has become this. What will you do now?"

Brand thought it was a good question. But it was not the only one. Now that the Halathrin were free, would they not wish to preserve the staff whose timber was sacred to them? And if so, what was he to do? He had no heart to fight them, or to fight Kareste. And yet he *must* destroy the staff.

Also, what of the power within him? He had freed it, and in doing so it lit up the path laid out ahead of him. To be sure, he did not seem to see his future as clearly as the Halathrin girl had done, but he saw it nonetheless.

His destiny was to become a lòhren. To serve the land. The magic inside him made it so, and he felt the connection. Yet magic was a thing that he distrusted, and all the more so now.

These matters were not all, either. Over and above them, calling to him from his childhood, was the voice of his own people. His responsibility as a lòhren would be to the whole land and not just a small and faraway community of little consequence to others. Even if it was everything to him.

He saw before him two futures, two separate paths. He wanted one, and not the other. But would fate allow him to choose?

He did not think so. He had been put on the path of a lòhren at every step of this quest, since perhaps even long before. Every move he had made, though he had not had any alternative, had brought him to this point. He had a feeling that it would continue, and that troubled him. It troubled him more than even an elùgroth, for the thought of becoming a lòhren *scared* him.

2. The Call to Serve

They were all gathered around Kareste. Harlinlanloth's words hung in the air, but whether or not Kareste believed them was another matter.

Slowly, Kareste reached for the staff. Brand wondered if he should have taken it before, while he could. Kareste had been true to her word and freed the Halathrin from the sorcery that bound them to the beasts, but did she have the strength to destroy the thing that gave her so much power?

She clasped the staff and used it to help her stand. Brand wanted to help, but he knew that reaching out toward her could be seen as an attempt to take the staff itself. That might be all that was needed to tip her thoughts in the wrong direction.

Kareste stood on wobbly legs, and she leaned on the broken staff. Unexpectedly, Brand thought of Aranloth. How many times had he seen the lòhren stand just so? But Aranloth's choices were made long ago. With Kareste, anything was still possible.

There was determination on her face that Brand had not seen before. She had always been strong willed, but a decision of one kind or another now seemed graven on her face as an image was onto stone.

She looked at them all, and though she was travel stained and dirty, though she was spent from their long journey and exhausted from the latest fight, he had never seen her look more beautiful. But the shadow was still in her eyes, and they seemed dark to him. He could not glimpse even a fraction of what she thought.

Then she turned her gaze directly on him as though the Halathrin were not there. She blinked a few times, and then she shrugged.

Brand watched her, uncertain. The Halathrin seemed calm, but underneath their exterior he sensed enormous tension.

Kareste stirred, and then spoke. "My choice is made. I promised Brand that I would destroy the staff, and I don't care what Durletha thought," she pointed at the witch's body, "I have power, and I *will* have more, for there are many things wrong in the land that need righting. But I will not achieve it with Shurilgar's staff. Even now, I fight its lure. If it isn't destroyed, and destroyed soon, I'll succumb."

The Halathrin looked at her gravely. After a few moments, Harlinlanloth spoke.

"It is so with you and your kind. But it is not so with us. The staff is a sacred thing. Long we protected its other half, hid it from the world, revered the memory of who once, long ago even to us, was lost. We could do so again, for we seek not to use its powers. We are not tempted."

Brand turned to the Halathrin girl.

"You know that there's another half, but do you know how it's used? How it's used even as we speak?"

Harlinlanloth looked at him with troubled eyes.

"Nay," she answered. "Only that the elùgroths possess it."

"Then I shall tell you. It's used in a siege. The enemy encircles Cardoroth City. Elugs, and all manner of other dark things, including elùgroths, draw on its dark power. The staff that is sacred to you is used by them to break down the city's defenses. Brave soldiers, and brave lòhrens, die to protect what they love. And though they fight, though they fight to their last breath, yet still the enemy will overcome them. At least, while the enemy wields the power of the staff."

He paused, allowing an opportunity for consideration of his words, before he went on.

"Even Aranloth cannot defy such power forever. It may already be too late, for long have Kareste and I tarried when we could have destroyed the staff earlier. And as you no doubt know, to destroy the one half is to destroy the other, for the power that infused it, when it was one, binds it still as two. Cardoroth may so be saved, and not only that, but great evil could be prevented that otherwise would follow as surely you know it must, so long as the power remains in the possession of the elùgroths. I don't wish to cause you, you who have been through so much, distress. But the staff must be destroyed. Not just for the sake of Kareste, not just for my sake, not just for Cardoroth, but for the whole land."

When Brand ceased speaking, there was silence. It was perhaps the longest speech he had ever made, and he thought he could have done better. But at least his thoughts were in the open. But how the Halathrin would react to them, he did not know.

The bulk of the Halathrin seemed ready to speak, but the girl silenced them with a slight gesture of her hand. She, it appeared, was their leader.

"This is no small thing for us," Harlinlanloth said. "We must speak amongst ourselves for a while."

She looked at Brand, and though he could not read her intentions, he saw sympathy in her eyes.

"Yet I hear you," she continued. "There's truth in your heart, and I sense it in your words. But this is a choice as even the wise should dread to make. On the one hand is the risk to Alithoras – on the other the veneration of one who is no longer alive, and yet who, while he lived, gave all he had, even the ultimate sacrifice, to protect the land."

She shook her head slowly. "To destroy the last remembrance of him is a dishonor beyond endurance to those who saw his deeds and heard his words. And most of my kind are accounted among that number. To them, in the end, I must justify my actions."

Brand did not answer. Instead, he gave a small bow. He understood what she said, and she understood the argument he had made. Nothing else needed saying, not yet, at least. And he hoped it never would.

The Halathrin withdrew. They gathered beneath the shadows of the nearby fringe of trees. They were close enough that Brand could hear the murmur of their voices, but not so close that he could understand them. But he did not wish to listen in anyway; theirs was a private conversation about things that he would never be able to truly understand.

He mused on his feelings. The power that was in him had been woken, and there was no way to cause it to slumber again. It was like a fire; having been sparked to life it must burn. He could not turn it back any more than a flower could refuse to bloom when the heat of approaching summer warmed the earth. Its time had come.

He closed his eyes and felt what he had sensed for some time: the need of the land. The land, from whence all power and life ultimately came. It called to him. He felt its demand to serve. It was the call that rumor and legend from everywhere in Alithoras claimed lòhrens heard. He knew it now for the truth.

But what of the Duthenor? What of the usurper who ruled in place of his father? Small things perhaps in the greater scheme of the world, in the face of the vast threat to Alithoras. But not to him. Could he heed a call, no matter how just and right, when his heart yearned for something else, equally just and right in its own way? Did he have the power to refuse the call? If he did, *should* he?

These also were questions that even the wise would dread to make. To serve without belief, without power of will and conviction of heart, was not to serve at all. It would only open the door to defeat, for the enemy would take such weakness and use it ruthlessly as a tool for their victory.

And yet there was no real way to refuse the call. The land outweighed all else. But why *him*? He did not believe in fate, did not believe that the future was set in stone. Let the land call another who could better answer! Yet who was that?

Brand's mind began to reel. He had no answers, was not even sure if he was asking the right questions. Perhaps he should run. If he were fast, if he fled far away, perhaps he could outrun them. And that thought became suddenly strong, for as he considered what would happen if he did that, he perceived with greater clarity the great shadow of the tasks that lay ahead of him. And even the hint of them was daunting. It was a mighty destiny, but not what his heart wanted. He steeled himself with an iron will: first, he must see things through with the staff.

Kareste, as always, sensed his mood. More importantly, she perceived his doubts, and was as direct as always.

"We don't need them to destroy the staff," she said. "If we must, we can do it while they talk."

Brand studied her for a moment. "Haven't *you* had a change of heart."

"Don't make light of it. I know now better than everyone the power in this thing." She gripped the staff tightly. "And the temptation. It would lead anyone into

426

evil, into the very heart of darkness. It must be destroyed, whether the Halathrin will it or no. Aranloth should have seen to it when he had the chance long ago. And I'll do it now, while I still have the will to do so."

"Maybe so," he answered. "But I don't think either of us have the power to burn it. Lòhrengai will not obliterate elùgai, and to try to do it that way is only going to bring the power within it into opposition. It couldn't be done quickly either, and then you'd have some very upset Halathrin to deal with." He paused, looking over at them thoughtfully. "The deed needs their cooperation, if we can get it. They see the thing as something different from what we do. And if we can get their cooperation, it will need much timber and a great fire. As I said, I wouldn't care to invoke lòhrengai to destroy it. That is to open yourself up to the staff itself, for such power can go both ways, and who knows how the power within it would react?"

She tilted her head. "I hadn't thought of that. Do you really think it's possible?"

"I don't know. You're more learned by far than I in such matters. But I think in truth that few ever walked the land who understood the powers of one of the great masters such as Shurilgar. Besides all of that, the Halathrin deserve better."

"Maybe so," she said. "But people rarely get what they deserve."

He did not answer that, and she shrugged. "Anyway, it was a thought. We'll do it your way, but I hope you can read these people better than I can. I have no idea what they'll do from one moment to the next."

Brand gave his own shrug. "Me neither, but as I always seem to have to do, I'll trust to my luck. I think they'll agree."

Kareste raise an eyebrow. "You have more than your fair share of luck. But we'll see. One day it'll run out. I just hope it isn't today."

She stopped talking, and he knew why. The Halathrin were returning.

"But it might be," she whispered a moment later under her breath.

3. Old as the Bones of the Earth

The Halathrin approached. Their visage was stern, and their eyes glinted with steady determination. It was the unwavering glance of immortals who endured through time, and the force of their will was honed by the long years so that their mind, once decided on some course, was not easily swayed.

There was a shimmer about them. It was stronger than before, for now that they seemed to have some purpose the power that was in them was focused. Just what they could do, and how strong they were in body and mind, Brand could not tell. But their powers were greater than that of human kind.

He felt tempted to draw his sword. This might yet become a fight, though he was still not sure if he could do that. He was sick of killing, but he began to feel that deep down inside him the urge to fight for Cardoroth, and for those who had placed their trust in him, was still there.

He waited, stony faced. He could not read them, but he was confident that they could not read him either.

Harlinlanloth came to stand before him. She was tall and proud. A light burned in her eyes, and though he could not read her, he knew this at least: her spirit was as proud as her manner, and though she was a gentle soul, there was also a fire in her that once woken would flare and burn and consume. As an enemy, she would be implacable. As a friend, loyal to death.

His heart pounded loudly, for he sensed in her a kindred spirit. But he betrayed no outward sign of his emotion.

Harlinlanloth stood still and looked at him intently. "Know this," she said with quiet force. "This decision is not easy for us. The wood of the staff comes from a sacred grove of elms in our forest realm. That alone makes it more precious than you can understand. But the trees grew on a mound, the burial place of our great king who led us to these shores during our exodus, for the Halathrin do not entomb their dead in stone as is the custom among men. It was from one of those sacred trees that Shurilgar stole the timber for his staff."

She paused. All was quiet about them. The hills were gray ghosts and the tarn silent as death.

"Yet we are not unaware that afterward the staff was possessed of an evil power. Yet still it remains a token of the living tree and the rest of the grove that Shurilgar razed by fire and elùgai. The staff alone, though broken in two, is all that remains of our memorial. For still no grass grows nor any flower or tree on the flame-blackened mound. You could never understand what a sad sight that is to us."

"Lady," he answered softly, "I understand death and tragedy."

She did not look away. "But you don't understand the bearing of it through years uncounted." She paused thoughtfully and then continued, a hesitant tone in her voice. "Though one day you will." She took a deep breath and went on with greater certainty. "So much of our story you may already know. Aranloth knows it, and it is clear that he set you on the path of this quest. But what you don't know is this."

The Halathrin girl swept her arm out imperiously behind her to indicate the other Halathrin.

"We are twenty," she said. "We are always twenty, for once there were twenty trees. We are the Drinhalath, the preservers of what was lost, the memory keepers and the guardians of the little that remains. Our lives are pledged to guard it. And in truth, we have no power or authority to agree or disagree with what you want. That is a decision for our king and his counselors. And yet," she said slowly, "a decision must be made, and made now else it will come too late for your people. And maybe ours also, for out in the world it may be that we cannot preserve our charge. So it proved in our own realm. We could not protect it there. And under our laws, the decision falls to me."

Brand felt for her. There was a hint of doubt in her eyes, of the anguish that she hid. For it was an impossible choice that she must make. And he knew what that was like.

"I lead the Drinhalath," she said. "The decision rests with me. Know this!"

Her voice changed, and he sensed that a sudden decision lay behind it.

"Our ways are not your ways, and there are consequences for any choice I make. But though we're different, the last remnant of sacred wood is as precious to us as your people are to you. We love what we love, and for us the memory of a loved one does not fade. For we who are immortal live longer and deeper in the past than those who live more briefly."

Kareste stirred and might have spoken, but Harlinlanloth went on.

"I don't mean to say that you love less, only that experience with your kind has taught us our differences. We live in the past as much as the present, and our thought encompasses both at the same time."

431

She paused a moment, and then shifted her gaze back to Brand.

"Know this, also. The Halathrin have long guessed where Aranloth secured the second half of the staff. That place is far away from here. You could have destroyed it there, but rather you came here to free us, at risk to yourselves and with the risk of delay to your people. We're in your debt, and we take such matters seriously."

Harlinlanloth bowed again, and so now did every Halathrin behind her. This, Brand noticed, was a deeper bow, as graceful as their every other movement, but somehow more formal this time. There was something behind Harlinlanloth's words that he could not quite grasp.

She straightened and spoke again. "We are in your debt, and as you made sacrifices for us, we will make them for you. The staff will burn."

There were tears in her eyes as she spoke, and a catch in her voice that tore at his heart.

"Lady," Brand said, "I would that it were not so."

"It is what it is," she answered, "And sometimes wishing is in vain. Yet still do we appreciate your thoughts. And though the staff must be destroyed, we would do so with dignity and in memory of he whom it commemorates."

Brand nodded. "How shall it be done?"

"There are funerary rites that are important to us. We would perform them."

Brand did not answer, but bowed in accession.

The next little while was solemn. In silence they each collected what dry timber they could. This they stacked into a large bier. After some time, it stood waist high and stretched out in a square with each side twice the length of a man. When it burned, Brand knew, it would burn with great intensity. And that was well, for though it was made of wood, he did not think Shurilgar's staff would catch fire easily.

Harlinlanloth approached Kareste. Gently, she reached out for the staff. Kareste gave it to her, and though her face betrayed no sign of struggle, Brand sensed that it took much force of will to pass it over.

Harlinlanloth laid the talisman gently on top of the bier, and then the Halathrin stood around it. Brand and Kareste stood back a little way, and watched in silence.

Harlinlanloth led the Halathrin in some sort of chant. Brand could not pick up the words at first, for it seemed to him that while it was the Halathrin tongue, there were many words and phrases that he had not heard before and he could not guess their meaning. Yet one phrase he understood: *Eleth nar duril.* This the Halathrin repeated frequently – lie in peace.

Kareste whispered to him, for evidently she understood more than he, or had learned of this rite from the lòhrens.

"They invoke the blessings of the sun and moon, of the sky and grass, of the forest and field. They seek oneness with all that was and all that will be, and they speak to the spirit of the departed, asking him to lie in peace, to be one with the universe as they will after him. They ask him to wait in tranquility until they are joined again, and the broken is mended, and the lost is found."

Brand was not sure what to make of it. But he saw the expression on the faces of the Halathrin, and whatever he thought did not matter. They believed, and it was a moment of great emotion for them. No matter that Halath, king of the Halathrin, had died thousands of years ago. It seemed to him that they felt his death as keenly now as they must have on that very first day.

433

Immortality, perhaps, was not so great as people made out.

The chanting continued without cessation, yet one of the Halathrin peeled away at some sign that Brand did not see. The warrior walked in stately fashion, stepping in time to the sonorous chanting. Soon, he plucked a handful of willow leaves that hung over the tarn. He returned, stepping in the same manner, and as he came to the bier he scattered the leaves over its top.

Before the warrior finished, another of the Halathrin peeled away. He also marched in the same fashion, yet his pace was slower, and the chanting became even more deliberate and deeper.

This warrior stooped and gathered soil from the edge of the tarn in his hands. It was dark and loamy, enriched be years of uncounted leaf falls.

The man returned. With graceful movements he spread the soil over the bier. And even as he did so, Harlinlanloth was already moving. Hers was a grace beyond even the others. She moved at a pace so stately, so elegant, that she barely seemed to move at all, and Brand could not take his gaze off her. There were tears on her cheeks, but her eyes shone with determination, and her voice did not falter.

The Halathrin girl reached the tarn. She ignored leaf and soil. Instead, she bent, scooped the dark water into her cupped hands, and stood again all in one fluid motion.

She returned to the others. Not one drop of water was spilled, and then with a sudden movement she cast the water over the bier. It glistened on the staff. The Halathrin chanting rose to a higher pitch, and it gathered pace. The ceremony, symbolizing many things beyond Brand's comprehension, was obviously drawing near its end.

The chanting was now high and remote. He understood little of it, but there was a beauty in its sound that transfixed him. He realized that the words and the rite were old; old even to the immortals. That was why he could not understand it, even though he spoke their tongue. It was a part of their heritage so ancient that it no doubt preceded their coming to Alithoras. It was old as the bones of the earth beneath their feet, and it meant something to these people that he could never understand. It was ancient even to them, bringing to life a language that they spoke eons ago in a land beyond the shores of Alithoras.

Unexpectedly, there was a slight falter in the chant. Brand looked to Kareste, and he saw that she was uneasy. And she did not look at the Halathrin, but out into the woods. Whatever had disturbed the immortals had disturbed her, and then he remembered the words of Durletha just before she died: *I will have the staff now, even if I must kill you, for others come for it…*

4. The Fire of the Sun

Gilhain stood atop the battlement. The noon heat beat down, and the sky was bright. He grinned to himself. He knew that he should not, not amidst such terrible waste of life, yet he did.

Shorty had been his champion and had defeated Hvargil. He had also escaped the sorcerers. This was a set of events to bring chagrin to the enemy, and what displeased them was good for Cardoroth – and his sense of humor.

He stood a moment longer, enjoying the feeling. There was satisfaction in being able to do so, but soon he must turn his mind toward facing the next threat, whatever it would be. Certainly, there would be more attacks, more elugs coming against the wall, but what else?

Aranloth was beside him, and he spoke into the silence. It seemed to Gilhain that the lòhren uncannily read his thoughts.

"Who knows what the enemy will do now?" he said. "They've been rebuffed, but not beaten. They'll come against you again, but they won't do so in the same way twice."

Lornach and Taingern were there also. They looked at each other, but only Taingern spoke.

"We'll be ready," he said.

They were simple words, but Gilhain felt the force of will that lay behind them. It was in the way the two men stood also, for they were warriors and they were riding high on confidence. They looked like they could proceed through the gate and take on the enemy just by themselves.

Gilhain understood the feeling, but he knew it would not last. He put an arm around each of their shoulders and stood between them. Together, they looked out over the battlement.

Aranloth stood a little apart, but he leaned against a merlon and looked out also. But though the lòhren's eyes gazed in that direction, Gilhain knew that he was not contemplating the enemy, but rather Brand. Where was he? What was he doing? Gilhain knew those same questions very well; he had asked them often enough himself.

There was no attack as yet, and it seemed that there was no sign of one building, either. Gilhain dropped his arms from the shoulders of the two Durlin and sighed.

"This is a good time for me to walk along the battlement and give some heart to the men, if I can."

"You always do," Lornach said. "More than you know."

They strolled along the battlement. They went slowly, for it was an oppressively hot day. The other Durlin, those who remained alive, joined them. And even Aranloth trailed along, a frown on his face and apparently deep in thought.

They came to an archer restringing his bow. "How goes it, friend?" Gilhain asked.

The man gave a slight smile. "Well, your Majesty. The light is good, and I have plenty of arrows."

Gilhain clapped him on the back. "Well spoken. If only you had an arrow for every enemy in the host and the time to shoot them all."

"Have them line up for me," the archer said with a straight face, "and I'll oblige you, Sire."

Gilhain gave him a wink. "Watch them closely," he answered. "And I'll see what I can do."

They moved on. Gilhain spoke to anyone and everyone as he walked the Cardurleth. Most of the soldiers merely listened though, for these were quiet and grim men. It was usually only the extroverts who spoke to him, and that was fine by him. These were the people who made jokes and lightened the mood. The others need not join in to benefit from that. Morale was like a fire: it was either sparking to life or dying. Only rarely did it burn steadily. And Gilhain knew it was his job to keep it burning, to keep it burning against the dark.

On they went, and Gilhain had spoken to a great many before he turned around and started to head back toward the rampart above the gate: his normal spot from which to direct the defense. He stopped and talked just as frequently as he had on the way out, and there was much grim banter. He took extra time for those who manned the Cardurleth despite a wound, yet who had chosen to remain with their regiment on the wall.

Gilhain had met all types of soldiers: the steely eyed, the mentally scared who joked to hide it, those who cared neither for life nor death but rather sought oblivion after some personal tragedy. He had met them all, talked to them all and understood them all. For he was at times all those things himself.

They eventually came back to the archer. His bow was long since restrung. Now, he was inspecting his arrows, checking their heads and shafts and red fletching.

The king nodded to him. "Those are long shafts," he said.

"Aye," the archer answered. "But I have long arms and the bow is well-matched to me."

"How far can you fire?"

The archer considered the question for a moment.

"With these arrows, close on three hundred yards."

"And how far can you shoot with accuracy?"

"That's a different thing altogether. Perhaps a third as far, depending on conditions."

Gilhain rubbed his chin. "That's further and more accurate than most."

The archer grinned at him. "I'm a tall man, and strong. I've been shooting since my youth, and there have been times when I went hungry if I missed. That sort of thing teaches a man to shoot well."

"I don't doubt it," Gilhain said. He looked out speculatively at the enemy host. "You could land an arrow among them?" he asked.

"I could, but at that range it would do very little damage."

"True," Gilhain said. "But should you see an elùgroth somewhere in the front ranks, it might be worth the attempt. If you strike one thus, there's ten gold pieces in it for you."

The archer grinned. "I'll see what I can do."

"Good man."

Gilhain looked out at the enemy again. They were not quite so far away that the archer faced an impossible challenge. Yet it was very nearly so.

He paused where he was a moment, studying the host. Something seemed to be happening among it, for there was movement in its center. But the host was so massive that he could not really see anything that far away. It waited there impatiently, a dark mass commanded by its dark masters. From both sides it stretched out wings to encircle the whole city. But Cardoroth was large, and those wings were stretched thin. They were not for attack but merely to ensure no one left or entered the city.

Gilhain gave a small sigh. How many times had he studied the host? And how many times had he found a weakness? But it did not matter, he would keep on looking and thinking. And even if he found no weakness, then this much at least he could be grateful for: the enemy did not build and employ siege engines. They did not use them in their homeland, either among the elugs or Azan. The land was not suitable, being mostly mountainous and rough. Nor were there walled cities. And anyway, they preferred to fight just as they did here. The elùgroths took pleasure in it, and they worked their soldiers up into a mad frenzy. Sometimes, Gilhain thought, they would attack the wall with nothing but hands and teeth if their masters asked them to.

There was movement along the rampart, and then Arell was there. She gave Gilhain a quick curtsey. "Your Majesty," she said. Then, she pointed her finger firmly at Lornach. "*You*," she continued. "You haven't come by for your examination as you said you would. Are you a fool? Do you know what sort of injuries you may have sustained in your fight with Hvargil? Do you know that some injuries are internal and not apparent straight away?"

He started to speak, but she cut straight through whatever he would have said.

"Don't bother to answer that. I *know* you know. I've told you these things myself often enough."

She turned to Gilhain. "This is unacceptable. I'm responsible for treating any injuries to the Durlin, but I can't treat them if they don't cooperate."

Gilhain turned to the short man. "Well, Lornach, why haven't you done as she requested? It seems to me that there are very good reasons for what she asks."

Lornach gave the healer a hard look, but it did not fool Gilhain. He knew the bond that was between Arell and all the Durlin, Brand especially.

"My lord, as it happens, I *did* report to her for an examination."

Gilhain glanced at Arell. "Is that so?"

Arell snorted. "If by report for an examination he means that he rolled his eyes at me, pointed to his arms and legs and said 'all still here,' before walking off, then yes, he's been examined. I wanted more than *that* though." She returned Lornach's stare. "But he pleaded that he must report to you directly. I only let him go after he promised to come straight back. But he never did."

Lornach clapped a hand to his forehead. "That reminds me, my lord." He pulled from a pocket in his white surcoat the cloth belt Gilhain had given him to wear as his champion. "This is yours, Sire."

He reached out to give the cloth to Gilhain.

"Don't change the subject, Shorty. You can keep the cloth – you may need it again someday. But for now, go along with Arell. You know she's right."

Lornach tucked the band of cloth away again. "But Sire, she lectures me all the time on what to eat and how to exercise and—"

"More likely," Gilhain interrupted him, "she tells you not to drink so much beer."

Lornach pretended to look surprised at the comment, but the answer he was going to give died in his throat and a sudden wariness came into his eyes.

Gilhain looked around for the source of Lornach's alarm. Immediately, he saw it. A vaporous fog had begun to rise from the stone floor of the battlement.

"Drùghoth!" Aranloth yelled.

Gilhain knew what they were. He had seen the sendings before, nearly been killed by them. But there was something different about them, now. Not only had they appeared this time in broad daylight, but the last had brought with them a chill that left ice everywhere. These brought with them heat, and though they seemed less distinct, less solid than the previous ones, they moved more quickly. And already they formed up into nine vague forms and swept toward him.

The eyes of the sendings burned with a white hot hatred, and in their hands they bore curved swords that glinted and sparkled like the water of a lake when the sun strikes it with slanting rays.

The forms of the Drùghoth were gray and wavery, and their approach was something like the shimmer of heat rising from a hot surface. As they drew near they gained more substance, and it seemed that sparks flew from their keen-edged blades, and their eyes had become like glowing embers.

There was stunned silence on the battlement. Gilhain drew his sword. He heard the same sound of steel slipping out of leather sheaths behind him. The Durlin were close, Lornach closest of them all. But it was Arell who found herself standing between him and those who had been sent to take his life. Arell the healer. Arell, who cured rather than killed.

5. A Dark Shadow

Brand felt a violent chill in the air, and a shadow obscured the already mist-dimmed sun. The chanting of the Halathrin continued, though he heard faltering notes within its rhythm.

And then, even as they reached a crescendo, the Halathrin abruptly ceased their ritual. Brand understood why. An elùgroth was come.

The sorcerer walked calmly around the narrow trail at the edge of the dark tarn. With him were elugs and hounds.

The world seemed to stand still, and into the dread silence the elùgroth spoke.

"A pretty little ceremony, for a nobody who is long dead."

Surprisingly, some of the Halathrin laughed. There was joy in the sound, their voices filled with a mirth that no human could match. For even as the immortals tasted of bitterness that men did not know, so also were they confident in their remembered joys.

Brand felt his heart lighten at the sound of their voices.

"Long dead, perhaps," Harlinlanloth answered. "Yet not a nobody. Halath did more than most to stymie the plans of your master. That is why you try to sleight him. And your hatred therefore speaks eloquently of his success."

"Yet I am still alive," the elùgroth said coolly, "and he is still dead."

443

"All things die," the girl replied. "Even Halathrin. Even *elùgroths*."

She said the last word with a venom that he had never heard before. He knew the speech of her people, yet nothing had prepared him for the emotion they could put into words. For them, words were power, they were the embodiment of thought. So he had learned, but to hear it was a different thing.

The elùgroth gave the impression of being less impressed.

"You will die now. All of you. Mortal and immortal, and the staff shall be mine."

The girl looked at him, still calm. "We are well matched, and these others," she pointed to Brand and Kareste, "are not without resources."

"I am Khamdar," the sorcerer said. "And I do not fear the threats of young girls, immortal or not. Even less do I fear the stuttering powers of mortals who reach out beyond their station and ability."

The great hounds spread out behind him, hulking things of tufted fur and muscle, eager to pounce at their master's word. Growls throbbed in their throats and the claws of their massive paws ripped the damp earth. Behind them the elugs, less keen perhaps, but still deadly in their way, took up positions.

Brand glanced at Kareste. He saw that exhaustion still hampered her, and something passed between them. She nodded. He would fight Khamdar and delay him, and while that happened she would destroy the staff. It was ready to be burned, and once a fire was lit it would take hold of the bier rapidly.

A moment later he saw her look at Harlinlanloth. There was a slight flicker in the eyes of the girl. The Halathrin understood and would be ready.

Brand saw also in Harlinlanloth's face the resolution that it must be so, else evil would always seek the staff, no matter how or where it was guarded.

Brand turned his gaze back to Khamdar. The sorcerer stood still, and yet he seemed to grow. As though a shadow fell over him, darkening and lengthening, he became taller, thicker, more massive. Nor did the growing cease. In a few moments he towered above them all, a gigantic form, clad in black, blocking out the mist-dimmed sun. Red fire, like flickering embers, ran and sparked along the length of his wych-wood staff.

The enemy had become massive, and Brand had no answer to that. But he attacked anyway, for that was who he was. He refused to let any obstacle, no matter how great, intimidate him.

The Halathrin blade earned long ago by one of his ancestors flashed. Khamdar, for all his size and power, seemed surprised. Brand took advantage of that and flung himself forward fiercely. Yet still the elùgroth had a chance to send a spurt of wicked flame from his staff.

Brand rolled and ducked. He came to his feet again, but the elùgroth had backed away. Now, the hounds and elugs raced forward. And yet Brand was not alone to face them all. Suddenly, the Halathrin were with him.

The immortals did not swell in size. Yet, in seeming defiance of the dark shadow that fell over them from the expanded elùgroth, the light that seemed to always shimmer about them shone brightly, and their pale swords glittered. They headed for the hounds and elugs, and Brand was free to keep driving at Khamdar.

The elùgroth backed farther away, but it was a feint. What he did next surprised Brand. There was a shimmer and disturbance in the air, and then Khamdar seemed to sprout wings. Great clouds of darkness billowed behind him, and he rose from the ground. With a giant leap his

445

chill shadow passed above Brand and then landed behind him. Then the shadow moved toward Kareste.

Brand turned and raced after the elùgroth. Even as he ran he drew and flung a dagger, but it passed into the shadow with a sizzling sound. There was a scattering of red sparks, and then the blade fell smoking and broken to the ground.

Kareste had already set flame to the bier. She sensed the danger behind her and turned to face it. Instantly, she gestured with her hand and a wall of flame sprang up between her and the elùgroth.

Khamdar hesitated, but only for a moment. That was all that Brand needed. He was upon his enemy again, his sword flashing, and Khamdar spun around to face him.

The two of them fought. The massive elùgroth swung his staff in a mighty down-handed blow. Brand darted to the side. Fire erupted from the ground in a crimson plume where he had just stood, and the earth heaved and scattered rocks and dirt.

Brand stepped in, stabbing with the point of his sword. Khamdar deflected the blow with his staff, and then swung it around again. It whooshed over Brand's head, all shadow and streaking fire as he ducked, and then he moved in to attack again.

This time Brand led with Aranloth's staff. He did not swing it as a weapon; instead, silver-white flame sprang from its tip and he lunged forward with it.

Khamdar was ready. His own staff, gigantic as his swollen body, swept it to the side. The sudden jolt knocked the weapon from Brand's hand. Yet he summoned flame to the sword in his other hand instead and continued to drive forward.

Khamdar seemed shocked. There was doubt in the burning eyes that looked down as though from a great

446

height, but still he sent a bolt of lightning sizzling through the air.

Brand dodged, feeling the heat of a hundred deaths pass him, and then the scream of a Halathrin from somewhere behind who had not seen it coming, or who had not moved as fast.

Brand glanced back. One of the immortals, charred beyond recognition, fell to the ground in a smoking heap of ash and bubbling metal from ornaments and blades. Brand knew he had made a mistake by looking behind him. He gritted his teeth and turned, but Khamdar had already used the momentary distraction to advantage.

The sorcerer had turned also and passed through the fading wall of flame that Kareste had raised. He knocked her aside as Brand watched, and she seemed too exhausted to even try to stand in his way. She fell into a crumpled heap.

Nothing now stood between Khamdar and the bier, and he reached for Shurilgar's staff that lay at the top of the burning heap of timber.

Brand, a sinking feeling in his stomach, leapt after him.

6. Relentless Swords

The Durlin leapt into the fray, but Arell was there before them. She ran at the sendings, crashing into them and causing them to stumble and slow. She paid for her bravery, for a spark-bright sword slashed through the air and struck her. What damage it did, Gilhain could not see. But smoke coiled up from the wound.

Arell was not done yet. In the midst of the attackers she drew a knife from her boot and stabbed. It sunk into the sorcerous flesh of the one who had struck her, but did no apparent harm.

The creature, too close to slash again, elbowed her out of the way, and though the blow would certainly have hurt, she recoiled as though with great pain, and wisps of smoke drifted from her clothing. Another sending struck at her, and she stumbled and fell, and even as she tumbled to the ground it delayed the enemy, for now they must trample over her body.

Arell had given the Durlin the little time they needed. They were gathered now around the king, and their swords met the spell-blades of the enemy. And though steel rang against steel, or its sorcery-created semblance, the weapons of the Durlin had little effect on the vaporish bodies of the attackers.

One sending broke through the ranks of the Durlin. It reached out with its blade, lurching toward the king. He deflected the strike, flicked back his own blade in a killing blow, but the thing still came at him.

Gilhain backed away. How could he fight something that steel could not kill? He spared a glance at Aranloth.

The lòhren was not that far away, but he was being attacked himself. Two of the creatures had spark-filled hands around his throat. Where their blades were, Gilhain did not know. Perhaps the lòhren had disarmed them, or maybe the hatred of the sorcerers who sent these things was so great that only the violent and slow death of their enemy would satisfy them.

There was a scream ahead of him, and a Durlin died. His white surcoat burned, and a flaming sword erupted with a spume of fiery blood from his back. A moment later another Durlin perished.

Gilhain stepped back further. He did not wish to retreat, yet he had no choice. He knew also that it was only delaying the inevitable.

And then Arell was among them again. Her clothes were rent by blade; blood-soaked ash stained the cloth around the tears, and pain showed on her face. What had happened to her knife, Gilhain did not know. How she was even alive, he knew less. Yet she was there, and in her hands was a bucket.

Gilhain sidestepped and dodged another thrust of a fiery blade lunging to kill him. He made no attempt to strike back. That was useless, and he endeavored now just to defend himself. He had thought that Arell would use the bucket as a weapon, but she did not.

The healer came up behind the sendings. And then she tossed water at them in a high arc. It fell down on them from above, splashing and sizzling as it struck the backs of the attackers. Steam rose in the air and unearthly cries of pain with it. But the attackers kept on coming.

Arell had done more though than get one bucket of water. She had gathered a half dozen soldiers and they each came behind her with their own buckets. These they had gathered from the back of the rampart where they were kept to help wash blood off the battlement floor.

The soldiers flung the water in their buckets at the same time. A wall of flashing water struck the sendings. Screams rose into the air and the spark-glittering swords dimmed and fluttered.

For once, the blades of the Durlin suddenly seemed to have more effect, and each strike caused pain and injury. The creatures screamed again, but then they gathered themselves and drove forward. Their swords burned once more, and the Durlin backed away.

"Water!" yelled Arell, and soldiers raced to retrieve it. But the buckets were further away now for the closest had already been used.

Time seemed to slow, and Gilhain knew that death hovered in the air all about him. There was a growing rumble, and then a crack of thunder. The sky darkened; a gust of air hit his face, and the sendings seemed a little less certain.

Gilhain spared another look at the lòhren. He was free of his attackers, and they seemed to shrink from him as he stood tall and spread his arms wide.

Thunder cracked again. There was a flash of light in the sky, and then the heavens opened. It rained. Nor was it just normal rain, but a downpour such as Gilhain had rarely seen.

In just a few moments water flowed in great rivulets across the stone floor. Massive drops smashed into Gilhain and the Durlin, wetting their clothes clean through. And the sendings hissed and smoked and writhed. The water was anathema to them, and their bright blades dimmed and then vanished, dissolved into the sorcerous air from which they had been summoned.

The sendings writhed and collapsed. In moments there was nothing left of them but a drift of steam and the faint echo of a faraway cry of pain. The elùgroths who sent them suffered for their demise, and a moan ran through the enemy camp.

Arell returned with the soldiers, but their buckets were no longer needed. They put them down where they stood. Water ran from their hair and dripped from their faces. But with a final rumble the sky lightened and the rain ceased. It did not peter out; it just stopped.

Gilhain looked farther along the battlement and saw, not really that far away, that it was still dry. Aranloth had called the rain, and it had fallen only where he had wanted it to.

They all stood there in silence, dripping wet, and the hot noon-day sun beat suddenly down upon them again.

Gilhain's gaze turned to the two dead Durlin, yet before he could even think of what to do or say Arell was already moving. There were others, and though not dead they were wounded, and she moved to help them. How she did it, how she stayed on her feet, he did not know, for she seemed just as wounded as they. There was blood on her in several places, and darkened rents on the cloth of her clothes where the swords of the enemy had cut her, yet she seemed to pay no heed to her own problems.

Gilhain tried to catch his breath. He was too old for this, and he felt his heart flutter strangely in his chest. At the same time, he felt lightheaded. Only Arell knew of these symptoms, for he had experienced them before, and she had given him a tonic to counter them. She had also said they would get worse over time, and he believed her.

He did not think his courage would ever give out, but his body would; she had warned him in her direct but caring manner of that, and he knew the time was not that

451

far away. Closer, unless he could leave stress and toil behind for the twilight years of his life.

He thought as he rested. The relentless swords of the enemy would wear them all down in the end. He must do something, something different and unexpected to break the pattern that was destroying them. Only by doing the unpredictable, the completely unforeseeable, did he have a chance to upset the rhythm of the enemy. For no matter the setbacks they had, they always regrouped and attacked again. But the question was, the question that had haunted him for most of the siege, was what?

7. All the Days of Your Life

Brand leapt through the failing wall of flame. Beyond it was Khamdar, and the fire on the bier that had begun to rage.

The elùgroth was massive. He had become a giant, become more than any man could hope to fight. Yet Brand called forth the magic that was in him. A blue-white nimbus surrounded him, and it protected him from the flame.

But Khamdar was another matter. The sorcerer was a threat beyond Brand's capacity to deal with. And yet, even as he thought that, he caught the lie within it. Khamdar had increased his size, swollen into immensity. But it was illusion only, a deceit intended to cause fear and hopelessness.

And the thought that he was unable to fight him had been seeded by the sorcerer himself. Brand did not let that thought take root in his mind. He gritted his teeth, told himself that he was right, and even as he did so Khamdar shrank. He was become a man again, yet still one of the most dangerous men to ever walk the earth.

Khamdar must have sensed this change in Brand, for he hastened toward Shurilgar's staff. With a leap he was upon the bier and reaching into the flames for the talisman.

Brand was right behind him. Sorcerer or no, he could not stab him in the back. Perhaps Khamdar knew that, and so risked this moment of vulnerability. Instead, Brand dropped Aranloth's staff and reached out with his own hand, gripping the back cloak of his enemy, and the bony shoulder that lay beneath it.

A moment thus they struggled. And then Brand's hand reached around and clutched the elùgroth's throat. His grip was strong, trained since his youth in weaponry, and an iron will guided it.

The elùgroth turned, for he had no choice. And with a heave Brand pulled him away from the bier and sent him sprawling to the ground.

Brand swung around to face his opponent, putting himself between the elùgroth and his goal. The fire on the bier swelled and crackled behind him. The elùgroth rose from the dirt like a swaying snake, a creature that would not be pinned down in one place, a creature that no one could predict where it would go and what it would do next.

And like a snake the elùgroth prepared to strike. His face was contorted by inhuman rage, and wicked flame burned at the fingertips of his left hand, but just at that moment three Halathrin propelled themselves into him. They knocked him flying and went down with him in a mess of flame and tangled limbs.

Brand looked for Kareste. She was nearby. Three hounds were growling at her, their tufted fur risen in hackles, saliva dripping from their fangs. She held them at bay, lòhren-fire stuttering from her fingers. But the fire was dying and the hounds getting ready to leap.

Brand did not hesitate. He threw his sword at them. The Halathrin blade spun and wheeled in the air, silver light burning at its edge. It smashed into the beasts with a spray of fire, but he was no longer even looking at them. He had turned, leapt back, and grabbed Aranloth's staff from the ground.

There, for a moment, he hesitated. The elùgroth had thrown off the Halathrin and was ready to leap into the flames of the bier again to retrieve Shurilgar's staff. But at the same moment Brand saw one of the hounds, the great ruff of fur around its neck burning with a wreath of flame, crouch to leap at Kareste.

He did not know what to do, and had no time in which to make an impossible decision. But even as he hesitated there was a strange sound. It was a thrum, or a scream, or a mighty screech. It was like no sound that he had ever heard, and he felt it vibrate as much through his bones as he heard it with his ears.

From the bier rose a plume of black smoke, thick and turgid. Thunder cracked in the sky and the earth rumbled as though the very hills of Lòrenta had come alive and begun to march. A gale rose, slapping into Brand's face and bending the plume of smoke. Sparks flew in the wind: red, green and wickedly hot.

Above them, the dark plume bent further, reaching down toward them, and its shadow was cold with evil. Closer it came, and then a gust of wind howled and dispersed it.

"No!" screamed Khamdar. It seemed as though there was agony in his voice. The elùgroth reached out toward the bier, his fingers opening and closing, but the staff was gone, and the bier roared with flame so hot that he stumbled back from it.

The hounds howled. The elugs moaned. Khamdar fell to his knees. Almost, Brand felt sorry for him, for he did not like to see anyone or anything suffer.

"It is done," Kareste muttered. "For good or for ill."

Harlinlanloth spoke quietly, solemnly. "Thus passes the last symbol of Halath, he who died for his people. Now, only memory exists, but memory shall endure even through the long ages yet to come."

Brand looked around. The few hounds and elugs that were left alive scattered. Khamdar had lost control of them, but the elùgroth remained. Slowly, he stood.

Brand took a step toward him. But he was not alone. Kareste shuffled on weary legs near him, and the Halathrin gathered close.

Khamdar eyed them all. He made no move or threat. His wych-wood staff was gripped but loosely in his hand. And then he stretched forth his free arm, long and clothed in a ragged black sleeve, and spoke.

"You shall pay for this, Brand of the Duthenor. Listen and hear, for my words are truth."

The elùgroth's voice was cold and remote, and a strange expression had come over his face. Brand had seen something similar before on Aranloth, but only when the lòhren spoke with foresight.

"Everything you touch," Khamdar said, "will wither before you. Everything that you reach for, shall fall from your grip. All that you want will disappear. You shall not know joy, nor friendship, nor love."

Brand stood still, frozen in place. This was not foresight, it was a curse, and the elùgroth continued with relentless calm.

"Your luck will always run out. Ill-fortune will follow you. That which you do not want will come for you, that which you seek shall remain hidden. The great shadow of death will walk by your side all the days of your life, dogging your every step. You will never be free of it, and you will know that not even death, *least* of all death, will allow you to escape your woe. And yet you will die, for I will kill you. I will destroy you in fire and smoke, even as you destroyed the staff. And I shall tread over your ashes, driving them into the barren earth."

A great quiet settled over everything. It seemed that even the hills of Lòrenta listened to the curse, for there

456

was power in the elùgroth's voice to command the very stone that lay at their roots. And the dark tarn looked up at them all, motionless as an unblinking eye to bear witness.

Brand was shocked, shocked and surprised as he had never been before. For he had expected a fight, expected anything from the elùgroth, but he had not anticipated this.

Yet he would not cower. In response, he gave a nonchalant shrug.

"That's been my life already. Perhaps it's the life of all who live." Then he stood taller, and a hardness came into his eyes. "Your words mean nothing to me. But this sword," and he raised his Halathrin blade before him, "is something that I well trust. It's in my grip, and it will not fall. Nor will it disappear. Nor will it turn to ash and smoke. And soon you shall feel the truth of *my* words."

Brand stepped forward toward his enemy.

8. The World Shall Tremble

Gilhain felt the loss of the two Durlin who had died. Death had claimed many lately, but he had known those two, known them well, for he spent most of his time with those who guarded him, more so than even with his family. He sighed. Would there ever be an end to the dying?

The bodies of the two men rested now in the Durlin chapterhouse; two young men, hand-picked by Brand, loyal to death. And though they would be honored, though their families would be well looked after in times to come if Cardoroth somehow managed to survive, they were still dead. There would be no wives for them. No children and grandchildren. It was not just the men who had died, but their futures with them.

All over the city it was the same. Nearly every house was in mourning, for they had been touched by death. War was a waste; it was an unthinkable waste. And how many had been killed that otherwise would have become great poets, or sculptors, or healers or merchants? They were all gone, would all never be, and the ghosts of the future haunted Gilhain as much as the dread of the present.

He felt the sorrow of the Durlin who were around him. It filled the air and even the irrepressible Lornach was subdued. All their faces were grim, and they would be grimmer tonight when the funerals were held.

The evening was no time for a funeral, but there was no choice in things these days. The days were for the

458

living to fight for their lives. The night was for funerals and dark dreams.

Gilhain straightened. He must not allow himself to become depressed. The whole city was watching him, and if he faltered they would follow; and the city would fall. He was sick of being attacked, of the enemy reaching out with the specific purpose of claiming his own life. He was sick of it, sick of it all, but he must play his part until the end.

Noon approached. The enemy massed again below, and it was clear that another attack was imminent. The men on the wall waited stoically. Everything they did lately was stoic, but they had little choice in that.

The soldiers stood quietly; the elug war drums thrummed away in their disconcerting beat. Gilhain was sick of them too, but he must bear things just the same as his men.

The dark ranks of the elugs chosen to attack marched to the front of the main host. They were a seething mass of enemies, fueled with a will to destroy and the sharp swords to bring their aim to fruition. Malice emanated from them, a darkness borne not just of hatred and the desire to kill and destroy, but also of foul sorcery whose depth was unplumbed and that knew no limit.

At that moment, with the defenders waiting in silent dread and the enemy poised to unleash the horror of war, there was a gust of wind. It touched the enemy first, moving among its ranks and troubling them, bringing their drums to a standstill. And then, with a light caress of the Cardurleth it lifted up banners and pennons, touched the faces of the men, and passed over into the city beyond.

Aranloth straightened. His eyes widened, and his hands formed white-knuckled fists.

459

"What is it?" Gilhain asked, whispering into the silence. "What new deviltry do you detect?"

The lòhren began to tremble. His eyes glittered, but as he seemed about to answer there was a crack of thunder.

A great boom rippled across the empty sky like the peal of a bell so vast that all the world would not contain its ringing. It seemed at once to reverberate through the battlement and to also come from the farthest ends of the earth.

At Gilhain's side Aurellin muttered. "There are no clouds."

Taingern and Lornach stepped closer to him, and Gilhain felt a shiver run up his spine.

They all looked around. The wind grew and hammered at them, beating at the white surcoats of the Durlin who surrounded the king.

Thunder boomed again. The wall trembled. Screams rose from the enemy camp, from its center where the tent of the elùgroths was pitched. The war drums started to beat again, wild and erratic, and then they died away into expectant silence once more. The elugs preparing to charge the Cardurleth milled around uncertainly.

The Durlin drew their weapons, but Aranloth glanced at them and spoke.

"Put them away!" he commanded. "Watch and see, and think of Brand, for just now, no matter the empty leagues that separate us all, he is thinking of us."

There was a third crack of thunder, louder even than the others. The very earth seemed to shudder. The enemy host fell to their knees and lifted their voices up to the heavens in a great moan.

The world seemed to stand still. And then a great plume of smoke, thick and black, filled with sparks and roiling power, rose above the enemy host. Like a vast tower, mighty as a mountain, it leaned toward the city as though to overshadow all Cardoroth, and then it was torn away in shreds and tatters by the gusty wind.

The enemy moaned and wailed. The darkness dispersed and the bright sun gleamed in the sky. As though a great burden had somehow been lifted from his heart Gilhain looked around in wonder.

All about him men were smiling and breaking into laughter. They felt it too, whatever it was, though they understood it no more than he.

Aranloth stood tall. It was one of the few times that Gilhain had seen him smile, a smile free of care that seemed to make him look almost like a young man again. Tears ran down his clear-skinned cheeks, and Gilhain realized that the true Aranloth stood before him. Not Aranloth the lòhren, bearing a great burden and masking his thoughts from the world, but just Aranloth.

And yet he was still a lòhren. His white robes glimmered, and the power that was in him, always present but usually hidden, shone forth. That force was unveiled, and it wreathed him from head to toe.

Aranloth moved. Slowly, he raised high his arms. And then he spoke. His voice was resonant, and by the power that was in him his words carried over all the battlement, and Gilhain guessed even over all the city.

"Behold! Brand of the Duthenor, Brand the Durlindrath, Brand who left this city on a quest, fulfills it! At great risk, battling perils and temptations you cannot guess, he has struck a mighty blow at the enemy. He has destroyed a source of their power, a staff that aided them, that enhanced their strength and gave the elùgroths might. No more! So, remember Brand in your hearts, for he has just now saved your life. If he returns, honor him with great honor!"

There was a sudden silence, and then a ringing from the city. Bells tolled. Soldiers cheered. City folk threw

461

their hats in the air and danced and laughed. Even the Durlin, eyes still alert for any threat, spared tight smiles for each other.

Gilhain felt his wife's hand in his own, and suddenly everything seemed right with the world. But that feeling could not last forever.

Within the hour, out of the disorganized mess of the enemy camp, strode three dark figures. They were tall, black clad, and angry.

They came before the Cardurleth. And when they spoke, the power that was within them carried their voices, for all three spoke as one, to everyone on the wall.

"This is not over, old man. Still we have the blades to bury you. Still we have the relentless swords of a numberless host to cut you down. We will *not* stop. We *will* prevail. That is as certain as day follows night, and then the night comes again. We will reduce this city to blood-stained rubble, and the world shall tremble at its fate."

As one the elùgroths ceased to speak. As one they turned and walked back toward their host.

Gilhain watched them go in silence, but Aurellin broke it.

"There was truth in those words."

Aranloth shrugged. The Durlin looked to their king.

Gilhain gazed out at the enemy. And then he also broke his silence.

"And there is truth in what I say now. We will prevail, for we have been given a chance beyond hope. Now, we shall turn defense into attack. Now, the hunted will become the hunters." He pointed out toward the dark host below. "The enemy shall learn to fear us. Too long we have stayed behind the great wall of Cardoroth. Now, Brand has given us an opportunity, and I will take it."

462

They all looked at him for a moment, different expressions on their faces. Most, he thought, were wondering if he were mad, if the pressure had finally unsettled his mind. He merely smiled at them, for a plan had come to him, a strategy that while of enormous risk could bring enormous benefits.

Aurellin, who knew him so well and knew that he had not lost his mind, narrowed her eyes at him.

"What are you planning?"

"Listen," Gilhain said. "This is what we'll do, and may fortune favor us."

9. More than You Seem

Khamdar stood there. The curse had left his lips, his black heart having given vent to the evil within it, but his arm remained stretched out, and the ragged sleeve that covered it hung like dead ribbons of flesh from a rotting corpse.

It did not matter. Brand advanced on him, and with him came all the others. A few moments the elùgroth studied them, his shadow-haunted eyes gleaming with hatred.

"This is not the end," he whispered.

Brand made no answer, but continued forward, his steps slow but confident.

Khamdar did not turn away to flee. By some art beyond Brand's comprehension he merely became more and more shadowy. In a few moments he was gone, nothing but a shadow flickering amid the fringe of trees marching up toward the hills, if even that.

"He is gone," Kareste said, and there was a great weariness in her voice.

Brand reached out with his thought. He found that the more he tried such things the easier they became. But he discovered no trace of his enemy. Yet he knew that they would meet again, at least once.

"What now?" Kareste asked.

Brand sheathed his sword. "For me, I must return to Cardoroth. The staff may be destroyed, but a massive host no doubt still besieges the city."

"I'll come with you," Kareste said without hesitation. "Though I don't see what help we can bring to them from without."

"We shall see," he answered. In truth, he did not know either, but he felt that that was where he should go.

The Halathrin were looking at him, those who still lived, and he bowed to them once more. They were a formal and ceremonious people, and they seemed to appreciate such things.

"Thank you," he said simply. "It was nice to meet the fair folk of legend." He would have said more, but Harlinlanloth had begun to smile, if sadly, at him.

She returned his bow with a curtsey, but the smile never left her face.

"So quick to see us off, Brand?"

"No, my lady, but you and your band have done all that you can do. I had thought that now you would return home and take news to your people of these events."

"I have already sent a messenger," she answered. "As for having done all that we can do, perhaps you're right. Then again, perhaps not."

"I didn't see anyone leave," Brand said with a frown.

She shrugged. "The Halathrin are skilled in such things. But it is of no matter. What does matter is this. We have a grudge against this Khamdar and his brethren, both for our people and also for ourselves. We will come with you, and what we can do – well, we shall see."

Brand bowed again. This was more than he expected.

There was little talk after that. They quickly prepared to leave, holding a ceremony for the dead and interring them in the earth. The bier still burned. Soon it would become coals and then nothing more than ash on the wind.

They left, and the fire dimmed behind them. Kareste led the way, for she knew Lòrenta and the surrounding lands better than everyone else. Brand followed her, brooding on his thoughts and problems. The Halathrin trailed behind, fanning out but moving in silence.

Kareste turned to him some while later. "I had not thought they would come," she said softly.

"Nor I," he answered. "But it's fitting."

"How so?"

"They've been wronged," he said, "and this is their chance to redress that."

"Revenge?" she asked. "I hadn't thought you the type."

"No. I'm not. But if you let people walk all over you, you only encourage them, and any others who see it to do the same. Sometimes you have to fight back – not because you want to, but because you must."

"It's a fine line."

"So it is, but you've just now walked on the right side of it. You destroyed the staff. It could've given you great power, and the capacity for revenge against the elugs who long ago wronged you and your family."

She looked away. "Perhaps," she replied at length. "But if I know where that line is, it's because you showed me." She paused again. "Truly, you're more than you seem. You know more than I think about many things, and you guess even more still. And you always have a few surprises up your sleeve. But I'm no longer surprised that Aranloth gave you his staff. Not in the least. And I think that now you have a greater appreciation of what it meant that he did so."

It was Brand's turn to look away. She had struck nearer to the truth than he would have liked, and it reminded him of his problems.

He was a warrior, perhaps one day a chieftain if he could free his people from their usurper. He wanted nothing else, especially not magic that he did not trust. But now a choice lay before him; to follow his heart's desire, or to accept a burden of responsibility and power that he did not seek, nor was wise enough to handle, and that in the end would see him weighed down with the cares of the world as was Aranloth. It was no way to live. But could he live with the knowledge that he refused to heed the call of the land, and the people who lived in it?

He did not answer Kareste, but he felt her eyes on him. She guessed much of what was going through his mind, and as he had left her free to make her choice, thus did she leave him to his. It was strange how quick, and how complete, the reversal of their situations had been. But fate was full of these little twists. Or if not fate, the chances of life.

But fate, or chance, or design did not matter. They never had to him before. He would forge his own path. At least, as soon as he knew what it should be.

10. Strife and Mayhem

Brand and his companions came down from the misty hills of Lòrenta. They were leaving that mysterious land behind them, and many strange things had happened there. Not Brand, nor Kareste, nor the Halathrin would ever be the same again.

An unusual feeling surfaced in his mind as he rode. Things had changed for him. Some for the better, some for the worse. But most related to the future, and he could not see where that led, for he had two paths before him and did not know which he should choose, if he even *had* a choice. And it was not in his nature to endure uncertainty or doubt. He must consider, and then decide on his action. Fate could go hang itself. But even as that thought crossed his mind so too came another: maybe for once in his life there was a power outside himself that was greater than his own will.

The Halathrin kept mostly to themselves. They were a strange people, quick and agile on their feet, keeping up with the pace of the horses. Brand had slowed down several times, but Harlinlanloth had only grinned at him and waved him imperiously on.

Brand did not quite know what to make of her. At times she seemed like any other young girl, but at other times she showed that she was a leader of people, and that she had an understanding of the world, born of years of living beyond his count, and a maturity that made him seem as a child. It was yet another strange feeling, and he sensed that she reveled in the fact that he did not understand her. In that respect, she was like most young girls that he knew: she enjoyed being a mystery but wanted him to solve it at the same time. Perhaps he would accomplish that. Perhaps he would not. Either way, he liked her.

The Halathrin travelled silently, almost invisibly, and Brand remembered that the famed Raithlin, the scouts of some of the Camar tribes in ancient days, had learned their arts from such as these.

"So," Kareste said, interrupting his thoughts. "What's your plan? Lead us to Cardoroth and get us killed?"

She had changed, but not in all ways. Her tongue could still be sharp. But that may have been because she knew he was thinking of the Halathrin girl. Kareste, for all her power, could also act like a young girl when the mood was on her, even if that was seldom.

"Hopefully not," he answered.

"Then what is it?"

"I don't know, but Cardoroth is where I must go. I'll think of something as we travel."

"Humpf!" Her tone was even more dismissive than usual, but he noted that she did not speak of going elsewhere.

Her question was nonetheless a good one, notwithstanding her ungraciousness. What aid could he bring the city, and his friends, now? But even as he considered that his earlier thoughts of the Raithlin came back to him. They were always few, but as scouts their job was to spy out the situation, report back on enemy movements, and at need sow strife and mayhem among the enemy. He was not a Raithlin, but with the Halathrin beside him, could they not kindle some sort of discord among their opponents?

It was a thought, it was the beginning of a plan, but it needed more work yet. Much more. He dared not even mention it to Kareste for she would tear it to pieces. And so she should. He must come up with something that she could *not* tear to pieces, no matter how much she tried. If he could do that, then maybe he was getting somewhere.

Eventually, they reached the Great North Road. It was empty and void of any sign of recent travel. Brand paused there a while to give the horses rest. He dismounted and Kareste followed suit. He chafed at the delay, but it was best to keep the horses fresh while they could, for it was impossible to say what hard riding might lie ahead.

One of the Halathrin approached. It was not Harlinlanloth, as usual, but a seemingly young man.

The warrior reached him, a slight frown on his face. His hair was that strange silver-white that seemed to predominate among his people; he had a slight scar that marred his face and his voice, when he spoke, though melodious in its way seemed rough compared to Harlinlanloth.

"The land here has changed little," he said casually. "I'm called Narinon, and I trod this road many times in my youth before the Camar came to dwell near our home in the south."

Brand, though he knew he should not have been, was somewhat shocked. This seemingly young man had been alive in a time that was no more than myth and legend to the people of Cardoroth. And there was an edge to his voice as well; it seemed that some of the Halathrin would not have destroyed the staff had the choice been theirs instead of Harlinlanloth's.

The warrior did not appear to require any reply to his comment. He carried on, almost, but not quite oblivious to Brand's surprise.

"Once, I even walked the mountains of the north, Auren Dennath as we call them. It was a fair land, and

470

the memory of that lingers in my mind. Gladly I would walk there again."

"But the Halathrin no longer travel abroad," Brand said. "They stay in their forest realm and the land, and its people, miss them."

Brand knew it sounded like a compliment, but there was a rebuke hidden within it. The Halathrin no longer ventured beyond their borders to help fight elugs. They had not done so since the Elu-Haraken, what most just called the Shadowed Wars. Brand did not really blame them, for they had suffered much, but if this warrior resented the fact that the staff was destroyed to help protect the free peoples of Alithoras, he may as well know that resentment could be a two-edged sword.

The warrior made no sign that he took offence, yet Brand was sure that he understood exactly what had just been said.

"What are the mountains like?" Brand asked. Having delivered his rebuke, he wanted to change the subject; and talk of those mountains always stirred him for some reason.

"Dangerous," the warrior replied. "A small misstep there could be death, but that is so in many places of the world."

Brand did not answer, and the warrior went on. "There are ice flows and chasms and storms wild as anything you have ever seen. The wind howls among the peaks and the caves moan when the snow flies and the sky is dark. But those days are not the only ones. At other times the world is still. Nothing moves over snow so white that it nearly blinds the eye, and the pines, dark green and scented, march away over slope and ridge, through valley and dale, and a man could walk beneath their shadow all the days of his life, however long that be, and not walk the same trail twice."

Brand began to feel his blood stir. "And what of summer?"

The warrior laughed. "Summer is short, but the days are beautiful beyond your comprehension. The daytime sky is bluer than any gem of the earth, and at night the stars shine so bright that you feel that if you climbed a mountain you could reach up and pluck them all from the sky."

"And what of the elugs who dwell there?"

"Yes, there are elugs there, or there were. Rumor is that they still haunt the caves and dark valleys. They are one of the dangers, that is true. But they are not the only one. There are other dark creatures also, but the mountains are vast, and you can walk for day after day without seeing such as they, perhaps even weeks. And at those times, in certain places, and one in particular near the source of the river that flows down to fill Lake Alithorin, there is peace and tranquility such as even we Halathrin cherish, for it is found in few places on earth."

Brand did not like this man, but there was a certain passion in his voice when he spoke that was eloquent, a certain something in his words that found an answer in Brand's heart.

"Does this place have a name?"

"Of course. We call it Limloth, which in your tongue would be 'Still-peace,' or something similar."

"A fair sounding name."

"It's a fair place, fair beyond your imagining – even as Harlinlanloth is forever beyond your grasp. The one is likely too dangerous for you to reach, frail mortal that you are, and the other, the other is too bright for mortal eyes to endure. Her spirit is greater than yours even as the mountains rise above the plains. To try to get too close is to risk falling as from a great height."

Brand raised an eyebrow. There it was, the cause of this warrior's hostility. Now, he realized how things stood. But there was no time for this. Other things needed doing.

"I'll think on your words," he said coolly.

"That would be wise."

Brand looked at this warrior more closely. He was fair, pretty as a girl in many ways, but there was a steel in him, and a confidence too. This was a warrior who feared little, least of all expressing his opinions.

Time slowed. Brand looked him in the eye, and then he smiled. The warrior did not know what to make of that, but he did not withdraw his gaze.

There was a commotion behind them, and then one of the Halathrin stepped forward and pointed.

"Someone comes!" he said.

They all looked to where the man pointed. South, a long way away down the straight line of the Great North Road, a lone figure walked.

It was no wonder that the Halathrin had seen him first. They were reputed to have excellent sight, far better than an ordinary man's, and yet Brand could see the figure also.

Brand considered the situation. There was nowhere to hide for there were no trees here, and the land was flat and the grass not long. Besides, if they could see the figure, likely enough whoever it was had long since seen them: they were many and there were horses among them.

"What do you think?" Kareste asked. "If she had heard the warrior's words of warning to Brand she gave no sign.

"There's nowhere to hide," Brand said, "and perhaps no reason either. He's only one, be he friend or foe."

The warrior with the scar pursed his lips. "Few times is a stranger in a strange land a friend."

Brand leaned on Aranloth's staff. "I haven't found that to be the case, myself. But I'm not as old as you, nor as wise."

The warrior did not answer. However, Brand felt Harlinlanloth's gaze on him. Her expression was unreadable, but he knew by the very fact that she looked at him, and then shifted her gaze to the warrior, that she guessed exactly what had passed between them. What she thought of it, he could not tell.

"Travelers are rare these days along the road," Kareste said, seemingly oblivious to what was going on. "It could be an elùgroth."

"Or it could be anybody," Brand replied. "We'll wait and see."

Kareste looked at him speculatively. "Trusting to luck, again?"

He gave her a wink, but did not answer. After a moment she looked away, the lòhren look of inscrutability on her face, and he knew that she also had heard or guessed what had passed between him and the warrior.

He watched the lone figure approach. He did not think it was an elùgroth, but there were others who sought Shurilgar's staff. Would they know it was destroyed? Probably those with enough power would sense that it was gone. But then, who was it that came toward them?

11. Now is Our Chance

They gathered around and listened as Gilhain spoke of his plan. He talked to them quietly, but nevertheless with excitement. And as he did so, he felt the anticipation of great events quicken his pulse.

"We've defended for a long time," he said. "Now, the enemy is in disarray. The staff is destroyed, the elùgroths are distraught, and the greatest sorcerer among them all is gone, drawn away from the attack by Brand." He paused, allowing his words to sink in. "What," he asked eventually, "does all that mean?"

"Trouble for Brand," Lornach said with a tight smile, and there was some laughter.

Even Gilhain saw the humor in that. The men around him, even as he did himself, used humor as a weapon against despair. And a potent weapon it was. Perhaps one of the strongest.

"And what else?" he asked, when the moment had passed.

Taingern spoke, quiet and thoughtful as always.

"The whole host is driven by the elùgroths. If they're in disarray, the enemy horde, mostly elugs, are in a worse state. It's the elùgroths who give them all purpose and direction."

Gilhain nodded slowly. He could not afford to move quickly here.

"And how can we take advantage of that?"

He waited patiently. He had deliberately not just explained his plan. It would be better to lead them to it, to understand the situation themselves and to make it their own.

Aranloth also remained silent. He, Gilhain was sure, knew exactly what the plan was going to be; at least the thrust of it, if not the details. And the fact that he remained quiet signified his agreement. If not, he would already have spoken. What he was doing, just as Gilhain himself must do, was time things well. The lòhren would speak at the right moment, and not before.

It was Lornach who answered Gilhain's question, and he was, as always, direct.

"You would send out a sortie to attack them?"

Taingern rubbed his chin.

"It's something we haven't had the chance to do before."

Gilhain looked from one of them to the other, but he did not answer.

"No," Aurellin said, adding her voice to the discussion as she always did, with quiet force. "I think he means a little more than a sortie."

The two men looked at their king, realization dawning on their faces, swiftly followed by surprise. Gilhain studied their reaction and liked what he saw; if he could surprise these two men he was a chance of surprising even the best leaders among the enemy host.

"Yes," he said. "I mean a bold attack." He allowed his voice to rise a little, allowed the passion that was in him to bubble up. A king could just give orders, but a good king did more than that: he motivated his men and inspired them.

One at a time, he looked both men directly in the eye and held their gaze.

"Now is our chance to do damage. Real damage. If we don't, they'll just regroup over a period of time and then start the process of wearing us down again."

476

"It's a great risk," Taingern said. "It might work, but it could fall apart as well. If they're not as disorganized as you think, then they'll counter attack. And we could lose many men, perhaps even have the gates taken by the enemy, and the end would then follow swiftly."

"That's true," Aranloth said. "Yet we all know that swift or slow, the end will come anyway. Unless we can do something *unexpected*. Gilhain has hit upon it there. Now is our chance, our only chance to strike, and I advise that we take it. We may lose our gamble, but we may win also. And if so, it would greatly even the odds. Without something else in our favor the enemy will do just as Gilhain says – wear us down."

Taingern, Gilhain knew, was naturally cautious. That's why he watched him the most closely. If he could win him over, he would have the others. Not that he needed to win anyone over. He could just command. Yet that was a slippery slope, and if people did not believe in what, and how, they were fighting, they did not drive themselves so hard.

Taingern continued to think his way through it. Gilhain glanced at Lornach. That one look was enough to see that he was all for it. After all, that was his way; he was an adventurer.

Then the two Durlin glanced at each other. They did not speak. Taingern could read the other man's face and intentions even better than Gilhain could. For all their differences, they were close. A moment Taingern held his friend's gaze, and then there was the slightest of nods. Few would even have noticed it, but Gilhain was watching. And it was what he had been waiting for.

"I've decided," he said. "We'll do it."

No one disagreed with him. They recognized that the decision was made, and they trusted his judgement. Especially when it coincided with their own.

Aranloth ran a hand through his hair. "A word of advice?" he asked.

"Always," Gilhain answered.

The lòhren pursed his lips and tugged at an earlobe. Evidently, he was still thinking his way through something and refining it.

12. Strange things are Abroad

They waited. And they waited quietly. No one showed discomfort or nerves, but they all must have felt those things. Brand did, and he did not think the others more courageous than he.

The figure drew closer. It was, after all, only one person, but nevertheless he relaxed a little as it neared and he could see that it was not an elùgroth.

There was a staff in the figure's hand, that much was clear. But there was no black cloak, no sense of menace. Whoever, or whatever it was, it was not a creature of evil.

They continued to wait. The figure came on, hastening down the road. It used the staff to help it walk, but it did not really need it. Brand was sure of that.

Soon, it was close, and Brand knew, with a sense of relief, that this was a friend rather than a foe. It was a lòhren, and there were few people that he would rather have met.

The lòhren was an old man. Frail even, or at least giving the appearance of it. He seemed older even than Aranloth, but was no doubt younger. Few, apart from the Halathrin, had seen as many seasons pass as the leader of the lòhrens. Yet regardless of seeming age or frailty, Brand never underestimated the strength of a lòhren, nor judged them for what they seemed. Aranloth had taught him that.

The old man shuffled near to them, and then stopped. For all his haste he did not appear out of breath. He gave Kareste a curious look, and then he bowed gracefully to the Halathrin.

"Well," he said in a matter of fact voice, "this is a surprise. Not a normal situation at all, with Halathrin and a lòhren just standing around on the road. What's going on?"

Brand considered him. He had said he was surprised, but in truth he did not look in the least bit startled. And though he recognized the Halathrin for what they were, and Kareste as a lòhren, he had said nothing about Brand himself. Perhaps that was mere random chance, nothing more than an expediency of time. But could it have been that he had omitted any comment because he did not know if Brand was a warrior or a lòhren? If so, Brand thought, he was not the only one.

Kareste took the lead and explained things to him. She did not hold back, for this man was a lòhren and she trusted him. Even so, Brand was a little surprised, for she said much and showed great respect.

Quickly, Kareste explained about Shurilgar's staff, how the Halathrin had been trapped by elùgai into the form of otherworldly beasts, and of their fight with Khamdar and the destruction of the staff.

The old man looked interested throughout, and he listened carefully, giving her his full attention. But he showed no surprise at anything.

"There is much news there, and some of it is new to me. I come from the south, the far south, and there is trouble brewing down there also. But that isn't all."

He leaned casually on his staff, but his eyes were intent as he continued to speak to them.

"Evil is abroad in the land. Beware! Not just elùgroths, but things darker and older. And they are vengeful."

480

For the first time since his arrival the old man looked directly at Brand.

"Now I know why. The staff drew them, woke them, but not all are yet dormant again. Beware! Strange things are abroad, and for some their hatred of you is personal."

"What things?" Brand asked.

"Just strange," the old man said enigmatically.

"Come with us to Cardoroth," Kareste said suddenly.

The old man thought about that. He seemed troubled, but that came across more in the time he hesitated to answer rather than in any facial expression.

"You might need my help," he answered. "Yet I have my own task. News of the south must reach the lòhrens. They'll need to hold council, perhaps then we can follow you, though you'll reach Cardoroth first. Some will come no matter what, that I promise. But at the end of the day Cardoroth will not stand or fall because of lòhrens. There are lòhrens and elùgroths enough there already. Its fate will be decided by other things."

The answer fell short of what Kareste obviously wanted, but she accepted the lòhren's decision with uncharacteristic meekness. Brand knew the old man could do nothing other than he had. Lòhrens were few in Alithoras, and the evils of the world many. They could not be everywhere at once. What could be done for Cardoroth they must do themselves, that and the soldiers of the city.

"Time is short," the old man said. "We'd better go our own ways."

The gave their farewells and parted, but the old man looked back over his shoulder at them and spoke to Kareste.

"Congratulations," he said.

"On what?"

481

"You passed your test. This I know – it's in your eyes. But we all pass such a test. Or fail…"

The old man walked away, but his words echoed in Brand's mind. They were said to Kareste, and yet the lòhren had glanced at him just as he had spoken. It was only a momentary flicker of his eyes, but Brand was sure of it.

The whole thing troubled him. How could the lòhren know that he faced a great choice himself, that he did not know how to proceed with his own future, and which task to take up?

Then he felt stupid. Of course, it could be more, but Aranloth's diadem and his staff were symbols, and not just a means to aid him. He should have known as much from the beginning. Symbols of exactly what, he was not so sure. But the old man had read the signs and understood them better than he.

"Who was he?" Brand asked Kareste.

"I don't really know."

Brand found that hard to believe, given how freely she had told him of what had been happening and what their purpose was. That doubt must have found a way to show on his face.

"Don't look at me that way. It's true. I don't even know his name, but I've seen him before. There are lòhrens … and then there are lòhrens."

She gave a shrug, and her face was thoughtful as she watched the old man hasten away into the distance.

"He may not have lived as long as Aranloth," she guessed, "but I bet he's wandered farther. Some of us travel, going from place to place among all the lands, everywhere but the far south where the elugs dwell. And *he* may even go there. That sort are healers and lovers of nature rather than advisors, as is Aranloth. But even they return from time to time to Lòrenta. They seldom stay

482

long. You can also be sure that that old man has power, though I'm not sure if he ever uses it. Lòhrens are a strange breed." She glances at him sideways. "There's not really any one type…"

Brand pondered her words. What she said was true. But still, he had never heard of a warrior-lòhren, nor a chieftain-lòhren, nor a bodyguard-lòhren. He could only answer one call at a time.

13. Hilk Var Jernik

"An attack is good," Aranloth said. "But where should we strike? Some targets are better than others."

Gilhain knew instinctively that the lòhren had a specific target in mind, but he decided it was best to wait for him to reveal it.

"As Brand always says," Lornach offered, "Strike at the head of the snake. It's no good cutting the tail off bit by bit."

Aurellin flashed a grin at the Durlin. "You're a bold one, that's for sure. The elùgroths control the enemy, but they're secure in the midst of the host. We could pour the entire army of Cardoroth out the gates without hope of reaching them."

Lornach grinned back at her. "Maybe so, but if an army doesn't suffice, the few might accomplish what the many could not."

Gilhain knew the lòhren had something in mind, but he did not think it was this.

"No," the king said with some force. "I'll not throw lives away in some mad scheme to try to infiltrate the enemy by stealth. It can't be done."

Aranloth sighed. "It *is* a mad scheme, my king. But I would not go so far as to say it couldn't be done. In point of fact, it *has* been done before. Twice that I know of. Nevertheless, it's not what I recommend ... at least not now, and not by us."

"Then what *do* you recommend?" Lornach asked.

Aranloth folded his arms across his chest. "You're right when you say that we must attack the head of the snake, but if that's beyond our reach, then what is next?"

They looked at him blankly. Gilhain thought he saw where the lòhren was going, but he was not sure so he remained silent.

Aranloth laughed. "Come now. If the head is beyond reach, then the next best thing is the heart. Where then is the beating heart of the enemy? What sets its rhythm? Come! The answer is simple enough. You've been hearing it now for a long time, and cursing it."

"The drums," Aurellin said.

"Yes," Aranloth answered. "The war drums of the elugs. They're sacred to them. They govern their life, awake or asleep, always beating. And they beat out the rhythm of destiny to that cruel folk. Destroy them, or damage them, stop them or slow them and the elugs will be reluctant to do anything."

"But how?" Lornach asked. "The drums are at the back of the enemy host, better protected even than the elùgroths themselves."

"Ah, Shorty," Aranloth said. "You're one of the best fighters I've ever seen, but you're not a strategist."

"No," Gilhain said. "But I am. And the answer is simply this – cavalry."

"Exactly," Aranloth said. "Cavalry. The war drums are sacred to the elugs. They're part of their rituals. Part of their life. They drive them on, and that's why they're at the back of the host. But cavalry can reach them. Riders could sweep out the gate, swing wide around the enemy, break through the picket lines and strike at the rear."

"Yes," Gilhain said. "Perhaps they could do just that, with luck and the right captain riding at their head, but returning would be harder. Much harder."

485

Aranloth nodded in agreement, but he did not say anything.

"It's a risky thing to attempt," Taingern said. "All the more so for the elùgroths will be aware of this weakness in their troops and will have taken precautions against such an attack."

Aranloth nodded, but again did not speak.

"No doubt there are precautions," Gilhain said. "But in all this time we haven't attempted such a thing. If we're quick, we can take them by surprise. Perhaps."

There seemed no real disagreement with the plan. Nor were any others offered. It was time to cast the dice, and Gilhain knew who he would risk such a plan with.

He gave orders to a nearby soldier, and the man scurried off in search of the person his message was for.

"So," Taingern said. "Which cavalry unit did you choose? And which captain did you send for?"

Gilhain glanced at Aranloth before he answered, and he saw that the lòhren was also interested in the response.

"None of the five." He said.

"But there *are* only five units," Taingern said with a frown.

"There are five *regular* units. Each a thousand riders strong, each with a well-respected captain. But for this mission, we need something different. We need someone bold, someone who knows that they may not come back, but who won't let that stop them. And better a few hundred of the most daring riders you've ever seen than a thousand ordinary horsemen. Speed will be their weapon here, not numbers. That is their only chance to get back in the gate when their job is done."

No one answered this. None of them knew there was a unit of irregular cavalry. Only Aranloth did, and

486

judging by the serene look on the lòhren's face, he agreed with the decision.

It was not long before the captain came. Gilhain gave him his instructions privately, but he sensed the eyes of the others on this new man, assessing and judging him. And well they might, if they could, for this was no ordinary man.

Hilk Var Jernik looked him steadily in the eye while he was given his orders. He was one of the few men that Gilhain had to look up to when he spoke, and that was something that he was not used to.

The captain towered above six feet, and his shaved head with the long scalp lock trailing down his back made him seem taller. The jagged scar down one side of his face, and the heavy gold earring added to the picture of a man who did not blend in to any crowd.

He was certainly different from most men, not least in his expressionless face when told of the mission. Instantly, he understood the great dangers, and the great benefits if it could be accomplished, but he gave no sign of emotion at all.

Gilhain finished speaking. "One last thing," he said. "I'll not order any man, or those he leads, into such a dangerous mission. Will you do it?"

The man looked back at him. For the first time there was some emotion on his face, even the slightest of grins, as though he looked forward to this challenge.

"Of course, my king. I'll do it. It's what I'm here for, what my men are here for, exactly this kind of mission. But I'll offer them the same choice that you just offered me."

"Good man," Gilhain said. "And good luck."

They shook hands and then the man was gone, his long strides carrying him away with seeming eagerness.

When he was gone the others came over and discussed him.

"An unusual looking man," Lornach said.

"And not of the aristocracy, as the other cavalry captains all are," Taingern added.

"None of that is relevant," Gilhain said. "Tell me what you think of him as a man, as a leader of other men."

"He didn't inspire me with confidence," Taingern said. "He was too quiet, too withdrawn into himself. But a man may be like that and yet still be bold at need."

"And you, Lornach?"

"I feel the same as Taingern. But time will tell."

"Indeed it will," Gilhain answered. But there was a slight smile on his face, and when he turned to Aranloth there was a knowing look in the lòhren's eyes.

The sun was lowering, but much of the afternoon remained. The enemy host still showed no sign of attacking. The elugs at the forefront of the horde milled about nervously. Of the Lethrin, there was no sign. They remained hidden away somewhere in the host, licking their wounds from their previous humiliation. The elùgroths made no move. Their tent was dark and still. No one entered and no one left.

Hilk Var Jernik watched the enemy through the bars of the West Gate, the Arach Neben as the people of Cardoroth called it. He watched and waited while his men, three hundred of the best riders in Alithoras prepared. It was quiet in the city. It was quiet out among the enemy.

"It won't be long now, Jinks," his lieutenant said to him.

Jinks nodded quietly, and the man went back to oversee the preparations. Jinks, the men called him. It was a strange nickname, but he liked it. It was a play on his name, but more than that. It was a play on fate itself. For a jinx was something in the nature of bad luck, and yet they called him that in defiance. They knew he made his own luck, and they followed him without question.

They were all his extended family, he supposed. Mostly part of the same clan, and that explained their loyalty to some extent, but not completely.

What knit them together most tightly was that they were not of the Camar race, not even originally from Cardoroth at all. Their grandparents had migrated with other families from the west less than a hundred years ago.

The lands of his ancestors were grasslands, grasslands bordering a river. The stories went that they loved that country dearly, but pestilence had devastated them. Their numbers were too few to survive in the wild lands. And at that time the world was becoming a darker and more dangerous place. The stories went that elug attacks from the north had grown frequent, and there were too few warriors to stand against them forever. So, their numbers dwindling and their hope with it, they packed what they could carry and came east to the great city they had heard of, but had never seen and could not be sure really even existed.

But it *had* existed, and they had found a welcome there. And though they integrated, and learned a new language and took up the ways of the foreigners, still they kept their identity. They stuck together, and they kept the one great skill that they had mastered on the grasslands: horsemanship.

Some of them said that their tribe was distantly related to Brand's people. Some held that they were descended from the lost race of the Letharn. Jinks, for his part, thought they were a mixed breed, coming from both those roots and more beside. But it did not matter. They were his people, and he was their leader. He had earned the king's favor and risen to the rank of captain. It was no small feat for a man from a proud but poverty stricken people.

Jinks walked back a little way and mounted his horse. The three hundred riders were nearly ready behind him. The Black Corps they were called, and their mood was grim enough to match their name. He had told them what the plan was. He had told them they would probably die, but if they rode well, they may yet live. The trick would be surprise and speed. He smiled to himself. He had given them the freedom to reject the task, but they had not. Not one of them. He was proud of them, and by the end of the day all his people, all the poor and dispossessed, all those looked down upon by some of the native Camar; they would be proud of the Black Corps too.

He looked back and assessed the men. They were rough, just like him. Some were close relations, some distant; but he could trust them all. They were in this together. He knew each man, had recruited them himself, mostly from the poorest of his people. Many were criminals. He had given them a new home. He had fed them, put a roof over their head. In return, they had to work. Those who did not were ejected from the unit. Those who did – bonded. He saved them from a bad life, and they were loyal. To him and the others. They were as brothers.

He reviewed their weapons, measuring them up for the task ahead. The sabre they used was standard cavalry equipment. It was light, sharp and curved; ideal for the slashing attacks riders employed. Their stirrups were shorter than average, for the speed of the horse and

490

maneuverability of the rider were critical factors that longer stirrups hindered.

The boots of the riders were of soft leather for comfort, but they also provided protection. The men wore no real armor; they relied on speed and they kept the weight of their equipment to a minimum, and the riders were also mostly small in stature, or at least very thin as was he.

But they had armor of sorts: stiffened leather greaves and jerkins. It was surprisingly resilient against sword strokes. Some wore caps of the same material, but Jinks did not think they helped much. Also, the legs and arms were the areas they were mostly struck at, being closer to reach for any attacker.

There were a few men who had the shaved head and scalp lock that he liked. These were mostly his close family. They held to the old ways of their ancestors longer, but it was a custom quickly growing out of favor.

Out of the three hundred one third carried a special bow. The black wood of its limbs was lacquered, and the weapon was small and lightweight, but nevertheless strong. Not as strong as a longbow, but still strong.

All of his men, archers or not, wore the standard black cloak pinned at the shoulder with a silver brooch. His fingers traced his own, feeling the outline of a galloping horse fashioned of jet. It was the only bit of jewelry that they wore, though some few others also sported the single gold earring that he did.

Jinks sighed. Another dying custom. And more than customs would die soon. Perhaps all of them were about to face death, and there would be fewer of his people left in Cardoroth. If the city survived, his people would disappear within a few more generations, absorbed into the great mass of the Camar race. It was inevitable, but there were worse fates than that. Cardoroth had welcomed and nurtured them. It was their home now, the same as for everybody else.

Drilk, his lieutenant, gave a sign, and Jinks knew the men were ready. There was nothing much to say now. They all knew what awaited them, and what needed saying he had said earlier.

"Good riding!" he wished them. They were the customary last words before an attack. "For the Black Corps, and for Cardoroth!" he added, which were not.

He held up his right arm, his light sabre gripped tightly. When it came down the soldiers who manned the gate would open it, and the riders behind would begin to gallop. There would be no fanfare here, no blowing of horns. There would be nothing to mark their venture, nothing to give away to the enemy even a second's notice of what was happening, nothing except the sound of steel shod hooves on cobbles.

But that was as it should be. The horses were what counted, for the men had a bond with them: the horses were the only thing that kept the men alive on the field of battle. And the men loved them.

Jinks dropped his arm. Slowly, the gate opened. The charge began, at first a trot and then a growing clatter of steel on cobbles until it rumbled as thunder in the vault of the tunnel.

Four abreast they rode, passing through the very same tunnel that their ancestors had used to enter the city long ago. Jinks thought they might be proud of the Black Corps if they could but see them now, riding to serve the city that had let them in.

In a grand column, the rush of wind and dark against their faces, they streamed out of the shadowy tunnel and came into the light. The road was heavily trodden and stained by blood. Elug bodies littered the way. The riders picked their way through the wrack of previous battles

492

and the stench of death, and then wheeled gracefully from the road and onto what once had been green grass. It was now dust, the lush grass having been beaten down by countless elug boots.

Behind them many men filled the empty space they had left behind: foot soldiers left to close the gate and guard it against their return. He wondered how long the gate would be kept open. Gilhain would do so as long as possible. But if the enemy seized the gap between host and gate, the riders would be stuck outside the wall.

They charged ahead. The thunder grew to a deafening roar, and a cloud of dust rose slowly and hulked behind them.

The enemy was encamped to their right: unready perhaps, but like a living beast, massive and restless, and able to turn and respond. But how quickly?

Clear now of any obstacle, un-harassed as yet by any foe, the riders began to race in earnest.

A ring of sentries was thrown up around the whole city. It would not be hard to break through it and come at the enemy's rear. It was getting back that was going to be the problem, at least for those who survived.

The Black Corps could yet have a victory but suffer the ultimate personal defeat. But they were here for Cardoroth, not for themselves. And it was the result for the city that counted the most.

Jinks glanced back over his shoulder. His men were with him, and he knew it was in thought as well as deed.

14. A Great Honor

The days passed without event. Brand did not mind that. Each day saw him and Kareste ride, and the Halathrin spread out behind them, loping in their wake with an easy growing stride that ate up the miles.

The days were long and hard, and the nights watchful. Brand could not be sure what enemies were out there somewhere ahead, but few things in Alithoras were swift enough to pursue them.

They stayed on the road and headed north. It was dangerous to follow a beaten path, but the long sight of the Halathrin gave them an advantage; they would see an enemy before the enemy saw them.

About five days into their journey they neared the southern end of Lake Alithorin, and the dark forest that surrounded it.

There were indications that the road had been used: the old marks of the elug army that now laid siege to Cardoroth remained. And there were more recent tracks, mostly riders, but who they were and what their destination was, Brand did not know.

Somehow, the Halathrin kept up with them. Marching men could cover a surprising amount of ground in a day; not quite as much as a horse, but a lot. The Halathrin, it appeared, could do better. The fast pace of the horses did not seem to trouble them at all.

And when there was no danger, and when the way was clear all around them, the Halathrin sang as they walked. But sometimes they ran, and when they did so they moved with the gentle lope of a wolf, and Brand had a feeling that they could run all day and all night.

"They could beat us to Cardoroth, if they wanted to," he said one day to Kareste. "They can out pace a horse."

"So the legends say," she answered. "And they seem to be right. But what are they going to do when they get there?"

Brand shrugged. "That, I guess, we'll have to wait and see."

"Patience is a great virtue," she said a little tartly, "for those who have it."

That night they camped, as usual, well off the road. Brand built a small fire. The Halathrin returned to the camp after gathering some gnarled tubers, and these they roasted in the embers for a long time. When they were done, they let them cool and then distributed them. The tubers were quite starchy, but very sweet.

The night began to grow old. Many of the Halathrin wandered off, finding a place to sleep. Brand stayed near the dying flames, and Harlinlanloth came over to sit beside him. From where she sat on her blanket, wrapped up in her cloak a little way off, Kareste watched with dark eyes.

Harlinlanloth talked to him for some time, asking questions about Cardoroth and the king, and especially of Aranloth. Her eyes glanced often at the lòhren's staff that he carried, but she said nothing of that.

Their conversation was free and easy, and when she laughed it was like the peal of a golden bell and as though the sun shone at night.

She did not speak much of Halathar. Only that she liked trees, as most of her kind did. Trees, tall and green, thick trunked and ancient. She spoke of dim forest trails, and the task of her band, which was considered a reward for service.

"It's a high honor," she said. "We are each the best at something. I can sing, and chant, and work what you might call magic. One of the others is the best with bow and arrow, another can run faster than the wind."

Brand noticed that some of them had found time to construct bows and arrows – he was sure they did not have them before the journey began.

"Another is good at hunting," she continued. "And he," she pointed to one of her companions who seemed to be asleep, "can mimic animal noises and bird calls. Another can outswim fish."

It took Brand a while, but eventually he realized that this was not a random conversation. She was giving him knowledge of the band so that he would know what skills they had, and how best they might be used in any plan against the enemy.

"Lady," he said to her earnestly. "Why tell me all this? I don't command your band. I'm grateful that you've come – more grateful than I can say, but you're in charge of your own people."

She smiled at him sadly. "Always your kind and mine misunderstand each other. Truly, we're in your debt for what you did for us. That places us in your service. You command us, for the moment at least, until our errand either fails or succeeds. Not only that, you have the greater knowledge of the lands we travel and the enemy we shall soon face. You lead, and we shall follow."

Brand was surprised, and that rarely happened to him these days.

"But you're wiser than I. You're older, smarter, more experienced. Really, if anyone should lead, it's your place to do so."

She grinned at him suddenly. "Older? Yes, by far. But you need not be so blunt about pointing that out. As for

496

wiser and more experienced, that has nothing to do with how old someone is. And you know it."

He was quite uncomfortable, but she looked at him sternly.

"You must learn to accept this, as you must learn to accept other things that lie beyond your power to change."

She smiled at him enigmatically, stood gracefully, and then left to rejoin her own people.

He looked over to Kareste who still watched him, her eyes unfathomable.

"Why me?" he asked.

"You know why," she answered. "You know exactly why."

He bit his lips. "I'm *not* a lòhren! I don't have the skill or knowledge or power to deal with different people, different lands, different races. I'm only a wild Duthenor. I've been told that often enough, and it's mostly true."

"That's not what I see when I look at you. Nor, it seems, what the Halathrin see. You are what you are. You will become who you will become. Accept it, as she advises, or run from it – if you can."

They did not speak after that. Soon, they laid out their cloaks and went to bed. It grew dark, for a cloud cover was beginning to build. As the night wore on, it became very gloomy.

Brand slept. Oblivion took him, and he had no memory of any dreams, pleasant or otherwise. When he woke, and he woke suddenly, it was some time before dawn, but not by much. Something had alarmed him, though he did not know what.

Everyone else remained asleep. The Halathrin kept watch; they had said that they needed less sleep than men. But they slept too. He saw only one that sat upright. He was atop an old tree stump, still as a stone, but then his head moved. His posture stiffened also. That he sensed something, the same something that had woken Brand was obvious. But what?

Brand took some deep breaths. Slowly, his hand reached out to the hilt of the sword that was always nearby, even when he slept. And then he waited, all his senses alert. He heard nothing. He saw nothing. Yet his heart began to pound in his chest.

15. Like a Spear

Jinks led his men at a gallop. The thunder of the horses rolled over the open lands surrounding the city. The enemy was massed to one side now, and they rode parallel to that. They were not within bowshot; neither within reach of the inferior long bows of the enemy nor within shooting range of their own black cavalry bows. Nevertheless, they were close enough to make out individual faces of elugs, and to see their surprise, even their fear.

But that great mass of the enemy to their right was not their target. Jinks changed direction once more when they reached its far edge. He struck out to the right, the horse he rode changing direction smoothly, the column behind him wheeling as one with his every move.

Four riders abreast was the column, and like a spear they hurtled toward the thin line that stretched out, vulture like, from the main host to surround the city with dark wings.

There was some attempt at resistance from the line, but then the elugs scattered like sparks in a gale. They had no bows. They had no pikes, nor did they even carry spears. Most of all, they did not have the training to stand before cavalry. Therefore, they did not have the courage to do so, for to hold firm in the face of a mounted charge took confidence and heart that few armies in Alithoras could muster. And that confidence came from training and practice, and finally from success in the field.

One elug, taller and fiercer than most, did loom up before Jinks. The creature held high its scimitar, preparing to make a slash, but at the last minute it panicked in the face of the rush of horsemen. Yet Jinks leaned forward, his own blade sweeping out and flicking across the elug's face. There was a spray of blood and a scream lost in the thunder of hooves, and then he was through. None fell beside him, and he did not think they would lose a single man breaking through the line, but this was not the hardest task that lay ahead, far from it. That was still to come.

Along the left flank of the enemy they now galloped. Some attempted to turn and face the riders, forming a shield-wall in defense. Jinks ignored their uncoordinated effort and rode on. This side of the enemy encampment, though ripe for an attack, was not their target.

A senior rider galloped beside him. The man smiled grimly. Another rode with the banner of the Black Corps unfurled on a staff. His lieutenant was some way back to reduce the chances of them both getting killed at the same time. But their mission here, though dangerous, was simple. Little leadership was needed.

The enemy host was massive. The column galloped what seemed a long time, and still the host hulked to their right. It seemed much bigger down here on the ground than it had from the wall.

Finally, they came to its rear and turned right again. The back of the army was a disorganized mess. There were wagons of food and supplies lined up in disorderly fashion and scarcely guarded. The enemy evidently had no fear of attack from Cardoroth, or from elsewhere in Alithoras. If there was time, Jinks would teach them that fear. But his primary job was to accomplish what the king had sent him to do: destroy the drums. And there they were! A long row of them.

The drums were large contraptions, covered in some thick, sun-bleached hide stretched taught over their wooden frames. Rusted iron rings hung from the sides, and long poles passed through them enabling four elug bearers to lift and carry them. And carry them they did, wherever the army went. A fifth elug served as the drummer.

Jinks veered toward them. As one his column of riders moved with him. There was a kind of channel between the supply wagons and the main host. Down this the column flowed like a river.

The drummers fled, but the pole-bearers held their ground and others came forward from the host to join them.

The hooves of the horses thundered. Jinks felt the blood of his body pound in his ears. The mad rush of battle was upon him, but not for nothing had he been made a captain. There was still a part of him that looked, analyzed and coolly considered. He had always been thus, and the greater the danger became the more this part of him came to the surface.

He saw at once that the elugs coming forward from the host were of a rarer breed. These were taller and stronger. They were better equipped too, drawing straight broadswords rather than the usual elug scimitar. The enemy was not as unprepared as they had looked. He must consider the possibility of a trap, but he was committed now, and trap or no trap, this attack was going to go ahead.

One thing, beyond any doubt, was to the advantage of the riders: the elugs did not carry spears. A defense could be made by warriors against cavalry, if they had courage, if they were battle-hardened and if they thrust a wall of spears before them. Without the spears, bravery was seldom enough.

Jinks led his men forward in their charge. The elugs held their ground, setting themselves for the clash about to come. The two forces drew close. Neither side flinched. Jinks took a deep breath. This was the moment; this was the moment that his people earned their place in Cardoroth. Or this was when his people died.

16. If Only I could See

Gilhain bit his lip. He did not normally show any emotion. As commander, it was his job, first and foremost, to be steady. Victory and defeat should not register on his face; that way men knew he was levelheaded, no matter the situation. That way he inspired confidence. He commanded first, and only allowed himself to feel emotion after his decisions were made. At least, that was what he strived for.

He stopped biting his lip. "If only I could *see*," he said with vehemence.

Aranloth turned to him. "Well, if you cannot see, then I shall tell you what's happening."

The lòhren turned away to look over the battlement again, an expression of intense concentration on his face as he peered over the seemingly endless ranks of the enemy.

They all looked at him strangely. "Surely," Gilhain said, "you can't see that far?"

Aranloth shrugged but did not break his gaze. "I can use lòhrengai to enhance my senses. It's no great thing, but it comes in handy. And Jinks, though you cannot see him, isn't really that far away. What I'm doing is only a slight stretch of natural sight."

Gilhain did not trust himself to answer. The lòhren made light of his powers, or else took them for granted as everyday things, but to others some of the things he could do were astounding. Perhaps that was one of the reasons he always shied away from revealing his abilities:

it was yet one more thing that separated him from normal people.

The lòhren did not speak again for a little while, but when he did his voice, though low, held a thread of tension all the way through it.

"They ride," he said. "Even as I watch, they turn and drive toward the rear of the enemy. The elug war drums are there, as we knew they would be. But they are not undefended. The riders move well – I didn't know Cardoroth had such good cavalry. I trusted Jinks since first I met him, but he has done better even than I guessed. His men move with grace and precision."

"I've kept a close eye on him, and on his training," Gilhain said. "He commands a special troop. They are the best. The ordinary cavalry is drawn from Cardoroth's aristocracy, and they are more or less chosen by hereditary. Jinks is different. I let him choose his own men, scoundrels mostly, but I let him do as he pleases, because he gets results."

"They *are* good," Aranloth nearly whispered. "I see now a band suddenly breaking away from their column and riding ahead of the others. They gallop parallel to the elugs. Now, they draw their bows. Short arrows fly. A spray of shafts thickens the air. Incredible! The riders turn swiftly. It's marvelous to see. Back they come in the opposite direction and spray the enemy host again. What skill! They can shoot left and right handed, shifting their small bows as needed."

Gilhain nodded. "Jinks introduced that himself. He picks ambidextrous men, and as I recall, he was proud of the innovation when he told me of it."

"Now they turn again," Aranloth continued. "They ride very close this time. The arrows fly once more. Behind them the other riders take up a new formation. The arrows flit through the air, and the elugs fall, though the small cavalry bows aren't so powerful as to kill through armor, even just the hardened leather of the elugs. But many fall down anyway, wounded and bleeding."

Aranloth paused, watching intently, and everyone held their gazes fixed to his face.

"Now they wheel away leaving a gap," the lòhren went on. "The other riders surge forward. These have spears. They ride. They ride! Into the mass of the enemy they ride! There is a clash of flesh. Horses are down! Men have fallen with them. The elugs hack at the riders driving through their ranks, but the leather greaves on their shins help, and the speed and momentum of the horses helps more."

Aranloth gripped the edge of the battlement. His fingers were white where they clamped around the stone, but his voice remained steady, though not without emotion.

"Elugs screech and yell. The riders ride on. The pennons on some of their blood-wetted spears stream behind them. They voice no battle cry, but they slay in silence. Wait!"

Aranloth fell silent a moment. His face paled. "Jinks is killed! Hold! The press of the enemy is in the way. I cannot see clearly. No. He is down, but not yet dead. Three elugs pulled him from the saddle. Now they are joined by others and they try to kill him, but riders drive into the fray. Jinks is up again! Now he leaps once more on his horse's back and the riders all gallop on. He is at the rear of the column now. They wheel away!"

Gilhain watched his friend in silence. Almost the words of the lòhren drew a picture in his mind. He need not see the events unfolding far away to envision them.

"The archers come forth again," Aranloth said, "and more arrows spray. This time they are set with fire.

505

Those men were not idle while their comrades clashed with the foe. Oiled rags flare, hissing through the strife-torn air. I have never seen that before, not so many at once so accurately fired. The arrows fly from up close. The drums are struck. They are pierced many times, both through their frames and the tight skin drawn over their tops. Flames catch. They have not got all of them, but many, very many."

Aranloth looked on grimly. He spoke slower now, his voice more measured.

"Yet more elugs rush forward. They try to put out the flames. The riders with spears come forth again. Jinks has planned for just such an event. The hard years of training show. They ride through and kill many. Among them now are some who cast their spears. But now they loosen water bags. I don't understand. Ah! They're not water bags but bags of oil. These they fling onto the burning drums and they burst. The skins must be very thin. And lo! Those drums they hit will not beat again!"

Aranloth laughed, and those around him grinned fiercely.

"Now they are off, all back in one column. They ride swiftly! Their work is done! Jinks leads them again. Now, they return."

"How many drums did they destroy?" Gilhain asked quickly.

"Thirty or forty. At least," Aranloth answered.

"And how many left?"

"Perhaps only ten," Aranloth said after a searching glance. "And some of those are damaged as well."

"It's as much as we could hope for. Perhaps even better than we could ever have hoped for. But how many elugs were slain?"

"Hundreds," came the sure reply of the lòhren.

"That's not really that many, but it never was going to be. This was about the drums, and uncertainty. We *have* taught the enemy that they're not safe. No matter where they are. None are safe."

"That is so," Aranloth said. "But it's not over yet. It's not over by far."

"Yes. They still have to make it back."

"No," Aranloth answered. "That's not what I mean."

17. All Dead Men, Now

Jinks kept riding. He was tired, and his horse more so. Not only that, there was a gash in its left foreleg. It bled profusely, but at least so far, it was not greatly hindering his mount's speed.

The column needed to hasten back toward the gate if it was any chance of making it home: but before him Jinks saw opportunity.

His riders had achieved their goal with the drums. It would have an impact on the elugs, much more a mental one than a physical, for they believed in a range of superstitious nonsense. But nonsense or otherwise, what mattered was that they believed it. Therefore, the destruction of their drums would hinder them. But now, beyond hope or expectation, was an opportunity to inflict real and physical damage.

They had not known when they planned the sortie that there were supply wagons here, so close to the drums. The king knew more about elug armies than most, and Aranloth more even than he. They would have talked the situation over before they summoned him, but if they had known the location of the wagons, they had said nothing, calculating the risks of finding and attacking them too high.

And there *was* great risk. Already the enemy would be moving to cut off their retreat back into the city. At least they would be if they were half competent, and a captain who assumed that his opponent was incompetent was the kind of captain who never lived to lead his men for long.

Jinks rode on, the mass of the enemy to his left, the wagon trains to his right. He was undecided, but not for long. It was for such decisions that he had been given command. He had freedom of choice here; the king encouraged that in his leaders. He wanted them to show initiative, to be bold when required, and to be cautious also, when that was needful.

Cardoroth remained badly outnumbered. The outlook was grim. Now, if ever, was the time to be bold. And so Jinks made his choice.

He gave a signal to one of the men who rode near him. This rider withdrew a small horn and blew a shrill note. The column of riders knew what that meant, must have guessed themselves that it was coming. They would have seen the same opportunity that he saw, would have just as quickly calculated the risks. But they did not hesitate.

The archers peeled away from the main column. They unleashed a hail of arrows, killing many of the scattered guards who stood before the wagons. The other riders came in, engaging the remainder with sword and spear. While this happened, the archers rode among the wagons.

There were no fire arrows left, but there was oil. This they cast over as many wagons as they could. Jinks had a quick look inside some, and he saw that they were stacked with sacks of grain and dried meat.

The wagons were close together. Jinks, for all his worry of underestimating the enemy, shook his head. Foolishness. There were hundreds of wagons, all in close proximity. His men could not burn them all, but they could get some, perhaps as much as a quarter if they were very lucky. And fire spread in such conditions.

In now they all went, riding slow, skirmishing here and there as necessary. Many dropped down on foot, for the wagons were too close to ride between. There they set fire to their wooden bases and canvas tops. Up the wagons went in flames, and black smoke roiled into the heavens. Jinks had never seen anything so grim and so pretty at the same time.

Out now from the host charged thousands of elugs. An elùgroth came with them. Jinks gave a signal and the archers galloped forth to meet them. It was token resistance, for so few against so many could not prevail, even mounted warriors against infantry. But it would slow down the charge and allow time for just a little bit more damage to be done to the wagons.

More went up in flame. Waves of heat beat at the riders, and a great roar and crackling filled the air. Jinks knew it was time to withdraw. It was now or never. They were already in trouble. Too long they had delayed, but the chance to wreak such havoc was worth it. They were all likely dead men, now. But they would *try* to return.

Jinks thought quickly. They could flee, yet to where? The enemy possessed cavalry. They were not as good, but Hvargil's force was a thousand strong. They would hunt the Black Corps down if they fled, for they could not allow such an attack to go unpunished. Nor could they allow such a force freedom to launch further assaults from the wilderness. It was better to fight now, to wreak more damage on the enemy and try to make it back to the city.

They swept out and away from the wagons to rejoin the archers. But even as they did so flame spurted from the elùgroth's wych-wood staff.

Men went down. Horses screamed. Jinks signaled again and the man nearest him blew his horn. The riders gathered together, forming a column again, and they wheeled and shot away in one formation.

510

Yet there was more fire; fire that leapt and bridged the gap, fire that hit one man and sizzled before jumping like lightening to another.

More men died. More lives were lost. Lives that might have been saved had they fled earlier. But Jinks knew in his heart that he had made the right decision: not for his men, but for Cardoroth. And his men knew that too.

18. Something Stirs

The Halathrin warrior atop the tree stump looked straight at Brand. Somehow, the immortal knew he was awake, though he had barely moved.

The warrior gave a warning gesture, but he made no other move except to slowly turn his head back and forth to scan the darkness.

Brand woke Kareste. All it took was a light touch to her shoulder and her eyes flicked open.

"What is it?" She whispered.

"I don't know. Something. Something out in the dark. Wake the others."

She did not ask any questions, but straightaway slipped from her make-shift bed.

Brand, crouching low so that he was not silhouetted against the horizon, made his way to the Halathrin guard atop the tree stump. The warrior was tall and thin. His face seemed chiseled out of marble, and his eyes gleamed in the dark. There was very little light, for the cloud cover was heavy, but it was near dawn and the first traces of the rising sun grayed the eastern sky.

Even in the dim light Brand could make out the alert look on the immortal's face.

"What is it?" he asked softly.

The Halathrin did not stop looking out into the dark, but he shook his head slowly.

"I don't know."

Brand waited beside him, silent and still. After a few minutes a light drizzle began. There was a pitter-patter of drops on the grass. The tops of the trees swayed at the touch of a slight breeze, and the air bit with a momentary chill.

Toward the center of the camp the near-dead embers of last night's fire began to smoke, hissing faintly at the touch of the water drops.

The others were all awake now, waiting and still, prepared for something to happen. But prepared for what?

In the distance a nudaluk bird called, knowing that dawn was at hand. A great flock of night-flying ducks passed overhead, their wings beating the dark air and their calls loud as they sought out nearby wetlands.

And then there were eyes in the dark. Some sort of beasts wandered around. Brand could not see them properly, but likely enough they were creatures of the elùgroth.

Khamdar was near, very near, but there was no sign of him. Nor did the beasts attack.

"What are they waiting for?" Brand whispered to the Halathrin.

"I don't know."

The drizzle grew heavier. Smoke was now thick in the air, for the rising breeze had stirred the old fire to life. There was no point in putting it out though. The enemy knew where they were.

Then out of the silence there came a sudden but muffled noise. Brand looked toward the camp. Two of the Halathrin were down. They thrashed on the ground, their faces blue even in the pre-dawn light. But no enemy was there.

Brand did not know what to do. Should he go back to help? Should he keep his eyes on the dark perimeter whence any attack must come?

He ran back into the camp. The Halathrin still thrashed, but their movements were growing weak. He saw that their necks were broken, and a sickening feeling overcame him. How could that have happened? There was no enemy in the camp?

As he stood there looking around wildly, Harlinlanloth came up to him. She seemed cool and resolute, but he sensed her feelings beneath that mask: the death of her companions was painful to her on levels beyond what a mortal could understand.

"Elùgai," she said definitively.

Brand cursed himself for a fool. Of course it was elùgai, of course it was Khamdar. And yet the sorcerer was not in their camp, and the beasts still did not attack.

Smoke roiled all around now, thick, swirling, turning and twisting under the influence of the breeze that had brought the drizzle.

A moment longer he stood there, undecided and uncertain, and then a realization hit him.

"The smoke!" he yelled. "The sorcery is in the smoke!"

He knew it was true, and even as he spoke the vaporous air grew suddenly hard. It was not yet around his throat, but he felt it creeping up his body like a disembodied arm seeking to strangle him.

Kareste was suddenly there. "The fire!" she yelled. "Put it out!"

But the smoke was everywhere now: tearing, twisting and tightening. And in the midst of the old fire's embers, something stirred. Sparks flew. A column of flame rose from the ashes, writhing in the dark air. An image was in it, and it was the semblance of Khamdar.

Sparks shot from the sorcerer's eyes, and they streamed from his hair. His arms were upraised. Strands of smoke, twining like rope, came from all his fingers. The camp shimmered with heat. The people were obscured by swirling smoke. A noise came to Brand's

514

ears, and it was the hissing of rain and steam in the air, but to him it sounded like laughter. And then the grinning image of Khamdar looked straight at him.

19. They Will Tell their Children

Jinks rode at the head of the column again. They had flanked the enemy host once more, and now the army was to their left. But ahead of them was the picket line that spread out around the city.

They raced ahead. The elugs in the line scattered, not even making an attempt to stop them. In a few moments all the riders were through.

"That was easy!" the man near him said, a fierce grin on his face.

Jinks thought so too. But the knowledge did not give him the momentary pleasure it gave his companion. It had been *too* easy. The elugs had not tried to hinder them, and that meant, likely enough, that they knew a greater hindrance was already prepared. No need to risk death when the true confrontation lay ahead.

And so it proved. Though he was ready for it, Jinks still felt his heart sink when they wheeled around the host again and turned left, left toward the Arach Neben and the safety of the city. But there was no safety to be found there.

What they had all feared had come to pass. The enemy had launched an attack against the gate. The soldiers of Cardoroth had come forward. Some of the best troops were there, and they fought with skill and ferocity. They would hold the gate open as long as possible, but skill and courage were not a match for far greater numbers.

And the elugs swarmed against the soldiers in seething multitudes. Slowly, surely, the men of Cardoroth were being driven back.

There was one last resort for Jinks to try. There were other gates into the city, and though the picket lines before them were strengthened in those places, just maybe they had not come forward to bar entry. Just maybe.

But then he heard the thunder of hooves, and it was a noise that was not from his own men. It was from farther away.

Hvargil's cavalry had come forth at last. Some came from the right, blocking the way back from where Jinks had just come. Others now appeared from the left, blocking that way too. The Black Corps was trapped, and every member of the regiment knew it. The column faltered, and many of the men cursed loudly.

Jinks slowed to a trot and his lieutenant hastened forward to speak to him.

"There's no escape from this," the man said.

"It would seem not," Jinks answered regretfully.

"None of the men will blame you, sir. We will surely die now, but it was worth it for damage to the supplies. A hungry army doesn't fight for long."

Jinks knew that this was true. His men had struck a great blow against the enemy, a blow when they were already of low morale. He had done more than could have been expected of him, and he had given the city he loved a greater chance of survival. But there were probably already other supply wagons coming up from the south. The wound his men had inflicted would, sooner or later, be healed by the enemy. Still, in the meantime, it might provoke an act of rashness that Gilhain could turn against them.

517

Jinks gave a signal. Without hesitation the column moved smoothly. They trotted now, forming a circle, their movements precise and even. Jinks, ringed by all his men, able to address them all now at the same time, spoke loudly.

"We will fight!" he said. "There's nothing left for it. We will fight, and we will take as many of the enemy with us as we can. And away in Cardoroth, the lords and the ladies, and those who looked down on us in our former lives, they shall know pride! They will tell their children, and their grandchildren that they knew us! The riders of Cardoroth. The Black Corps!"

The company gave a mighty cheer, and then they came smoothly out of the circle and formed a column again. Like a well-cast spear they drove forth, but not at the approaching cavalry to either side; instead Jinks led them directly toward the rear of the enemy attacking the gate. This would make it easier for the soldiers of Cardoroth to retreat and secure the Arach Neben behind them.

The Black Corps struck with precision, unleashing a hail of arrows and then smashing into the poorly defended rear of the enemy. There was great slaughter, and the elugs fell by the score. As the riders drove deep into the enemy ranks they heard from afar the sound of battle on the other side of the attackers, from the battle being fought near the gate.

Jinks gave another signal and the archers of the Black Corps broke away, half to the left and half to the right. They fired arrows, keeping the enemy riders away briefly, but their supply of shafts was growing thin. Their victory with the wagons was coming back to haunt them.

Hvargil's cavalry did not have their own archers to return the attack. Their charge faltered, but they regrouped and when they came again there were too few arrows to halt their charge.

The enemy now came at the Black Corps from three sides, surrounding them, for the rear of the elugs had also stiffened their resolve.

Jinks fought with his sabre, as now did all his companions. They were ringed around, pressed close, and the advantage of their mounts was reduced. Swiftly they began to fall in the face of such an onslaught and of the three hundred there were perhaps now only fifty men left alive. They were close now, all together for their last stand. Jinks was still there among them, his sabre broken and lying on the field but an elug scimitar in his steady grip instead.

The enemy riders closed in. The elugs at the gate were better prepared now, and they had turned a flank to them and commenced to advance, swords crashing against shields in a mighty tumult meant to intimidate.

Jinks glanced skyward, offering a momentary plea to the universe; but he knew no such appeal would be answered. The clouds hanging low overhead were dark. In an abstract way he noted that rain was on the way. Or perhaps even a storm. He squinted. Yes, definitely a storm. He could feel it build, and a gust of wind tossed his scalp lock.

All his men were steady about him. They knew what came next; it took no genius to contemplate that. He looked about him with a certain pride.

"One day is as good as another to die," he said.

Somewhere a horse snorted and stamped a hoof. Some of the men gave nods of agreement at their leader's words. Jinks worked his way to their front, getting ready to face the advancing elugs.

"One more charge at the enemy!" he shouted. "It will be our last, as well you know, but long will Cardoroth remember it!"

He gathered his reins tightly into his trembling hands, and was about to nudge his horse into a gallop. But at that moment a flash of lightning streaked across the darkening sky. Thunder pealed like the crack of doom and then rumbled away into the distance.

Jinks looked up at the Cardurleth, behind which lay all that he loved. Yet upon the battlement he saw Aranloth. And with him were now gathered other lòhrens. They had come to join their leader from their usual places along the wall, and they now stood in one group behind him.

Aranloth held his arms high. A white light was about him. Jinks looked, and he paused as he watched, the reins forgotten in his hands.

All about him leaves and dust and grass stems swirled in the air. The wind whipped into his face. Lightning once again cracked. This time it struck in the midst of the elugs before the gate. Jinks looked at the enemy. He heard their screams. He felt their panic. And he sensed their primal fear.

Again and again the lightning tore apart the sky and stabbed, dagger like, into the middle of the elug ranks. The smell of smoke hung heavy in the air. There were more screams, and at last the panic grew so great that the elugs fled. They scattered left and right, for there was no lightning to either side. A gap opened. Jinks saw, as though through a widening tunnel, the soldiers of Cardoroth before the gate.

Yet though he saw a chance of life, a chance to enter the city that he could not have hoped for, straightaway it was dashed. No man would dare such a storm, for now the lightning struck ever more swiftly, and a vortex of dust and debris spun where the elugs had but recently blocked the way. No man had the courage to risk that road, no matter what lay at its end.

Jinks shuddered, and then looked up at Aranloth. The lòhren in his turn looked down upon him. From all that distance Jinks sensed his gaze, and then something more. Dimly, as though from very far away, he heard the lòhren's voice. And it was filled with urgency.

"Ride! Ride to the gate! Fear no storm! Fear no lightning. Ride! Ride and live!"

Jinks looked at his men. A moment thus he hesitated, and then he acted.

"We ride!" he called. "The storm is our friend. Ride now and live!" His command echoed the lòhren's words.

Those of the Black Copse who yet lived looked at him in disbelief, but when he kicked his own horse forward they followed.

The riders gathered speed. Lightning hissed in the air all around them. It sizzled and boomed. And yet ... and yet Jinks noticed that no scorch marks showed on the ground. Nor had any fires started amid the dry and trampled grass. Most of all, there were no dead bodies of elugs. Where the army had stood, the field was empty of stricken corpses as surely there should have been.

"It's illusion!" he yelled to his men. On he rode, and his men rode in a tight group behind him. The vortex of air spun upward and disappeared. The soldiers before the gate retreated back into Cardoroth.

Jinks rode onward. Now there were dead bodies, but these elugs had been killed by steel and not lightning. Their wounds were proof of that.

And then beyond any hope that he had foreseen, Jinks led his men into the tunnel of the Arach Neben. It was dark. Behind him he heard the clang of the great gate as it shut.

Soldiers were now all around, helping him and his riders down. They began to tend the wounded and they led away exhausted mounts. This was not easy, for some of the horses had become terrified and they pranced and shied and only the soft and repeated words of their riders brought any semblance of calm.

Jinks looked around. He saw that less than fifty of the three hundred had made it back alive. But the enemy had suffered a major defeat.

It was worth it. And his men had absolved themselves of guilt; the pickpockets, the confidence men, the burglars and the tricksters. That was worth it too, for guilt was worse than death, and his men, every one of them, knew it. And he knew it too, and even as his legs gave out beneath him he exulted, for his people had become a legend that would endure so long as Cardoroth stood.

20. Tall and Terrible

Khamdar, or at least the image of him that hung in the smoke, grinned. Fire curled from his mouth. His hair streamed rivers of fire.

The sorcery of the elùgroth was great. They all seemed trapped by his power. Some were pinned to the earth by smoke become substance. Some were being choked. Brand was thrown back to sprawl helpless on the ground.

He lay there, half stupefied by the force that had hurled him away, but his mind still asked questions and groped for answers. Why had he been hurled away? Slowly, the answer came to him: to keep him away from the fire.

Slowly but surely, he began to stand. It took all his strength. The smoke tried to pin him down and then, like a seeking hand, it reached for his throat.

Nevertheless, he pushed forward. Having come to his feet he stepped, and his steps, though each one seemed like climbing a mountain, were inexorable.

The force thrown against him redoubled, but he pushed forward anyway. He had a grudge against Khamdar. The sorcerer had dogged his steps for a long time now. Khamdar had killed many innocent people. The conflict between them had become a contest of will against will, and that was what really lay behind the struggle. The smoke was little more than illusion.

Sweat broke out all over Brand. He was dripping wet by the time he neared the fire and gasping for breath.

Khamdar rose in a plume before him, tall and terrible. Brand ignored the image. He knew that his blade could not hurt such a phantom. Instead, he deliberately struck into the fire itself and scattered embers wide and far.

Again and again he struck, and then he was kicking as well. The fire flared brightly. He felt the heat of it, and then it was gone. Khamdar simply evaporated. Smoke clogged the air, but now, though thick, it was nothing more than a reeking cloud that drifted without intent.

Brand looked around. Some of the Halathrin were dead. This was yet another crime added to Khamdar's long tally. One day, Brand knew with sudden certainty, there would be a reckoning. Khamdar would be held to account, or Brand himself would die. There was no doubt in his mind that that time would come, and he had a feeling it would be one day soon. Brand knew that he did not have the sorcerer's skill, perhaps not his power, but nevertheless that day of reckoning would come, and the elùgroth would know fear as he had never known it before. Silently, Brand swore it.

The living Halathrin looked bleak. Harlinlanloth, grim as the others, looked determined also.

"We will make him pay for that," she said, as though she had read his thoughts. "It is one more evil against us, one more call for justice that will one day be answered."

He realized that she had not perceived his thoughts at all. It was just that she felt about the sorcerer exactly as did he.

"You and I both," he answered. "I have my grudges, and you have yours. He shall not escape us."

Kareste shook her head. "Dreaming of revenge against such as he is sweet, but that's all it is – dreaming. Khamdar is greater than us, and he nearly beat us all though he was but now a phantom. The real him is miles away. If you would oppose him, bear that in mind. Fear him, and fear him greatly. Fear him, and you might yet live. Fear him the more so, for our band grows weaker after every encounter."

Brand cocked his head. "You're right, and yet why did he send a phantom against us? Perhaps he is scared even as are we?"

None of them had any answer to that, and soon they moved on to the ceremony for the funeral of the fallen Halathrin. This was not so elaborate as the earlier one, yet still it had that somber feel to it, that sense of otherworldliness that the Halathrin brought to everything they did.

Without making it obvious, Brand studied Harlinlanloth. She showed little overt emotion, and yet he saw the deep sorrow in her eyes. Nobody understood death, and the immortals, who experienced it so rarely, must understand it less.

When she was done she walked past Brand, and her momentary glance stabbed him to the heart. She was hurting, and there was nothing he could do to take the pain away. It was one more mark against Khamdar, one more crime for which Brand would hold him to account – if he could.

They struck out to the east and toward Cardoroth. Ever they watched for Khamdar, or for some trap that he had left for them to spring, some ambush of beasts or men or elugs. But they saw nothing. Nothing at least until the Halathrin pointed out to Brand the tracks of the elùgroth.

Khamdar, like all elùgroths, wore boots. And a design was worked into their soles: a drùgluck sign. Brand had heard something of it before, but the Halathrin warrior traced the marks with his fingers and then spoke to him quietly.

"The mark of ill-omen. He wants us to see it. It is a warning."

They went on, and sure enough the marks became much plainer. Khamdar had made no attempt to hide his passing, even at times going out of his way to deliberately stand in damp earth to leave a trail. Evidently, the drùgluck was a warning, but a warning of what? That he was nearby and would attack again? Or that his prints led in one direction only – to Cardoroth, and that he would wreak havoc there by way of revenge?

21. The Future is not Fixed

The enemy host was in rampant turmoil, and Gilhain enjoyed it.

"Not since this siege began," he said, "have they been in such disarray."

Aranloth grinned. "No, and it's worse even than it looks."

"How so?"

"Because the elùgroths know that Khamdar returns. And though he failed in his attempt to stop Brand, that does not mean that he will accept *their* failure. He would have hoped that Cardoroth would have fallen by now, and he will blame them that it hasn't, and he is no easy master to serve."

"Why should they fear him?" asked Taingern. "He is only one and they are several?"

"In this case the one is more powerful than the several joined together."

Gilhain scratched his chin. "It poses a question though. Brand is resourceful, but how could he have succeeded with the likes of Khamdar trying to stop him?"

Aranloth looked away. "We always knew that Brand's quest was near impossible. But there is more about him than even you guessed. If we are ever reunited, I think you will see a change in him."

Gilhain did not ask further questions. He caught the faint sense that he was broaching a subject about which the lòhren would not reveal more. Clearly, there was something going on that only Aranloth or Brand knew.

Or perhaps only Aranloth. Sometimes the lòhren kept secrets just for the sake of it. Gilhain stopped himself there; that was an unworthy thought. The lòhren said and did what he could. When he kept secrets, there were always reasons for it.

Lornach chuckled. "We're always too serious here. Let's just enjoy the moment instead of analyzing it. What matters most is that we pulled the enemy's beard, and they don't like it – not one bit."

Taingern grinned and put an arm around his Durlin brother.

"That's the truth. Between us all we've disrupted the plans of the enemy more than they ever thought we could. And Jinks has just landed a mighty blow."

"And yet not a killing blow," Aranloth said. "The elug host will suffer in morale and loss of supplies. Hunger will weaken them, but there is still some food, and more supplies will arrive in time."

The lòhren grew more serious as he spoke, not heeding Lornach's suggestion to enjoy the moment. "And make no mistake," he continued. "The elùgroths will drive them on no matter what. They're desperate now. We've won a battle, but we haven't won the war."

Aurellin spoke little at times like these, but when she did, they all listened.

"But what final stroke can there be?" she asked.

There was silence then, and Gilhain felt, one by one, that the gazes of those around began to rest on him. He was the king; he was the great strategist.

"I'm trying to think of one," he shrugged nonchalantly. He made light of it, but the same question burned in his soul and he knew it would run through his mind from now on, day and night, waking and sleeping.

"And do you have any ideas?" Aranloth asked.

"Nothing yet."

"Nor I," the lòhren said quietly.

It was not long afterward that the elùgroths came. There were three of them, and behind each was a shazrahad, the strange elders of the Azan people who fought with the elugs.

Slowly they walked. Their black robes were so dark that they seemed to absorb all light, yet their skin, pale and sickly, stood out all the more for its contrast. But there was little skin to see; the robes covered all except for hints of their grim faces and their bare hands that gripped tight the wych-wood staffs.

They stopped before the wall, and stood motionless. The silence on the battlement was vast. Into that silence their leader spoke.

"Come forth, old man."

No one doubted who he meant. It could only be Aranloth.

The lòhren stepped to the edge of the rampart, and he leaned casually against it. Slowly, insolently, he winked at his three adversaries. They were, perhaps, too far away to see it, but they could not have missed his overall mannerism, nor the contempt that dripped from his voice when he answered.

"Have you come to thank me for my little show? If I don't say so myself, it was impressive. Especially given that it was all illusion. But the elugs believed it, and that was what counted in the end."

Gilhain held his breath. The lòhren was deliberately insulting the enemy, challenging them. It was the sort of thing that Brand would do, and suddenly he saw the likeness between the two men. Strange that he had not noticed it before.

The elùgroths scowled. That much was visible even beneath their cowls.

529

"Your time has come," their leader said. "Khamdar returns. He nears, and so too does the end of Cardoroth."

Aranloth scratched his chin. "I've heard that kind of thing before. And I've heard of Khamdar. He has some notoriety. But you three? I don't know you. Come back and talk to me in a thousand years or so – if you're still alive."

The elùgroths made no move, but enmity radiated from them in waves. If hatred alone could destroy, then the Cardurleth would have crumbled to dust.

Aranloth laughed. "I will give to you a warning," he said. "You seem to think that Khamdar's return is something to worry about. Know this!"

Suddenly the lòhren was not casual any more. He stood straight and tall and the very air about him seemed charged with eldritch forces. It was one of those rare moments when he revealed the power that was in him, and the elùgroths backed away several paces.

"I am more than a match for Khamdar," the lòhren declared. But he is not destined to die by my hand, though die he will, and he will wither in flame and great anguish. You, on the other hand, have no particular destiny. I could snuff you out even as we speak."

Aranloth pointed at them with a white-robed arm, and they stepped back yet again.

"Parley!" they cried. "We come as messengers!"

Aranloth lowered his hand, but his voice rose and swept out, out to the elùgroths and beyond to their army.

"Dogs!" his great voice boomed. "Begone. I will not kill you, at least not now. But beware of Khamdar. You are more likely to die at his hands, for he suffers fools not lightly, and you have failed him. The tide now turns. Cardoroth stands, and the black mass of your host shall recede as the sea before unassailable cliffs."

Aranloth seemed to stand even taller. About him was a flicker of white light, pale silver as the moon, piercing bright as the midday sun.

"Go!" the lòhren commanded, and the elùgroths fled. The shazrahads ran behind them, stumbling and tripping in their flight.

The moment passed. Gilhain let out a long breath, and then he gave a slight bow to the lòhren.

"That was a nice performance. Even as Jinks has seeded doubt and mistrust into the enemy, you have given greater hope to our own men who defend the walls. Even *I* believed what you said about Khamdar. But in truth, I think there are none in Cardoroth who can kill him if it is not you, but that will also keep the enemy thinking and worrying."

Aranloth seemed normal once more. The power that was in him was hidden again, but the remnant of it still lingered in his eyes.

"It was no act. I saw him. In fire and anguish he shall die. And the other elùgroths with him. I gave fair warning to them. They are in great danger, but they will heed me not."

Gilhain did not know what to make of that. The lòhren's manner was strange. But he had seen this mood on his friend before.

"Really? You saw the future?"

Aranloth looked away, his bright eyes surveying the host on the ground below, but his expression was one of deep thought.

"I saw one of them."

"Is there more than one?"

Aranloth looked back. His eyes were an old man's now, and his posture subtly different.

"Of course. There are many, but as the future draws near, the possibilities dwindle. Things become more

531

certain, and most definitely harder to change. I see glimpses of what may yet be from time to time. Some never come to pass, though many do. The future is not fixed as many believe, but events gather pace now, and Khamdar's future and our own, whatever they be, rush now upon us. It is just that there are now fewer possibilities. Two only now remain, most likely."

"But it's better that you saw Khamdar die than us."

Aranloth sighed. "It was good to tell the enemy that. But I must say to you that I have also seen Cardoroth fall to ash and firebrands, and the booted foot of Khamdar on your slain body while he proclaims his victory to the heavens."

22. Stealth

Long days and long nights passed. The Halathrin kept a keen guard, but no further attack was made against the group.

"Khamdar hastens," Harlinlanloth said one morning as they all prepared to set out again.

"How can you tell?" Brand asked.

"The length of his strides has increased. That means he is walking faster."

Brand was not much of a tracker, but he understood that. He also knew that there were no other tracks: the elugs and hounds had scattered and were no longer under the elùgroth's control. Either that, or their master had sent them elsewhere, perhaps even sent them to flank their pursuers and come against them from behind in another attack.

Brand studied the ground. The imprint of the elùgroth was clear, the drùgluck sign clearer still.

"What of his servants?" he asked. "Where do you think they've gone?"

The girl shrugged. "As you already guess, they may have fled, or they may yet seek to ambush us. There's no way to know."

"Small wonder that your scouts are anxious."

She smiled at him. "You couldn't track a bear up a snow slope, but you don't miss much else of what's going on. My people are on the alert for an attack from behind as much as the front, and rest assured, they will not be taken by surprise."

Kareste joined them, leading her saddled horse. "You both worry too much. Khamdar knows of the skills of the Halathrin." She turned to Harlinlanloth. "Your people have better sight and hearing than men. No elug is going to sneak up on you, and not likely the hounds either. Khamdar knows that, and that's why he hastens. He has nothing to fear from our little band. But if his army has taken Cardoroth, then when he reaches them he will turn the whole lot loose to find us."

That was a disturbing thought, and not one that Brand had really considered before. In his heart he knew that Cardoroth still endured, but if not, the small group around him was heading toward the biggest ambush in history.

"What do you think, Harlinlanloth?"

The Halathrin girl tugged absently at her hair. "It could be even as she suggests, Brand of the Duthenor."

"That's a cumbersome title. Just call me Brand."

She let her hair go and smiled. "Brand it is then, Brand."

He laughed. "And I think I'll just call you Harly."

She gave a bow. "A short name for one who has lived as long as I, for we Halathrin tend to gather names to us as the years pass rather than discard them. But I like it."

Kareste mounted her horse and began to move forward. She did not say anything. The Halathrin formed up their travelling positions: some to the front, some to either side, and some behind. One loped far ahead and disappeared. He would scout for them.

Brand and the Halathrin girl stayed in the middle of the group, and she strode beside his horse.

"It's long since I've been here," she said. "But we must be close to a great lake."

"We are," he answered. "Lake Alithorin is close. Its southern shores are only a little way over there." He

534

pointed the direction with Aranloth's staff. "That means we're somewhat hemmed in," he paused before going on. "Perhaps we should stop following the elùgroth's trail. We know where he's going, but if we continue to follow, our enemies will find us all the sooner."

The morning passed, and Brand was undecided. To their left marched the flank of the forest that surrounded the lake. It was dark and silent. To the right were more open lands. Behind lay many things that he would rather forget, and ahead was danger.

Danger. It was a feeling he knew all too well. It seemed that since his childhood he had always been pressing forward against it. He was sick of that fight, sick of pushing against the unknown, of taking on enemies and finding ways to defeat them. One day he would lose, for though he had more luck than most, a time came for every man to die. And the more he pushed the sooner that day was likely to come.

Did he really have to go to Cardoroth? Had he not already played his part? Surely not even Aranloth or Gilhain could ask more of him than he had already given. And the diamond, the massive diamond the king had given him was a just reward. He was a rich man, a man who could find a life of ease and pleasure in other places besides Cardoroth.

The morning passed in silence, and he turned his mind to what troubled him most. There was power in him, magic that he had not asked for nor wanted. He guessed it had always been there, a latent thing that maybe gave him greater insights from time to time and helped him survive his encounters with sorcerers before. Perhaps that was not such a bad thing. While latent he was still in control, but magic had a life of its own, for it came from the land. Aranloth had seen it in him, and put him in a position where it had a chance to come to the fore. Thinking about things, this quest may not have been the first time that the lòhren had done that.

But things were different now. The power inside him had been used, used consciously and deliberately. It was awake, and not easily, if it all, would he be able to suppress it. One thing he knew for sure was that if he went ahead he would be forced to use it again to try to survive. And that would give it greater power, bring it closer to the surface. Even now he felt it run through his body as he considered it. It was a part of him, linked to his body and mind, yet he knew that in some strange way that he was just as much linked to it. It was an entity of its own, and now that it woke it placed thoughts in his mind, gave him knowledge and instincts of how to use it. How else could he have learned so fast and contended with the creatures that he had, and lived?

He brooded on this a long while as he rode. The Halathrin loped at a matching pace, easily maintaining it the whole morning. At times they ranged out, at other times they closed in, all depending on the terrain.

As Brand worried these ideas around in his mind the same way that a dog might gnaw at a bone that had long since been stripped of flesh, a new thought occurred to him. To where could he run to avoid his fate? If Cardoroth fell, which city would be next? The enemy wanted them all, would destroy everything in the north if it could. The more he ran from things the faster might they catch up with him. It was something to think about, for no one knew were the enemy in the south would strike next.

The Halathrin gathered in close. It was noon, and it was time for a rest and a meal. The horses needed a spell also, for it seemed that they tired more easily than the Halathrin. Brand was sure the immortals could keep on going for the rest of the day.

They stopped on a small hillock. It had a rocky outcrop at its top and a litter of boulders and loose stones spilled over its near-barren sides. From here, they could see far. On the other hand, they could also *be* seen. Every decision had consequences, and there was rarely a wrong or a right way to do things, just an acceptance of which consequences were preferable.

They finished their meal and then remained silent. They all knew a decision must be made, and they waited on the outcome.

Harly spoke first. "We cannot keep following the elùgroth," she said. "We know where he is going, and we should not make ourselves targets by staying on his trail."

"Agreed," Brand said. "But where shall we head? To the left of his trail or to the right?"

Harly looked him in the eye. "We should go to the right. The lands are open there, and we cannot be ambushed."

Kareste shook her head. "We should go into the forest to the left. We can hide there and sneak close to the enemy host unobserved."

Harly kept her gaze on Brand. "That is an unwholesome forest. It is dark, it has always been dark, and I sense that it is still so. There are many stories of that place, some from of old when my people dwelt there. Dangers lurk amid the shadowy trees, and it would be hard to guard against ambush."

So the argument went for some time, back and forth between Kareste and Harly. At length, they grew quiet.

Harly kept her steady gaze on Brand. "You lead us. It is your choice. You have heard the arguments for and against. You lead, and we shall follow."

Brand sat on a slab rock. The day was dark and gloomy. The clouds above were heavy and pregnant with rain, but none fell yet. That would change, he knew.

He considered things. Was life always like this? So many choices? And each choice had consequences, and he could not see them all.

Nevertheless, he looked at the situation logically. Their small band could not launch a frontal assault on the enemy host. They must work by stealth. And though to the right felt better, to the left offered the concealment of the forest. It offered what they had most need of: secrecy and the ability to come into reasonable proximity of the enemy without being seen.

He made his choice, and he felt better for having done so.

"We go into the forest," he said, agreeing with Kareste. Harly showed little emotion, though he sensed that she was taken aback by the decision. Still, she was as good as her word and without further argument prepared her band to fulfill his choice. Kareste said nothing, but he felt her brown-green eyes searching his face.

The group began to move once more, and they turned left into the forest. The Halathrin stayed close now, and none of them ranged out. Nor was there a scout. Harly herself spear-headed their progress, and they moved at a walk once they passed the tree-line.

The day wore away and they rode toward the vast expanse of Lake Alithorin. Harly led them along a path so faint that Brand doubted anyone but a Halathrin could have found it.

The trail, such as it was, snaked to and fro. It did not seem to head anywhere in particular, but it always took them deeper into the tall stands of pine. It swiftly grew dark beneath the tree canopy, and the air was humid and pungent with the fresh smell of pinesap and the fetid odor of decomposition. Bright orange fungus flowered in lush growths on fallen trunks and hoary lengths of gray-green moss trailed from overhead branches.

The travelers slowed even more. Here, in the shadowy dark amid the trees, it felt like another world. And not a pleasant one.

Brand swayed in the saddle to avoid a low hanging trailer of moss.

"There's definitely something creepy about this place," he said quietly to Kareste.

She ducked under the same trailer of moss. "Woods are woods."

"Not in this case, they aren't. There are things in this forest to fill you with fear. At least as much as Khamdar."

She gave him a sideways look, an appraising kind of glance, but did not answer.

Not long later Brand saw the first signs of fog. There was always fog near the lake, and it contributed as much to the gloomy feelings of the forest as the shadowy paths beneath the trees.

The fog reached out, drifting from the water and stretching forth groping tendrils amid the tree trunks. Moisture clung in a film over the pine leaves and dripped from their needle-like ends. It was deathly quiet, and they saw no wildlife.

It grew darker still. Not because the woods thickened, but because the barely seen clouds far above became heavier and deeper. The silence became so oppressive that Brand felt the need to talk loudly. Yet he dared not talk at all, for who knew what was about them, watching even now, or that would be drawn by the sound of his voice?

And then the rain began. It was soft at first, little more than the fog that already creeped around them. But soon it increased. At last there was a sound, but it was only the drip-drip noise of water drops falling from the ends of leaves.

The leaf mould soon grew muddy, and the smell of fungus and decay grew strong. Even the dark green leaves of the pines looked mournful, and the wet trunks of the trees took on the appearance of a host of tall warriors, grim and determined.

Just on dusk the weather turned even worse. The rain became heavy, and though its intensity varied, it did not remit. It was a bad night, being both wet and cold, and the morning after was no better.

The rain was too heavy to travel, but they had to do so anyway. By mid-morning it had grown even heavier, and instead of becoming lighter beneath the trees as the sun climbed, it was gloomy as a midwinter's night.

The rain fell in waves, and each one seemed a greater downpour than the last. The earth beneath their feet had turned to mud, but they struggled forward, heads down, plodding away relentlessly.

The attack came in the midst of it all. Elugs loomed to the left, springing out of the tree-shadows. There were perhaps twenty of them. From the right several beasts leaped, howling suddenly as they sprang.

Even the Halathrin, the best scouts in the world, gave no warning under the terrible conditions. Their skills were rendered near useless by the weather, and they were as surprised as Brand and Kareste.

Yet the Halathrin reacted quickly. Those nearest the elugs drew their weapons swiftly, and they met the attack with fierce determination. The beasts went for Brand and Kareste, for they slipped between the unprepared Halathrin and came straight at their target.

540

Brand drew the blade of his forefathers, and it glittered coldly in the dim light. But at the same time fire sprang to the tip of Aranloth's staff. The power in him came unbidden now at times of danger, and he knew he would never be able to stop it from doing so. All he could do was use it sparingly, that would be the key. By doing so he might be able to ensure that he used the magic rather than that it used him. But he had no time to worry about such things.

A hound leapt at him, and his instinct with his sword was stronger than his awakening knowledge of magic. He swayed to the side, his arm loose and relaxed, and he slashed the full length of the sharp blade along the creature's belly.

Blood sprayed from the hound. When it landed, its entrails slipped and gushed from its belly over its legs. It tried to turn and leap again, but it stumbled, its black-clawed paws caught up in a mess of gore and intestines. Brand spun away from it. It was dead even if it did not know it yet.

Kareste sent a ball of fire flying into another hound. It pranced to the side, but the lòhrengai still caught it a glancing blow and in a moment the ruff of fur around its neck caught fire. It howled, a terrible sound from so close, and would have attacked anyway, but Kareste kicked it in the head even as it voiced its pain. It writhed on the ground, but did not get up again. Together they faced the remaining two hounds.

Brand was slower to act. Kareste sent a sheet of fire at them, and it caught them full on. They fell, rose to their feet again, their hair alight, and then they yelped and rolled on the wet earth. Brand stepped toward them, the flame on Aranloth's staff flickering silvery-white in the gloom, but the beasts came to their feet and fled.

541

Kareste and Brand turned around, but the Halathrin needed no help. A dozen elugs lay dead and the rest were disappearing into the shadowy forest from where their attack had started just moments ago.

The pine woods were quiet except for the receding noise of their attackers as they fled.

In the ensuing silence Harly held up her hand. The rain had momentarily eased, and without the noise of it they heard another sound: the beat of war drums.

"We're close," Harly said quietly.

"Yes," Brand answered. "Closer than I thought. It's hard to find landmarks in this forest."

Kareste came forward. "The rain doesn't help, either. But something has happened. Can't you hear it?"

"Hear what?" Brand asked. "I can hear the drums."

She shook her head adamantly. "Yes. The drums. But listen. Can't you tell the difference? There are far *fewer* of them?"

Brand tilted his head and listened carefully. "You may be right. But it's hard to tell. Everything seems muted within the forest."

"Something has happened," Kareste insisted. "There are fewer drums. Much fewer – I swear it. I don't know what's been going on, but *something* has happened. I guess this much at least – the enemy has not had everything their own way."

Brand did not know about that. He was not sure of the drums either, but if she said so, he believed her. But for once, he was glad to hear the drums anyway, either lots of them or few of them. For it meant the siege still continued. Cardoroth still defied the enemy, and had not gone under.

He turned to Harly. "I'm sorry. Perhaps we should have done what you advised. The forest turned out more dangerous than I expected."

She smiled at him. "Maybe. Maybe not. But this much I think is true. These elugs and beasts weren't the same as the ones we saw with Khamdar. I don't think he sent them here to wait in ambush in case we came this way. I think they were just a patrol, and we were unlucky enough to come their way. It was bad luck, and we could just as easily have had the same kind of ill-fortune if we had gone the way I suggested. There are sure to be patrols all around the enemy host, and we could have run into them no matter where we went."

They pushed on soon after. The rain grew heavy again, and as they moved along it seemed to Brand that they were like mist-phantoms moving through a wet forest. The Halathrin were almost invisible, and they made no noise. Soon, he knew, they would reach a point where they could look out and see the enemy.

But what then? Dare he put into action the plan that was slowly forming in his mind?

23. Why do they Wait?

The beat of drums, of elug war drums – of hate and malice and fear, snaked through the air and up to the Cardurleth. But to be sure, the drums were far fewer than they once were, and their clamor had a thready sound to it like the heartbeat of an old man upon whom death crept near; like, in fact, the pulse Gilhain heard thrum in his chest when he overexerted himself.

The drums were at the heart of the superstitious elug nation. Gilhain knew this, as did all Alithoras. But Aranloth had recently told him more. The lòhren had traced their origin for him, back into the prehistory of the elug race. It was lore that only the lòhrens would possess, and the elùgroths, of course. Those two opposing forces who went back as far as the elugs, or farther, themselves.

The drums were in the blood of the elugs, a part of their race-memory. They predated by far the Halathrin exodus into Alithoras. The unceasing beat was a religion to them, and it marked and measured their life, and the lives of their ancestors back into dark oblivion.

The drums were not just instruments of war. They beat wildly at elug birth ceremonies, and they muttered darky at elug burials. The drums were the heartbeat of their life, and there were words and meanings in their rhythm and tone beyond human comprehension. Small wonder that they were also tools of the elùgroths, implements of control, for the sorcerers ruled all in the south with an iron grip and had long since usurped all means of domination in the races subject to them.

544

The drums thrummed now before the Cardurleth, fewer by far, and the elugs were disheartened. Gilhain understood better now why that was so. Fear ran among the enemy. Superstition and dread were its companions. The elugs were scared of the riders who had attacked them, brought low their drums and returned in fire and storm into the fortress from whence they had come. They were terrified of another such sortie, and they feared just as much being sent to attack themselves.

But their greatest fear was the elùgroths, and the elùgroths drove them on. War was inevitable. Attack was inevitable. Death was inevitable, for the sorcerers would not give up. Nor, Gilhain knew, would he have done so in their place. No matter the setbacks that they had received, they still dominated the situation. And when Khamdar returned, their strength would be all the greater. Yet still, there was a sense of desperation among the enemy. A feeling that time was running out.

The enemy host now began to seethe like a swarm of ants below. The elùgroths drove them on, the shazrahads whipped them forward. The horde was imbued with a dark spirit, with the very will of the sorcerers themselves. They prepared now for a great assault, an assault that might never end. Wave after wave of attackers would come without respite, and perhaps even the whole host, charge after charge, was going to be thrown against the Cardurleth. Nothing would be held in reserve.

"It builds and builds without end," Taingern said. "Why do they wait? Why not unleash the storm upon us?"

"Because we feel it, and that's reason enough," Gilhain answered. "The storm builds, and death is in the air, just as a real storm builds in the east."

He pointed to the dark clouds piled deep, cloud upon cloud toward the sea. Bad weather was coming from the

545

ocean, but worse trouble was on the ground before them.

"They will let fear erode our will before they strike, but when they come it will be with thunder and lightning, and their charge will be a gale of bodies, of elug warriors driven by the malice of the elùgroths like leaves before a great wind."

Aurellin clenched her fists. "And they do something else also. To reduce us, and to fortify themselves. Look! They gather now the dead riders from the field!"

It was true, Gilhain realized. The bodies of the Black Corps littered the ground, for three hundred had left but few returned. Many of their horses were dead also, laying like carrion on the trampled grassland before the Cardurleth. Yet man and horse both began to jerk and twitch.

Gilhain swallowed hard. Dead men rose to their feet. Dead horses heaved up off the ground to stand on trembling legs. Blood seeped from mortal wounds. Cold entrails spilled from the bellies of horses.

The men pulled arrows from their bodies and let them fall. They straightened broken limbs. All the while they made no sound.

At length, the riders mounted. Slowly, unhurriedly, but with great precision they formed a wedge and took up a position before the Cardurleth, before the Arach Neben, the gate that in life they sought but never reached.

And when the riders found and held their position, though they were silent, the elugs voiced their age old battle-cry that had been heard before cities had fallen for long ages in Alithoras:

Ashrak ghùl skar! Skee ghùl ashrak!
Skee ghùl ashrak! Ashrak ghùl skar!

The chant flowed ceaselessly. It had neither beginning nor end. All the while the beating of the drums that remained grew louder and faster. The stamping of boots thundered, and a low rumble filled the cloud-dimmed sky above the horde.

The king knew what the chant meant.

> *Death and destruction! Blood and death!*
> *Blood and death! Death and destruction!*

Gilhain drew himself up. He did not speak. Now was not the time. Yet he would not be cowed. If death had come for him at last, *still* he would not be cowed.

He watched in silence as the enemy brought forth timber gathered from the pine forests that surrounded Lake Alithorin. It was green, and fresh leaves still sprouted from the many twigs and branches left on it. What this was for, he could not guess, but Hvargil's riders carried it fearfully.

Although Gilhain did not know what purpose the ceremony unfolding before him served, and the re-animated corpses of his own riders sickened and troubled him greatly, he noted with some slight satisfaction that Hvargil himself was not there.

The enemy cavalry took their burden of timber, and they circled the dead riders of the Black Corps. It was an eerie thing to see: the living riders gathering round the dead that sat silently upon their slain horses. And the first piled their burden of timber near to the second.

The drums beat faster, and Aranloth stirred. He spoke, his voice subdued, barely a mumble.

"There is a third thing the enemy will yet do."

"What?" Gilhain asked.

"I sense that Khamdar has returned. He is behind this, for the other elùgroths lack both the strength and skill. His power is enormous, his will dark, and his anger great at the loss of Shurilgar's staff. But the other elùgroths aid him."

"What will come next?"

Aranloth either did not hear, or chose not to answer, but he seemed to gather himself in readiness.

The drums beat faster, and their note changed. At the same time, lifting up and soaring from the midst of the dark host, came the sound of elùgroth chanting. It was a deep and strong sound, harsh and unharmonious, but powerful all the same.

"Do they attack us?" Gilhain asked.

Aranloth answered this time. "Not quite," he said. "Not in body at least. But in mind. Watch, if your heart is strong, and you will see."

Gilhain watched. All on the Cardurleth watched.

Smoke roiled from the ground where Hvargil's riders had placed the timber. It churned under the hooves of their horses. Hvargil's cavalry flowed back into the main host and disappeared, but the smoke, and the dead riders, remained.

Sparks gathered on the conifer branches laid on the ground. Black smoke billowed into the dim sky, and from the thickening clouds a drizzle fell. Soon it became rain, falling in torrential waves, but the sparks and growing flames did not go out.

Smoke billowed, thick and choking, into the air. Fire, like a living thing, took hold of the timber. The branches of the conifers seemed to move and thrash, falling in on themselves as the fire consumed them. But from that seething mass the fire flickered, rose and spread. And then, red and wicked, it leapt from dead horse to dead horse, from dead man to dead man.

548

The horses did not scream. The men did not cry out. They stood in silence while the flames took hold of them.

Gilhain wanted to look away, but he could not. The fire sizzled and popped. The heads of some of the men snapped back. Limbs twisted and writhed as the fire played over them. Then, unbelievably, the horses began to trot, flame spraying from their nostrils as their dead lungs breathed out, sparks flying from their hooves.

They were all dead, men and horses both. But they began to rush forward, and though the flame burned with a great heat, it consumed but slowly.

Yet, the fire *did* consume. The riders drew their swords, and the flesh of their hands melded like hot wax onto the hilts. Their hair burned away. Their faces, once proud in life, began to melt. The skin tightened and drew tight about their skulls in smoke and flickering flame. The stench of death filled the air, and it reached even to the top of the Cardurleth. Yet the riders came forward without pause.

The living riders of Hvargil were now out of sight. But the dead riders held everyone's attention. What would they do next?

The wedge before the gate wheeled and turned with precision. It was a mockery of what they did in life, yet the skill remained to them. Gilhain gasped. Was it possible that the spirits of these men were somehow still in their bodies? Surely no mere sorcery, no animation of dead flesh could mimic the hard-earned expertise of the riders?

They came again toward the battlement. Now even the thick hides of the horses smoked and charred. Hair and flesh burned away. Gilhain saw in many places the red muscles and the white-gleaming bones that drove the animals on. He felt sick, but still he watched. Terrible as it all was to behold, he *must* watch, for something would come next. The elùgroths no doubt executed this plan with more in mind than the desecration of the dead.

The horses snorted red fire. The wounds of the dead men seeped steaming blood, and its falling drops hissed in the air before turning to dark smoke. All along the Cardurleth the men watched in horror. They were silent and pale. They had no words to voice their fear or disgust. Some vomited over the walls. Some fainted. Gilhain gritted his teeth and waited. There was nothing else he could do.

And then the dead riders gathered pace. Swift they came now. The war drums beat with frenetic glee, and behind the wedge of riders the elug horde broke into a charge, screaming in maddened rage, filled and fueled by the sorcerous will of the elùgroths.

24. Have I not the Right?

Brand stood with the others. It was dark, but they had come to the fringe of the forest. The shadowy woodlands lay behind them, and ahead was Cardoroth. The people he loved were close, and the sight of the city that he called home brought a film of tears to his eyes. It was not his home by birth, but he had grown to love it even so.

The city was vast, but it was so gloomy that he could barely see it. It was day time, but the dark clouds had gathered thickly and they unleashed their burden of rain in great torrents.

Out of that darkness came a flash of light. It was all silver and white, and the brightness illuminated much that he could not see before. The enemy host stood out, and the Cardurleth, all of red stone as was much of the city. It seemed that the walls were smeared in blood, and perhaps they were, but they looked like that all the time. It was not a pretty sight, but he loved it anyway.

The Halathrin gasped. It was an ancient city, but to them it was new. They had not seen it before, and well did Brand remember his own reaction to the red stone when first he saw it.

"It always looks like that," he said, but they gave no answer.

And then, as the light faded, they saw the enemy swarm. The horde commenced an attack against the wall, and even in the gloom and rain-swept air, they could still see the outline of the host as it charged, and dimly they heard the wild yells and cries of a maddened foe. Like a deeper shadow amid the gloom it seethed forward, a thing of deep darkness that would swallow the city before it, and then the world after.

There was silence among the watchers. Eventually, Kareste broke it.

"What now?" she asked.

"Now," Brand answered quietly, "I go into the heart of that army, and I find Khamdar and his brethren, and I kill them. If I do that, if I cut the head from the snake, then the army will wither." He paused, allowing his words to sink in, and then he spoke again. "But I do this alone. I don't ask any to come with me."

They looked at him in stunned silence. It was Kareste, once again, who spoke.

"*That* is your plan?"

He shrugged, and then winked at her for good measure. Humor was the best way to deal with fear.

"It's as good a plan as any. And actually it'll be easier than I thought. I hadn't counted on the rain, but that will help conceal me."

"Not once you get close the enemy, it won't."

"I'll also use lòhrengai to make Aranloth's staff and my cloak look black. I think I can do that."

"How quick you are to follow your fate."

"I do what I must ... because I must. But after that, we shall see."

"So it always is with you. You do what you must, not what you want. I cannot see the future, but I can see that that will never change. Nor should it, I suppose. That much you've taught me, and much else besides. So, I do now what I also must do. I'll go with you."

Brand shook his head. "No. It'll be easier for one to slip into the enemy army than two. I'll go alone."

Kareste held his gaze. "Would you shame me? Would you make me less than you? You gave up much for me,

552

risked everything on my behalf, and now I do so for you. That also is as it must be. Don't demean my choice by arguing with me. Have I not the right to risk all to help you, as you risked all to help me?"

He *was* going to argue. He was going to find a way to talk her out of it, but he looked back into her eyes and felt the truth of her words. She would not be swayed, and he would only diminish her choice if he tried to.

A long while he looked at her, and a long while she stared back at him. Eventually, he bowed his head slightly, reached out to her and gave her a tight hug.

"You're right," he said. "I don't like it, but you're right, and I'm proud of you. Nevertheless, I won't forgive myself if you get hurt."

The Halathrin watched without speaking, but there was a strange look in their eyes.

Harly eventually approached. When she spoke, her voice was very quiet.

"We also will go with you." She held up the palm of her hand to stop Brand from talking. "We do this for you. But we do it for ourselves and our kind also. Most of all, we do it for Halath, he who died for our people. We understand what you now try to do, for everything you do is for others, even as Halath did. We will follow his example."

He looked at her and slowly shook his head. "Harly, I can't disguise you. You're too fair, too bright, too beautiful to enter the enemy host unobserved. I don't have the skill to change everybody's appearance."

The Halathrin girl smiled at him. "If you have half the skill with lòhrengai that you have at flattery, you could do it with ease. But it doesn't matter. This is a thing I can do for my band, albeit in my own way."

Brand did not argue. He needed these people just as he needed Kareste. At the same time, he did not want anyone to go but himself. Yet, at the end of the day, he had no right to try to deny them the opportunity to do what they felt in their hearts that they had to do. No more right than they had to deny him.

After a few more moments they formed a column. Brand was at their head, Kareste at the rear and the Halathrin between. They had to leave the horses where they were, and their packs also. But Brand took the diamond that Gilhain had given him. He was not about to leave that behind. Then, solemnly, they left the concealing fringe of trees and marched down the rain-slicked slope toward the enemy camp.

25. The Light Grows Brighter

Aranloth spoke, and his voice carried all over the Cardurleth.

"Take heart!" he commanded. "These are the bodies of those who once were our comrades, but their spirit is gone. Sorcery uses them now, raises them up, puts their feet in the stirrups and makes the horses pace. Remember your brothers for who they were, and know that these are no longer they."

The riders charged. Fire leaped and darted beneath the cold hooves of dead horses. A haze of smoke gathered, and it rose into the air, and the riders rode upon it, angling up into the very air themselves, climbing upon dark sorcery toward the top of the rampart.

The stink of burning flesh was everywhere. The stench of opened entrails accompanied it. The eyes of the enemy, who once were comrades, burned and sizzled in their sockets, staring without emotion or pain, staring inhumanely, staring as the dead horses galloped.

The defenders fired arrows. They hurled spears and javelins. These implements of war stuck in the riders, but the enemy rose higher, rode closer, came on without any interruption. The dead were already dead. Neither death nor pain nor the tactics of battle concerned them.

The horses snorted flame. The riders neared. The skin of their faces peeled away to reveal the haggard grin of death, and flames curled around the white teeth protruding from bony jaws.

Blood spurted from their wounds, falling down, boiling and sizzling like a ghastly rain on the barren earth below. And then, as the riders approached, it splattered on the stone of the rampart.

Men fled their stations. Suddenly, loud and horrible, was the sound of iron-shod hooves on stone. The smell of corruption was overpowering.

At that moment the lòhrens finally acted, for this was an attack beyond skill and courage of arms. A white light sprang forth. It was soft, silvery, reminiscent of a midwinter moon. But however soft the light started, it swiftly grew and encompassed the riders even as they reached the Cardurleth.

On the rides came, unstoppably. Yet the lòhrengai did not seek to block them, to oppose elùgai with its own might. Instead, it took the force thrown against the city and transformed it. The riders rode, but they continued their upward ascent, being just barely deflected from their destination.

Up they rode. Higher and higher. Up and over the battlement and then above the city beyond. The silvery light grew brighter. And for all the horror unleashed there was now a sense of peace, for the light bathed everything as though the very moon itself hung pregnant with argent beauty in the sky.

The light was no ordinary light. Peace came with it, release and ease of spirit. And hope. Hope most definitely, Gilhain felt. It was unexpected, unlooked for, more powerful than any darkness.

Somewhere far below in the city a bell tolled. And as though that were a signal the light became suddenly blindingly bright. Gilhain cast his eyes downward, and saw at the edge of his vision, or beyond the vision of normal sight, a fleeting glance, faint and shimmery as though from a great distance, of green grasslands and a silver river winding through them.

556

Gilhain thought of the origin of the Black Corps, of the refugees to the city and from the land whence they had come.

Even as he thought of their homeland, the riders now high above gave a shiver in their saddles as they wheeled once more in precision, and then, banking away to the left like a flight of white doves, they disappeared. And the silvery light with them.

Gilhain let out a long breath. They were gone. The light was gone. But a lingering sense of peace remained for a while, but that too, with each beat of his heart, began to fade.

It was dark again. Almost night-dark. Water ran as a sheet over the stone, for at some time that he did not quite realize it had begun to rain in a mighty downpour. Men rushed back to the front of the battlement.

But the enemy host below, driven now by powers beyond recall, swarmed as a dark wave and crashed upon the wall.

26. The Storm Breaks

The nearer they approached, the better Brand saw the unstinting attack of the enemy on Cardurleth. His heart swelled with pride; not just of Gilhain and Aranloth, not just of the Durlin, but also of the everyday soldiers who had defended the city since even before he had left on his quest. They had endured. They had borne attack after attack, suffered horrors that could not be described. And still they stood, awaiting some final hope, hope that for all they knew would never come. But *still* they endured.

He was proud of them. And he felt a great love of the city wash over him. It was always thus, he knew. The greater the danger the more something, or someone, was appreciated. But cities fell even as did people, and he knew in his heart that nothing was permanent. The history of Alithoras taught him that, and his own life had brought home the message even more strongly.

Cardoroth had endured. But nothing lasted forever, not even great courage, and soon, very soon now, the end must come. The city teetered on the edge of fate, and the next few hours would send it into oblivion or light it as a beacon of hope for the whole land.

The small band made their way through the rain, which grew even heavier. Brand reached out with his thought. He drew the downpour about himself and his companions. It whipped and lashed at them, and thereby helped to obscure them from the army they approached.

He felt power, and he felt the lòhrengai that was in him pulse through Aranloth's staff. It was there because he made it so, because he had chosen to wake it, and very gently the staff began to glow. As it did so, he brought his mind to bear, concentrated on the gloom that was about him, and the flicker of silver light turned darker, transformed slowly and surely to black.

Brand thought about what he had done. He had not changed the color of the staff, but merely the light that sprang from it. It was a subterfuge, rather than a real change. He knew, instinctively, as he knew so many other things about lòhrengai, that to make real change, or to create something from nothing, was the hardest thing of all. To take something that already existed, and to transform it, was much easier. But still not easy, for doing such things taxed the mind just as physical effort taxed the body.

The gloom of the dark day, and the rain and the scudding clouds above were all around him. He had used that subdued light, that atmosphere, to bring forth darkness of his own, but he did not stop with the staff. He did the same for his clothes, making them appear black, creating a shadow about himself to make it seem that he wore an elùgroth's cloak.

All the while he heard a soft chanting behind him. The words were in the Halathrin tongue, but they were harsh and guttural and he did not know their meaning, though they seemed tantalizingly familiar.

He turned and looked at the Halathrin. Their once beautiful forms were become grotesque. Fangs sprang from their gray-lipped mouths. Their skin had become gray-green even as that of the elugs. Their limbs were now long and ungainly, and the hair on their heads, spilling from beneath now-tarnished helms, was lank. They wore also the leather jerkins of elugs, the cheap armor stained by blood and grime.

The one at their front leered at him evilly, and with a shock he realized it was Harly. A shiver ran down his spine, and she laughed at him, showing wicked fangs and a lolling red tongue. He suppressed his revulsion and winked at her, which made her laugh all the louder.

He turned to the front again, leader of this band of savages, and pulled about him a sense of menace and power.

Soon, they came to a picket line of miserable elugs with their cloaks wrapped tightly about them and their heads bent low to keep their eyes out of the rain.

Brand did not hesitate. To try to hide, to try to slip through was death. He walked brazenly at them. The elugs looked up at him, and he stared back, and he allowed his hatred of Khamdar, his hatred of the enemy to fill his eyes. He imagined crushing his foes, sweeping them into oblivion with steel and lòhrengai. The elugs saw the look in his eyes, the malice-laden glance of an elùgroth, and backed away.

A path opened, and they went through the gap. And then, within a hundred paces they were within the enemy host itself. Elugs milled all around them. At times, there were Lethrin. Then, suddenly and unexpectedly, he nearly bumped into a man of the Camar race.

Brand hid his shock, for shocked he was. But then he pieced it together. Hvargil must be here somewhere. And that made him wonder what strange things had happened in his absence. For even as much had happened to him, clearly much had happened here also.

He headed toward the center of the host. There they would find the elùgroths. He had no need to try to track them down by guesswork, for he heard sorcerous chanting ahead, and then the voices of hundreds of elugs join in. Some dark elùgai was being worked, and Brand hastened. Already the wall was in danger of falling from the great attack hurled against it, and this new stroke, whatever it was, could mean the end.

560

He looked up, but could no longer see the bulk of the Cardurleth, only the top of it dimly through the obscuring rain.

The clouds, thick banks of black and deep-sea blue that piled one upon another, roiled ominously. A storm was about to break, and Cardoroth was at its center. There was a boom of thunder, and it was not sorcery. Nature was about to unleash its fury, uncaring of man or elugs, peace or battle. And about the edges of the storm jagged shafts of lightning flashed and leaped, spearing toward the earth as though the sky made war upon the earth.

Ahead, Brand finally saw the elùgroths. Soldiers cowered motionless about them, crouching low to try to shelter themselves. Brand and his small group were all that moved, all that dared to move when it seemed that the fury of the sky would break the world apart.

On Brand strode. On his band came behind him. None stood in their way, for all scattered at his approach and he felt the fear that elùgroths generated among those they led. It sickened him, but the power of it fueled his pride also. For the first time he knew what every lòhren had felt before him: temptation. And he knew he must always be on his guard. Power was a lure, a trap for the unwary, a golden path that led to blackness. Better now did he understand what Kareste had gone through.

On he walked, and fear stabbed at his heart like the lightning that seared the ground. Here was Khamdar, and he was not alone. His brethren were with him, and a horde of elugs and dark foes at the sorcerer's beck and call.

Brand slowed. His heart turned to ice, and he knew at this moment that death was likely, nearly certain, and that life and hope were as distant from him as clear skies and bright sunlight.

He faltered, and he sensed the fear of those behind him like a wave. This was madness. This was suicide. This was stupidity. Maybe, just maybe, they could yet turn around and leave the host even as they had entered it.

A buffet of cold wind slapped him in the face, but he did not feel it. His mind raced, but as it did so he thought of all those who had died by Khamdar's hand. And how many defenders of Cardoroth had fallen? And what if the city succumbed? Perhaps, just perhaps, he could prevent that, or at the least hinder the enemy. If he died, it might be better than living with the guilt of not trying to protect those he loved. Not just Gilhain and the Durlin, not just Aranloth. But the people of Cardoroth, the women and children who might yet see the sun shine again, even if he would not.

Brand made his choice and strode forward again. Like a wave, the others followed in his wake, drawn forward by the strength of his will. They all went now to their deaths, but they went with one purpose, and they went as brothers and sisters to meet their fate.

They saw the elùgroths more clearly. Lightning flared and crashed all around them. In its flickering light, the dark forms of the sorcerers were clear. They sat in a wedge, their wych-wood staffs held in their laps, their voices rising in a chant of dark magic, of magic that one way or another would be hurled at the city they strove to destroy.

And beyond, illuminated by the same fitful light, was the Cardurleth. The enemy swarmed against it, engulfed it as a dark tide. How could the defenders hold? Yet hold they did.

Brand felt something smash against his arm. And then something else struck his shoulder. It was hail, and it felt as though the very sky began to hammer the earth and all who stood upon it.

The elug host wailed. The massive Lethrin wrapped their arms about their heads. Brand strode on, and the elùgroths kept chanting.

The hail grew much larger and fell in a heavy blanket. As swiftly as it started it faltered, and then, just as swiftly again, it fell once more. This time the hail-stones were even larger, and they fell so thick that the ground was become white and the noise of their battering was a roar in Brand's ears.

But on he strode, and his band followed. They were near the elùgroths now, but they were also near the Lethrin who stood adjacent as an honor guard. And the Lethrin looked and watched, their heads coming up despite the hail, and their hands reaching down for weapons.

At the very end, Brand had been discovered. To fool elugs was one thing, but the Lethrin who guarded the sorcerers was another. They knew better than the rest of the army who their masters were, and what they looked like.

Brand stared at them, hatred and power in his eyes, emulating the elùgroths. But the Lethrin could not be deceived. They were about to sound an alarm, but the Halathrin were already acting. Their bright swords glittered amid the gloom, flashing like little streaks of lightening.

Brand and Kareste raced toward the elùgroths. There were only six left, for evidently they had not had things all their own way during the siege. But it was still a fight of three to one, and Brand did not like those odds.

They had not reached them when the elùgroth at the head of the wedge looked back, alerted by the sudden noise and mayhem behind him. It was Khamdar, and even as he looked Brand saw swift recognition in the other's eyes.

Khamdar cried out in a tongue that Brand did not understand, but the rest of the elùgroths obviously did. They lurched to their feet, their chanting forgotten, and hatred burning like fire in their dark eyes.

27. Burn!

The elùgroths spread out. Khamdar was on their right, and it was toward him that Brand looked. Kill the leader, and the followers would flail about like a headless snake.

Khamdar, for all that he was taken by surprise, acted with speed and determination. Crimson fire spurted from his staff. The sorcerous flame flashed through the air. Rain sizzled. Steam billowed upward. But Brand was ready, and he held Aranloth's staff before him, and his drawn Halathrin blade also.

The attack struck, and Brand took that power, felt the skill and strength that lay behind it, and managed to deflect it upward until it pierced the dark clouds above.

He did not wait where he was, but sprang forward. If he were to have a chance against Khamdar he must not fight him on the elùgroth's own terms, elùgai against lòhrengai. He must bring his sword to bear, use his skill as a warrior. It was a small advantage, and it could not compensate for the disadvantage of fighting someone far more powerful, but it was all he had.

Khamdar struck again. The hail that lay on the ground between them seethed and rose into the air. It coalesced, and then like an arrow shot at Brand.

Brand had no answer to that. Not with lòhrengai, but he did not need to. He dived and rolled, coming up again many yards from where he had stood. Still, he felt the whoosh of air by his body as the ice-arrow sped past him. And then he heard screams from the elug camp behind as the sorcerous attack killed unintended victims.

But Khamdar did not care. His cloak billowed about him as he moved in closer himself, driving toward Brand even as Brand came toward him. That was off-putting, for it showed that the sorcerer feared neither staff nor blade.

From the left, Brand saw lights flicker. Kareste was in a battle of her own, but he dared not take his eyes of his enemy. That was death.

A ring of crimson fire sprang up around him. It began to swirl, but even as it did so Brand reached out with his thought. He joined his power to that of the elùgroth's. The fire intensified, and the whirling increased. The air about Brand shimmered with heat, but the whirlwind of fire lifted up from the earth and soared away into the roiling sky.

Rain dripped down Brand's face. His body was covered in sweat. He felt chilled to the bone, for this was a life and death struggle. But he took heart.

Somewhere behind him now the Halathrin battled the Lethrin, and that fight continued. So too did Kareste's struggle. Light and fire sizzled from her direction, and he saw the crumpled forms of several elùgroths.

Brand and Khamdar closed. His Halathrin blade gleamed with lòhrengai. He cut and thrust, but Khamdar spun to the side, and like a whip his wych-wood staff came down. It struck Brand on the face, and he reeled back.

Pain shot through him. Anger rose. In a fury he leaped forward. Aranloth's staff was forgotten. He attacked with his blade, and he drove in, swinging, sweeping and stabbing in a mad rush. But for all the speed of his attack, it was not without skill. Every move was calculated. Every technique honed by years of practice and fighting experience.

566

But he did not break through the elùgroth's defenses. The sorcerer was like a shadow, and no matter how fast Brand was, he could not get ahead of him. Yet still, Khamdar had an opportunity to attack himself. He dodged and leaped, his every thought bent on staying alive.

But, as Brand knew he must, he began to tire. And that was the moment that the sorcerer had waited for.

Khamdar struck with great speed. He had learned his lesson previously and did not speak or taunt. He raised his staff in his right hand, but it was from his left, held low, that fire spurted.

Like jagged lightning it hissed, sizzling and steaming through the air. Brand ducked, but not quick enough. A vicious blow caught him on the shoulder and sent him staggering back. His cloak burned, and smoke spiraled upward.

Some instinct long dormant within him rose to the surface. Before he could even think about it his mind reached out and pushed the fire away, but Khamdar was not done.

The sorcerer now sent flame from his staff as well, and Brand spun further back. He fell to the ground, and then rose again. A nimbus of silver light shone from within him, protecting him against the attack. Yet he was tired in both body and mind.

His protection faltered. He swayed on his feet, and the attack against him intensified. Suddenly, a figure was leaping from the side of his vision. He thought it was Harly, but it was not. It was the Halathrin with the scar who had warned him away from her.

The warrior sped across the muddied earth. Khamdar saw him, and hesitated. Then, he pointed the staff at him and sprayed him with fire. The warrior dove to the ground, but he was hit. He came up again, now between

Brand and the sorcerer. He raced in, covered in flames, burning as he ran. Khamdar leaped back and now attacked with both streams of flame.

The warrior screamed. He fell to the ground, but even as he did so he hurled a small dagger.

Khamdar was swift yet again. The dagger burst into flame and shot off to the side to land in the mud, where it smoked and hissed.

The Halathrin warrior did not live to see his attack fail. But Brand was still alive, kept that way by one he had thought was not his friend.

Brand used the brief moment of respite wisely. He reached out with his thought, conscious this time of what he was doing, and drew the rain about him as a protective shield.

Khamdar drew himself up. Slowly he walked toward Brand, and fire spurted from hand and staff. The new attack knocked Brand backward again, but somehow, he kept his footing.

Brand struggled to move forward to meet his enemy, but Khamdar laughed.

"You are outmatched, fool."

Brand made no answer, and he took another step forward.

Khamdar shook his head. "You are dead, but you know it not. Watch then! Learn what true power is, for I am greater than you, and my skill, honed long ages before you first drew breath, is beyond the reach of your thought."

The sorcerer drew himself up. Tall he stood, and terrible. Blackness was about him, and it was not the gloom of the storm that raged all around them. It was a blackness of spirit. Brand felt as though he looked over the edge into a bottomless pit. And thither, into the great dark, he knew he must fall.

"Burn," Khamdar said. "I foretold that you would perish in flame and anguish, and thus it comes to pass. Burn!"

And Brand felt the full force of his enemy's will. It was a crushing power, greater than his own, steeped in malice that itself struck him as a blow over and beyond the sorcery.

The protection that Brand had drawn about himself was stripped away. Water sprayed up and outward. He stood there, so tired it was all he could do to stay on his feet. Some last instinct flickered to life and a silver-white nimbus surrounded him. He knew that he could not last long, that this protection would also be taken from him.

"Burn!" the elùgroth screamed.

Scarlet flame swept through the air. It sent Brand spinning. Somehow, he again stayed on his feet. Somehow, the nimbus survived, but it flickered fitfully, nearly gone as was Brand's will to live. There was only so much a person could endure, and he knew he had gone past his limits.

"Burn!" Khamdar said again. His voice was quieter this time, but the will behind it even stronger. The elùgroth waxed in power as he saw his enemy succumb.

Brand felt the nimbus of power about him die. With a final flicker it went out, but then, beyond his comprehension, Kareste was before him, protecting him. Somehow she had survived, abandoned or won her own battle, and she was come to his aid.

But that hope was short lived. She was as exhausted as he. With a negligent flick of his wych-wood staff Khamdar sent a stream of flame at her that knocked her down to the muddied earth. But he did not follow up on that attack. He looked again at Brand.

"I will kill her when I am done with you."

Slowly, the elùgroth walked toward him. As though from a great distance Brand heard fighting behind him. The Halathrin still engaged the lethrin. There could be no help from them.

Brand was outmatched, outfought, and he knew it. Too young was he in his power, too unskilled. He had no choice but to wait for death, because the power to fight was no longer his.

By some immense force of will he stayed on his feet, unwilling to die on the ground, a beaten and defeated thing. Khamdar was not right: he *was* dead but he *did* know it.

And yet, one last gamble came to his mind. He had not the power to contend with one of the great elùgroths, yet had he not survived thus far by deflecting his enemy's attacks, rather than opposing them force to force? Might not he have one last hope? His instincts had not yet surrendered, and nor would he.

He drew forth from an inner pocket the diamond Gilhain had given him. At the same moment, Khamdar spoke again, and his voice was a command.

"Burn!"

The single word, louder than thunder, cracked the air.

Khamdar levelled his staff. Wicked flame ran along its length, and Brand saw the light of that same sorcerous flame in his enemy's eyes.

The flame leaped. Intense, murderous, bent on his destruction.

Brand welcomed it. He opened his mind, drew it in with his thought. He became one with its roiling fury, but he did not fight it. He did not resist it. He felt its heat, and relished it. He felt its hunger, and knew insatiable desire. He felt its rage, and knew madness. It enveloped him, became his body, and a pillar of wicked flame rose as a towering inferno about him.

And then two other elùgroths staggered toward Khamdar and joined their power to that of their master. The flame intensified. Dimly, Brand heard the roar of flames, the lustful cries of elugs and a single heartbroken scream from Kareste.

All the while he drew in the force that pummeled him, drew it in and guided it into the hard diamond. On it went, relentlessly. The elùgroths showed no mercy. They burned, fueling their elùgai with hatred, spending themselves utterly in their lust for destruction.

But when their strength faltered, when their power one by one drew to an end, Brand was still there. And in his hand the diamond shimmered with trapped power. It was no longer hard in his grip, but soft like clay. He could shape it with his fingers, and he sensed that what had gone into it must come out. It was caught there like a beast in a cage, but there was no substance on earth that could long hold such power trapped.

The last remnant of flame about his body flickered and died. He stood before the elùgroths, unharmed and implacable. His will to live was greater in the end than their will to kill.

Brand stepped toward them. Somewhere behind him lay his sword and staff on the scorched earth. High he held the diamond, and the elùgroths, even Khamdar, were shocked and fearful. They shrank from him.

He heard Kareste gasp in shock, but he did not look at her. His mind was fixed on his enemies, on the enemies of all mankind.

"Thus I cast your curse back into your teeth, Khamdar. Burn. Burn and perish, for there is no place for such as you in the world. Burn and pass from Alithoras, and as you die, think of the many that you killed. Think of them, and feel their vengeance."

Brand released the sorcery caught in the diamond. It leaped out, and like chain-lightning sprang from elùgroth to elùgroth. But the force did not spurt out slowly as it had been gathered in. The release was sudden, and the swift outlet of such power cracked the air more loudly than the thunder of any storm.

The earth trembled. The Cardurleth seemed to sway, and the elùgroths screamed.

Up into the heavens the wailing rose. The lesser elùgroths fell to the ground. Khamdar stayed upright, and he staggered toward Brand, one hand reaching out in supplication or attack. But then he too stumbled and fell.

Brand did not relent. The last of the force stored in the diamond shot outward. The clothes of the elùgroths burned, and their flesh with it. The muscles of their limbs withered away in smoke. Fat flared and dripped like sputtering candles. Their eyes sizzled and smoked leaving blackened holes, and their faces shriveled, revealing the white bone beneath.

The elùgroths died. And their wych-wood staffs turned to a fine ash. All about them the hail still fell, yet where the elùgroths burned the heat was so great that the ice melted. Water ran with blood, and burning streaks of fat hissed and bubbled.

Brand stood there. There had been shock and despair on Khamdar's face before it melted away. And though Brand had seen men die before, had killed many himself, yet still what he had seen would haunt his dreams as long as he lived. But he did not feel sorry for the elùgroths. Justice could be as cruel as any crime, but that did not make it wrong.

The elug host moaned. Brand looked around. He did not know when it had happened, but he had fallen to his knees. Nearby were dead Halathrin, and dead Lethrin also. But still some of the immortals were left alive. Harly

572

was one of them, and she held his gaze a moment. Her eyes were wide and there were emotions in them that surpassed his comprehension. Too much had happened, and he was too weak to stand, let alone think.

But hammering at his vision was something else that finally seeped through to his consciousness. The elug host was fleeing. In a mad rush they ran, abandoning the siege. Their leaders had died in fire and anguish, and the storm raged at them like a living thing. Bereft of the malicious will that had infused them, fear drove them instead.

Brand looked to Cardoroth. From the city came an army. Real, or a phantom of his exhaustion, he did not know, but he could not keep his eyes on it. He fell to the ground and rolled onto his side. From his hand ash scattered, all that was left of the precious diamond.

Dimly, he saw Kareste and Harly run toward him. They reached him and held his hands. He did not at first understand the worried looks on their faces, and then he felt the pain in his chest. He looked down, and saw the hilt of a dagger sticking out from his flesh. An elùgroth dagger, marked on blade and hilt with the drùgluck sign.

Khamdar had killed him, and he had not even seen or felt the dagger thrown by his enemy. But life was sweet. Kareste and Harly were alive. Cardoroth still stood.

He felt the hands of the two girls grip tight his own as oblivion claimed him. Just as it did, though all was dim and shadowy about him, he felt other hands upon him, gentle, firm, skilled. And then there was only darkness.

28. Filled with Power

Not for the first time, Gilhain marveled at the men who defended Cardoroth. They fought against all odds, and without any real hope.

The enemy swarmed the walls. They came without stint, hatred in their battle-cries and madness in their eyes. That madness was born of the elùgroths, of that the king was sure, but however it came to be, it was only its presence that mattered. For the elugs fought with a fury that he had never seen before.

The elugs did not give up. Death swept them aside by the hundreds, but they no longer feared it. They fought as creatures possessed, and when one fell another took its place. So it went, and it seemed without end.

Blood ran over the stone floor of the rampart. Bodies lay there, dead and maimed. Others were maimed but not dead. The living fought for their lives, trampling all that lay beneath.

In contrast to the fury of the enemy, the defenders fought with grim quietude. There was, almost, a sense of peace among them. Perhaps it was really so, for Gilhain still had a lingering sense of tranquility from Aranloth's white light. But be that as it may, with or without Aranloth, the men fought to save and preserve while the elugs fought to destroy. That was in some ways a small difference, and in others enormous. It was, Gilhain knew, a bigger difference than any of the other things that separated them. The men did what they must do, live or die, and hatred did not drive them.

Afar in the city all was silent. The people had gathered in the streets. They watched, but did not talk. The Durlin stood around the king, drawing closer to him for the final confrontation that must come soon, for this could not continue. They guarded him until the end.

Aurellin was there, as she always was. The storm broke, and wind and hail lashed the battlement. It was hard to see, yet still Gilhain sensed that the very air seemed to shiver, to draw back and away from the violence of the storm.

The air shimmered, yet something appeared that was not air or rain or hail. It had the form of a man, though many times larger.

And it was no man, but a devil raised by the elùgroths. Black wings sprouted from its muscular back. Horns, twisted and curved, grew from its massive skull, towering above its head like a crown of evil.

With a bellow as loud as thunder it stepped forth, and the Cardurleth trembled at the weight of its tread. The soldiers scattered. The creature paid them no heed, but came for Gilhain, its eyes burning with the light of hatred.

The Durlin stood before it. But before them stood Aranloth. And he was not as he usually appeared, an old man of uncertain humor and old regrets. He revealed now his full power, showed the might that was in him. For dark as the devil was, wrapped in shadow and evil, the lòhren blazed with an inner light. He would contend with this thing, and even as its shadow fell over him, the devil paused.

Aranloth had no weapon, but the massive beast, a thing of rippling shadow and muscle, drew forth a mighty sword that smoked and flickered with wicked light. The blade was bent, tooth edged and longer than the span of a tall man.

575

Aranloth cocked his head, but made no move to flee or to attack.

"Stay!" the lòhren commanded. Even as he spoke he held up his hand, palm out.

The beast hesitated, and the shadow and wicked light ebbed and flared uncertainly along the blade of its sword.

Aranloth spoke again, but it seemed that he did not address the devil, but rather those elùgroths who had summoned or made it.

"The moment is upon you," he said. "Choose now, and choose swiftly, if it is not already too late. Pull back, Khamdar. Take your host and go."

Khamdar answered through the beast; through twisted mouth and cruel fang his voice rang out.

"Those are empty words, old man. Your hope is dead. I will kill you, and the glory will be mine. The honor and the praise of he that I serve will raise me unto godhood. Verily, I would not retreat now though the spirits of all those that I have vanquished joined together to kill me. Let them come, for they are dead and I am on the brink of ultimate power!"

"So be it," Aranloth said softly.

The lòhren bowed his head. The beast took a step forward. Aranloth did not move.

Hail beat around the two figures. Lightning flickered and hissed nearby. A sulphurous smell filled the air.

The devil lifted high its sword. Fire darted in its eyes and shadows writhed about it. Its great arm bulged with muscles, and it gripped the black hilt with a taloned hand.

A moment thus it stood, ready to strike. Aranloth waited, and then the creature dropped the mighty blade to the battlement.

There was no noise, no clang, no rattle of metal against stone. The sword ceased to exist the moment the creature let it go.

And then the beast turned and looked behind it. Gilhain watched, rooted to the spot by fear or fascination. Which, he did not know, but he watched.

The devil shape tensed, and the face of the creature showed surprise. Suddenly, it seemed more human. It wavered, great folds of shadow billowing about it as its dark wings trembled, and then it was gone, gone in the blink of an eye as though it had never even existed.

The onrush of elugs faltered. Many had gained the wall because it was unmanned, yet most had held back, just as scared of the devil as were the defenders. No one seemed to know what was happening.

But now men began to come back to their positions, and there was great turmoil in the host below. A light flashed, sharp and bright. Then there were more and more flares and bursts of power. On it went, and it seemed that the world stood still. Only the storm moved, venting its fury, but the two opposing armies seemed paralyzed.

Finally, a burning light, too bright to watch, pierced the rain-thick air, and screams rose up from far below, full of pain and anguish beyond any cry that Gilhain had ever heard. Then a boom rolled across the battlefield as though the earth itself cracked asunder.

The enemy host suddenly moved. At first, everything below seemed a mad panic, but quickly it became evident that the horde was breaking up, scattering, taking flight.

"What's happening?" Gilhain asked.

Aranloth seemed tense, and his eyes were distant. But then he answered.

"More than we could hope. But when you trust in such as Brand, hope is rarely cheated."

"*Brand?*"

"Aye. Brand. He has come, returning to us over the long leagues of Alithoras, and there are others with him. And they attacked the heart of the enemy, the head of the snake as he would call it."

"The elùgroths?"

"Verily. And rejoice if you can, for death is a bitter thing to all, to evil as much as to good, but they are dead. All of them, including Khamdar. That is why the enemy flees."

Gilhain thought. But not for long. There would be time to rejoice later. For now, he must act. Swiftly he issued orders for the regular cavalry to leave the city and harry the enemy, lest they regroup.

"Tell them to harass the elugs," he instructed the messenger. "Kill them. Give them no peace. Find their supply wagons, or what is left of them, and target them wherever possible."

And then the king watched and waited from atop the Cardurleth. The enemy retreated, and the riders of Cardoroth pursued.

A small group was left in the middle of the field, and suddenly Aranloth's voice rang out.

"Brand is wounded!" the lòhren yelled.

Before those words were finished it seemed that Arell was already moving.

Gilhain did not know what to feel. Somehow, beyond hope, they had won. But at what cost?

Aurellin slipped her hand into his. He bowed his head, and gently squeezed her. She squeezed his hand back.

"Cardoroth will endure," he whispered.

But Aranloth heard him also, and it was the lòhren who answered.

"And yet the shadow is not vanquished. Only its long arm is injured."

The truth of those words struck home to Gilhain. They had won a great battle, but the war was only beginning. It would be fought in other times and places. No doubt, it would be fought here again, even if in another fashion. But his time as king was drawing to an end. Another must soon bear the burden, for he was growing too old to continue as he had done. His time in Alithoras was nearly spent, but there was another to take his place. Another, who was prepared to give his life for all that he loved, if he had not already done so.

29. Can You Deny Her?

Arell knew what she was doing. She had no lack of confidence, no lack of skill, yet still she worried about Brand.

The dagger of the elùgroth had gone deep. The blade had slipped between his ribs. That in itself was unusual, for the ribcage was good at protecting the vital organs of the body; that was one of its purposes. But the blade had apparently not penetrated far enough to touch his heart or damage his lungs.

So far so good. But why was he so ill? She looked up from her ministrations and saw Aranloth and several others had come down from the battlement, but it was the lòhren who was most important just now.

"Do the elùgroths use poison on their daggers?" she asked.

The lòhren shook his head. "That's unlikely. They have no aversion to such a thing, but they have better means of protection at their disposal."

That was good news. But then another thought occurred to her.

"What about sorcery?"

Aranloth frowned. "That's certainly possible," he said. He peered closely at the dagger for a moment, and then knelt down. Tentatively, he reached forward and brushed his fingers against the hilt that protruded from Brand's chest. He did not grasp it though, and Arell saw him flinch as his skin touched it.

Several moments passed, and Arell held her breath. At length, the lòhren stood.

"There is elùgai infused into the blade, but it is not of a kind that would hurt Brand. The spells woven about it are of sharpness and seeking. They are potent, but they would have only helped the blade bite deeper. We can be thankful that whoever threw it had poor aim, otherwise it would have found what it sought."

"And what was that?" Gilhain asked.

Arell answered, thinking aloud more than anything else.

"The heart, no doubt. And it was close too, but Brand's luck has always been good."

"That's exactly right," Aranloth confirmed. Though whether he was talking about the dagger or Brand's luck, Arell was not sure. Perhaps both.

"Then I think I know what the trouble is," she said. "He's exhausted. Exhausted to the point of death, as only a man with the will of Brand can drive themselves. And the dagger, though not the main problem, could well push him over the edge."

"What then is the treatment?" the king asked.

"I'd like to get him back into the city where I can do things properly, but he may not survive that long. So, I'll draw the dagger out here. If he survives that, then his body can start to heal, and then he may regain some strength."

"Do as you must, Arell," the king said. "I have confidence in you."

Arell did not answer. She had spoken in matter of fact tones. It was her job to do so, for it gave confidence to those who watched the treatment. But most of all, it brought to the fore that part of her mind that analyzed and assessed, that diagnosed and initiated treatment, and by concentrating on that it kept the other part of her mind that felt and feared, suppressed. And just as well,

581

for if her emotions got loose on her she would fall to pieces. She could not let Brand die!

Swiftly she made her preparations, dabbing an unguent around the wound that would help protect against infection. She prepared cloth, in case of bleeding, and then she put both her hands to the hilt of the dagger. She must be steady here.

She took a deep breath, and then she gradually let it out, withdrawing the dagger very slowly at the same time.

Brand moaned as the blade began to move. She gave a curt nod, and several sets of hands immediately pressed down upon him to keep him still so that he could not hurt himself.

The blade slipped free, but it was not easy. Wounds were often like that; extra blood and tense muscles put pressure on blades that made it so.

The dagger was a wicked looking thing, and it dripped with Brand's blood. Swiftly she put it down and inspected the wound.

She could see little, and had no way to know if there was dirt or other foreign material in there. If she had time and leisure, she would have considered trying to clean it, but that had its own dangers, because no matter how careful a healer was, there was always the chance of introducing foreign material that had not been there before. Often, whatever caused infections was so small that it could not even be seen.

Arell resorted to what had often worked well for her in the past. She drenched the wound with a special fluid. She gave her clients a long-sounding name for it, but the king and the Durlin knew it was merely a kind of potent spirit brewed by those who had no taste for wine or beer. Many healers would use wine for such a purpose, but she had found that the spirit gave better results. Barok, one of her great enemies in the profession berated her for this, claiming it broke tradition. She did not care about tradition though, she always sought the best results.

When she was done she applied a poultice. This also helped to fight infection, but its main purpose was to promote quicker healing and the drawing together of the edges of the wound.

If there was no sign of infection in several days, she would consider stitching it together. But if she did that too early, then it was possible that puss could build up inside, and that made infections worse.

She applied a bandage over the poultice, and then she was done. Brand would live or die now by his own will, by the natural strength of his body.

Those who had held him down were two girls. For the first time Arell allowed herself the chance to look around. One was an ash-blond woman, fierce and keen-eyed. The other ... the other must have been one of the immortals, a Halathrin. And she seemed as sweet as a summer's day, though there was steel in her also.

Brand had kept strange company outside of the city, and much had evidently happened to him. The Halathrin did not venture beyond their forest realm, at least not these days, and there must be quite a story to this. But one thing about the two girls was the same, and she felt a pang of jealousy: they each felt for Brand. Their worry and their fear for him were palpable things. It was something that Arell had often seen when treating patients – the frightened concern of those who loved them.

Whatever jealousy Arell felt, she suppressed it. It was not her way, and it would do no good. Besides, it was clear that Brand had touched their hearts in some way, and she could not hold that against them. Had he not done the same to her?

Nevertheless, the three of them eyed each other off. But it was the fierce looking one, the one with the shadow of past pain in her eyes, that surprised her by speaking.

"I'm Kareste, and you must be Arell. Brand has told me of you."

"I'm sure he has."

There was a flicker of a smile on Kareste's face. "He said you were a great healer, and I believe him. He will not die, of that I'm certain. You won't let him. But, I won't be here when he wakes up. Tell him," she paused, "tell him that I said goodbye. Tell him that I've much to think about and consider. And tell him this also. I'll be back. One day I'll appear again, unexpectedly, just as I did when we first met."

She looked fierce for a moment, and there truly was a shadow in her eyes, but it was more than past pain.

Arell nodded. This girl obviously had many issues to work through.

"I'll tell him."

Arell stood, and the two of them exchanged a stiff curtsey. Kareste was ready to leave, but her glance fell on Aranloth and she paused. A long time they looked at each other.

The lòhren bowed to her. It was a thing that Arell had not seen him do even for the king.

"Well have you chosen," he said when he straightened.

She smiled at him, and her face changed completely.

"Good was my guide, and good was he who sent him to my aid. For did you not know that we would meet?"

Aranloth shrugged. "Perhaps. I hoped. But nothing is certain."

She bowed and started to walk away, but not toward the city. Then she turned to face the lòhren again.

"Brand will live. The healer-girl will care for him, and she will see to it. Thank him for me."

"I will. And when you're ready, return to Lòrenta. Your staff is there, and it would be better in your hands than lying unused in a dusty chamber."

She looked at him and smiled again. It was a happy smile, but a sad smile too.

"I'm not sure the other lòhrens are ready for me."

"All the more reason to return."

Her smile flashed fiercely, and then she turned and left.

The days passed, and they were long. But the nights were longer, for the pain grew worse. Yet, day by day, night by night, under the steady ministrations of Arell, Brand grew stronger.

Within a week he was walking around and receiving visitors. There were many of those, and the catching up with old friends and the exchange of news and the storytelling of recent events filled many hours.

He missed Kareste, but he understood that she needed time alone. He missed Harly also, for once he was on the mend she had come to say goodbye.

"This city is no place for me," she had said. "I yearn for the wild lands, the lands of forest and grass, and the stars up above at night."

He understood that as well. He understood it better than most, for he was like her.

"Don't forget me," she said.

"Never," he answered.

"Nor will I let you, for I suspect we shall meet again."

"Really? Halathar is far away. It may be that even my wandering feet never reach there."

"Perhaps not. But my feet wander also. And one day, when you leave this place of stone, this swirling storm of hustle and bustle behind, look for me in the quiet wilderness."

"I will always look for you," he said. And then she and the remnant of her band were gone.

The king came to see him, and he shook his head and laughed at the fate of the diamond.

"Perhaps you were never meant to be wealthy."

"Maybe not, but I'm rich in other ways."

Gilhain nodded sagely at that, and then he returned the knife, the knife of his ancestors marked with the sign of Halathgar, that he had given to Brand once before when this had all begun.

"I will keep it, this time."

Taingern and Shorty came to see him also. One was quiet and reserved, the other rowdy and jovial. But whatever their manner, he felt their love. But even Shorty grew subdued when they spoke of the Durlin who had died protecting the king since Brand had left the city.

All the while Arell kept a close eye on him, and when he grew tired she chased the two visitors away in quick order. Shorty, however, winked at him slyly before he went through the doorway.

The days passed, and Brand grew stronger. He was well enough to return to his own room, even to resume duty as the Durlindrath again. But Arell did not allow either, and he did not argue.

Yet, one bright morning when the sun shone and the sky was clear, he felt restless. And he knew the cause of it.

He took up Aranloth's staff and diadem, that Arell had stored in a closet, and went looking for the lòhren.

Aranloth was not hard to find, and after speaking to several soldiers Brand tracked him down. He was atop the battlement, where he was said these days to spend much time gazing out at the empty space where the enemy had once camped below.

"Ah," the lòhren said without turning. "The day has come at last, Brand."

Brand stood beside him and looked out at the view. The ground was ripped and pockmarked. In places, the earth was scorched. Yet green shoots were rising up from the trampled earth, and in the distance the pinewoods around Lake Alithorin were so green as to appear almost black.

Brand leaned the staff against the stone and put down the diadem.

"Why not tell me that you knew?"

Aranloth turned to look at him. "You know the answer to that."

Brand let out a long sigh and nodded.

The lòhren looked him steadily in the eye. "In the staff, that long I have born, since before the fall of the Letharn empire, there is only the memory of enchantment. The diadem, however, is different. If you better knew its history, you would better understand its virtue."

"So, what now?" Brand asked.

Aranloth turned his gaze back out to the empty countryside.

"You feel the call of the land, do you not? And in her voice are the dreams and hopes of all who would live in Alithoras, of all who would not succumb to the shadow of the south. Can you deny her?"

Brand shook his head.

"The land knows you well," Aranloth said. "The land from which you came, to which you will one day return. No servitude is it to serve her. She lays no bonds upon

587

you. Yet bonds there are, for you lay them upon yourself. Do you accept this?"

Brand looked at the land below. Alithoras stretched out all around him, and though he could only see this small bit of it, he felt the rest.

"I will serve," he answered. "I will become a lòhren."

Aranloth did not answer, and after a moment Brand spoke again. This time, his voice was soft, barely more than a whisper, and the words he chanted were ones that he had long held dear.

> *Tum del conar – El dar tum.*
> *Death or infamy – I choose death.*

"I had thought," he added, "that those words only applied to serving the king. But they hold true for other things as well. They hold true for serving the whole land, and not just a part of it. They hold true for serving, and protecting, all who live in it."

Aranloth seemed surprised. "Yes," he said eventually. "They're fitting words for a lòhren as much as for a Durlin. More fitting than you could ever guess. For though you have no way of knowing this, they were uttered long ago, long before the Durlin existed, long before the Camar came east. Once, they were spoken in the very halls from whence you brought forth the second half of Shurilgar's staff, and the sound of them was like a death-knell to an entire empire."

Aranloth looked out over the battlement, but Brand knew the lòhren's eyes saw nothing. His mind was on some event, some recollection of so long ago, so world-shattering in its way that even its distant memory moved him in a manner that Brand could not understand.

"Strange, very strange that you should speak those words now, speak them in the context of a lòhren and not a Durlin. And all the more now do I feel that this is the right path for you."

Brand was not so sure of things. "What will be, will be," he said.

The lòhren's mood suddenly shifted, and he laughed. "You of all people don't believe that. You, who have foretellings hanging over your head wherever you go, and ignore them all."

Brand shrugged, but did not answer. He wondered just who, or what, Aranloth saw when he looked at him.

And Aranloth did look at him now, his mood changing again to one of warning.

"Remember this, and remember it always. You are now a lòhren, though you have much yet to learn. But your serving may take a different form than you think. Even to those who wander the paths of the future, its ways and its twists and turns are often unseen. Remember that in the days ahead."

Brand looked at him, looked at his oldest friend in Cardoroth, and felt the full force of those words. Aranloth knew something. And Brand had a feeling that the future held surprises for him. He smiled to himself, for it was a feeling that he liked.

Epilogue

A breeze touched the tops of the pine trees. Dusk was drawing close, and in the forest darkness had already descended, deep and impenetrable. Thus it always was in the woods that surrounded Lake Alithorin, and thus it would always remain.

Beneath the fringe of that forest, atop a hill, several pairs of eyes looked down coldly at what they saw. The landscape shone eerily under the slanting rays of the dying sun. The light flickered, shifted and changed as it danced to the movement of the cloud-wreck on the horizon, the remnant of the terrible storm. Those clouds, fired red by the lowering sun, seemed like blood poured across the western sky.

But redder still was the great wall of Cardoroth. Blood was on it, and it reeked of death. Blood was soaked into the soil, and the remembered screams of the dying hung in the air, though all that could be heard by the ears of the watchers was the rustle of pine leaves and the sounds of small animals scurrying in the shadows, hunter and hunted, playing their own battle of life and death. Those creatures recked nothing of men, thought nothing of the battles that had been fought. And they cared even less.

But the eyes that watched, or rather the minds that directed them, cared and understood. And they felt the joy of the city and the people who lived there, and it chagrined them. And they felt the terror of the fleeing elugs, and though that excited them, it disturbed them more.

One of the great masters had fallen, and there were few in the world like him. Just how it had happened, they did not know, but one of them sensed the involvement of Brand. Brand of the Duthenor come west into lands that had nothing to do with him, come west into lands to kill and destroy.

The death of Khamdar was a great event in Alithoras, yet it was a small thing beside the death of one other that Brand had killed.

Ginsar stared out through the falling night. She paid no heed to the cold glinting of the stars that sparked to life like far-away campfires in the dark sky. She thought nothing of the forest behind her, though it had been her home for years beyond the count of mortal men. She thought of nothing but Brand, and the more she thought, the greater the cold fury that burned within her grew.

"The battle is lost," she said to her three companions. "Khamdar underestimated Brand. That is a mistake I will not make, for I am not of the south as was Khamdar, and I have watched Brand closely over the years – and I have learned."

One of the black-cloaked elùgroths next to her spoke, and his voice was wary, for he had seen this mood on his leader before.

"But Mistress," he said, "if the battle is lost how can you attain revenge on Brand? He is safe in the walls of the city."

Ginsar turned to look at him, and her expression was cold, colder than the void in which the stars burned out their life surrounded by oblivion.

"I am Ginsar, and my power is great. Khamdar failed, but I will not, and the death of Brand will atone for my brother whom he killed. And for all Khamdar's power, he could not foretell the future as do I."

"And what do you see, Mistress?"

She looked back at Cardoroth, and a smile touched her lips, but it was colder than the black void.

"Brand thinks that soon he can leave the city, that his duty here is done. But that is not so. His duty will pin him here, like an insect crawling over stone and squashed beneath a booted foot. And that will be the death of him."

There was a pause, marked only by the rustle of the breeze through pine needles.

"How so, Mistress?" one of the other elùgroths asked after a moment.

Ginsar stood, silent as a stone, and whatever thoughts and plans spun through her mind, nothing showed on her face.

"This much I will reveal to you. The way to Brand is through those he loves. And one that he loves most will place a burden on him, and the care of a child."

There was another pause. She said nothing, and the elùgroths grew anxious.

She turned to them and grinned, and power was in her glance, unwavering and potent. But there was madness in it also. This the elùgroths recognized, but it mattered not. She led, and they followed. Thus it had ever been, even with her as it was with her brother, the master that they had served before they had taken her as mistress.

"The child is the key," she said. "I will use him to lure Brand to his downfall. And never will one have fallen from such heights to such depths. Never will one know such pain and regret. And I will draw it out, and savor every moment though it be unendurable torment to him."

"And what of the child himself?"

"Ah. The child. Such sweet revenge, for with him I can condemn Brand. Yet the child is also an enemy. Verily, that youth is born of the line of she that we hate most in all the world."

The elùgroths pondered this. After several moments and secret glances among themselves, one spoke.

"Mistress? Who is it that we hate even more than Brand?"

She looked at him coolly, and he trembled.

"Think, O fool. Think!"

One of the other elùgroths bowed, and glanced slyly at his discomforted brother. "Mistress. She that we hate is Carnhaina, and the child must be descended from that ancient witch."

Ginsar tossed back her long hair, black as the shadows of the forest. It was a girlish gesture, and, coming from her, was so out of place that it unnerved even the elùgroths.

"So he is, and destroying the boy and Brand together is fitting beyond description. For though the witch has been dead many centuries, still does her spirit linger in the city, watching and helping. And the destruction of Brand and the witch's descendant will drive my revenge deep into her long-dead heart, and her anguish will add to my ecstasy."

The stars wheeled above. The night wore on, and Ginsar revealed her plans to the elùgroths. And even they, dark souls though they were, blanched.

Thus ends *Victorious Swords*. It brings the Durlindrath trilogy to a conclusion. Yet the growing power of the south, and the madness of Ginsar, imperils all of Alithoras and more of the desperate struggle is told in book one of the Son of Sorcery series: *Prince of the Magic*.

Sign up below and be the first to hear about new book releases, see previews and learn of upcoming discounts. http://eepurl.com/Rswv1

Visit my website at www.homeofhighfantasy.com

Encyclopedic Glossary

Note: the glossary of each book in this series is individualized for that book alone. Additionally, there is often historical material provided in its entries for people, artifacts and events that are not included in the main text.

Many races dwell in Alithoras. All have their own language, and though sometimes related to one another, the changes sparked by migration, isolation and various influences often render these tongues unintelligible to each other.

The ascendancy of Halathrin culture, combined with their widespread efforts to secure and maintain allies against elug incursions, has made their language the primary means of communication between diverse peoples.

For instance, a soldier of Cardoroth addressing a ship's captain from Camarelon would speak Halathrin, or a simplified version of it, even though their native speeches stem from the same ancestral language.

This glossary contains a range of names and terms. Many are of Halathrin origin, and their meaning is provided. The remainder derive from native tongues and are obscure, so meanings are only given intermittently.

Some variation exists within the Halathrin language, chiefly between the regions of Halathar and Alonin. The most obvious example is the latter's preference for a "dh" spelling instead of "th".

Often, Camar names and Halathrin elements are combined. This is especially so for the aristocracy. No other tribes had such long-term friendship with the Halathrin, and though in this relationship they lost some of their natural culture, they gained nobility and knowledge in return.

List of abbreviations:

Azn. Azan

Cam. Camar

Chg. Cheng

Comb. Combined

Cor. Corrupted form

Duth. Duthenor

Esg. Esgallien

Hal. Halathrin

Leth. Letharn

Prn. Pronounced

Age of heroes: A period of Camar history that has become mythical. Many tales are told of this time. Some are true, others are not. And yet, even the false ones usually contain elements of historical fact. Many were the heroes who walked abroad during this time, and they are remembered still, and honored still, by the Camar people. The old days are looked back on with pride, and the descendants of many heroes yet walk the streets of Cardoroth, though they be unaware of their heritage and the accomplishments of their forefathers.

Alar: *Azn.* A strain of horses raised in the southern deserts of Alithoras. Bred for endurance, but capable of bursts of speed. Most valued possession of the Azan people, who measure wealth and status by their number. In their culture, where a person on foot is likely to die between water sources, horse-theft is punished by torture and death.

Alithoras: *Hal.* "Silver land." The Halathrin name for the continent they settled after the exodus. Refers to the extensive river and lake systems they found and their appreciation of the beauty of the land.

Alith Nien: *Hal.* "Silver river." Has its source in the mountainous lands of Auren Dennath and empties into Lake Alithorin.

Anast Dennath: *Hal.* "Stone mountains." Mountain range in northern Alithoras. Contiguous with Auren Dennath and location of the Dweorhrealm.

Angle: The land hemmed in by the Carist Nien and Erenian rivers, especially the area in proximity to their divergence.

Angrod: One of the ancient names of the witch better known in present times as Durletha.

Arach Neben: *Hal.* "West gate." The great wall surrounding Cardoroth has four gates. Each is named after a cardinal direction, and each also carries a token to represent a celestial object. Arach Neben bears a steel ornament of the Morning Star.

Aranloth: *Hal.* "Noble might." A lòhren.

Arell: A name formerly common among the Camar people, but currently out of favor in Cardoroth. Its etymology is obscure, though it is speculated that it derives from the Halathrin stems "aran" and "ell" meaning noble and slender. Ell, in the Halathrin tongue, also refers to any type of timber that is pliable, for instance, hazel. This is cognate with our word wych-wood, meaning timber that is supple and pliable. As elùgroths use wych-wood staffs as instruments of sorcery, it is sometimes supposed that their name derives from this stem, rather than elù (shadowed). This is a viable philological theory. Nevertheless, as a matter of historical fact, it is wrong.

Aurellin: *Cor. Hal.* The first element means blue. The second appears to be native Camar. Queen of Cardoroth and wife to Gilhain.

Auren Dennath: *Comb. Duth.* and *Hal. Prn.* Our-ren dennath. "Blue mountains." Mountain range in northern Alithoras. Contiguous with Anast Dennath.

Azan: *Azn.* Desert dwelling people. Their nobility often serve as leaders of elug armies. They are a prideful race, often haughty and domineering, but they also adhere to a strict code of honor.

Barok: A healer in Cardoroth. A man held in high regard by the profession he represents. Distantly related to the king on his mother's side. It is believed by some that he obtained his position as chief physician via political influence. Others argue that, his family being wealthy, they bribed the king's chancellor in order to obtain the favored position for one of their own. Be that as it may, it is well known in Gilhain's court that the king dislikes him. This likely stems from an older cause, however. In his youth, the king required stitches. Barok inserted them, but miscalculated the date of their removal. The process, undertaken many days later than it should have been, was painful. Gilhain still bears the scars on his arm, not just of the initial cut, but also the faint point marks where the string was pulled from his flesh.

Black Corps: An irregular unit of cavalry for Cardoroth. Formed by direct command of the king. Its leader, Hilk Var Jernik, was appointed its captain after the king had seen him ride in a competition. At that time, he was of low rank in the regular cavalry. His officers commended him, but said he was willful and unsuited to command. The king researched his military exploits, overruled the commanders, and ensured the Black Corps answered directly to the throne rather than the leadership of the regular cavalry.

Brand: A Duthenor tribesman. Currently serving King Gilhain as his Durlindrath. By birth, he is the rightful chieftain of the Duthenor people. However, an usurper overthrew his father, killing him and his wife. Brand,

599

only a youth at the time, swore an oath of vengeance. That oath sleeps, but it is not forgotten, either by Brand or the usurper. The usurper sought to have him killed also, but without success.

Camar: *Cam. Prn.* Kay-mar. A race of interrelated tribes that migrated in two main stages. The first brought them to the vicinity of Halathar; in the second, they separated and established cities along a broad sweep of eastern Alithoras.

Camarelon: *Cam. Prn.* Kam-arelon. A port city and capital of a Camar tribe. It was founded before Cardoroth as the waves of migrating people settled the more southerly lands first. Each new migration tended northward. It is perhaps the most representative of a traditional Camar realm.

Cardoroth: *Cor. Hal. Comb. Cam.* A Camar city, often called Red Cardoroth. Some say this alludes to the red granite commonly used in the construction of its buildings, others that it refers to a prophecy of destruction.

Cardurleth: *Hal.* "Car – red, dur – steadfast, leth – stone." The great wall that surrounds Cardoroth. Established soon after the city's founding and constructed with red granite. It looks displeasing to the eye, but the people of the city love it nonetheless. They believe it impregnable and say that no enemy shall ever breach it – except by treachery.

Careth Nien: *Hal. Prn.* Kareth nyen. "Great river." Largest river in Alithoras. Has its source in the mountains of Anast Dennath and runs southeast across the land before emptying into the sea. It was over this river (which sometimes freezes along its northern stretches) that the Camar and other tribes migrated into the eastern lands. Much later, Brand came to the city of Cardoroth by one of these ancient migratory routes.

Carist Nien: *Hal.* "Ice river." A river of northern Alithoras that has its source in the hills of Lòrenta.

Carnhaina: First element native *Cam.* Second *Hal.* "Heroine." An ancient queen of Cardoroth. Revered as a savior of her people, but to some degree also feared, for she possessed powers of magic. Hated to this day by elùgroths, because she overthrew their power unexpectedly at a time when their dark influence was rising. According to dim legend, kept alive mostly within the royal family of Cardoroth, she guards the city even in death and will return in its darkest hour.

Carnyx horn: The sacred horn of the Camar tribes. An instrument of brass, man high with a mouth fashioned in the likeness of a fierce animal, often a boar or bear. Winded in battle and designed to intimidate the foe with its otherworldly sound. Some believe it invokes supernatural aid.

Chapterhouse: Special halls set aside in the palace of Cardoroth for the private meetings, teachings and military training of the Durlin.

Crenel: The vertical gap on a battlement between merlons. The merlon offers protection, the crenel an opening through which missiles are fired.

Drilk: Lieutenant in the Black Corps and second in command to Jar Van Hilk. Married to Jar's sister. Their extended family operates a horse stud that produces mounts not just for the Black Corps, but also the regular cavalry of Cardoroth. The leaders of the regular cavalry often complain to the king that the best horses are held back from sale. The king advises them to make better bids at the auctions.

Drinhalath: *Hal.* "Drin – a group of people united in one purpose, Halath – a long-dead Halathrin king." The Drinhalath is an order chosen by the living king from the people as a reward or honor for some great service or deed to the people. The service itself, of protecting the remains of the memorial, lasts for twenty years.

Drùghoth: *Hal.* First element – black. Second element – that which hastens, races or glides. More commonly called a sending.

Drùgluck: A pattern of three slanted lines, going from right to left and each one longer than the previous. Used by elugs as a warning to stay away from a place because it is a sacred area that serves as a gateway between the spirit and normal worlds. Such areas are used in ceremonies and invocations for help or retribution against enemies. It is believed that at certain cycles of the moon and seasons the barriers that separate the worlds are weakened and the gateway opens. Also marks a place where the effects of elùgai linger or where there is some unspecified but lethal danger. Often it signifies all three at once.

Durletha: *Hal.* "She who is as enduring as stone." A witch of Alithoras whose birth was before even the rise of the ancient, but now forgotten, Letharn empire.

Durlin: *Hal.* "The steadfast." The original Durlin were the seven sons of the first king of Cardoroth. They guarded him against all enemies, of which there were many, and three died to protect him. Their tradition continued throughout Cardoroth's history, suspended only once, and briefly, some four hundred years ago when it was discovered that three members were secretly in the service of elùgroths. These were imprisoned, but committed suicide while waiting for the king's trial to commence. It is rumored that the king himself provided them with the knives that they used. It is said that he felt sorry for them and gave them this way out to avoid the shame a trial would bring to their families.

Durlin creed: These are the native Camar words, long remembered and much honored, uttered by the first Durlin to die while he defended his father, and king, from attack. Tum del conar – El dar tum! Death or infamy – I choose death! This man was a pupil of the lòhren Aranloth.

Durlindrath: *Hal.* "Lord of the steadfast." The title given to the leader of the Durlin.

Duthenor: *Duth. Prn.* Dooth-en-or. "The people." A single tribe, or sometimes a group of tribes melded into a larger people at times of war or disaster, who generally live a rustic and peaceful lifestyle. They are raisers of cattle and herders of sheep. However, when need demands they are fierce warriors – men and women alike.

Eleth nar duril: *Hal.* "Lie in peace." Part of the Halathrin funerary chant.

Elugs: *Hal.* "That which creeps in shadows." A cruel and superstitious race that inhabits the southern lands, especially the Graèglin Dennath.

Elùdrath: *Hal. Prn.* Eloo-drath. "Shadowed lord." A sorcerer. First and greatest among elùgroths. Believed to be dead or defeated.

Elùgai: *Hal. Prn.* Eloo-guy. "Shadowed force." The sorcery of an elùgroth.

Elùgroth: *Hal. Prn.* Eloo-groth. "Shadowed horror." A sorcerer. They often take names in the Halathrin tongue in mockery of the lòhren's practice to do so.

Elu-haraken: *Hal.* "The shadowed wars." Long ago battles in a time that is become myth to the Camar tribes.

Exodus: The arrival of the Halathrin into Alithoras from an outside land. They came by ship and beached north of Anast Dennath.

Foresight: Premonition of the future. Can occur at random as a single image or as a longer sequence of events. Can also be deliberately sought by entering the realm between life and death where the spirit is released from the body to travel through space and time. To achieve this, the body must be brought to the very threshold of death. The first method is uncontrollable and rare. The second exceedingly rare but controllable for those with the skill and willingness to endure the danger.

Forgotten Queen (the): An epithet for Queen Carnhaina.

Free Cities: A group of cooperative city states that pool military resources to defend themselves against attack. Founded prior to Cardoroth. Initially ruled by kings and queens, now by a senate.

Galenthern: *Hal.* "Green flat." Southern plains bounded by the Careth Nien and the Graèglin Dennath mountain range.

Gavnor: A lòhren of Queen Carnhaina's ancient court. Driven by desperate need he attempted to Spirit Walk, though he did not have sufficient skill. He saw deeply into what was, and what yet may be. But he was assailed. He had neither the skill to attempt to defend himself, nor to return to his body. He was lost in the void, from whence none had ever returned. Yet Carnhaina recalled him, revealing herself as a great power, greater than most lòhrens or elùgroths. But Gavnor was changed by the experience. He withdrew from the court, renounced his stature among the lòhren order, and wandered the land as a lover of nature. It is said that his power was increased, and he may well yet still live. But none have seen him for long centuries.

Gernlik: *Cam.* A Durlin.

Gilhain: *Comb. Cam & Hal.* First element unknown, second "hero." King of Cardoroth. Husband to Aurellin.

Graèglin Dennath: *Hal. Prn.* Greg-lin dennath. "Mountains of ash." Chain of mountains in southern Alithoras. The landscape is one of jagged stone and boulder, relieved only by gaping fissures from which plumes of ashen smoke ascend, thus leading to its name. Believed to be impassable because of the danger of poisonous air flowing from cracks, and the ground unexpectedly giving way, swallowing any who dare to tread its forbidden paths. In other places swathes of molten stone run in rivers down its slopes.

Great North Road: An ancient construction of the Halathrin. Built at a time when they had settlements in the northern reaches of Alithoras. Warriors traveled swiftly from north to south in order to aid the main population who dwelt in Halathar when they faced attack from the south.

Grothanon: *Hal.* "Horror desert." The flat salt plains south of the Graèglin Dennath.

Halath: *Hal.* King of the Halathrin. He died thousands of years ago. He led them on their exodus to Alithoras. Revered and loved as a great ruler. Originally, one of the main opponents of Elùdrath, leader of the elùgroths who sought dominion over Alithoras.

Halathar: *Hal.* "Dwelling place of the people of Halath." The forest realm of the Halathrin.

Halathgar: *Hal.* "Bright star." Actually a constellation. Also known as the Lost Huntress.

Halathrin: *Hal.* "People of Halath." A race named after a mighty lord who led an exodus of his people to the continent of Alithoras in pursuit of justice, having sworn to redress a great evil. They are human, though of fairer form, greater skill and higher culture than ordinary men. They possess an inherent unity of body, mind and spirit enabling insight and endurance beyond other races of Alithoras. Reported to be immortal, but killed in great numbers during their conflicts with the evil they seek to destroy. Those conflicts are collectively known as the elù-haraken: the Shadowed Wars.

Harlak: *Leth.* An ancient name of Aranloth.

Harath Neben: *Hal.* "North gate." This gate bears a token of two massive emeralds that represent the constellation of Halathgar. The gate is also known as "Hunter's Gate," for the north road out of the city leads to wild lands full of game.

Harlinlanloth: *Hal.* "The mighty power of gentle water over long years." Current leader of the Drinhalath. Puissant in a form of Halathrin magic.

Harly: See Harlinlanloth.

Hilk Var Jernik: Captain of the Black Corps. A man of rare courage, intellect and judgement. Sentenced to a year's servitude into the army of Cardoroth after being convicted of theft in his youth. So much did he impress his superior officers that they recommended him for promotion. This was denied by the aristocratic leaders of the army. The king, however, saw his worth as a man and promoted him.

Hvargil: Prince of Cardoroth. Younger son of Carangil, former king of Cardoroth. Exiled by Carangil for treason after it was discovered he plotted with elùgroths to assassinate his older half-brother, Gilhain, and prevent him from one day ascending to the throne. He gathered a band about him in exile of outlaws and discontents. Most came from Cardoroth but others were drawn from Camarelon.

Immortals: See Halathrin.

Jinks: See Hilk Var Jernik.

Karappe: A great healer of antiquity. Responsible for many of the medical treatises still used today among the Camar peoples. He lived to 109 years of age, and remained sprightly well past his hundredth birthday. Famous for recommending two mugs of beer, or one glass of wine, a day as good for health.

Kareste: A mysterious girl who helps Brand. She possess potent magic.

Kardoch: A hero of ancient lethrin society. Revered by them, and at times worshipped by them. It is believed that the elùgroths stamp out the latter practice. They have no room in their rule for reverence of anything save their own power, and the power that they ultimately serve themselves.

Khamdar: An elùgroth. Leader of the host the besieges Cardoroth.

Kirsch: A race of men who established a mighty empire across Alithoras. Yet they predated even the Letharn and nearly all knowledge of them is lost forever.

Lake Alithorin: *Hal.* "Silver lake." A lake of northern Alithoras.

Letharn: *Hal.* "Stone raisers. Builders." A race of people that in antiquity ruled much of Alithoras. Only traces of their civilization remain.

Lethrin: *Hal.* "Stone people." Creatures of the Graèglin Dennath. Renowned for their size and strength. Tunnelers and miners.

Limloth: Hal. "Still-peace." The "loth" element is the same stem as appears in Aranloth's name. However, in this context it means a powerful or mighty sense of tranquility, a sense of serenity that has a prevailing effect on a person rather than as a force to achieve some physical impact. The name refers to an especially peaceful area in a high and remote section of the Auren Dennath mountain range.

Lòhren: *Hal. Prn.* Ler-ren. "Knowledge giver – a counsellor." Other terms used by various nations include wizard, druid and sage.

Lòhren-fire: A defensive manifestation of lòhrengai. The color of the flame varies according to the skill and temperament of the lòhren.

Lòhrengai: *Hal. Prn.* Ler-ren-guy. "Lòhren force." Enchantment, spell or use of arcane power. A manipulation and transformation of the natural energy inherent in all things. Each use takes something from the user. Likewise, some part of the transformed energy infuses them. Lòhrens use it sparingly, elùgroths indiscriminately.

609

Lòhrenin: *Hal. Prn.* Ler-ren-in. "Council of lòhrens."

Lòrenta: *Hal. Prn.* Ler-rent-a. "Hills of knowledge." Uplands in northern Alithoras in which the stronghold of the lòhrens is established.

Lornach: A Durlin. Friend to Brand and often called by his nickname of "Shorty."

Lost Huntress: See Halathgar.

Magic: Supernatural power. See lòhrengai and elùgai.

Merlon: The vertical stonework on a battlement between crenels. The merlon offers protection, the crenel a gap through which missiles are fired.

Narinon: *Hal.* "Spear-water, a swimmer or diver." A member of the Drinhalath. In love with Harlinlanloth, though aware that his feelings are not returned. Bears a facial scar due to a fight with a lethrin in an ancient battle. The lethrin did not survive, but his dying stroke nearly killed the Halathrin warrior.

Netherwall: One of the ancient names of the witch better known in present times as Durletha.

Nudaluk: *Cam.* A bird of the woodpecker family.

Otherworld: Camar term for a mingling of half-remembered history, myth and the spirit world.

Raithlin: *Hal.* "Range and report people." A scouting and saboteur organization. In Camar society, they derive from ancient contact with, and the teachings of, the Halathrin. In Halathrin history the roots of the order predate the exodus.

Red-fletched arrows: Cardoroth is famed for having great archers, and the greatest of them always use the red feathers of the Cara-hak turkey for their fletching. The bird is revered by them as a creature of luck, and it is considered ill fortune to shoot one. But many a farmer or hungry hunter does so, and the feathers are never wasted. But a wide variety of feathers are used from different bird species for arrow making, though all are dyed red before use.

Sellic Neben: *Hal.* "East gate." This gate bears a representation, crafted of silver and pearl, of the moon rising over the sea.

Sending: See Drùghoth.

Shadowed Lord: See Elùdrath.

Shazrahad: The Azan who commands an elug army, or serves as a lieutenant of an elùgroth.

Shorty: See Lornach.

Shurilgar: *Hal.* "Midnight star." An elùgroth. Also called the betrayer of nations.

Sight: The ability to discern the intentions and even thoughts of another person. Not reliable, and yet effective at times.

Slithrest: One of the ancient names of the witch better known in present times as Durletha.

Spirit walk: Similar in process to foresight. It is deliberately sought by entering the realm between life and death where the spirit is released from the body to travel through space. To achieve this, the body must be brought to the very threshold of death. This is exceedingly dangerous and only attempted by those of paramount skill.

Sorcerer: See Elùgroth.

Sorcery: See elùgai.

Surcoat: An outer garment. Often worn over chain mail. The Durlin surcoat is unadorned white.

Taingern: *Cam.* A Durlin. Friend to Brand.

Tombs of the Letharn: The ancient burial place of the Letharn people. All members of the population, throughout the course of their long civilization, were laid to rest here. It was believed that to be interred elsewhere was to condemn the spirit to a true death, rather than an afterlife. The dead were preserved, and returned even from the far reaches of the empire. This was withheld from perpetrators of treason and heinous crimes. These were buried in special cemeteries near the river. Petty criminals were afforded an opportunity to redeem their place in the tombs on payment of a fine determined by the head-priest.

Tower of Halathgar: In life, the place of study of Queen Carnhaina. In death, her resting place. Somewhat unusually, her sarcophagus rests on the tower's parapet beneath the stars.

Unlach Neben: *Hal.* "South gate." This gate bears a representation of the sun, crafted of gold, beating down upon a desert land. Said by some to signify the homeland of the elugs, whence the gold of the sun was obtained by an adventurer of old.

War drums: Drums of the elug tribes. Used especially in times of war or ceremony. Rumored to carry hidden messages in their beat and also to invoke sorcery.

Wizard: See lòhren.

Wych-wood: A general description for a range of supple and springy timbers. Some hardy varieties are prevalent on the poisonous slopes of the Graèglin Dennath mountain range and are favored by elùgroths as instruments of sorcery.

From the author

I'm a man born in the wrong era. My heart yearns for faraway places and even further afield times. Tolkien had me at the beginning of *The Hobbit* when he said, ". . . one morning long ago in the quiet of the world . . ."

Sometimes I imagine myself in a Viking mead-hall. The long winter night presses in, but the shimmering embers of a log in the hearth hold back both cold and dark. The chieftain calls for a story, and I take a sip from my drinking horn and stand up . . .

Or maybe the desert stars shine bright and clear, obscured occasionally by wisps of smoke from burning camel dung. A dry gust of wind marches sand grains across our lonely campsite, and the wayfarers about me stir restlessly. I sip cool water and begin to speak.

I'm a storyteller. A man to paint a picture by the slow music of words. I like to bring faraway places and times to life, to make hearts yearn for something they can never have, unless for a passing moment.

Made in the USA
Lexington, KY
14 February 2018